GOD DUST

A Novel
by

Doug Kane M.D.

Chapter 1

No one wanted to see the CIA psychologist, especially Alex. His experience with psychobabble in rehab had been more than enough for a lifetime. Therapists usually assumed he was just another snotty, stubborn doctor and treated him with restrained contempt. He wasn't that way at all. Life just sucked at the time.

"Dr. Senna will see you now."

Her voice t-boned his train of thought. He slid a five-year-old copy of <u>Southern Living</u> back into the rack and shook his head. *Okay, let's get this over with.* He gave the pleasant twenty-something girl behind the glass a whoopee-shit-I-can't-wait eye roll and headed down the hall.

At some level, he knew Ella's eyes followed his six-foot athletic frame as he left the waiting room. She'd been stealing peeks at him through the sliding glass windows that gave her a false sense of cover. It was his last visit. He guessed she didn't have enough time to figure him out or understand why she cared. At nearly twice her age, he wondered why this young woman was drawn to him. *Maybe she likes depressed men whose lives have been turned upside down,* was the best he could come up with.

Dr. Carol Senna's office favored function over style. Two cheap, comfortable chairs faced a desk littered with manila file folders, a phone, and an out-of-date desktop computer. Several partially filled bookcases gave it the learned look. The obligatory framed diplomas, licenses, and certifications hung on the wall behind her chair, no doubt meant to promote a casual feel, as if visiting any psychologist was ever casual.

Alex stumbled through a tedious battery of psychological tests with minimal cortical energy expenditure. In other words, he didn't give a flying flip. Much to his disappointment, Director Cunningham never mentioned his high anti-authority scores. There was one thing Alex couldn't get around—his history. Cunningham knew him all too well.

Dr. Senna's weekly summaries clearly revealed that Alex didn't fit the mold. *So why was the agency interested in him?* That bit of mystery had its allure. Alex sat in the chair furthest from her desk, smiled and took a deep breath. Today, he would suffer through his last session before reporting to Director Cunningham.

"Hi Alex. How are you?" Dr. Senna smiled and sat in the chair across from him, not behind her desk as usual. Typically, she wore slacks, no makeup, and kept her auburn hair in a neat French braid, but that day, she'd ramped it up a notch with a fitted skirt, a little makeup, and her naturally wavy hair was flowing just below her shoulders. Her soft green eyes and upturned lips briefly caught Alex's attention for the first, and last, time.

"Fine, and you?"

"I'm good. Today is our last session. We can cover any lingering questions or concerns we may wish to discuss. I thought you might want to talk about dealing with grief, since it's such an important issue for you." She smiled, not patronizing, just a sincere smile.

"Really? Okay, fine. I'll tell you how I feel about it," snapped Alex. "I resent how losing my wife and daughters has forever reshaped my thoughts and view on life. My dreams for them, for us, are gone. There's no going back. I can go to therapy and read dumbass self-help grief books for the rest of my life—it won't bring them back. Only time will soften the sting, but I'll never be the same. There's nothing to talk about, Carol; it is what it is—period. Thanks for your help. I have to be at Camp Peary by noon." He stood, reached out his hand, and stared hard into her eyes. They shook hands. She gripped for a moment longer.

When he turned to leave, she murmured, "If you need to talk, you can call me. You...you need to know that. CIA psych guidelines."

"Got it. Thank you. Goodbye, Carol."

◇◇

It was a long two-and-a-half-hour drive from the Pentagon to Camp Peary. Visiting nearby Colonial Williamsburg was on his wish list—Camp Peary was not.

The nine thousand acre facility was acquired by the US government during WWII for Seabee training. It was affectionately referred to as "The Farm," a moniker it earned in 1943 when base commander Captain J. G. Ware decided it would be nice to have a pig farm right at the base's center. His foul-smelling venture infuriated recruits and became the brunt of jokes in local papers. After several months he cut the pork, but the name remained. In 1951, The Farm became an official training facility for the CIA.

The Camp Peary exit sign on Route 64 made it clear that the property's whereabouts was no secret. The first thing Alex saw when he drove in was the visitor's center. The welcome mat ended there. Armed soldiers stood behind explosive proof barricades— ready to shoot. Alex was told to drive up to a kiosk where he scanned his ID, fingerprints, eyes, and face. After several minutes, he was ordered to step out of the car. One of the soldiers scanned him, then his car with an explosives scanner.

"Go ahead, Dr. Winthrop," said the soldier, now looking more relaxed. He cautiously drove the two-lane road toward his destination, chiding himself for worrying about being blown to bits for crossing over the white line or grinning too broadly. To his left, he saw several nondescript buildings scattered around in random clusters. He passed what appeared to be residential housing and caught a glimpse of the airstrip along the York River. Most of the land was undeveloped and blanketed by flat forest. The river was partially hidden by tall cordgrass that created a maze of narrow waterways. Along the shoreline he saw a Police boat moored to a weather-worn dock. As he began to turn away, his eyes were drawn to a stunning pearl white egret standing on the furthest dock post. His heart rate and breathing slowed. In five seconds, a bird did more for him than five sessions with Dr. Senna.

All in all, it wasn't what Alex expected. There were no men dressed like ninjas lurching around swinging from ropes or scaling buildings, and no Aston Martins with machine guns hidden behind their headlights.

A few minutes later, he spotted his turn, marked with a plain white metal sign that read "Administration." There were three identical single-story brick buildings, evenly spaced and lifeless. His map directed him to park in front of the one where a patch of grass hosted an American flag. A very bored-looking soldier sat just inside the first set of glass doors. Alex presented his ID to the young man. Once satisfied with Alex's credentials, the inner door buzzed and the lock clicked open. Unfortunately, the soldier only held the button for a few seconds. When Alex pushed on the door, it had already relocked itself. He walked over to the desk and bent over so he could look the soldier straight in the eyes.

"Don't fuck with me, I'm not in the mood."

"I'm sorry, sir. I apologize, sir." The young man swallowed hard and held the buzzer until he passed.

◇◇

"Dr. Winthrop, good to see you. Have a seat." Director Cunningham's office reminded Alex of the principal's office at his elementary school; off-white painted cinder block, a metal desk, desktop computer, two monitors, and three worn wooden chairs. Cunningham's Pentagon office was much more plush. "I'm sure you are wondering what's going on."

Alex nodded. "That's an understatement. I thought I was just going to work in Olivia's lab, not get thrown into spy-world."

"I didn't want to tell you too much beforehand."

Alex glanced around the room. No windows. Only an analog clock with a dangling cord hung on the wall behind him. "You guys probably make taking a crap mysterious."

"Not really, but the toilet paper dispenser requires your ID. If you happen to forget it...well...you won't forget it the next time." Cunningham grinned and leaned back against his chair.

Alex relaxed. *I'll be damned. The bastard has a sense of humor.*

Cunningham was prepared for a less-than-cordial meeting. Alex's hard-headed independence didn't put him off. Classic machismo was a trait he admired. Sometimes it was what it took to succeed—and stay alive. He pulled his chair under the desk and patted a stack of three-ring notebooks, sending a "these are for you" message. Alex rolled his eyes.

Cunningham's face showed the wear from thirty-four years of managing clandestine operations. If something went wrong, his ass was on the line. It was exhausting. The no-frills intimidator was beginning to waver. With wisdom came regrets. In his free moments, he thought less about getting bad guys and more about the three grandchildren he rarely saw.

"We want to thank both of you for your cooperation. Especially for your help with the Broken Cure Project. The data you collected is invaluable."

"Broken Cure Project? You never mentioned it had a name...pretty catchy. I like it. Just one of many projects, I suspect. But for this one, you sat by and watched as a drug meant to save lives was transformed into a delivery system for death so you could learn how it worked? How many people died, Cunningham? How many? I'd say that's pretty broken. It's just too bad we had no intention of being part of it. Left a bitter taste in our mouths, to put it mildly."

"Get off it, Alex. Don't forget, we never asked you and Dr. Nilsson to break into Altiva and steal data. That was your bright idea. Where did you think it would all end up? Did you think you'd blow up a major pharmaceutical plant and just walk away?"

"Wait a minute. Unless my memory fails me, it was your men who brought in the fifty-gallon drums of rocket fuel."

"We had no choice but to finish up your little dog and pony show. Let's move on, shall we?"

"Screw you!" Alex stood up and started to leave.

"Dr. Winthrop—sit down! Please. Stop playing games. You know damn well you can't walk out. I'm sorry going back into practice didn't work out for you, but you know you're obligated to help us. We set Dr. Nilsson up with her dream—her own lab— and she's thriving. You don't want to screw that up, do you?"

"Right," said Alex. "I guess you're right. Olivia is thriving. You've got me by the balls. You like that, don't you? Okay, what is it you want me to do, Director?"

"Dr. Nilsson is a very special lady. Brilliant scientist. How is your relationship with her?"

"I'm banging a hot blue-eyed, blonde Swede. What could be better? We're fine, but why's that your business?" Alex leaned forward, gripping his armrests.

"Things will go a lot smoother if you two are getting on well...working...in happy harmony. Are you going to marry her?"

"Marry her? I don't know. Are you a matchmaker or just up for a little girl-talk? I think she wants to, but, you know, I've got baggage...like you...issues to work out." He stopped short of saying, "Like a few dead bodies here and there." The man was right about one thing— he couldn't just walk out.

"Yes, of course. Alex, the recent pandemic has sped things up a bit. Labs are still working furiously around the globe. Information is being shared instantaneously. Chinese authorities can't appear to be holding back data or silencing researchers. We see an opportunity. After your training and some time in the lab, we may need you to go to China. We have a man, Dr. Hu Chau. He's a geneticist and nanorobotics expert at Huazhong University of Science and Technology in Wuhan. We've received preliminary information that they've engineered a virus that can remain invisible to our immune system. That much I understand." Cunningham shrugged and waited for Alex to respond. He didn't.

"Chau said the virus is unique, not typical genetic engineering. It has the ability to replicate a molecule he referred to as a biorobot. Some kind of nanorobotic thing. I have no idea what he's talking about. I figured you might. Anyway, it seems we aren't the only ones capitalizing on the pandemic-related research frenzy. At the same time, they've created a vaccine that was given to their people along with their COVID-19 vaccine. Alex, the pandemic has spawned a new arms race, only this time, it's viruses, not nukes."

"This shit never ends, does it, Director? Tainted drugs that cause rare diseases and viruses that kill off selected populations. I'm sure the list goes on and on."

"I'm afraid it does. I've arranged for you to undergo twelve weeks of training. Sort of a 'spy light' course. You'll be done by the end of February. So you'll be spending Christmas with us." Cunningham pushed a laptop across his desk and handed Alex one of two three-ring binders. "This is mostly general information, but you will need to refer to it. The laptop requires fingerprint and ocular recognition to boot up."

Alex looked at the binder in front of them. He wanted to tell Cunningham what he could do with it— but he didn't. The cost/benefit ratio was too high.

"This is all very interesting, Director, but what's your point? What do you want from me?"

"I'll tell you when it's time. Things could change."

Chapter 2

1907

The screen door snapped shut behind him with the sound of a cracking whip. "Grandpa, can we go to the river?" yelled Simon as he ran out to the front porch where Doc Stevenson was blissfully dozing after their Sunday meal.

"What is it, boy? You 'bout scared my hair off."

"I sayed, can we go to the river?" To make sure his request captured his grandfather's full and undivided attention, Simon locked his arms around his leg and sat on his foot.

"If it's alright with your momma."

"It is."

"There's one problem, son."

"What's that?"

"I can't very well walk to the river with you all wrapped around my leg. Fetch my limb saw so I can cut this thing off."

"Yer funny, Grandpa."

"Tell that to your g-ma."

"Yessir, I'll be right—"

"No, no, Simon, I was pulling your leg. Get your shoes...and maybe you should ask your momma if you can go...in case she forgot."

Simon looked at the floor with reddening ears.

An ancient willow, now twice the size it was when he built the house, stood proudly, a stone's throw from where he sat. Its silvery green leaves, reaching toward the earth, swayed so gently in the breeze that the old doc nearly fell back asleep before Simon returned.

August in Lake County, Tennessee, was steamy hot. Free blacks and poor whites worked the cotton fields. Right after the war, many blacks went north. For those who left, not knowing what lay ahead was much less important than the exuberance of being free. For others, home was home, and families wanted to stay together. They settled on abandoned land or became tenant farmers working for their previous masters. Within several years, farm owners desperate for cheap labor drew more blacks to the area than had ever lived there before the war. Whites were displaced and none too happy about it. Over time, freed slaves built their own churches and communities. A new norm settled in. Free but separate—far from equal.

Going north was not the panacea many had hoped for. Doc Stevenson explained this to the children. "Just knowing you are free makes all the difference in the world, no matter where you live." He despised slavery despite being raised where it was a way of life. Even when he first opened his practice, he took care of slaves. That certainly didn't help his social standing, but he stayed busy just the same. After all, he was the only doctor within thirty miles.

Doc compared the full bloom cotton fields to a summer snow. Simon agreed, even though he'd never seen more than a few flakes. Pristine white puffs coated the fields each July, creating a welcome sight. A good harvest filled local pockets with profit. Doc was convinced less sickness stalked the community when the crops boomed. Nature was kind that year. The summer dry spell had waited until August. About half the cotton had been harvested.

Holding hands, the pair set off down the narrow dusty lane toward the Mississippi. Simon only stopped asking questions when he had to breathe. When Doc couldn't keep up, he would try to slow Simon down with a tale or two. He would time his words and phrases so that there was never a pause long enough for Simon to start jabbering. They took turns: jabber-tale-jabber-jabber-tale, and so on. A winning formula for both.

"Let's go to the green spot," asked Simon, just like always. The "green spot," as he called it, was a twenty-five-yard swath of dense greenery that jutted out from Doc's back field to the riverbank. According to legend, it was precisely where the fault occurred that ran under the river during the great earthquake of 1811.

As they neared the river, the sandy soil gave way to pure powdery sand. Simon filled his cupped palms with the golden-brown sand and raised it to his nose. "It smells like carrots, Grandpa." Doc had been puzzled by the green spot for years. The flora there was rich and diverse, unlike the surrounding riverbanks. They always stopped to admire Doc's favorite—a dense patch of purple orchids. There were loads of little critters for Simon to capture and ask his grandpa about. The little patch of land had only been noticed by a few curious folks over the years. Neighbors thought of it as his property and didn't wander in.

The roar of the river required them to speak louder with every step. Simon's high-pitched little voice and Grandpa's partial deafness didn't help matters. Doc would resort to just nodding his head, hoping Simon didn't notice, but he did. The boy was just too polite to show it. He learned that from his momma. His mother, Sue Ellen Parker, always seemed to know how to handle sensitive relations. Doc said she got it from his wife, Edith, when, in fact, it was obvious that Sue Ellen took after her father. The Stevensons were blessed with the gift of grace.

A bald eagle swooped down thirty feet or so in front of them, snagging some helpless little mammal. Their field of view filled with airborne color as goldfinch, bluebirds, and rose-breasted grosbeaks appeared out of nowhere, heading somewhere—away from the eagle.

"Yeouch! Ouch! Grandpa, it hurts!" squealed Simon.

By reflex, Doc snatched him up into his arms. "What's wrong, boy?"

"My toe."

Blood slowly dribbled from the tip of Simon's left big toe. He'd kicked the sharp edge of a buried stone as he slithered his feet through the cool sand. It was just a bit more than a scratch, but the sharpness of the stone made it bleed freely. Doc wiped it with his cuff.

"Oh, poor boy. That must hurt. Looks like it'll be alright. Don't think we'll need the limb saw." Simon pouted, not quite ready for Grandpa's humor. "Wanna go home?"

"No. Please? Can we stay?"

"Sure. We can soak it in the water. That'll make it feel better."

Simon was silent for the last thirty feet before reaching the natural levee that stood about four feet above the water. The sand went from cool to hot as they stepped out of the dense foliage. They both climbed down to the water's edge and sat. Doc gripped Simon's hand as he surveyed the treacherous, powerful river that had swept away more than one unsuspecting child.

"Let me see your cut."

Simon pulled his foot from the muck and plopped it onto Grandpa's lap. Doc examined the dirty little foot.

"It must be your other foot, Simon."

"No, Grandpa. See? This one's fine."

Doc paused for a moment, re-examining Simon's foot. Then he turned his eyes toward the hazy blue sky and focused on a slow-moving cotton-ball cloud. An indescribable peaceful feeling surged through him. He couldn't feel the pressure of his butt on the sand. The river's roar went silent—just for a moment.

"What's wrong, Grandpa? You look funny."

"I was just thinking."

"Thinkin'. Thinkin' 'bout what?"

"Simon. It's gone. Your cut is gone."

Chapter 3

"Alex, have you seen my keys?" Olivia's impatient plea reverberated down the hall, loud enough to stir him from his restless slumber.

"Keys?" he mumbled. *I don't even know where I am.* It had only been a week since he'd moved down from Providence. His waking mind hadn't accepted the change. By the time he started to reply, she was already in the bedroom nabbing her keys from the bedside table. As she turned to leave, her fresh scent wafted over him, bringing a smile to his face. Reluctantly, he sat up, planted his bare feet on the floor, and peered between partially drawn curtains. He watched as several streetlights fizzled out, giving way to the oncoming sun.

"Hey, honey," shouted Alex as Olivia race-walked back down the hall.

"Yes, what?"

"Wait a second."

"Alex, I'm in a hurry. I told you I needed to go in early."

He went to the hall clad in his favorite baggy boxers and put his hands on her shoulders. Olivia had seen them dozens of times, but every time she saw the faded image of Bugs Bunny, she chuckled.

"Honey, I'm sorry," he said, with a look she couldn't ignore.

"What for?"

"Six months ago, I told you we didn't have to stay here under their watchful eyes. We haven't even talked about it since then.

Why are you grinning?"

"The juxtaposition of incongruity...it's...it's too funny."

"Huh? The juxtapo-what?"

"It's just hard to take a man in Bugs Bunny underpants seriously."

"Well, I am serious, so stop laughing at me."

"Sorry. I know you are. Alex, it's okay. My work is going well. I like it. You will too, once you're up to speed. I have to go. See you at the lab. Love you."

"Yeah, Olivia, I know you're happy here. Okay. Love you too."

Six months ago, leaving the country looked like their best option—so he thought. Now, Olivia seemed to have forgotten all about it. His momentum to get out from under his past—their past—had come to a screeching halt. Their plan to disappear and start a new life in Argentina was now nothing more than a desperate thought during a desperate time. Alex had made a commitment, like it or not; he needed to follow through.

◇◇

Alex spiraled up five levels of dimly lit parking garage before he found a spot to park. He pulled his briefcase off the passenger seat. *Briefcase? Really?* In all his years of medical practice, he'd never used a briefcase. Once again, he felt like a poser. As crazy as it seemed, he missed Puerto de Anapra. They were only there for a month. One intense month that felt like a lifetime. Staying in the moment was easy when he was immersed in a life-threatening adventure with a smart and beautiful woman. Now, his mind whirred away, looking for trouble in a vacuum. No matter how he cut it, resuming a normal life was a lot harder than he'd expected.

The chilly March wind ruffled his carefully combed hair as he looked up at ten stories of brick. A tinge of anxiety flushed through him. That first day in a new school kind of feeling. New sportscoat, pants, and shiny shoes completed his nerdy ensemble.

He'd had enough experience in research labs to know everybody wore jeans and casual shirts covered up by lab jackets. Yet he still wanted to make a good impression. With one hand, he straightened his tie, while the other fumbled with his key fob and the two IDs he needed to get into the lab. Glancing at his picture ID, he read, "Alexander Winthrop, M.D., Vanhusse University Medical Center." He read it again. The photo he'd emailed security was seven years old. Looking at it brought tears to his eyes. It was taken when he, Julie, and the girls first moved to Providence for his new job at Rhode Island General. Not a day passed without the cold, hollow memories. After a couple stuttering deep breaths, he pushed his grief aside.

The new job was going to be a challenge, not only because he didn't feel qualified or have a clear grasp on what he would be doing, but because his heart wasn't in it. It was a job—just a job. Like being hungry and all you have to eat is raw, unseasoned tofu. Olivia assured him that his natural thirst for knowledge would eventually light him up. Alex didn't choose his new position; it was offered to him. It was the only way he could be with Olivia, and, at the moment, he didn't have any good alternatives. Olivia had used her influence. Fair enough, but Director Cunningham did the heavy lifting. It would now be easier for Cunningham's minions to keep an eye on both of them.

◇◇

"Hello. Ed? Hey, I was just thinking about calling you. Give me a minute. I need to stuff myself into an elevator."

"Don't fart."

"Geez, Ed, you know I love farting in crowded elevators. Okay. I'll try not to."

Alex got off on the fourth floor. To his left were windows that ran down the entire length of the hall. On his right were laboratories spaced thirty feet apart. Each gray metal entrance door was labeled with a number and the name of the lab director.

He walked to the window and looked down onto a courtyard that separated the research building from the main hospital.

"Okay. I'm back. How are you?"

"Fine, fine. How's it going? How's it going at Rhode Island General? You've been back in practice now, what, six months?"

"I was. It…"

"Was? What do you mean 'was'?"

"It just wasn't working, Ed. I really thought it would be okay, but it wasn't."

"Wait a minute, what are you talking about? You quit?"

"Yeah, I resigned from the RIG three months ago. I'm going to help Olivia with her research. So happens her project needed some clinical input—help planning for clinical trials, and such. Somehow, she convinced them—"

"Alex. Stop. Who is Olivia?"

He hadn't told anyone, not even his close friend, Ed, about his time in Mexico. Everyone thought he'd been in rehab. Quite convenient. After all that went down, it was hard to fathom that nobody in the RIG's upper management suspected Alex was involved. At least one of them knew Alex was asking too many questions.

Spencer Health, a national hospital chain, had entered into a joint venture with Rhode Island General a year earlier. The four-hundred-and-twenty-bed city hospital had been in financial trouble. The hospital conglomerate claimed they could stop the hemorrhaging. Altiva Pharmaceuticals in Puerto de Anapra Mexico had more than a "preferred customer" arrangement with Spencer Health.

Olivia was fired from Altiva because she knew too much. Together, she and Alex learned Altiva was making more than just generic drugs. Nobody said a word about Altiva Pharmaceuticals burning to the ground. The CIA had orchestrated an impressive cover-up.

"Oh God, I never told you. She's my girlfriend...a biochemist; she specializes in cellular toxicology. She has a lab here at Vanhusse University."

"Vanhusse?"

"Yep. She came down here a few months ago. I followed." Alex felt his face flush. Ed was an old friend and he'd told him nothing about anything that was going on.

"Meet her in rehab?" asked Ed.

"Yeah, something like that."

"Alex, are you okay? It hasn't been very long since…"

"I know what you're thinking. It does seem too soon, but, Ed, a lot has gone on. It's a long story. I love her. I can't help that. Can't wait 'til you meet her. You'll see why...I…"

"I'm sure she's special, Alex."

"Look, I gotta go. I'll call you. Can't be late for my first day on the job, right?"

"Okay, call me."

He never did.

◇◇

An odd odor permeated the hallway. The smell of animals mixed with the sweet sting of organic solvents. He could only describe it as a "lab smell." Alex passed a couple of men in long white coats chatting in the hall. They ignored him. "Olivia Nilsson Ph.D." was stenciled on the door of lab #3. Peering through the narrow vertical window, he saw rows of typical dull black soapstone lab tables. Several people were busy doing whatever they were doing. He swiped his pass-key and pushed his thumb into the print reader. Two women glanced over at him as he opened the door. One turned back to her work after looking him up and down with a slight smile. She seemed to like the look of this six-foot, trim, fit man with wavy brown hair and hazel eyes. The other, a stocky brunette with no makeup, wearing jeans and a long white coat, greeted him.

"Hi, I'm Dr. Winthrop, the new guy. Is Dr. Nilsson available?"

She nodded her head and looked at him with faint suspicion. "I'm Jan Whitorsh. Welcome. We heard you were joining us. I'll get Olivia."

"Thank you."

She left him standing there, nervously fiddling with his keys. After an awkward thirty seconds, he saw Olivia walking toward him, smiling. He stopped fidgeting. She looked great, even in her unadorned and stained lab coat. Jan was already back at her workbench.

"Good morning," she said in her business tone. "I'll show you your office."

"Hi hon…" he started to say but cut it short when Olivia glared at him. He got the message.

"They moved this little desk into my office for you. No other room."

"Perfect. I'll be more comfortable with you. By the way, why'd you ditch me this morning?"

"I told you last night that I had to come in early to change a water bath."

"Oh yeah, I forgot."

"Alex, you forgot—twice. Let me take you around, meet everybody, and tour the lab."

She introduced him to six busy people whose names vaporized somewhere between his ears and his memory. One was an M.D. research fellow, two were Ph.D. candidates, and three were lab assistants. He recognized some of the standard lab equipment, but most of it looked like something out of a sci-fi movie.

They walked by an office decorated with at least a dozen three-foot-tall stacks of journals. A narrow serpentine path led to a desk. Olivia pointed and said, "That's Dr. Bullock's office. Shane

Bullock; he should be back in the morning. He's the guy I told you about whose background is virology, but spends most of his time collaborating with the nanorobotics group. That work goes on in there." Olivia pointed to a solid steel door. "Access requires fingerprint and eye recognition. Let's go back to my...our...office." She bent to drink from a water fountain. Next to it was a sink with two upward pointing nozzles. "Eye wash station and here's a fire extinguisher—just in case."

Alex grinned while reading the inspection tag. "Just in case my eyes catch on fire?"

"Of course," chided Olivia, shaking her head.

Back in their office, Alex plopped down on his chair and spun to face her. "I guess I'll get over it," said Alex.

Olivia tilted her head. "Get over what?"

"My suspicion of nano-scientists."

"You know that's what we do here. I've told you about the progress we're making with the murine tumor model. One of our nanomeds shows ninety percent binding to tumor cells in vitro. Our drug delivery methods are coming along faster than I imagined. It's also part of what you will be working on." Olivia shook her head and let out a loud sigh.

"I know, I know. It's just a little hard to shake my suspicious nature sometimes." Alex felt a blush of shame. He wished he'd kept it to himself.

"Sorry. I think it just hit me too," she whispered. "Here we are together, once again, looking at nanorobotic drug delivery. But this time, Alex, it's about doing good...really."

"I'll try to remember that. Oh, your boss-lady scientist thing turns me on. Must be a storage room around here somewhere..."

Olivia shot him a sly grin. "Maybe we can do a little dominatrix when we get home tonight."

"Very funny, boss-lady."

She closed the office door, pulled him close by his tie, and kissed him. "Now, let's get to work."

"Okay. Great. What the hell am I supposed to do?"

"Here." Olivia handed him a couple pounds of journals and stapled articles. "This week, try to read as much as you can. Then we'll show you how things work around here."

"Do I get a sticker or some candy if I do well?"

"No, smartass, all you get is a vanishingly small chance of not making a fool of yourself."

"I feel better already," he mumbled, looking up from the intimidating stack of research articles. On the job, he'd always been in control. It wasn't an ego thing. He just didn't know how not to be.

"Alex."

"What?"

"Last week, before he went out of town, Shane told me he needed you to work with him for a while. Dr. Brown approved it. Here's the details." She laid an envelope on his desk.

"Brown? Department chairman, right?"

"Right."

"Crap. That's not what I signed up for. Tell him no."

"I can't. Cunningham…he told Bullock to use you if needed. It's probably just temporary."

Alex's face turned cold. He was furious. Olivia watched and waited until his clenched fists started to relax.

"I'm sorry. There's quite a push to get his antiviral nanomed project completed before the onslaught of SARS-CoV-3 or some other nasty virus. Anyway, I thought you loved virology."

"I do."

◇◇

Alex intermittently glanced out at the Nashville skyline from their newly renovated twelfth floor apartment while setting the table for dinner. For a moment, he stared across the Cumberland River at Nissan Stadium, home of the Tennessee Titans. It reminded him of Boston, residency, his wife Julie, and their apartment that overlooked Fenway Park. It was an eerie feeling, living in an apartment with a woman he loved, overlooking a stadium—again. Starting over. Maybe this would be the last time.

Olivia had told him "I'll just be a few minutes" over an hour ago. He couldn't complain. They were both on "doctor time." A six-pack of Samuel Adams was calling to him through the refrigerator door. *A couple beers would be nice, but I'd drink all six and go buy more and then I'd be looking for what I really wanted.* Over the past month, he'd thought more and more about drinking. *Could be worse.* He guzzled a glass of sparkling water and clicked on the TV. The news highlighted the St. Patrick's Day parade and pubs packed with beer-swilling Irish in New York City. Great timing.

The front door beeped, announcing Olivia's entrance. He turned off the TV.

"Hi, honey. I'm home," she bellowed, even though Alex was sitting on the couch eight feet away.

"Hi. Your cigar, martini, and two gluten-free valium are waiting for you."

"You know I quit cigars, silly. I might take you up on the others." Olivia smiled and put her arms up for a hug.

"Sorry. Just ran out. You'll have to settle for water Tylenol...and cooking dinner."

"Oh boy. Can't wait."

She held him around the waist, studied his expression, and tried to read his eyes. "How are you coming with the articles?"

"Great. I'm ready to extract some RNA and whip up a few bots. Not. But I did get through several. I'll try and finish a couple more tonight."

✧✧

The sun had set, leaving the city lights sparkling through the wall of glass that spanned their apartment. Nashville, country music, and southern accents are three things Alex never gave much thought to. When he did, it wasn't flattering. His stereotypical views had already begun to crumble. Olivia warned him never to assume that a southern drawl was pathognomonic for stupid. Nashville's vibrant music scene made his new home almost palatable. As a teen, he had dreamed of being a famous musician. Nashville rekindled the fantasy. Olivia was in her element. Being back at Vanhusse was a homecoming. A rebirth. It was there where she'd done her breakthrough research that led to her landmark article on cellular toxicology assays. Unfortunately, that notoriety led to her ill-fated decision to leave academics for a job with Altiva Pharmaceuticals. After that blew up, quite literally, she never in a million years thought she'd get a second chance running her own lab at a university. A second chance that came with a price. CIA Director Cunningham made it clear from the start that she was to work on developing an assay that could determine the presence of nanorobots in cells, drugs, and various biological environments.

How enduring would a relationship built within a crisis and glued together by a common enemy recalibrate to their new life? Alex feared that if he squeezed, it could break. Letting this mystery solve itself required patience. A virtue in short supply.

Now they were safe, living a normal mundane American life. It was strange, new, and full of uncertainty. External threats had been seamlessly replaced by internal concerns. The personal cost of living in an affluent society.

◇◇

"Alex, did I tell you I got approval to hire Melinda?" Olivia poured herself a glass of her favorite dry red wine. Alex stared as the Beaujolais led her to the couch.

"No. You mean Melinda...what's her name...the one that helped us, right?"

"Duh. Yeah, that Melinda. Melinda Taylor. She finished her dissertation and got her Ph.D. several months ago. I'm so proud of her. We've been talking for a while."

"When is she moving down?"

"This week. She starts work the week after next. She's sad about leaving her sweetie behind." Olivia poured another glass of wine. She liked to drink. Alex was surprised that she never drank too much. It was getting harder for him to be around it all the time.

"Her sweetie?" asked Alex, putting down an article on membrane potential that had just about lulled him to sleep. "She's married?"

"No."

"Is he coming down?"

"No." Olivia cleared her throat. "It's a she."

"You never told me she was gay. Doesn't matter. It's just something people usually mention."

"Ah...she's sorta gender fluid...bi."

"Well, I hope her fluid doesn't interfere with her work."

"Not funny, you bigot. I know you're just screwing with me, but, Alex, that's not funny."

Alex rubbed the back of his reddening neck. He didn't like being scolded. "I know, and yes, I was just kidding. My bad. You well know that I don't give a crap what somebody is as long as it doesn't interfere with their work. Period. Does knowing she's bi change the way you feel about her?"

"No. I mean, yes...maybe. We were together non-stop for two years at Yale, and I never picked up on anything. She dated a guy part of the time, but that was it. Don't get me wrong, but I think I'm a little jealous. Not physically. It's just that we've always been so close, and she's never hit on me. I get the feeling she's not sure yet. I just hope she's happy either way."

"Okay, wait a minute. Just because she's a bit fluid doesn't mean she's gonna hit on every chick she meets. Come on now, you're not sounding very woke. And I'm sure she didn't just start having bi tendencies at age twenty-whatever. I suspect it's a big step to accept that you're not straight."

"Woke this," Olivia said, patting her crotch.

"So, when did you join a fraternity?"

"I wasn't at all crass until I met you." She sashayed into the kitchen, swirling her glass.

"Good. We're making progress. Anyway, I guess she's the only one outside of the CIA that knows about our escapades with Altiva."

"She knows very little. Just enough to be suspicious."

"Cunningham must know about her, don't you think?" asked Alex.

"He asked me about her, of course. I told him she ran some tests for us and that's all. That's the truth. We never gave her too many details. No doubt he already knew plenty about her. After I told him about the skills she could bring to the table, he was sold."

"Too easy, maybe?" He pulled the chicken out of the oven. "Looks done," he said, not wanting to explain himself.

"What do you mean, Alex?" Her eyes narrowed. "What do you mean?"

"Relax. I'm sorry. I'm suspicious and I don't even know what of. I'm sure it'll work out fine. Can't wait to meet her."

"She must have passed the background check, interviews and whatever else, or it never would've gotten this far, right?"

"True."

Chapter 4

Charles Davenport was soaked with sweat. It took effort just to raise his head and gaze aimlessly around the small Pucallpa airport. Non-stop chit-chat in Spanish, Romani, and Portuguese accosted his ears as he waited for his flight to Lima. The Latam puddle-jumper was six hours late. A tiny man wearing a crumpled oversized khaki uniform attempted to answer the obvious question. The man, probably of Shipibo lineage, shrugged his shoulders. "Seis horas...is good, señor. Latam es late."

Charles limply nodded and sat back down, gripping his worn leather satchel under his arm. The moist heat was crushing. His head throbbed. The lingering fevers and sweats from Dengue fever were almost intolerable. Intermittently, he dozed and dreamt vivid, confusing dreams. He didn't know if they were from Dengue or the ayahuasca the shaman had him drink.

◇◇

Bogota El Dorado International Airport. Charles read the sign twice. *How the hell did I get to Bogota...so fast?* It had been twelve hours since he'd boarded in Pucallpa. He didn't remember anything since getting off the plane in Lima. If there were no delays, he'd land in Nashville in seven hours and finally climb into bed by around 2:00 a.m.

Stateside reality seeped into his mind as he stared down at the Atlantic during the last few moments of dusk. Thoughts of his father brought tears to his eyes. It was hard to shake. His dad was battling multiple myeloma—and losing. The last-ditch series of chemo had done nothing but make him sicker. *There's got to be something that'll work.* His father, Ron, had accepted that death was close at hand. Charles had not. Their relationship had never been good—Ron referred to his son as that leftist "rage against the machine" liberal and Charles called his father a right-wing fanatic. His mother, Maggie, would just shake her head. She'd given up trying to make the left and right get along. In her mind, it wasn't a big deal. They loved each other and that was all that mattered.

No sooner had he dried his swollen eyes, the name Melinda popped into his tangential mess of thoughts. Melinda Taylor was the love of his life until they parted ways after graduating from the University of Tennessee. She came to mind as he tried to recall natural remedies thought to treat cancer. At first, he had no idea what her name had to do with his cancer thoughts, then, he remembered—it was her childhood stories.

Two of them stuck with him. One was about the formation of Reelfoot Lake, just a few miles from her home in Lake County, Tennessee. In 1811, a powerful earthquake erupted from the New Madrid Fault along the Mississippi. It was so severe that it caused flooding of hundreds of acres that remained today as Reelfoot Lake. According to the Chickasaw, the earth split under the Mississippi. The southern edge of the fault rose so high that the mighty river flowed backwards, poured over its eastern banks, and submerged the bordering cypress forest, forming the shallow lake. Charles was fascinated. He'd lived his entire life in Tennessee and had never heard about it. But it was the second story that triggered his brain to retrieve Melinda's name.

◇◇

A shrill voice announcing the jet's descent into Nashville startled him. His mouth was parched. The remainder of his cup of water was soaking into his pants. He stood and held on to the seat in front of him and waited for the dizziness to pass. Before squeezing into the aisle, he rummaged through his satchel, reassuring himself that he had all his notebooks, phone, and digital mini-recorder. Finally, he had the last bit of information he needed to complete his text on the social effects of indigenous medicine. He was confident that the published text would advance him to full professor. So far, the promotions committee at Middle Tennessee State University had passed him over on the basis he hadn't met the publication standard. According to Charles, one of the committee members had it out for him.

If his notes and recordings were not just philosophical meanderings conjured up while tripping on ayahuasca, he might have a chance. The book was intended to be purely academic, not a treatise on his personal psychedelic experiences. During his numerous journeys to the world's most remote locations, he'd tried about every hallucinogen the earth had to offer. It was fair to say he liked to trip, especially on Middle Tennessee State's tab.

✧✧

At 2:30 a.m. he drove up his gravel drive and parked behind his house. He grabbed his suitcase and walked up three steps onto the porch. The old wooden boards creaked under his feet, reminding him that he'd been meaning to fix them for the past three years. A pole light illuminated the new roof trusses poking above the row of trees that ran along the field behind his house. When he first moved to Fairview, it was a sleepy town of eighteen hundred residents. Nashville's growth spurt pushed it to nearly three thousand. Charles' bucolic five acres and updated 1800s farmhouse was quickly surrounded by development. He didn't like it, but his soaring property value made it easier to swallow. He made a bee-line to his bedroom and flopped on his bed, still dressed and oblivious to his cat's pleas for food. Apparently, Mango was tired of the dry food Charles left in his feeder two weeks earlier.

He slept like the dead. When he awoke, he stripped and stumbled his way into the bathroom. A half hour later, when the water heater had drained, he reluctantly stepped out of the shower and reveled in the feeling of being clean. The cold crocodile-infested waters of the Amazon were hardly inviting. He was baffled by the Shipibo, who seemed undaunted by the risk. Before he could dry himself, his phone rang. "Oh, for chrissakes," he yelled as he ran around the house wrapped in a towel in search of the irritating device. "Hello. Oh, hi, Mom."

"Charles! You're back from your latest adventure?"

"Yeah, I got in late last night. How's Dad?"

"Not so good. A lot of pain. He's not eating—"

"What are you going to do?"

"What can we do, Charles? We're just waiting for tests to see if the last round of chemo helped...Doctor didn't seem to have much faith in it. He said, if anything, it'd just slow it down a little."

"Got to be something."

"Don't start in again about your silly natural remedies."

"Mom, you're just brainwashed like everybody else."

"Charles, please, none of your conspiracy theories. Not now. Anyway, you're supposed to be a scientist, not some kinda flake."

"You sound like Dad."

"Well?"

"Tell him hi for me. I'll be back in touch soon. Bye."

"I will. Bye."

Anything mainstream annoyed him. He didn't trust corporations or the medical establishment. The unproven powers of folk-medicine easily gained his trust. Unfortunately, his dad didn't share his enthusiasm. Ron refused to try the Juca fruit he'd brought from Brazil or the Carctol from India. Before he left for Peru, Charles brought his dad some CBD oil, hoping its recent popularity might convince him to try it. No such luck. His dad's biting final words on it had been "Just 'cause some primitive tribe uses it, or some wacky natural-organic company spokesperson says it works, you believe it. Nothing would shatter Charles' belief system. It was his life, and his identity as a medicinal anthropologist.

His mind latched on to the story, the other story, the one that tied Melinda's name to his thoughts about cancer treatment. It was about a strange healing remedy found along the banks of the Mississippi by an old country doctor over a hundred years ago.

◇◇

Charles booted up his laptop and sat with his fingers poised above the keyboard, then he typed: "Melinda Taylor Ph.D." She was on page two of his Google search. He read the short blurb about her on the Middleton University webpage. Old wounds kept him from calling her. He still cringed when he thought about how he pleaded with her not to move. For her, missing out on her dream of going to Yale for grad school was unthinkable. She loved him, but when his wants got in the way of her future, he'd crossed the line. Her parting words, "Charles, a needy guy is not attractive. It's a turn-off," struck him like a block of ice. Over time, his embarrassment morphed into a smoldering resentment. "Dammit!" he shouted, slamming his laptop shut. He got up and leaned his forehead against the doorframe. *But I still love that bitch. Will she ever take me back?*

Chapter 5

Moving to Nashville to take a real job and be a real scientist, working alongside the renowned Olivia Nilsson at Vanhusse was a dream come true. Bittersweet just the same. Tears ran down Melinda's cheeks as she put her last files in a box. The notes and pictures pinned to her six-by-four-foot corkboard hit her the hardest. An impatient knock on the door yanked Melinda away from memory lane. She turned to see Gwen's stocky frame, close-cropped blonde hair, and a bad mood enter her office. Gwen's eyes bore into Melinda's. They were both silent for an uncomfortable few seconds before Gwen put her hands on her hips and said, "So you're really doing it."

"Doing what?" answered Melinda, knowing well what Gwen was talking about.

"Moving. What else would I be talking about?"

"Yes, moving. I told you a month ago and several times since. I'm sorry. You know I can't miss this opportunity." Suddenly, she remembered how she left Charles. A sucky déjà vu. This time was different; she was leaving more behind than just a lover. Her fertile prime was slipping away. She wanted a husband and children. At least she thought she did. The words wouldn't come. She couldn't muster the courage to tell Gwen. In time, she'd tell her. Maybe once she got settled in Nashville.

"Melinda, you know...you know I can't leave now. I've only been teaching for a year. It would look bad on my resume. I've got to stay for at least three years so it doesn't look like I'm a problem. You know that."

"You have to stay just as much as I have to leave. You can visit, get a look at Nashville, right?"

"Great. Rednecks and country music. I'd fit right in."

"You might be surprised. Hold the door for me...please?" Melinda asked. "Please? This box is heavy."

Gwen shook her head, pulled the door open, and stepped aside. As Melinda stepped over the threshold, Gwen blurted, "Is Olivia gay?"

"No. She's not. She's living with a guy."

Melinda took a few steps down the hall, turned back to Gwen, and said, "I'm sorry." Gwen didn't follow her out to her car. *Maybe a clean cut-off is the best thing. It'll give me time to figure this mess out.* On the way out, she paid extra attention to the gray cinder-block walls, the speckled linoleum floor tiles, and the impotent water fountain that only pushed the water an inch above its fixture. A last look and silent goodbye.

Her phone started ringing. It was Charles' ringtone. *Perfect timing. Good grief.* She set the box on her trunk. They hadn't spoken in years. She'd assumed it was long over between them. But there was no denying the butterflies. No, she hadn't gotten over him. She let it ring.

This time, she wasn't towing her belongings in a U-Haul. Vanhusse was paying her moving expenses. Proof her real career had begun. Except for the nagging shame of ditching another lover, she tingled with excitement. The job at Vanhusse was exactly what she needed. In just two days, she'd be starting her new life.

The movers were gone. She slowly drove down her driveway for the last time. The sixty-four-year-old two-bedroom house she'd called home for five years looked nicer in her rear-view mirror. She assumed the litany of disconnected memories would soon fade, with one exception—Gwen. For the time being, that file would remain closed.

Chapter 6

Olivia sat on the steps in front of Music Square East, one of Nashville's many new chic apartment buildings just a few blocks from Vanhusse University. The tenants, for the most part, were under forty, either well-off Vanhusse students, or young professionals. At any moment, she expected some polite young person to ask her whose mother she was and if she needed help with directions. Nope. She remained anonymous. Invisible to eyes under forty. Working in academia had a strange effect on her perception of age. She generally felt a kinship with the swarms of Gen Zs she was immersed in, while at the same time feeling strangely out of place. If she came upon a group of students, even some of the interns and residents, they would immediately go mute. *Am I that damn scary?* Her cell rang.

"Hello. Melinda. Hi! How are you?"

"Great. Excited. Where are you?"

"I'm outside your groovy new home. You'll see me...I'm the old person on the steps."

"Oh, poor baby, are you having a moment?"

"Yeah, I'm forty-four and feeling ancient."

"You're gorgeous and don't look a day over thirty-seven."

"How do you know?"

"I still have some old...very old pictures of you."

"Just park and get over here."

"Yes, ma'am."

◇◇

A warm March breeze greeted Melinda as she stepped out of her car. She shed her L.L. Bean windbreaker. The sidewalk was abuzz with motion and animated conversation. The newness of the bustling city sent a feeling of thrill and expectation through her body. She caught a glimpse of Olivia between puffs of white blossoms and delicate branches. Two newly planted early blooming Callery pear trees flanked the entranceway. The blossoms were stunning, but they gave off a faint odor of dead fish.

"Welcome to Nashville, future famous scientist," greeted Olivia.

"You mean future chief test-tube washer?"

"Well, yeah, but I'm sure you'll advance in a few years."

Melinda sniffed at the air. "What's with the stinky trees?"

"They're pretty and grow anywhere. I guess that's why they're here. They overlooked the smell issue. It's nice to have something around that's producing oxygen, right?"

"Of course."

"Apartment 222. It's really nice."

They stepped into the glassed-in vestibule, bumping through three blonded girls who never looked up from their phones.

"Here's your pass-key. The manager lady gave me a temporary code for the pushbutton to use when the movers got here. You'll have to reset it." When they got off the elevator, Melinda's apartment was the first one on the right. "Well, here it is, 222. Let us in."

"Oh, Olivia, it's perfect." Melinda beamed as she took in her first glimpse of the apartment.

"Good. Glad you like it. You're welcome to stay with us until you get set up."

"No, no, I'm fine. I see my mattress made it, so I'll be fine. Thanks. When do I get to meet your awesome beau?"

Olivia smiled. "Yes. He is awesome. Let's have dinner Wednesday. Sound good?"

"Perfect."

"Glad your security clearance went smoothly. It's a pain. Please bring the rest of the paperwork with you. Okay, so here's your itinerary. Wednesday morning, you will have the typical orientation to Vanhusse and the lab. Then we'll have dinner at our place around six. At seven thirty, Cunningham and his DOD buddies will grill and intimidate you for about an hour concerning our department of defense work. It won't be bad, really…just protocol. I'm sure you've noticed they have zero sense of humor."

"Got it. No joking with the men in black."

"Exactly. After that, we'll get drunk."

"Roger that."

"Okay. Hate to rush, but I've got to get back to the lab. See you then. I'll text you our address. Call if you need anything."

◇◇

Where's my Keurig? was the first thought to enter Melinda's sleepy head. Then she remembered seeing a coffee bar on the first floor. Bingo. Off she went. By her second cup of coffee, she'd made a plan on how to attack the formidable task of unpacking. Her phone rang. It was Charles.

"Hello." She pretended not to know who it was so he wouldn't think she'd saved his number and ringtone.

"Melinda?"

"Charles?"

"Yup. It's me, Charles. How are you?"

"Great. You?"

"Good, good. Listen, I'm sorry about the way things ended. I was a dick. I should've been excited for you. I…"

"No worries. I wasn't too smooth with all that either."

"Melinda, I wanted to ask you about something."

"Okay. Shoot."

"Remember the story you told me about the old country doc?"

"Of course. Why?"

"Well, I'm an assistant professor at MTSU in medicinal anthropology. My focus has been the social impact of folk and indigenous medicine. I wonder if you could tell me more about his alleged discovery, or maybe you know someone I could talk to about it."

"First, I want to congratulate you, and second, what's MTSU?"

"Middle Tennessee State Un…"

"Oh god, yes. Sorry, how could I forget? In Murfreesboro, right?"

"I'll bet nobody ever asked you what Yale was."

"Ah…no. True, but Yale's been around for like two hundred years, so… Anyway, I've been at Middleton for a while and nobody's heard of that either." Several thick uncomfortable seconds hung in the air. Charles wished he'd shut up and Melinda felt embarrassed. "Why don't we meet for coffee?"

"Okay. Sure. I'll catch a plane to Vermont this afternoon."

"I guess I forgot to mention that I'm here in Nashville. Just got here last night."

"Really? You're kidding? Great! What are you doing here?"

Melinda was a little reluctant to tell him that she was now at another snobby upper-crust university. "I've taken a job at Vanhusse."

"Oh. Shit. That's wonderful. I bet you're freaking excited. I looked there, but they didn't have a position in med anth. I can be downtown in thirty minutes. Is today good?"

"I haven't even started to unpack, so maybe…"

"I can help you. I'm off today."

"Okay. I'll take you up on it. Music Square East, Apartment 222."

"Got it. I'll be a couple hours. Bye."

"Bye."

Crap, what was I thinking? I hope he doesn't think I'm interested in anything more than moving my furniture around. Not yet. Not until I've seen what he's turned into. The first thing she did was rummage for some nicer clothes and her make-up bag.

◇◇

The door buzzer sounded. It was the first time she'd heard it. It sounded like a high-school fire alarm designed for the hearing impaired. The owners of Music Square East probably got them in a package deal with the Callery pears. She looked at the small screen showing the vestibule. There he was, smiling into the camera and waving.

He'd lost a lot of hair. She had a few crow's feet and her boobs were a bit less perky. Both were self-conscious, each expecting the other to look exactly like they did eight years ago. After a low-contact hug and a few pleasantries, they got to work. Melinda gave orders and Charles obeyed. Neither of them liked being told what to do unless it made complete sense from their perspective. Moving furniture and boxes didn't warrant any deep debate, although lesser things have been the final straw for many. Conversation quickly filled the time.

"So, what raised your interest in my old Tennessee story?" asked Melinda.

Charles turned to her, set down a lamp and put his hands in his pockets. It was a habit he had when he was nervous. He quickly pulled them out when he saw a tiny change in her expression.

"I suspect that powder or potion, whatever, that he made probably had some effect on his community. It would be an interesting vignette for my book."

"Well, if his powder didn't, the way it ended sure made an impact, at least for a while." She held her tongue, not wanting to argue that his reasoning seemed weak. After all, Charles was the expert, and they'd only been around each other for a few hours. "I take it you remember the gist of it?"

"Yeah, I have a few questions and I'd love some details. Was it ever documented?"

"I don't know, but I suppose there may have been some newspaper articles."

"Any living relatives who might have some details...saved clippings?"

"His great-granddaughter is living, but…"

"Really? Maybe I could talk to her?"

"...Not sure she'd wanna dredge it up."

Chapter 7

1907

Flatboats stacked with cotton were a common sight. Simon waved at each one hoping to get a wave in return. It was all part of their river ritual. He didn't understand why only the men going downstream waved back. Many boat owners sold their boats for lumber when they got to New Orleans. Paying a crew to fight their way upstream could slash profits in half.

The moist air cooled as the sun closed in on the horizon. Doc hadn't paid attention to the time. He was still deep in thought, in wonder of Simon's vanishing cut.

"Oh my, son, we better be gettin' home."

"Aw, Grandpa, can't we stayed a while?" Simon pleaded, like always.

"Come on, let's go. We'll round up some leftovers."

"Aw, please?"

"...and a nice big slice of apple pie."

Simon shot up the levee like a jackrabbit. When they reached the green spot, Doc reached down and scooped up some of the sandy soil and eased it into his pocket, burying a few pennies. After a few steps, he had a sudden urge to pull that pocket inside out and wipe it clean, pennies or not.

◇◇

Doc was proud of his barn. It stood straight and tall, not a loose board to be found. Hay was neatly stacked and the horses had comfortable quarters. In the back, behind the stalls, he had a room that was as nice as the rooms in his house. It was his study and laboratory where, over time, he'd put together an impressive collection of equipment. Bell jars, test tubes, decanting flasks, alcohol burners, tubing, a Chamberland filter, bottles full of chemicals and medicine, and of course, his prized microscope.

Bookshelves were crammed with books on pathology, microscopy, and infectious disease. There was a separate shelf for his journals where he'd meticulously documented experiments, observations, and conclusions. The earthy smell of the barn punctuated by horse-talk was comforting and familiar. The office chair, made from hickory with its cracked leather seat cushion, was perfect for his ever-widening derriere. He'd salvaged it from a local bank that closed during the war. From that chair, Mr. Goldman made or refused loans to local farmers who needed money for seed. War and the Department of Agriculture's free seed distribution program killed his loan business.

In the days before Tommy Dunn, the pharmacist, came to town, Doc measured out doses of medicine and compounded ointments and potions on a daily basis. He'd brought most of the labware to the barn from his office, now that Tommy was doing the drug work. He still made some of his signature powders. A handful of his patients wanted Doc's powders and salves, or nothing at all.

There was always something to study, even cuttings from diseased cotton plants. Edith was certain he'd fall asleep and one of his lamps would set the barn on fire. She reminded him so often, he'd greet her with, "No fire and the horses are calm, honey," as he slipped in the front door after a night of tinkering in his laboratory. Edith called it tinkering. He called it research. When the whiskey flowed, it became—life-saving medical research...on the verge of a major breakthrough. Spirits made him quite verbose.

✧✧

It was just before 9:00 p.m. that night when Doc went out to the barn. On average, it took about seventy-five steps to get to the barn door. He liked knowing things like that.

"Don't be too late, you have a slew of patients tomorrow," hollered Edith as the screen door clapped shut.

"Yes, de…"

"…and don't burn the place down."

"Yes, dear," he shouted over his shoulder, about five steps down the path.

It was his habit to check on the horses. They were startled by the grating sound of the barn door and wary of the fire coming toward them. Doc set the oil lantern down several feet from the stirring mares and gave them each a pat. "Don't you tell Edith I put that lantern down in here. She'd have a fit."

He went into his lab and lit two more lamps. Then he gingerly shook the soil from his pocket into a 100-milliliter beaker and studied it, tilting it back and forth in front of the lamp. *Maybe it's some healing material from a plant like aloe, ginseng, or some combination that made the effects more potent. Maybe Simon's cut closed up just enough in the cold river water that I plumb couldn't see it.* Setting it down on his long marble table-top that served as his lab bench, he chastised himself for going off on such an unlikely tangent. *Magic dirt? I must have eaten too much rum-cake with my rum.*

He poured a little on a piece of filter paper and pressed it with his forefinger. The black granules smudged like carbon, leaving behind a fine golden powder. The lighter-colored granules looked like ordinary sand. Using his Chamberland filter, he gently poured water into a small sample and watched it drip into a beaker. While holding the transparent amber fluid in front of his eyes, in a flash, it clouded up and became turbid, not unlike what he'd seen when titrating various chemicals. But with just water and filtered dirt? Strange, but not impossible. In keeping with standard practice, his next step was to prepare a slide and examine a sample with his prized Powell & Lealand microscope. It was one of the finest compound condenser microscopes money could buy.

Tiny circular and rod-like forms filled his view. Bacteria. He'd seen water turn turbid after several days due to bacterial growth, but in an instant? Impossible. The Chamberland filter should have kept any bacteria in the soil from getting into the beaker. He repeated his steps, this time capturing a drop of the clear filtered mixture on a slide and quickly putting it under the microscope before it became turbid. He stared through the tiny lens, holding his breath. In less than a minute, the empty appearing slide was teeming with life. Dividing bacteria could be seen in every field of view. Astonished and trembling with excitement, he grabbed his notebook and carefully described what he'd seen. After jotting down several lines, he stopped and threw down his pencil. *But if something in the dirt is promoting bacterial growth, then Simon's cut should have become infected—not healed.* The germ theory was still a subject of hot debate. Not for Doc; he thought it made perfect sense. Yet if that theory was true, this made no sense.

I need a live specimen. He scanned the floor as if some rodent would be there waiting to be plucked up. Unfortunately, the cats did too good a job keeping the barn cleared of varmints. At that moment, there weren't many options. He reached into the top drawer of his mahogany roll-top desk and retrieved his father's treasured silver handled, straight-edge razor.

Doc dropped the razor on his desk. *What if the wound became immediately infested with bacteria? What if it did nothing at all? What if it had nothing to do with Simon's vanishing wound? But…what if it did?* The polished steel blade reflected the lamp's shimmering flame. He tipped it back and forth, watching the light dance, and picked it back up. *A small cut into the epidermis—no deeper, just enough to test my theory. My thigh. Yes, a tiny cut on my thigh.*

He unbuckled his belt and pushed his breeches over his knees.

The blade cut easily as he drew its tip less than a half-inch across his thigh. He was careful not to cut all the way through his skin. The trickle of blood clotted almost instantly when he rubbed in a pinch of river sand. As he rubbed, the sand broke down into a fine powder and disappeared into the wound. *Sand doesn't do that.*

The barn creaked, yielding to a sudden gust of wind, scaring the horses. He dropped the razor into a flask of alcohol and downed a shot of whiskey before getting up to leave.

"It's just the wind, my dears," he whispered. "It's just the wind."

Chapter 8

Alex tapped his fingernails on the granite counter. Olivia didn't interrupt his thoughts. She wanted him to process the change in plans on his own. She hoped he'd take it in stride. Other researchers would jump at the chance to work with Shane Bullock, Ph.D. Alex took a deep breath, turned to her, and waited for her to finish slicing a tomato.

"I think working on Bullock's project will be good...once I know what the hell I'm doing."

"Yes." Olivia set down her dishcloth. "I'll miss not working with you, but it's really quite an honor to work with him...even if he is kind of condescending sometimes."

"Oh really?" Alex tilted his head as if ducking from the unwanted reveal.

Olivia grinned and patted him on the shoulder. "Yup. Just pretend he's one of those pretentious attendings you had during medical school."

"Thanks for the heads up."

"Alex, he needs some clinical input and probably needs some help with the animal physiology data. That's not an area he's well-versed in. He knows you're a smart doc, so if he intimidates you for not knowing something, you can do the same to him."

"Now that sounds pleasant." Alex shook his head and grinned. "Give me some background on BN27."

"Okay. Initially BN27, a nanomed, was developed by the

Department of Defense to create a secret antidote in the event China or Russia unleashed a virus as a biological weapon. This nanotechnology became critical to the government's larger biological weapons program. Sharing this with our adversaries would be a major and dangerous setback. Once word leaked out to a couple politicians outside the DOD, the moral card was played, causing a firestorm. The do-gooders finally quieted down when they understood the importance of protecting the technology. In exchange for their silence, if another pandemic hit, the DOD had to promise it would go into mass production and make BN27 available to everyone."

"Sounds messy," said Alex.

"It's a given when politicians are involved."

"But of course." Alex rolled his eyes.

"So," Olivia continued. "Bullock knew there was no way international demands could be met quickly enough without sharing technological secrets. A month after all that, COVID-19 hit, and BN27 wasn't anywhere near being ready."

"I guess it's best just to focus on making the stuff and worry about the politics later."

"That's the only thing you can do. Oh, Alex, tomorrow night…"

"Yeah?" Alex finished drying a plate and looked at her.

"Melinda's coming for dinner."

"Okay…and?"

"Director Cunningham and a couple guys from DOD are going to brief her on the rules of conduct, etcetera."

"Oh, dang, I forgot to tell you. I've got plans...I'm...I'm going to walk down Broadway and pick up cigarette butts. You know, civic duty."

"Very funny. Cunningham wants you to be here. He said you need a refresher course now that you're working with Bullock."

"Blah, blah, blah, I hear ya."

"For chrissake, it's not exactly my idea of a fun night either."

"I know that. Sorry."

"So don't be a smartass."

"You won't believe this, but I think I've heard that before."

Alex's expression became serious. Olivia knew what was coming next.

"Have you told her…"

"No."

"…how our little explosive Mexican 'vacation' ended up? That's fine. I'll do it. I'll give her a watered down, almost true version. Okay?"

"Thanks. You're more creative than I am. A better liar, too."

"I'll take that as a compliment."

For a time, they were silent. She washed, he dried, both oblivious to the rain snapping against the twelve-foot expanse of west facing glass.

◇◇

"Melinda should be here any minute. We wanted to have some time before the 'Men in Black' show up."

"Wow, you are really doing it up. She'll think it's our wedding china," said Alex.

"Wedding? Did I hear you say wedding? Let me sit down, I'm feeling faint." Olivia fanned herself with a plate.

"Oops. Maybe I should take my temperature. I might have encephalitis or something."

"Too late. Answer the door. And do not ask her about her girlfriend."

He gave her a "do you think I'm that stupid?" look as he reached for the door.

"Hi, Melinda. I'm Alex."

"I'm so glad to finally meet you. Olivia has told me so much about you." Her tone didn't set up a humorous comeback.

"Thank you. It's great to meet you. I want to thank you for

your help with our Mexico project. Your NMR and mass spec. expertise made all the difference."

"You're welcome. Whatever happened with—?"

Olivia shouted from the kitchen, "Geez, Alex, let her in the door, would ya?"

"Sorry. Come on in." Alex led her to the kitchen. Melinda and Olivia immediately engaged in intense catch-up talk. Alex leaned on the bar and listened intently until he realized he wasn't part of the conversation—at all.

"So how did things end up in Mexico? Sounded pretty scary," asked Melinda.

"Why don't you let Alex tell you while I finish up in here."

"Can I help?"

"No, no, go get the scoop from Alex. I'm fine."

Alex's ears perked up. Olivia shot him a wink. He turned and watched Melinda walk into the living room with a very large glass of white wine. *What are the odds of having two attractive female scientists in the same room?*

Alex took a deep breath. "I'll begin where we left off with you, okay?"

"Sounds good." She leaned forward, close enough for him to smell the wine and a faint whiff of perfume.

"Once you identified a nanobot in the drug, it all made sense. That was the key to why the drug was causing the deadly side effects. While we were putting all the information together, I got a call from Director Cunningham, who told me that our government had been investigating Altiva Pharmaceuticals. I have no idea how he knew about us, why we were there, or what we were doing, let alone getting my phone number. He—"

"He never told me anything about all that during my interview...and I never said anything about what I found. He caught me off guard when he said he knew about the first bioassays I ran for you."

"No. He wouldn't have said much. It's a major serious secret. Melinda, you can't mention any of this to anyone or we will all lose our jobs and face some serious charges. We're telling you this because you were so much help, and I'm sure you've been curious...suspicious that something sorta big was going on."

"Thanks. My imagination is sometimes worse than the truth."

"Probably not this time. Anyway, he wanted all the information we had to help them shut down Altiva. Which they did. But Cunningham had a problem. We knew too much. We had to swear to secrecy, and, yes, we are doing what we're doing in the lab because of him. Helping Olivia get a lab set up at Vanhusse has been great...but there are strings attached. You're coming into the fold and we know you have a pretty good idea what that means.

"Day to day, the lab runs like any other lab. The work is meaningful. You'll hardly know the government is involved, at least that's what Olivia says. The DOD provides the funding. We do the work. Olivia and the other section heads provide progress reports each month. The technology for some of the research is classified. Highly classified. They have to approve anything we do, say, or publish. You will get the serious low-down when they get here tonight. Welcome aboard."

Chapter 9

Shane Bullock already had his lab humming when Alex announced his arrival through the intercom. Olivia was right: he could smell what reminded him of his childhood guinea-pig cage. Stored mice and rats had the same musty odor. The lab was crowded with equipment. Four assistants worked silently with graceful efficiency. A well-oiled machine. Only Minji Tam and Dr. Bullock acknowledged his presence. Minji was several months away from getting her Ph.D. She was Bullock's favorite, a status that would assure her a great start as a young researcher.

"Good morning, Alex," said Dr. Bullock, looking over his reading glasses. He was a tall, rotund man with bushy gray hair and beard. "I'd shake your hand, but I need to maintain sterility. Do you have a pretty good idea where I am with my research?"

"A very basic understanding."

"Great. For now, I'd like you to shadow me. I'll explain in detail throughout the day while asking you to assist, hands-on as needed. Having said that, I need your help with the mice ASAP. You'll get it. I know you've had a good bit of lab experience. but I don't expect you to have a clue about the specifics of my work, yet."

"Sounds good, and I appreciate your patience."

"Our computer engineers have been working on nanorobotics for twenty years. What started out as not much more than theory has become a reality."

Alex nodded. "It still baffles me that man-made devices smaller than a cell's nucleus can be created to manipulate a biological system. Fascinating."

"Very fascinating. My part has been to describe the characteristics needed to bind viral genes intracellularly. Finally, we have a bot that can do it, at least in cell culture. The nanobot completely stopped viral replication. By the end of this week, we plan to inoculate mice with live virus. Your job will be to place arterial and venous catheters for monitoring. You will judge how sick they are. On days three and five, you will administer the nanobot-saline mixture intraperitoneally. Then, at 24, 48, and 72 hours, live tissue samples will be taken followed by sacrifice. Autopsies will immediately be performed followed by slide prep for light and electron microscopy. Not by you. Not at first anyway. Take an hour or so each day to get your skills up so you can help with that when we do the next batch. If I find evidence for nanobot binding and a drop in viral load, we can move on to dosage studies."

Bullock's eyes glistened. "Alex, if this works it will be the biggest breakthrough in the history of antivirals. Can you imagine a world without fear of viral pandemics? I have one bothersome concern...there's been some talk among the DOD about not sharing BN27 with our adversaries. If we were about to go to war, that might make sense, but how could we let another pandemic hit us and do nothing?"

Alex's eyes grew wide. He could feel himself flush. "You don't think they'd do that, do you?" He thought it best to act surprised.

"Honestly, I can't imagine it. Probably just talk."

"Yes. I hope."

"Oh, and Alex, this lab is separate from Olivia's. It's fine that she knows what we are doing, but you can't share specific technology or any DOD stuff pertaining to our work with her. I'm pretty sure she'll be involved later, but that's solely up to the

DOD."

✧✧

Olivia and Alex sat as far away from the raucous as possible. The hospital's cafeteria was packed at noon. The line moved quickly; efficient by necessity. Employees had no time to dawdle. Many chose to eat outside, still in the habit of social distancing. A lingering and likely a good habit to hang on to. People from every area of healthcare mixed among distraught visitors. Some were visibly irritated by the laughter and boisterous March Madness banter.

"I remember, during my residency, overhearing a young woman say, 'How can they be laughing when my son is dying?' as I yucked it up with a couple of my fellow interns. Sorta stuck with me. That's one of the reasons hospitals had separate doctors' eating areas. Over time, as hospitals pined for more control, many dismantled what they called "elitist" treatment of doctors. So it goes. Idiots. They just don't get it," said Alex.

Olivia, chewing a mouthful of sandwich, nodded, and said, "You know resentments are unhealthy."

"Oh no, you're going Dr. Phil on me."

Olivia, still chewing, covered her chuckle with a napkin. "How'd it go with Bullock?"

"He'll be fine. We are both aware we know a lot the other doesn't, so we'll get along fine. Still, I have to admit I'm a bit intimidated because this isn't my turf. He clearly has the home field advantage."

"Okay, so the egos are in check. What about the work?"

"You were right. We're starting animal studies this week. I get to... ah, try to put venous and arterial lines in mice? Even their biggest blood vessels are half the size of toothpicks. Why couldn't we use rabbits or maybe medical students, or something?"

"Good point. Why don't you put in an order for some?" she scoffed. "Hey, changing the subject, did you hear that there's been a small outbreak in China? Eight people with that bat flu I was telling you about. This 'bat flu' is a Nipah virus. You remember the outbreak in Malaysia had a seventy-five percent kill rate. It spread from fruit bats to pigs to humans. Not a clue where ground zero is, so they say. Of course, wet markets are top suspects. Chinese authorities say they've got it contained. We've heard that before. What's really scary is that six have died and the others are comatose. Damn. I can't imagine another pandemic."

"Just a matter of time."

Olivia gazed out at the courtyard, grappling with the possibilities. Alex stole her pickle. She looked back toward him but focused on a group of tables that were now empty, and said, "When I first got here, the cafeteria was still closed. The entire place felt apocalyptic—eerie. A palpable mix of fear, fatigue, and anxiety."

He nodded, recalling those days when the COVID-19 pandemic crept into months, then three years, leaving two million Americans dead. "Let's get back," said Alex, as he stacked the dishes, carefully balancing their paper trash on top.

It was a five-minute race-walk back to the labs. Like many older university hospitals, networks of subterranean tunnels and catwalks connected separate buildings that were added over many years. With growth confined by the inner city, they'd acquire contiguous properties when available. As a result, they ended up with a confusing array of buildings that appear to have sprung up from scattered seeds. Alex thought it added historical charm. Olivia found it irritating.

◇◇

It was after 7:00 p.m. when Alex left Bullock's lab and made his way to Olivia's office. He sat across from her, waiting for her to finish putting her daily data into her computer. It had been a pretty good day. Dr. Bullock and his lab staff were respectful and curious about his impression. They hadn't had a practicing M.D.

in their lab before. Alex didn't need another day of feeling like a loser. Olivia was right. She'd predicted he'd come alive with a good mental challenge.

"I'm ready. Let's go." Olivia shut down her computer. "By the way, I've noticed some of the women around here checking you out."

"So?"

"I'm ordering you five 'Property of Dr. Nilsson' t-shirts, one for each day of the week."

"God, I love it when you're jealous. So sexy. I'm sure you get more looks than I do."

"Not anymore. They're all afraid of me...I think it's my Swedish accent."

Road grit blew into their eyes as they stepped onto Medical Center Drive. Alex gripped her hand. She smiled and gripped back.

"Can't shake it, can you?" Alex asked as they walked through the dimly lit parking garage. Footsteps and car noise echoed from all directions, making it difficult to pinpoint where the sounds came from.

"Shake what?"

"I noticed you glancing side-to-side the whole way through the garage."

"After being followed for so long…it's a hard habit to break."

"I get it. I'm sorry. Probably not a bad habit when you're walking in here alone. Just watching TV and movies can make you think parking garages are filled with muggers and perverts."

"Well, they are, aren't they?"

"Yeah, probably. You carry your pistol, right?"

"Alex, don't be so naive. You know I'd never get through the entrance scan."

"What's this damn world coming to? Is it only acceptable for the innocent to be defenseless against their attackers?"

"Alex, you know the deal. It is what it is. Oh, I invited Melinda over tonight to give her a break from her boxes. Sorry I forgot to check with you. I ordered take-out...Chinese."

"That's okay. Sounds fine."

◇◇

Melinda figured out that walking to the lab was a lot quicker and easier than driving. As she neared her apartment, her cheery mood did a nosedive. Unpacking was a major annoyance. She couldn't figure out why, but she just didn't want to do it. Her bedroom was mostly set up. The kitchen was usable, but boxes still controlled most of the floor space. *I'll finish it this weekend. No ifs, ands, or buts!*

Gwen was on her mind as she entered her apartment and headed in to clean up and change clothes, but she wasn't ready to talk to her. As for Charles, things were moving too fast. She was gently putting on the brakes to give herself time to think. On the other hand, he was a big help with unpacking. Tonight, she had an excuse; she was going over to Olivia and Alex's.

Charles' recent obsession with the old doc's powder was strangely irritating, even though she was more curious about it than she'd let on. She'd first thought it had just been an excuse to call her. Apparently not. Folks from Lake County didn't talk about it. It was an unwritten rule. Back in the day, everyone loved and respected Doc Stevenson. Nobody wanted to burden his descendants with ancient rumors, especially Melinda. When her family moved to Lake County, Melinda became friends with the old lady next door, Geneva Brown, Doc Stevenson's great-granddaughter. Melinda knew her as Miss Jenny. That was what everybody called her. She still lived in the family home, the farmhouse Doc built in 1861. Miss Jenny and Melinda would sit on the porch swing for hours sipping sweet tea and talking. Melinda did most of the talking. She was a teenager and life wasn't fair. Miss Jenny patiently listened.

Chapter 10

1907

Before going downstairs for breakfast, he examined his leg. "My God, it's healed," he whispered. His heart raced with a surge of anxious wonder.

"Are you well?" asked Edith, pausing at the top of the stairs. Doc didn't usually sit on the edge of the bed so long on workdays.

"Yes. Fine."

"Best not dawdle. Your first patients will be waiting soon."

"Yes, dear. Oh, did you feel the tremor last night?"

"No. What time?"

"About 9:30."

"I was up. Didn't feel a thing."

Doc was perplexed but let it go. He was full of energy despite only four hours of sleep. The white shirt Edith washed on Saturday was stiff and wrinkled. She did the ironing on Sunday night when the iron had time to heat in the hearth after dinner. Somehow, they'd both forgotten until the embers had faded. He put on his gray breeches and buttoned his signature suspenders. When shaving, he stopped mid-stroke. Fragments of dreams suddenly emerged from his subconscious. He remembered atoms and molecules coming together to form chemicals. Chemicals arranged themselves into odd three-dimensional structures. He'd read a journal not long ago explaining a recent discovery of something called amino acids that made up proteins which sounded similar to what he'd seen. The advancements in chemistry fascinated Doc. Maybe that interest had been woven into his dreams. Standing at the top of the stairs, he whispered, "Dreams—just the nonsense of dreams."

It was a good thing his horse had memorized the route to his office because she never felt a tug on her reins. Doc was too distracted. Suzy waited patiently, swatting flies with her tail, until Doc snapped out of it and climbed down from the buggy.

Yet all that morning in his office, instead of jotting down clinical notes on each patient, he feverishly drew as many of the chemical structures as he could remember. One after another, the images came to mind. He wrote through his lunch break. Just before seeing his first afternoon patient, he stopped and stared at his pen, bewildered. *This thing is nigh on to drawing on its own.* Suzy didn't have it so easy on the trip home. Doc pushed her to a full gallop the entire way.

◇◇

Edith poured the dirty dishwater off the porch and set the basin by the door. The pigs heard the water splash. Table scraps were soon to follow. They watched and waited for Edith's return. There was only a bite or two. Like their dog, Butch, they seemed to enjoy just the thought of food.

Doc met Edith at the door, hugged her, and began to caress her breast. She put her hand over his, holding it still. She didn't push him away, after all, she was his wife. It wasn't like she wouldn't like sex with her husband again, but...

"Honey, what are you doing? What are you thinking?" asked Edith.

"I'd like to take you to bed."

"How can we, it's been years since...?" His inability to perform in the past had been so humiliating, he'd quit trying.

"Edith, I can't explain it. Feel it."

"Oh heavens," she said with a grin he hadn't seen in a long

time.

$$\diamond\diamond$$

Edith was sound asleep. He quietly got dressed and tiptoed toward the door, trying his best to avoid the squeaky planks. He gathered his notes and lantern, his mind racing.

The horses perked up their ears when he pulled open the heavy barn door. Certainly, they were puzzled when he walked past them without even a "hello." Once the lanterns were lit, he sat at his desk and busily copied all of the day's drawings into one of his lab notebooks. For hours, he jotted down thoughts and drew images.

A true scientist never trusts the results from a single experiment. He took the straight edge down from the shelf, passed it over his desk lantern's flame, unhooked his suspenders, and pushed his breeches down. This time, he was a little braver. He'd make more than a scratch. The blade cut through the epidermis and into the dermis. Blood flowed freely down either side of his thigh. After pressing a pad of gauze against it for a few minutes, he weighed out 0.1 grams of his river sand and rubbed it into his wound. Again, the bleeding stopped almost immediately. He pulled his breeches back up to his hips and wrote down his observations.

A loud scraping sound came from the roof. It creaked as if under great pressure. He guessed it was a sagging limb from the huge oak closest to the barn. He put the notebook back on the shelf, blew out one lantern, and used the other to guide him by the stalls and out into the night. Damp cool air ran over his skin. He took several steps down the path, turned, and looked up at the great oak. There were no branches anywhere near the barn. He studied the trees around the barn. None had branches near the roof. The horses had settled, hardly noticing him when he walked back to his lab for a little whiskey. Several gulps of warm whiskey stung its way to his stomach and quickly to his brain. A warm sense of relief came over him. With his notebook in one hand and lantern in the other, he secured the door and walked up the path toward the house.

Through the side of his eye, he saw a light as he stepped onto the porch. He turned and tried to focus. Two rhythmically bobbing torches were coming up his dirt lane. Three fast galloping horses came into view, silhouetted by a full moon. A few seconds later, he could distinguish two anxious riders and a third slumped over his saddle. They stopped between the house and the willow tree as if to ask permission.

"Doc, Doc, need yer help," shouted one of the men, holding his torch closer to his body to show he wasn't holding a gun.

"Who are you?" Doc yelled back.

"Jimmy Sanders and Jake Forrester. We work for W.R. Henderson. Tennessee Land Company. We got Jeb Henry, farm manager. He's hurt. Night Riders sliced him up good."

"Bring him in the house," said Doc, waving them in. "Put him on the kitchen table. I'll have a look."

The Night Riders were a local vigilante group who took it upon themselves to be the arbiters of justice, for the usual reason—local authorities didn't do enough. Their main target was the Tennessee Land Company, a callous group of outsiders that had been buying up land around Reelfoot lake, barring access to the locals. The waterfront had always been considered public domain. It was used for fishing, hunting waterfowl, and recreation. Many in Obion and Lake County tacitly supported the Night Riders' violent response. Doc detested the land company but drew the line at violence. That night, he felt differently. It took all the strength he could muster not to shoot all three of them. There'd be no repercussions. They were trespassing and it would be easy to imagine they'd come to Doc's house with nefarious intent. No local jury would give it a second thought.

"Take his shirt off," ordered Doc as he lit an extra lantern.

Edith heard the commotion and yelled down the stairs, "What

is it, dear? Are you alright?"

"Yes. Fine. Get me a pail of water."

She threw a tunic over her night clothes and went to draw the water. Doc pulled open Jeb Henry's shirt, revealing two long knife slashes. One started just below the left breast, stopping at his navel. The other ran horizontally across the full length of his abdomen. They were both deep and bleeding. He was pale from blood loss, but alert enough to show fear.

"Give him a few big swallows." Doc handed Jimmy a bottle of whiskey. "I'm going to get some supplies." Doc jogged out to the barn to get some gauze, suture, antiseptic, and a little chloroform. He picked up the flask of river sand, poured a small amount onto a piece of filter paper, folded it, and slid it into his pocket. *This will be a fine experiment, indeed.*

Edith held the pail until Doc was done cleaning the wounds. She'd learned a lot over the years and became his nurse by default. That was the furthest thing from her mind when she married the young doctor thirty-five years ago.

They met in church where Doc's father, James, was preaching. Doc was still thin and tired from his long tense journey back home from Philadelphia. The fresh medical school graduate was robbed and beaten by recently displaced Native Americans, near Green River Lake, Kentucky. Their despair was palpable. He had no malice. He'd been home six days when his eyes locked on Edith's. At that moment, they both knew they had found their mate. James preached on Sunday morning and doctored the locals every day and night. The Stevensons were well known in Jackson, Tennessee. Maybe too well known. Doc feared the responsibility of his father's legacy, but he'd promised to come back and join the aging man's practice.

Edith was raised with nine siblings on a farm in Crockett Mills, about midway between Jackson and Lake County. Thanks to the tireless efforts of Catherine Beecher, women were slowly being accepted into the field of teaching. Edith was one of the first female teachers in Jackson. By marrying Doc, she broke the unwritten rule that only unmarried women could teach. Some parents kept their children out of her classroom. She knew the risk.

They were abolitionists among slave owners. This caused a deep rift between Doc and his father. Their final decision to move came when General Nathan Bedford Forrest took on General Ulysses Grant's army in Jackson. Forrest successfully stopped Grant's campaign by destroying the railroad, but the Union army still occupied the city. They converted Edith's alma mater, West Tennessee College, into a field hospital. Looting and rape were commonplace. Choosing sides was nearly impossible. Neither of them could explain exactly what drew them seventy miles northwest to Lake County. Maybe it was the river.

"What's that?" asked Jimmy. It was obvious he could hardly stomach watching Doc treat the gaping wound.

"Medicine," answered Doc as he dabbed the river sand into the open lacerations.

"Looks like dirt or sand or something."

"Yes. It does, doesn't it?"

Jimmy said no more. He was smart enough to hush. They were lucky Doc was willing to help.

"Mr. Henry, rest up a few days. Keep it clean, dry, and covered. Come see me in four days—after sunset. And yes, I expect to be paid for my work."

◇◇

Each night after dinner, he returned to the barn and wrote down his dreams as they flowed into his consciousness. Two days after patching up Jeb Henry, Doc drew a rough image of DNA's double helix, complete with labeled nucleotide pairs. He recalled a paper written thirty-some years ago by Swiss chemist, Friedrich Miescher. He had identified a novel molecule derived from the nuclei of white blood cells, which he called nuclein. Miescher did not know this new material's structure or its function. Doc was certain that his drawings were intimately tied to the Swiss chemist's discovery. It would be forty-three years before Watson and Crick would become famous for revealing DNA's double helix structure.

He began to understand the images that flooded his thoughts. The common thread had to do with cell division, growth, and differentiation. Doc peered through his microscope for hours searching for clues. Cells from the tip of an onion root, of all things, revealed plenty of easy to see mitosis and cell division. Scrapings from inside horses' mouths, rat intestines, and plant samples all found their way into the lab.

It wasn't unusual for Doc to be preoccupied with something he was studying. Edith had grown accustomed to him coming to bed an hour or so after her. The only thing that drew her attention was his newfound ability and interest in sex. "God's Will" was her go-to explanation. Then, everything changed.

One night, a few days after Doc drew his first double helix, he'd been out in the barn reviewing his journals and sipping whiskey. It was close to midnight when he went back to the house. He carefully ascended the unlit stairway to the bedroom.

A gentle breeze came in through the west-facing bedroom window, keeping the room just cool enough to keep them from waking up on sweat-soaked sheets. For most of the summer, that wasn't the case. The window sheers swayed silently in the moonlight. Edith was sleeping soundly when he undressed and climbed into bed. He gently pulled back the covers and pulled her close to him. She awakened with a start when he rolled on top of her.

"Dear. No. Not now. Please?"

He gripped her left arm around the biceps, firm enough to make a point but not enough to hurt—so he thought.

"You're hurting me. Let go!"

She felt a sharp pain shoot through her face into the side of her head just before lapsing into unconsciousness. His fist had crashed into her face with tremendous force before he'd had a thought. Immediately, he kneeled at her side and wept.

"Edith, I'm sorry! I didn't mean to. It just happened. Oh, good Lord—I'm sorry." She awoke at the tail-end of his last "I'm sorry" with blood dripping from her nose and lip. At first, for a fleeting moment, she felt responsible. *I shouldn't have resisted. He meant no harm. It was his right.* Twice as quickly, she rejected that notion. Silently, she stared at him, shaking her head and pinching her nostrils shut to stop the flow of blood. She got up and left the room.

✧✧

She leaned into the open stone hearth to stir the eggs. The heat exaggerated the pain surrounding her left eye. She had only a sliver of vision between swollen, contused eyelids. An open slit crossed her upper lip where Doc's fist burst it open. Drinking her morning hot coffee was impossible. She turned away when he came into the kitchen.

"Dear God. I'm so sorry. I don't know what came over me."

He put his arms around her. She stood firm, covering her face with both hands. Her salty tears stung as they flowed over raw flesh. They sat at the well-worn pine plank table facing each other, but not looking. Doc said grace. They ate breakfast in silence.

He stood and clasped his hands together in front of him with tears in his eyes.

"Edith, I'm sorry. Please forgive me."

"Were you drunk?" She wanted an excuse, some way to convince herself it was a fluke, and unlikely to happen again.

"I'd sipped some whiskey. Yes, I did...but I wasn't drunk."

He should have lied. It was the right thing to do. He picked up his black leather medical bag and stepped out of the kitchen, giving Edith's grief more room. From the dining room, he called back, "Stay home and rest. I'll be fine."

The August air was already heating up. Doc didn't notice as he went out to put Suzy in her driving harness. Six separate components had to be strapped, wrapped, clipped and adjusted before Suzy and the buggy were ready to ride into town. Doc was able to do it in five minutes.

Jeb Henry rode up the lane as Doc tightened Suzy's belly-band. He turned his head to see who it was but stayed on task until Jeb was off his horse and walking toward him.

"Good morning, Doc. I'm sor—"

"You were supposed to be here last eve, Mr. Henry."

Jeb had gotten accustomed to unfriendly treatment from locals, which had only gotten worse. Once a welcome neighbor, Jeb was now a pariah who worked for the Tennessee Land Company. "Thank you, Doc. My wounds almost healed up overnight. You're something special, Doc. I brought you your fee."

"Show me the wounds," demanded Doc, masking his excitement. Doc's eyes opened wide as he stared at Jeb's torso and ran his finger along the suture lines. All that remained of the once gaping wounds were the stitches. "Follow me to town. I'll take out your stitches in my office."

Going to town was the last thing Jeb wanted to do.

◇◇

Weekly get-togethers were arranged after church each Sunday. It was Wednesday and lunch with her daughter, Sue Ellen, was planned. Edith had no way to cancel and no way to hide her bruises. Sue Ellen would not be satisfied with some unlikely tale, especially since the only one Edith could come up with was being stomped by the pigs.

Slices of smoked ham, bread, jam, cucumber, and tomato were neatly arranged on a small oak table on the front porch.

Decorative corner inserts flanked the post-tops, giving the wrap-around porch a distinctly Victorian look. It was Edith's favorite place to hide from the summer sun. The table was covered with a linen cloth and the napkins were perfectly folded. Sue Ellen rode up in her buggy, parasol in hand, as Edith brought out a pitcher of water. Her ever-present youthful smile greeted her mother from fifty feet. Edith kept her head down, shielded by the brim of her hat—until the last possible moment. Sue Ellen stopped cold at the first porch step.

"Mother!"

Edith's stoicism melted. She began to weep. Her body shook as if chilled to the bone. Their food sat gathering flies while Sue Ellen listened to her mother's attempts to explain and justify. She wanted to believe it as much as her mother. How could her loving father do such a thing? After fifteen minutes passed, Sue Ellen began to calm down. They both agreed it had to have been the whiskey. Their next priority was how to keep all of Lake County from gossiping. They decided Edith should not attend church that Sunday, even though that alone would raise a few eyebrows. Three days wasn't enough time for the bruises to fade.

◇◇

O'Brien's Grocery was doing very well. Yearly sales had doubled since Sue Ellen's husband opened the store. He'd already paid back the bank and his father-in-law, Doc. Grady was a hard worker and an astute businessman. More importantly, he was good to Sue Ellen and their son, Simon. Doc and Edith were grateful their daughter had found a good man. But he had a secret. He was a member of the Night Riders. Their newest addition.

Grady came in the door, balled up his grocery apron, and stuffed it into the hamper before giving Sue Ellen a kiss. At six feet, he towered over most men of the time. His broad shoulders, stocky frame, and fiery red hair kept any man within earshot from uttering a negative word about the Irish.

"What's wrong, hon?" Grady asked. He sat down next to her, brow furrowed, and waited for her to answer. She was still wearing the dressy skirt and fitted bodice she'd worn to visit her mother.

"I'm all right. Just tired."

"Did you stay late at Nannie's?"

Simon burst through the front door. "Pappa, you wanna see the frog I caught?" He tugged on his father's shirtsleeve.

"Not right now, son. Go and fetch some wood."

"Aw, Pappa…"

"Simon."

"Yes, sir."

"Sue Ellen, I know something's bothering you."

"Promise me you will just listen. It's my parents… Your prayers are all that's needed." Grady was extremely protective of his family. His mother was raped and murdered by outlaws during their journey west from Virginia. A year later, his father died of consumption. At twelve, Grady was left to raise his two younger sisters.

"I'm listening," he said.

"Father had been out in the barn last night, tinkering as usual. He drank too much whiskey. He got mad at Mother…over something, when he came to the house. He…he hit her, but he apologized immediately. You know how gentle he…"

"Gentle! You call that gentle? Hitting your mother? You think it's nothing? Damn him!"

He stood, walked around the room rubbing his head, then stared out the front door.

"No. I don't. Of course not…it's never happened before. You know that's not like him." Sue Ellen regretted telling him. He'd see the bruises Sunday anyway. They'd be visiting even if she told him Edith wasn't feeling well.

"I'm sorry. Yellin' doesn't help. We'll pray for them. I'm sure it will work out. He won't do it again."

"No dear. It won't happen again."

✧✧

Grady rode up to Tid Burton's place. Most of the Night Riders were already there, sitting around a long table in front of the house. Four children under twelve were running about. Grady wondered how they all fit in the little shack Tid had built a few years back. Tid fed his family with fish from Reelfoot Lake and what he grew from the small plot of land he called his own. He wasn't about to be kept from fishing by Judge Harris and his Tennessee Land Company. Judge was his name, not his title, but he wouldn't tell anyone who didn't ask.

The Saturday afternoon meetings were for planning their exploits against Judge and his workers. The Night Riders were men who needed the lake. Some had a little land to farm, but when a poor harvest hit or they ran low on chickens, they got out their fishing poles.

Tid Burton was tall and lanky. His cheeks were sunken, not from starvation, he just looked that way. Like a rattlesnake wearing a bonnet, a smile wouldn't suit his face. There were a lot of ideas being tossed about. "Let's burn down his house and torch his boat dock," suggested Alton Chance. "Why don't we steal their horses...beat up his workers..." On and on. Tid settled the men down, telling them they'd all go to jail if they overdid it, especially since they'd just sliced up Jeb Harris.

The Night Riders didn't only exert their brand of justice on the Tennessee Land Company, they'd go after any good candidates who needed a clear lesson. It was never their intent to kill. They only wanted to help their victims make behavioral adjustments. A good ass-whooping would suffice for most. More serious persuasions were reserved for the Tennessee Land Company.

Once most of the old business had been aired out, Alton turned to Grady and asked, "Do you have anything to add?

Anything you think we should look into?"

"I don't think so...well, then again, there's someone I want to send a message to." Grady knew he couldn't do anything himself, but he'd be damned if he would let Doc get away with hitting Edith. "This is touchy, and I don't want him hurt, just scared."

Tid looked over at him, shaking his head "Let's hear it."

"It's my father-in-law. He..."

"Doc Stevenson?" exclaimed Alton. A few men whispered. One spoke up, asking if it was because Doc tended to Jeb Henry.

Another man added, "I heard Doc had some special medicine that healed that scoundrel up overnight." Everyone liked Doc. He'd doctored many of them and their families.

"Yes, sir. Seems he drank too much whiskey and punched his Missus in the face. I, for one, can't stand for a man striking a woman."

"It is his right," said Michael James, the oldest of the group.

"Hell it is," barked Grady. Everyone stiffened.

"Maybe you should handle this yourself," replied Michael. "Leave it a family affair." Grady's face reddened, his fists clenched, then he drew a long, slow breath.

"I promised my wife I'd stay out of it."

"Who wears the pants at your hou...?"

Grady lunged across the table, grabbed Michael by the collar, pulled him over the table, and threw him to the ground. Tid pulled out his pistol and fired into the air.

"Stop it! Now!" he shouted. Tid looked back at Grady, then the other men. "Boys, we can't let a man in our county strike a woman. We might be more successful in conveying that message than young Grady here. He doesn't need any trouble from his wife. Can I get two volunteers?" Two hands went up. "Grady, you take them to the house, stay back, and wear your hoods. Just scare him. That's all."

✧✧

"Nah, you rest. I'll get the dishes. You can read to Simon," said Grady, on his way out the door to get some more water.

"Simon, get your new book. I'll read some to you."

Nearly out of breath, Simon plopped down on the bench next to Sue Ellen. He was fascinated by the book's many colorful drawings. Edith went to great pains to get a copy of Louisa May Alcott's newest book, *Jack and Jill*, sent from back east.

"I can read it, Momma."

"All right then, you can read to me." Sue Ellen wasn't sure what Simon had in mind. He was five and able to make out a few words, but reading a sentence was still a way off. She scruffed his red hair and said, "Let's hear it." Simon positioned the book, smiled, and assumed his most confident expression. He began to read, slowly, but he read. After the third sentence, Sue Ellen was stunned and speechless, unable to say anything until he'd completed another two sentences. "Simon! You can read? How? When did…? Grady, Simon can read!"

Grady stopped scrubbing a pot and went into the dining room. "Read? That's great. I guess he's a genius...just like his father." Sue Ellen shook her head and smiled.

"Simon, read for Pappa." After a couple more sentences, Simon stopped and looked at his parents, grinning ear to ear. Grady didn't seem quite as dumbfounded as Sue Ellen. He was too distracted.

"I need to ride down to the store and stock shelves. I'll be back in a couple hours."

"Tonight?" asked Sue Ellen.

"I didn't get it done yesterday. I don't want to do it on Sabbath, so there's no other time before Monday."

She wanted to ask him why he couldn't go after sunset Sunday, but it was obvious his mind was made up. There was no way to reconcile what her father had done. How long would the anger, fear, sadness, and uncertainty linger? Forever? She wanted the comfort of her boy and her husband. Grady had a different way of dealing with it.

"Don't be late."

"I won't be."

"Grady? Simon has learned to start reading in just two weeks. How can that be?"

"I don't know. God's will? That's the only answer I have."

◇◇

Thunder rumbled in the distance. Rain would soon follow. That suited Grady fine. The more noise and reduced visibility the better. He wanted to be invisible, inaudible, to hide from his sins. Blackie's whinny and bray suggested that she had a distinctly different opinion of the oncoming storm. Before mounting Blackie, Grady pulled out the feed sack that contained his newly sewn Night Rider's black hood and robe. As of late, Mrs. Burton had been a busy seamstress. He pulled it out of the sack, glared at it with temporary disgust, and spit on the floor.

By the time he met the other two men, it was raining hard. They donned their robes and headed toward Doc's farm. Grady loosened up on Blackie's reins in advance of the next thunderclap. All in all, Blackie was more composed than her master. When they reached Doc's lane, they could see light in the barn. That was exactly what Grady hoped to see. He didn't want to alert Edith. His ridiculous-looking hood and bad weather were good cover, but he didn't want to see her at all.

Grady stayed back, between the barn and house. The others rode to the barn and dismounted. His pulse pounded in his ears. The men had specific instructions: make verbal threats, but no violence. They walked quietly through the barn, hoping the horses would ignore them. The smaller of the two was carrying a short club that Grady hadn't seen. They pushed open the door and stepped into the lab. Doc was at his desk writing. There were three glowing lanterns spread through the room shining plenty of light on the intruders. Doc sprang to his feet, curiously glaring at the two men in ridiculous-looking get-ups.

"Who the hell are you?" shouted Doc as he took a step closer to see if he could identify the men by their eyes. The larger man stepped forward and grabbed Doc by his shirt collar. Before he could levy the threat, Doc punched the man in the face and threw him into the door. The other man brought his wooden club down hard on top of Doc's head, sending him backwards over his chair, knocking a lantern onto the straw-covered floor. Doc lay unconscious, crumpled near the edge of the spilled lamp oil. His attacker panicked and pulled his burly accomplice to his feet. They shoved open the barn door and mounted their horses.

Hearing the commotion, Edith ran from the house and down the porch steps, just feet from Grady.

The men rode up, shouting, "Let's go! Let's go!"

Grady looked back at the barn and could see the blaze rapidly growing. Edith recognized his horse and saddle. Two details Grady had overlooked.

"Grady?" she shouted above the hammering rain.

He kicked his heels in and turned Blackie toward the barn, hoping to save his father-in-law—when a shot rang out. He turned to see his mother-in-law grasping her belly.

"Why?" whimpered Edith as she dropped to the ground.

"You bastards!" shouted Grady. He reached for his gun, but before he got a shot off, both men pulled their triggers, striking Grady in the head and chest.

"We have to get his hood and robe off...put him in the barn...her too. Let the horses out!"

Neither man moved a muscle. They'd come to scare the old Doc and now they were transfixed by the ghastly scene they had created. Three good people—dead. They weren't killers. They just wanted to be able to fish and live where people treated each other like God intended.

Chapter 11

Mango was meowing at the door. She spent the days outdoors hunting but acted like she was starving when Charles came home. Cats kill for pleasure. She'd leave one or two perfectly good, edible-looking dead critters at the front door every day.

"Mango, what gives? You left your groceries at the door. Go ahead, eat it. It's free, for chrissakes, and I don't want it, thanks." Undeterred, Mango ran straight to her dish, then rubbed against his legs until he broke out the Friskies tuna-flavored, gluten-free entree. Another bit of science denial from the Ph.D. scientist.

"Shit, where's my phone? Wait a minute, Mango. Hello?...Hi, Mom. What's...?"

"Dad's not doing well. I'm meeting his oncologist at the hospital."

"What's wrong?"

"A lot of bone pain, not eating or drinking for the last couple of days. He needs an IV."

"He'll be okay, right?"

"His doctor thinks he'll feel a lot better after he's hydrated and increases his pain med."

"Good, good. Hey, Mom. Don't say anything, but I'm working on getting something that may help him. It's a long shot and it may be another month or so before I can get it."

"Charles, please, none of your flaky unproven remedies, okay?"

"Mom, it's something that a doctor discovered a hundred years ago that has amazing properties. It's been forgotten about all these years. … No. I'm not sure it's real, or if I can get any, but it's worth a try. You know, a lot of these old medicines work. I study this stuff. I have evidence. The medical establishment suppresses all the data."

"Charles. Stop. Do you really think that's true? Dad's oncologist is doing everything he can to help him. He'd tell him to take all your herbal, natural stuff if he thought it would work. He has nothing to lose. He doesn't want us to think he failed. That's the most important thing to a doctor. He's not paid off by anybody. Why don't you accept that?"

"Because I don't. They're all in cahoots."

"Good lord. Why don't you come talk to him?"

"That wouldn't change anything. Anyway, I'll come by tomorrow."

Charles fed Mango and cracked open a can of beer. He pushed open the screen door, dodged Mango's frantic exit, and sat on his slowly rotting front porch. Melinda was meeting him at Margot's for dinner. He guessed she learned to like French food at Yale. If Margot's served portions like most French restaurants, he didn't see any harm in filling up with beer. That familiar feeling of excitement and anticipation stirred in his chest. *I hope she's not yankin' my chain.* "Six fifty. Crap! I'll be late." He jogged to the bedroom, Mango in pursuit, and pulled on his charcoal gray wool slacks, matching sports coat, and white shirt. They were clothes he hadn't worn since his cousin's wedding eight months earlier. He never dressed up to teach class. "Oh yeah. I'm lookin' fly," he announced to the mirror, loud enough to scare Mango off his bed. Before leaving his bedroom, he picked up a partially smoked joint from a small clay bowl he'd brought back from Africa and took two quick hits. "Locked and loaded. Time to go."

◇◇

East Nashville had changed—gentrified, like many once undesirable and neglected parts of town. Longtime low-income homeowners were selling their homes to speculators for more than they ever dreamed of. But they lost their homes, their neighbors, and the comforts of familiarity. Their windfalls were hardly enough to purchase an equivalent home anything like the place they called home. Regrets soon followed.

Cranes reaching up over a hundred feet had become part of the skyline. Charles didn't notice them as he drove up Woodland Street to Margot's. He spotted Melinda sitting at a small round table covered in white cloth. She looked more beautiful than he remembered. Her brilliant black hair, olive skin, and high cheekbones reminded him of women he'd seen on the beaches in Rio de Janeiro. Her disclosed lineage didn't seem to fit. C'est la vie.

The restaurant was an aging brick building at the end of a row. A haphazard addition had been stuck on the angled outside wall for extra seating. At best, an interesting design element, in reality, a poorly planned afterthought. Melinda was drawn to its "authentic character'."

"Hi. I love your dress; it goes with the theme."

"Thanks. I think this is the first time I've seen you dressed up since graduation. You look nice."

Familiarity muted the tingle of mystery. It hadn't been that long since they'd laughed, fought, and spent time in bed. Courtship replay was awkward. Melinda couldn't be sure what her motives were. Define herself as a heterosexual? *"Don't be so stupid."* An illogical struggle between hormones, innate behaviors, and societal norms. Her maternal instinct had tilted the scale back to Plan A: find a man, get married, and maybe start a family before she hit forty. Charles seemed to be a natural fit. She loved him and always had.

Inside, Margot's was simple. Brick walls, exposed ventilation conduits, and ceiling trusses. A typical but comfortable look. They were greeted by a young woman, probably a student at one of Nashville's many colleges. Her hair was pulled back with a clip. A few loose strands floated about, giving her a faux classy but busy look. All the employees wore the same starched white shirt, black slacks, and black waist aprons. They were led toward a busy part of the restaurant. Charles pointed to an isolated table near the front window. The young woman smiled but silently clucked her tongue. She knew the server would be perturbed.

Melinda's new job and apartment gave her a lot to talk about. Charles listened, waiting for the right time to talk. After they ordered dessert, he wiped his mouth, pulled his chair up, and leaned in. They'd split a bottle of chardonnay. It was as good a time as any.

Charles cleared his throat and said, "I'm trying to finish my book up and was hoping to maybe talk to your friend...the relative of…"

"Geneva Brown. I've thought about it. When she dies, the legend dies with her. I admit I'd love to read Doc Stevenson's journals. Miss Jenny told me he kept extremely detailed notes."

"Legend? You don't think there's anything to his magic river sand?"

"No, Charles, I mean...as a scientist, there's no convincing evidence. It's an anecdote, a single testimony. The entire legend began with a farm-hand who claimed Doc Stevenson's medicine healed his wounds almost overnight. He told people that Doc rubbed some kind of dusty powder that looked like dirt into his wounds. The story spread like wildfire but died out as quickly as it started when Doc died in a barn fire. Later, Doc's grandson Simon found several jars filled with the sandy dirt in the remains of the barn. He took them to his mother, Sue Ellen, and told her he thought it was what Doc rubbed on the man's wounds. There's more to the story."

Charles grinned. "I'm on the edge of my seat."

"Miss Jenny told me that in his journals, Doc described a cut on his grandson's foot and several self-inflicted cuts he'd made into his own leg that healed miraculously. He suggested that the river sand sped up the healing. There was one other thing she mentioned, I'm not sure why, except she must have thought it was related. Simon, who was six at the time, supposedly learned how to read in a week, shortly after he cut his foot at the river. Likely just a coincidence. Simon was Miss Jenny's father. She said he was a genius. After the war, he worked as some kind of scientist for the Army. He was killed in a mysterious accident having to do with his research when he was thirty-five, right after Miss Jenny was born."

"So, you do believe it," said Charles.

"No, I didn't say that." Melinda tilted her head and pointed at his cheesecake. "Try it. It's really good."

"Wow, it is good."

"Let's just say I'm keeping an open mind. For a man of science, don't you think you're letting yourself be swayed by your hopes and not evidence?"

Charles sighed. "You may be right."

"I'm going to visit my parents next weekend. I'll try to reach Miss Jenny. Maybe she wouldn't mind chatting and letting us look at the journals."

"That would be great."

"One catch. I haven't seen my parents in a while. I should probably visit them alone...I think."

"That's fine. I understand completely."

"Great. There's a seedy motel nearby."

"Yeah. Didn't we stay there before?"

"No. That must have been one of your seedy girlfriends."

"We've done worse."

"That's for sure."

They laughed, then went silent for several seconds. Charles reached his hand across the table. She slid her fingers under his. He whispered, "I've missed you."

"I've missed you too."

Chapter 12

Alex leaned the box of catheters, IV tubing, and sundry surgical supplies against the window while waiting for the elevator. Sheets of rain peppered the glass in front of him, distorting his view. Faceless figures darted between buildings, dodging raindrops, seven stories below. The lab was humming along just like any other day, except there was more talking and no one was smiling.

It was confirmed. A dozen cases of bat flu, now known as Nipah-2, had been identified on the west coast and eight on the east. Four people were dead and scores of others with similar symptoms were clogging emergency rooms. Just a few days earlier, Chinese authorities had reassured the world their outbreak had been contained. All it took was one infected person flying from Nanchang to the U.K. to infect passengers who dispersed to seven countries. Two of them landed in the US, one in New York, and one in San Francisco. The havoc from COVID-19 was finally fading away. Some still wore masks, and for many, the loss of friends and family remained an open wound.

Alex fumbled his way around the lab's security door and set the box of supplies on a lab bench. Dr. Bullock was standing along the bench several feet away

"Alex. It could be over six months before a Nipah vaccine is ready," said Bullock without looking up from his work. "I think we're all going to have to work overtime on BN27 for a while. Are you in?" He asked. Alex watched him slide a pipette into a small rack and turn to meet his eyes.

"I…I'm in." replied Alex. Bullock tilted his head, holding his stare. For a second, Alex wanted to turn around and walk out. He was desperate to bury himself in something that would fill the hole, crowd out the negative mind-chatter, and give him a sense of purpose and direction. At the same time, he wanted to hide from obligation as if that would prevent him from losing something he cared about. "I'm in," he repeated. "One hundred percent."

"Good. I need you."

Alex cleared his throat. "So, have you heard anything about asymptomatic carriers?" That's what really fooled us with COVID-19."

"I talked to Holdsworth at the CDC. He said that the Chinese have tested a thousand people near the epicenter outside of Nanchang. So far, everyone who has tested positive is sick, very sick."

"Then spread should be easier to contain, right?"

"Usually, that's the case. It's a lot easier to isolate people with the virus when they know they're ill. But it looks like we have a big problem with this one."

"What's that?"

"It's highly contagious by day two and people don't have symptoms for four days, so they still have too much time to spread it."

The prospect of what was to come stopped Alex in his tracks. He squeezed the box of supplies so tight, the cardboard crumpled. At least they had a potential treatment. BN27 could potentially stop any RNA virus. The first small group of mice to receive BN27 showed resistance to an experimental strain of coronavirus. Complete safety data would take too long. Early calculations suggested that Nipah-2 spread five times as fast as COVID-19.

They'd be lucky to have dosing established before this pandemic spread across the country. Manufacturing BN27 was tedious and time consuming. Millions would die before the drug was available. Millions more would perish if the DOD dragged its feet on sharing the technology with Russia or China. Politics and public health never mixed well.

◇◇

"Lunch in your office?" Alex asked.

"Sure, come on over." Olivia dug into her bag and pulled out their somewhat mushed sandwiches. A news alert came up on her computer screen. **1800 US Deaths Reported.** Alex came in and began clearing journals off the smaller of the two desks. He took one of the two paper bags and shook out his tuna on rye and potato chips.

"You look worried. What are you reading?" he asked through a mouthful of chips.

"Alex, it says there's already been eighteen hundred deaths due to the Nipah-2—in less than a day! A thousand in New York and eight hundred out west."

"Wait a minute. We just heard about the first cases this morning. What the hell? Are you kidding?"

"No. I'm not. It says that the patients have headaches, go into a coma, then die from respiratory failure, shock, and coagulation problems...bleeding and clotting. They're doing the usual things: dexamethasone, anti-virals, prone positioning, all the tricks, but patients are flaming out too quickly. They believe most of the patients have had it for several days but then become deathly ill within hours."

"Did you hear?" Alex and Olivia jumped at the sound of Dr. Bullock's booming voice. His body filled the doorway. He leaned in, tightly gripping each side of the metal door frame.

"Yeah, we just saw the news flash about—"

"Not that. All the labs except ours, on the entire floor, are being emptied out to set up for on-site manufacturing of BN27. Trucks are off-loading equipment now." He breathed heavily, rattling the change in his pockets. "I had no idea the DOD was already tooling up for manufacturing. Shit. It's my drug, and they don't have the decency to tell me. So much for careful dosing and safety studies. Alex, do you have the preliminary data from that animal run?"

"Yes, and it's not so great. Only about sixty percent effective at the 0.4 milligram per kilogram dose."

"So, we need to try again with 0.8 mg." Bullock scratched his head. "Dammit, if it takes that much, it could take months to make three hundred million doses. Other countries will insist we give them the technology. How couldn't we?"

"Shane, I have an idea."

"I'm all ears."

"What if we gave it as an aerosol via a nebulizer directly to the lungs? It may be more effective, even at a much lower dose."

Bullock furrowed his brow. "What are you talking about?"

"Inhalers deliver an aerosol or dry powder directly to the lungs. We give other drugs that way as well...antibiotics, and a couple cardiac drugs. I've always thought it's an underutilized drug delivery method."

Olivia's ears perked up.

"I had no idea." Bullock walked in and sat on the edge of Olivia's desk. Alex took a quick bite of his sandwich and washed it down with Olivia's cold coffee.

"The virus gains entry primarily through the lungs. Lung and neurologic damage kill ninety percent of the victims. Now, theoretically, this could work, but it's no slam dunk. The nanomed has to be nontoxic to the airway, not cause bronchospasm, and of course, it has to be absorbed by lung tissue."

"And it has to stop the virus," added Olivia.

"No shit, Sherlock." Alex grimaced, realizing his comment

was a bit harsh. Two nervous lab technicians lined up behind Bullock waiting to ask him questions.

"In a minute." He waved them off. "Alex, do you know how to do this?"

"I need somebody to get us some patient nebulizers that I can rig up for the mice. I'll need to do it under a hood. Can I dilute it in saline?"

"Yes. That's fine. It won't hurt the formula. Alex, let's get on it. At the same time, we've got to try the 0.8 milligram per kilogram dose in case the aerosol doesn't pan out. We won't be using the coronavirus model anymore. We—"

Olivia stopped looking at her monitor and turned toward Bullock. "What do you mean?"

"We are getting a batch of live Nipah today."

"Nipah? Are we set up for that?" asked Alex.

Shane frowned. "Yes, but it makes me nervous. We've never had to handle a virus this virulent. I'm sure it'll be fine, but if it kills off my staff, it'll take our replacements a hell of a long time to replicate our work."

"That's a cheery thought. How do you think the staff will react when they hear they'll be handling the new killer virus?" asked Olivia.

"We'll find out when they see the freezer container with Nipah-2BF written on it."

"Put a smiley face on it and maybe they'll think the BF stands for best friend."

"Alex, that wasn't even close to funny," said Olivia.

"Sorry, I'll have to work on my Nipah humor."

There were now four people standing outside of Olivia's office staring at Dr. Bullock. One of them spoke up at the first pause in their conversation.

"Dr. Bullock, there are men in full PPE wheeling equipment down the hall. Why—what's going on?" Alex felt a chill as he sensed panic in the air. Bullock bolted up and almost pushed them out of the way as he went to the hall.

"Hey!" he yelled at the first PPE-donned man he saw. "I'm Dr. Bullock, this is my lab, and I'm in charge. Why are you all wearing PPE? There's no Nipah cases here. You're scaring the shit out of the staff...and the entirety of Vanhusse, if you don't take it off. Now!"

"Sorry, sir. We're National Guard. Just following orders."

"Shit. Get your C.O. or somebody to do some damage control before we have a mass exodus on our hands. He needs to talk to the staff and administration—now! How can I expect to get any work done if everybody's freaking out?"

"That would be Major Patricia Lane, sir. She's downstairs. I'll pass on your concern ASAP, sir."

"If you want me to finish creating the drug that's going to save your ass, you'll make it your number one priority, son."

"Yes, sir."

Equipment from the labs was stacked in the hall as crates packed with hi-tech drug manufacturing equipment were brought in to replace it. Scientists and lab directors fumed as they watched their delicate equipment get disassembled and shoved into the hallway. Demo crews tore up lab benches. Power tools whined. The deafening noise of a jackhammer soon drowned out everything else.

Chapter 13

Horns blared and middle fingers were getting a workout. Traffic in and out of Nashville was almost at a standstill. Charles and Melinda listened to the frightening news on NPR. There was no denying it—another pandemic. A tsunami after an earthquake was how the announcer described it. Once a few miles outside of Nashville, Route 40 West began to look pretty normal. Worn windshield wipers flipped across the glass at full speed, making little difference. Melinda reassured Charles that her fifteen-year-old Kia was in tip-top shape.

"I'm calling Olivia for an update," said Melinda.

"Okay. Wonder if she knows if this virus came out of one of our labs or one of China's?"

"I doubt it came out of any lab. Epidemics and pandemics happen just fine without any laboratory assistance. What makes you think it's some sinister plot?"

Charles decided to let that go for the time being. "Just saying," was all he said.

"Olivia. Hi. We finally made it out of Nashville. What's going on?"

"Hey, Melinda. I was just going to call you. Things have gotten crazy around here. I'm sure you've heard how fast this bat flu, Nipah, is spreading, and how deadly it is."

"I have, but—"

"Are you on speaker?"

"No."

"Good. The DOD people are setting up to manufacture the antiviral right here on our floor. They're emptying out all the other labs and bringing in equipment. They want everything done in one place in case things get out of hand so our research can continue uninterrupted while manufacturing is set up. That way, changes in formula and process will not be interrupted by travel or setting up another lab. Sorta makes sense, but right now, it's a cluster."

"Oh my God. Should I come back—now?"

"No, no, it may be a while before you get to see your folks again. I'll let you know, but you'll be back Monday anyway."

"Right. See you then."

"I'll call you with anything important. Bye."

"Bye."

Route 40W gets increasingly boring between Nashville and Memphis. Mountains, hills, and valleys disappear. The road becomes flat, straight and sedating. In Jackson, they went northwest on Route 412 all the way to Lake County.

"This is it, Tiptonville. You're in for a treat. I'm dropping you off at the Reelfoot Inn. Fifty bucks a night. You will be able to experience Reelfoot Lake firsthand. Just take the usual seedy motel precautions...Lysol everything, don't lie on the bedspread...stuff like that."

"But of course. I wouldn't go anywhere without a can of Lysol and rubber gloves. It just dawned on me; we'll be doing all that again anyway, pretty soon."

"Yeah. That takes all the humor out of it, for sure. I'll pick you up in the morning and we'll go see Miss Jenny."

"Okay." He gave her a peck on the forehead and watched her expression for more.

"If I go in there with you, my parents will know about it before we get our pants off."

"Good point. See ya later."

◇◇

Charles waited a few minutes in the motel office before ringing the bell.

"I'm a comin'," wheezed the seventy-five-year-old-looking fifty-five-year-old woman who was about five foot four and pushing two fifty. Smoke continued to flow out of her nose and mouth for most of the five minutes it took him to check in. She smiled and handed him a key attached to a piece of plywood the size of a paperback.

"Ya herra on business?" she asked, knowing full well that there wasn't any business to be herra for.

"No. Just visiting, ma'am."

"Jeyest visiting..." she repeated in a vague effort to draw out some more specifics.

Charles had the urge to say, "I'm in town investigating the murder of those two trans-homobisapiens," to give her a little something ridiculous to gossip about, but instead, he just repeated her words. "Jeyest visiting."

The rain had stopped and a mist hovered over the lake. It drew him to the water's edge to get a better look. Fog floating through ancient cypress was an eerie, almost magical sight. The lake shimmered in the remaining sunset. A great blue heron stood as still as the air on a knob of bald cypress a hundred feet away. He stooped to touch the delicate leaves of a featherfoil bathing in the swamp. Spring came to Tiptonville a couple of weeks ahead of Nashville. Plants he'd never seen before were beginning to push through the soil. Renewed life when death was closing in. Decaying leaves and remains of fish left behind by scavenging eagles gave the air a musty sweet smell. The odor was titrated right to the edge of unpleasantness.

The sun set, and the clouds scurried away. A full moon drew a streak of light across the lake. Charles sat on a bench where the only noise he heard was a faint ringing in his ears. The near silence gave way to a peloton of thoughts racing through his mind. His dad, Melinda, his book, the legend of Doc Stevenson's healing sand, the new pandemic, and even his advancing baldness came to mind. He was in no hurry to linger at the Cockroach Inn. He wished he'd brought some pot.

✧✧

"Good morning, sunshine," greeted Charles on the phone. Melinda was a morning person, Charles wasn't.

"Hi. Have a nice time with your folks?"

"Yes. They're thrilled that I live closer now. I talked to Miss Jenny. She said she'd let us see Doc's journals and sorta seemed excited about talking to you. It sounds like she just wants someone to know the story. I can tell she thinks it's important. She knows she won't be around for too long. Truth be known, she doesn't think any of us will."

"Come again?" asked Charles.

"End times. She believes the pandemic is the fulfillment of prophecy."

"You're kidding. She's one of those fruitcakes?"

"Charles, around here, you're the fruitcake. If she brings up religion—you're a Baptist, politics—you voted for Trump. Got it?"

"If you say so."

"I'll be by in ten minutes."

"Good. Maybe my can of Raid will hold out 'til then."

✧✧

They drove west on Lake Drive through town. Closed businesses and decaying buildings were a depressing sight. Small, dilapidated homes surrounded by yards strewn with long-dead cars and washing machines were standard fare. One of many towns where the jobs left, but the people didn't. Living off a government check was somehow a better choice. Fear of change locked people into a dead-end existence of poverty and

86

hopelessness. Blame and victimhood nailed the door shut. A little way up Cedar Street, they were greeted by flat fields of corn, soy, and cotton. They both took a deep breath as if driving through town had sucked the oxygen out of the air. Neither one of them said a word until they drove by the prison.

Melinda nodded toward the gray buildings. "Well, at least the prison provides a few jobs. Something to be grateful for, right?"

Charles gave her a bewildered look. "If you say so."

Stevenson's old Victorian home was off Pea Ridge Road. It ran parallel to the river and had been there since 1861. As the house came into view, they were both pleased to see it was very well-maintained. Miss Jenny was good with money. After ninety-four years of growth, her father's General Electric stock yielded her close to a hundred thousand a year.

Geneva Brown stood on the porch with a genuine smile they could see before parking the car. From the outside, the house looked like it did when it was built. The interior had been remodeled about the time Melinda left for college.

"Do I call her Miss Jenny?" asked Charles.

"Yes. And, Charles, if she happens to give us a sample of the sand...dirt...powder, whatever it is, I want your word that you won't touch it until I've looked at it in the lab."

"I thought you didn't believe there was anything to it."

"Your word, or we're getting back in the car and I'm taking you back to the Flea Bait Motel. Okay?"

"Yeah, yeah, sure. Shit, relax."

"Sorry. Sorta."

Miss Jenny led them into the room she called the parlor and turned on an ornate Tiffany floor lamp. A love seat with rose velvet upholstery and two floral-patterned high-back armchairs were arranged for close conversation. A burled walnut desk faced the window. On it were a stack of old composition books, newspaper clippings, and a small mason jar with a rusted lid.

Melinda and Charles shared a wide-eyed glance. The jar contained about two inches of the sandy dirt. Melinda was expecting Miss Jenny to tell the old tale and peruse a few interesting journals. She never expected Miss Jenny to have any of the alleged magic sand. They were both still staring at it when Miss Jenny started to talk. For the next fifteen minutes, Miss Jenny and Melinda reviewed the previous ten years.

About the time Charles' grin muscles were exhausted, Miss Jenny turned her attention to him. She probed his family history and asked about his education. When he tried to explain what medicinal anthropology was, she gave Melinda a cautionary glance as if to say, "Don't get mixed up with him until he gets a real job." All and all, she got the two answers that mattered the most: 1. He was Baptist, and 2. His family had always been in the south. If he'd said he was Catholic, she would have been obligated to ask about politics.

"I want y'all to know the entire story. Melinda, I know you've heard most of this. I have nothing to fear at this point. Before I die, I'd like to know if there is anything special about this sand. It's haunted me my entire life. It's probably nonsense, but I want to know. You two are scientists, so I hope you'll find some answers. I'm convinced that both my grandfather and my father died because of it. Maybe that's a silly notion...I don't know. If there's a good medical use for it, I hope you can figure it out. That would be the family legacy I'd like to leave behind."

They talked until noon. Miss Jenny served ham and biscuits for lunch, then they went through newspaper clippings and a quick look at the journals.

"Oh my God, Charles, look at this," exclaimed Melinda, about midway through Doc's first journal. "This is unbelievable. They didn't know this stuff back then. How did—?"

"Those look like amino acids, right?"

"Yes, but he drew reactions, enzymes, ring structures. It looks like he was figuring out how proteins were formed...in his head, for God sakes."

"Melinda," Miss Jenny scolded.

"Sorry. Oh, look at the time. We need to leave in a few minutes. Dinner with my folks."

"Alright, dear. I want you to take all this with you. I trust you will take good care of it."

"The jar?" asked Charles.

"Yes. Take the jar. Let me know as soon as you know anything. If it turns out to be plain old dirt, just throw it out if you like. I don't mean to be superstitious, and I don't believe in curses not given by God, but be careful."

"Yes, ma'am. Thank you. We'll let you know everything we find out," said Charles, who looked like a kid on Christmas.

"Thank you, Miss Jenny. I'm not sure how soon we'll know anything with this new pandemic coming on."

"Oh, Melinda, I thought all that COVID stuff was left-wing nonsense, but I have a feeling this one's for real. Those Democrats are gonna kill us all off sooner or later. But Christ will come first. You can count on that."

"Yes, ma'am." One last hug on the porch and they said goodbye. Melinda had a feeling it was the last time she'd see Miss Jenny. She turned quickly to hide her moistening eyes. "Love you."

"Love you too."

◇◇

A warm breeze from the west blew on their backs as they walked to the car. Melinda stopped and looked toward the river. The sun shone from a blue cloudless sky, drying out the last of the previous day's soaking.

Still scanning the river's edge, she raised a finger to her lips and said, "I wonder if the green spot is still there?"

"The green spot?" asked Charles, who was now studying the

jar.

"Put it in the car before you drop it. Yeah, the green spot. Didn't I tell you about that?"

"Maybe. Not sure. Tell me again."

"It's a little swath of land leading to the river that's really lush with growth. As a kid, I'd play there, until Miss Jenny told me not to."

"Okay, why?"

"Her father, Simon, told her it was where Doc got the sand. She told me there were copperheads and water moccasins there. That was enough to keep me away."

"Now that's interesting. Did you ever see any snakes?"

"No. But there was a lot of wildlife there, especially birds. The 'green spot' is tiny now, according to Miss Jenny. Over the years, the river took it. I guess it wanted to smooth out that hairpin turn. There's also been a lot of flooding over the past hundred years or so."

"Can we go check it out?"

"I'm curious too...but I think we've got enough for today. I'm sure she hopes I've forgotten about it, or she would have brought it up. There's another part of the story she didn't mention."

"What's that?"

"The 'green spot' is supposedly right where the Madrid fault split across the river during the earthquake of 1811, or 1812. Doc Stevenson believed that the unusual substance spewed up from deep within the earth's crust and landed there, mixing in with the sand and soil."

Chapter 14

He stopped mid-sentence as they neared the Route 440 exit ramp. With withering sighs and clenched teeth, they returned to a life besieged by yet another invisible enemy. COVID-19 at first brought fear and anxiety. Later, it turned to denial and frustration. Nipah entered the ring with an angry punch-drunk opponent. Except for an ambulance that blew by them and a convoy of troop carrier trucks, they were the only car on the road. It was estimated that close to twenty thousand people died from Nipah on Saturday. Their phones beeped with notifications. Martial Law was in effect. Like a scene from an apocalypse movie, but this was real.

Charles got a call from his department chairman of his department at MTSU telling him to start teaching online the following day. He'd had his mind set on a little romance when they got back to Melinda's apartment. That thought vanished.

"Where are you going?" he asked as Melinda turned onto West End Avenue, one exit short of Hillsborough Pike.

"Sorry. I wasn't thinking."

Centennial Park had been turned into a tent hospital. Military vehicles were on the grass, ambulances clogged the side streets, and healthcare workers in full protective garb hurried in and out of the tents. She took a right on Natchez Trace. Two soldiers with rifles blocked the road.

"Ma'am, are you a healthcare worker?" he shouted through

his face shield from ten feet away.

"No, sir. We're—"

"Aren't you aware of the shelter-in-place order?"

"I'm a scientist. I work at Vanhusse. My work is deemed essential." She grabbed her ID off the console and showed him.

"What about him?"

"He's also a scientist."

"Sorry, ma'am. Go ahead."

Charles sighed. "I wonder what they would have done if you didn't have ID?"

"Shoot us...like zombies."

"I hadn't thought of that."

"I guess you'll need to stay at my apartment for a while."

"Okay. Mango's a good hunter and there's still some food in his feeder. He'll be okay."

"Mango?"

"My cat. I thought I mentioned him to you."

"If you did, I thought you were talking about fruit."

"You thought I had a pet fruit? I haven't tripped that much, my dear."

◇◇

They both stared in disbelief at the congregating twenty-somethings yucking it up in the apartment building's cafe. No masks. No social distancing. They seemed to be treating the lockdown like a snow-day party.

"They keep this up, Music Square will have a lot of vacancies. The owners may not care about their lives, but they certainly don't want to lose the rent. I'm sure these kids have heard that Nipah kills the young at nearly the same rate as old people. Immortal youth. I'm calling management. No, better yet, I'm telling them right now. I sure as hell don't want to be basking in virions, or death for that matter."

"Well, have at it, I guess."

Melinda positioned herself where she thought everyone could see her.

"Excuse me. People." All eyes turned to her. "I'm Doctor Melinda Taylor. First off, is there anyone here who hasn't heard about the pandemic? I didn't think so. So, what in the hell are you thinking? Do you want to turn this place into a death camp, for chrissakes? It is up to every one of us to do whatever we can to mitigate the spread of this deadly pandemic. We are under Martial Law. Soldiers and police have the authority to intervene in any circumstance that threatens public health. You all are a threat! I will not hesitate to call them."

"Fuck you, lady," yelled a young hipster. Some nodded. Others glared at him. He was expecting full support.

"I hope your parents don't have to bury you."

"Melinda, let's go. You've made your point." Charles gently nudged her toward the elevator.

"Geez. I'm probably only five years older than that little twit. Let's take the stairs. I wonder what that is?" Melinda asked as she bent down to pick up a box in front of her door.

"Probably a bomb."

"If so, it looks like it's from Olivia. I'll take my chances." She opened the box on her kitchen counter. Charles set the box of journals and the jar of sand down next to it. "PPE, the whole ball of wax. Masks, shields, gowns, and gloves. Oh crap, it's almost eight o'clock. I'd better get to the lab. Make yourself at home, honey. You can use my desktop to set up your classes, or whatever."

◇◇

Humvees, sandbags, and soldiers had made a perimeter around the research building. Melinda passed through three checkpoints on her way to the lab. Equipment that had been hastily removed from the nine labs on her floor were stacked in the halls. Her phone rang just as she reached the lab. It was Gwen.

"Hi, Gwen."

"Melinda, sweetie, are you okay?"

"Yes. You?"

"I'm teaching from home. The school shut down the moment Nipah hit the news. So far, we're doing pretty well. Won't last...I'm certain some wayward student or anti-precaution conspiracy nut will bring it to us."

Melinda felt herself getting anxious. It was a bad time for more emotional challenges. "Gwen, I'm walking into the lab. It's crazy here. Our building has become a high security facility. I can't talk now. Sorry."

"Yeah. Sure. Talk to you later."

"Take care. Bye."

Olivia's lab looked like it had when she left. Maybe the staff was moving around a bit quicker, but overall, things looked pretty normal. It didn't matter how fast they wanted to work; most procedures required a fixed amount of time to complete.

Melinda found Olivia peering into a petri dish. She stood out of her line of sight until she set it down on the bench. "Dr. Nilsson?"

"Ah, hey, Melinda. You can address me as Olivia around here. You've got your Ph.D. now. The staff needs to know that I think of you as an equal, but I also respond to, 'Your Highness,' if you prefer."

"Thank you, Your Heinous. I needed a laugh."

"I give you an inch and you take a mile."

"Yeah, well...wonder where I learned that?"

"I'll only take credit for your good habits, Doctor."

"Dream on.... Okay, what can I do?"

"We're having delays in getting some supplies, so your work may be a little slowed up. That's not so bad. You have a lot to learn around here. Alex is super busy with Bullock in the virology lab. They're testing with Nipah now. That's made some of the staff very nervous."

"No doubt."

"Once Bullock's staff goes into his lab, they don't come out until they leave at night."

◇◇

Like a kid left alone with a cookie jar, Charles couldn't concentrate on setting up his online class platform. He got up and put the jar of sand in the spice cabinet and sat down to read Doc Stevenson's journals. They were mesmerizing. It was clear that the old doc was convinced that the sand accelerated healing. Nothing in the journals suggested an explanation. Charles couldn't figure out what all the chemistry had to do with the sand. At first, it appeared to be two separate lines of thought, but in time, it began to make sense. *Oh my God, he seems to be developing a knowledge base in chemistry, working his way toward figuring out something important about the sand. I'll bet that's it.* Charles had a decent background in chemistry, mostly pharmacology. He did some research to compare what was known in 1907 to what Doc Stevenson was drawing. Nineteen of the twenty amino acids had been discovered by 1907. The association between them and proteins had just been described by Emil Fischer a few years earlier, but few knew about this. Doc's drawings of proteins, nucleotides, and DNA were ahead of their time. His drawing of DNA's double helix predated the discovery by over forty years. *How is this possible?* Halfway through the first book, there was a page where Doc wrote about how he saw all the chemistry in dreams. Before his death, he was beginning to understand what it all meant.

There were reactions involving aromatic ring structures suggesting he understood organic chemistry and biochemistry that wasn't generally known for thirty years after his death. The writings and drawings became increasingly detailed. By the second journal, drawings of cell organelles began to appear with details beyond the capability of even the best light microscopes of the time.

The third and final journal was the most intriguing. Doc Stevenson not only recorded his fervent chemistry creations and experimental data, but as time went on, his entries contained descriptions of behavioral and physical changes that occurred— in him. On page 32, he wrote: *When opening the barn door with my usual effort, it swung open as if I'd used all my force and the hinges were freshly greased.* Two pages later, Charles read: *This evening when I came home, the sight of my dear Edith aroused me in ways I hadn't felt in many years, both physically and mentally. I dare say, Edith was as surprised as I was.*

The last several pages of the journal were hard to fathom. Charles began to pace back and forth. He couldn't believe his eyes. Doc Stevenson had drawn DNA components: phosphate groups, pentose sugar, and nitrogenous bases. Then he worked them into a structure. The infamous double helix. The final chemistry entries were the most bizarre. He'd sketched a series of reactions leading to the formation of RNA, but it was full of symbols Charles had never seen before. Off in the margins were sketches resembling lightning, wind, rain, fire, ice, and a river.

As he turned the last page, he found a folded piece of paper. It was a page torn from the journal. On it, Doc had written: *Dear God, forgive me. I struck her with my fist with more force than I possess. It happened ahead of any ability to control it. Is the devil in me, Lord? Was it the whiskey? I have no excuse. I did it. It was my fault. Dear Lord, I don't know if she'll ever forgive me. I've damaged the most important thing in my life. Not a drop of whiskey will touch my lips. I promise. I am at your mercy.*

Miss Jenny never mentioned this. If she knew about it, she had good reason not to bring it up. However, she made a point of dismissing the rumor that Doc had shot his wife before they burned in the fire. There were lots of rumors, but in the end, the final document on the fire stated that Edith and Doc Stevenson died in the barn fire along with their son-in-law, Grady O'Brien, probably caused by an oil lamp. There was no speculation concerning how the horses escaped.

Charles stood at the living room window peering down at the empty sidewalks below. Ambulances and military vehicles ran up and down Hillsboro Pike to his right. He didn't want to hear the news. There was nothing he could do about the rapidly rising death toll. They needed groceries, but the stores had likely been emptied out over the weekend. Restaurants were closed. *Damn! We could go hungry.*

Even when he spent weeks with the Shipibo, along the Amazon, he never went hungry. It took work, but everyone was fed and they were grateful for every meal. It wasn't something middle-class Americans thought about. When he first started gallivanting around the world, immersed among primitive tribes, he was struck by how happy and content they appeared to be. After a couple of years, he noticed a common thread. These people were consumed with the basics of living. People in first-world countries took food, shelter, family, and comfort for granted. He hypothesized that the further away we got from the basics the more miserable we became. Tending to family and survival needs was invigorating as long as it remained manageable. At times, he felt embarrassed by his "high-class" problems. Worrying about survival during a pandemic was a potent source of humility.

He went online and found that Kroger had six of the twenty foods on his hastily made grocery list. He was given a number to use for curbside pickup. Of course, there wasn't any toilet paper, napkins, or paper towels. There was a checkpoint right before Kroger's parking lot entrance, designed to keep people from lying about being out to shop.

On the way back, he tried to comprehend Doc Stevenson's journals. It all started with a small cut on his grandson Simon's foot. *Why did he think the sand had anything to do with the cut healing, versus the cold water, or maybe even a plant his grandson had rubbed against?*

And how did he get the nerve to rub it into an open wound? There was no mistaking that the old doc believed the river sand accelerated healing. Charles couldn't see it any other way. *But why did he cut himself night after night? Why did he write about his newfound virility, strength, and uncontrollable violence? What did that have to do with his experiments and where the hell did his prophetic chemistry knowledge come from?*

Chapter 15

Alex hastily put together a protocol for delivering BN27 by inhalation to Wistar rats that had been bred to be susceptible to human viruses. It had to work. Bullock put Alex in charge of the animal trial. If it failed, at least a week would be wasted. *How many lives could have been saved in a week?*

Fifty unsuspecting rats scurried about their cages, riled by Alex's presence. He was relieved to see that he was familiar with most of the equipment assembled in the twenty-by-twenty-foot animal physiology lab. It was similar to what he'd used before, only it was rat size.

The lab remained nearly unchanged for fifty years. Aging devices used to measure physiological data were stacked on dusty shelves. The adjoining animal operating room had been converted into a high-tech isolation pod. In the nineties, funding for molecular biology research took off, leaving most physiology researchers without support. Even science has fads, but Alex's lab assistant Levi Smitt still had his job. Rumor had it that during the late sixties he was the first black employee at Vanhusse to move from housekeeping or kitchen work to a position within the medical school. He was seventy-two, slow, and soon to retire. Nobody wanted to see him go. He was the heartbeat of old-school blood-and-guts research.

The first rat was placed in a plexiglass chamber designed for administering anesthesia. Levi set up the anesthesia machine to deliver the inhalant, isoflurane. Once the critter was zonked, Alex used a fiberoptic bronchoscope to guide a tiny endotracheal tube into the rat's trachea. The BN27 was then aerosolized through the tube and delivered to the lungs. After two or three rats, he was able to repeat the process every ten minutes. Without a break, he and Levi managed to get all fifty rats treated by late afternoon. Twenty-five with BN27 and twenty-five with placebo. The following morning, the rats would be inoculated with live virus.

At 6:00 a.m. the next day, Alex and two technicians experienced in handling contagion entered the animal lab—with a vial of Nipah. The animal O.R. had been transformed into a protective isolation pod. They each wore an airtight suit complete with built-in air supply. They entered the outer cubicle through a decontamination ante-room before entering the main pod. The caged rats were placed in a sealed glass isolation cubicle topped with a sophisticated ventilation hood. The cubicle was leak tested. Four sealed arm-holes, each with a flexible sleeve and glove, provided access. A solution containing Nipah was sprayed into the nostrils of twenty-five rats. The other twenty-five received saline as the placebo. Alex snickered at himself for trying to hold his breath as he worked. He was soaked in sweat by the time they finished.

He returned to the isolation pod at 2:00 p.m. The placebo-treated rats were lethargic—four were dead. None of the BN27 treated rats appeared ill. After several sweaty hours of measuring each rat's heart rate, respiratory rate, and temperature, it was obvious they were onto something. *This is almost too good to be true.* He found Levi cleaning equipment in the animal lab.

"Levi. Levi, it works! So far, the drug has protected the rats from getting sick. We'll give them a couple of days and see what we have. Either way, we'll need to do autopsies." Levi smiled a smile that went ear to ear. Over the years, he'd dutifully done his job without much praise. He'd seen a lot of success and a lot of failure. Later in his career, research docs started giving him credit in their publications. Times had changed.

"Yes, sir. That's wonderful. Let me help you do the autopsies. Done a lotta them."

"Thanks. I need you to teach me," said Alex.

Levi stood and reached out his hand. When Alex grasped his, Levi said, "Good work, Dr. Winthrop. If we're done, I'd like to head home."

"Sure. Go ahead, and Levi, you don't know how glad I am to have you helping me."

"My pleasure. Goodnight."

◇◇

The main lab was bustling with activity at a frenetic pace. Alex had the urge to retreat to the animal lab. His eyes opened wide as he surveyed the lab looking for Bullock. It was a sea of white lab jackets zipping about like waiters on a cruise ship. Then he heard Bullock's booming voice giving orders. Alex stood behind him and let him finish.

"Shane. Can I talk to you? It's…"

"Yeah. Alex, what do you got?"

"Good frigging news."

Bullock led Alex to his office. The central area in front of his desk had been cleared out. Years of journals, broken printers, and office decor. Last year's unwrapped Christmas presents had been pushed up against the outside wall.

"Eight hours after live virus exposure, twenty-one in the placebo group are sick and four are dead. None of the BN27 treated rats show any signs of infection."

Bullock's expression didn't change, but he nodded his head so fast, Alex thought he was having a fit. "With the 0.4 milligram dose? Okay, okay, yes, yes." His head bobbing slowed. "How will we give it to people?"

"I've been giving that some thought...and yes...0.4 milligrams. We can deliver with a metered dose inhaler, just like those asthma patients use. Self-administered, which speeds up distribution and delivery."

"That's fantastic, Alex. Otherwise, people would have to get it by injection. The logistics would be terrible—we've been through that before, and this time, it would be worse."

"Exactly. We need to get one of the pharma companies that makes inhalers on board now. I don't know how long it'll take them to pull it off. As a matter of fact, we need every inhaler company we can find."

"It's a bit premature to claim victory," said Bullock. "Our happy rats could still drop dead in the next few days, but I agree, we have to move forward. None of us like incomplete studies. But if people keep dying at the current logarithmic rate, we won't have time to even test it in human subjects."

"I agree. It will be spreading through the military and police soon. People have to go out for food. Our entire manufacturing process could grind to a halt."

Bullock pushed his chair back and took off his readers. "I think we may need to convert department office suites into living quarters. Hell, maybe even convert some of the labs on other floors...we can't afford to lose staff. Call Holdsworth at the CDC. Sandy, my secretary, has a list of names and numbers for us to contact. The governor, DOD, etcetera. Try to get a list of companies that make inhalers. I gotta get back to work. Let me know where things stand in a couple hours, okay?"

"Got it." Alex returned to the animal lab to make the calls.

◇◇

It was past 9:00 p.m. when Alex and Olivia walked out to his car. They couldn't help being suspicious of the air they breathed. The lab and home were the only places they felt safe. Before the hospital could issue strict guidelines for N-95 masks, gloves, sterile gowns, and booties, the virus had already started to spread among doctors, nurses, and support staff. The parking garage was nearly empty.

Once on Hillsboro Ave, Alex began to reveal the day's test results, hardly taking a breath between sentences. She hadn't seen him this animated since they were in Mexico.

"So, your results suggest that BN27 works preventively. What about using it for active infection?"

"Geez. Who knows? I suppose I could try it on the sick ones tomorrow, if any of them are still alive."

"Only problem with that is you won't know if the med did it or if they were going to survive anyway."

"Correct. It would only be suggestive, but you know it will be given to sick people anyway once it...if it...goes out to the public. Of course, at some point, we'll test for that."

"What's this?" asked Alex. There were blue lights flashing at the intersection of Lyle Ave. and Broadway. Three cars were ahead of them. Police weren't letting anyone through.

"Oh God. Alex, I see an ambulance turned over on its side. Looks like it was broad-sided."

"Someone ran the light. What a mess." He backed up and took a side street to their apartment.

The elevator door opened and a young couple froze in place. Four pairs of eyes widened in fear, each wondering if they'd already gotten too close. Alex and Olivia backed up a good ten feet to let the couple pass. Not a word was exchanged. Eyes speak a language everyone understands.

Alex and Olivia shared a knowing glance as they walked toward the stairwell. They were exhausted after fourteen hours of work, but it was worth walking up twelve flights to avoid the elevator's stagnant air. Their ears strained to hear footsteps echoing down the stairs. They decided they would duck into the closest floor if someone was coming their way.

"This is pretty ridiculous," said Alex, as they trudged up on yet another flight.

"Yeah, but Bullock really needs you now. You can't get sick."

"I know. Same goes for you. It does feel good to be needed and immersed in something. I could do without the pandemic part. Where are we?"

"Eighth floor, I think."

"Phew. I gotta start running again. I'm out of shape."

"Bullock said something about using department office suites as living quarters. Pulmonary and cardiology have call rooms and showers. Back in the day, on-call fellows would try to catch a little sleep there.

"Quite honestly, it might not be a bad idea."

"I haven't been in a call room for a while."

"Single beds, I bet."

"Most likely. That might be too cozy. We'd have to do something about that."

A rush of fear came over Olivia. She wrapped her arm around his and squeezed it against her side when they got to the twelfth floor.

"Are you alright?" he asked.

"Besides the overwhelming dread...yeah, I'm fine." Olivia had her keys in her hand but was so distracted, she just stood in a daze in front of their apartment door.

"I'll get it." He fished his apartment key from his pocket and let them in.

Olivia sat on the bed and pulled off her shoes. "This is the fourth time today we've dressed, undressed, and dressed again. It's getting old in a hurry."

"I guess we should turn on the news," yelled Alex while stuffing their clothes in the washer.

"Go ahead. It'll cheer us up while we fix dinner..."

Nipah had killed another thirty-eight thousand Americans the previous day. Existing vaccines for previous strains were ineffective.

Olivia didn't bring a glass of wine to the table. She brought the bottle. Alex squinted just long enough for her to notice. They both dug into their Healthy Choice microwave dinners without taking their eyes off the TV. Alex switched to the BBC channel to get the world perspective. Every country had cases. Western Europe, Spain, and China were hit the hardest. Russia, as expected, reported a fictitiously scant number of deaths. *They're no more truthful than they were during the COVID-19 pandemic.* Every news channel had various experts making all sorts of off the hip speculations. Democrats and Republicans had yet to start slinging blame. That wouldn't last. As long as any politicians were left standing, they'd eventually stoop to their habitual bottom-feeding behavior. Big city hospitals were way past capacity. Supplies were already in short supply.

"Since we're probably all gonna die anyway, I might as well start drinking." Alex grinned. His brain was always looking for an acceptable excuse.

"I know you're kidding, but, Alex, please don't say crap like that. It scares me."

"That was thoughtless of me. I'm sorry. Would you mind if we didn't keep any alcohol around the house for a while?"

"No. That's fine. The liquor store shelves will be empty soon anyway."

"I know, and that's a bummer because millions of alcoholics are going to go through DTs. You know that's why they kept liquor stores open during COVID-19, right?"

"What do you mean?"

"They didn't want all the E.D.s getting over-run with people going through withdrawal."

"No. Really?"

"Why else would liquor stores be considered essential?"

"Yeah, maybe so."

The internet was clogged with conspiracy theories. "Why do people do that?" Olivia fumed. "What do they gain from scaring people?"

"And the next question is why do so many people believe in them?"

"I suppose they like to hear stuff that goes with their worldview."

"For sure." Alex took his last bite. "If I ate two more of those, I might get full. Healthy Choice, my ass. It's healthy if you're in need of severe calorie restriction."

"Eat some ice cream."

"I will. Then let's get some sleep."

◇◇

Alex was standing at the living room window with a cup of coffee when Olivia's phone alarm went off. Four-thirty a.m. He went down the hall and leaned into the bedroom. She was sitting on the edge of the bed rubbing her eyes.

"Do you know what song that is?" asked Alex

"What song?"

"Your ringtone."

"No, and I don't care either."

"It's 'I'm a Man' by Muddy Waters. I just wondered if your inner child was a trans-gender blues lover."

Olivia went to the bathroom and sat on the toilet. "What the hell are you talking about?"

"Never mind. I'll talk to you when that friendly part of your brain wakes up."

"Good idea."

Olivia blew through two big cups of coffee and a yogurt. "I smell eggs. Did you have eggs?" The caffeine was kicking in.

"No. I just cooked them for the fun of it."

"Smartass."

"I love you, sugar-button." Alex bent down and kissed her on the neck.

"Sugar-button? That's a new one. I love you too. Sorry I was kinda bitchy."

"That's okay. Let's get going. Maybe we can get to the car without getting breathed on."

They didn't notice that the air was warm for April, or even that it was April, let alone April Fool's Day. On the horizon, the sun glowed orange, more like a sunset. They sat at a red light with no cars in sight. Soldiers stationed in front of closed stores discouraged looters from enjoying a pandemic shopping spree. Nashville's five large hospitals spewed several thousand tired workers onto the streets at shift change. Their replacements were just as tired.

◇◇

He didn't know what to expect when he went back to the isolation pod. If the treated animals were well, Bullock might push to get approval to pull the trigger on manufacturing. It would be the first time since the FDA came into existence that a drug was released without a human trial. NewHaler, a company that made inhalers for drug companies, hadn't called back with a final okay. There were several steps of bureaucratic gobbledygook to get through. The bottom line was always the bottom line.

Alex anxiously opened the door to the animal lab and went straight for the pod. One of the BN27 treated rats had died and two were ill. All the untreated rats were dead. Levi set up the autopsy instruments to be taken into the pod. Biosafety level four (BSL4) was new to him. Some of the support staff walked off the job when they heard they'd be working with Nipah. Levi stayed on board and adapted quickly. Alex called Bullock on the in-pod intercom.

"Shane, one test rat died and four are ill at grade 2. All of the placebo rats are dead."

"Okay. I'll call Governor Brewster, our DOD contact, and Holdsworth at CDC. I'm sure we'll get the okay for full-scale manufacturing despite not having any human safety data. Well, maybe I shouldn't assume anything. If we can start now, we could have at least a few thousand doses for NewHaler to work with."

"NewHaler's been dragging their feet. I'm sure they're waiting for a money transfer from Uncle Sam. Maybe tell your contacts to hurry up and get it done, for chrissakes. I'll get the autopsies done, samples to path, and hopefully have some frozen sections done by the end of the day. Blood sample results should be back then as well. At least we'll know if BN27 was causing any overt damage. Although far from true safety data, it could be released to the press to give the public some reassurance."

"Somehow, they've already gotten wind that we might be onto something. The problem with that is I'm afraid we'll get a mob demanding the drug even before it's ready."

"Damn. I hadn't thought of that. Hopefully, the National Guard can keep them off us."

"I'll ask for beefed-up security," said Bullock.

"You know what?" posed Alex before he realized it was a bad time for riddles.

"What?"

"I doubt we will have many who will refuse to take it," said Alex.

"You're probably right. People might ignore all the conspiracy bullshit."

"Later."

"Bye."

◇◇

Melinda pecked her phone, searching for news. Oliva half watched while chewing down a piece of unyielding rye crust. She took a sip of water and cleared her throat.

The DOD wanted Olivia to continue her work on nanorobot

detection. Up to that point, she'd been working on identifying various types of nanorobots. Not BN27. Now that Nipah had hit, she hoped to find a way to get involved.

She looked over her reports as she sat with Melinda at lunch. "Okay, so, I've got the preliminary results of the nanorobot detection assays. The MRI and modified NMR data for detecting larger metal containing nanorobots, those around 50-100 nanometers wide, or 1/100 the width of a human hair, was close to 97%. Which is great. However, smaller nonmetallic biologic bots, such as tetrahedral DNA, required gel electrophoresis and we could only identify 43% of the bots in those samples." They both knew the assay's sensitivity needed to be improved to identify the critical DNA matrix bots. But even then, it was still a major breakthrough for Olivia.

"Melinda, this is awesome. We are getting closer. I know it's way premature, but I'd like to know if our assays can detect the nanomed...BN27. We'll need to know if it's absorbed into tissue and at what concentration, right? That should give us a legitimate reason to get involved. I mean, what better way to test our methods?"

"Hell, yeah," said Melinda, throwing her sandwich down on the desk. Olivia jumped— surprised by Melinda's enthusiasm. "Even if we can't bet the bank on the results."

"I'll round some up after we eat...if Shane can spare a little."

"You said Alex was doing autopsies on his rats this morning. Do you think he could give us a tissue sample to check?"

"Absolutely. Great idea. I'll give him a call, and I'll hold on bothering Shane."

Melinda grasped Olivia's hand and said, "Thank you for getting me this job. I know this is a sucky situation...but I feel like I'm part of something and it's great working with you again."

Olivia wasn't sure how to react. She waited for Melinda to let go. "You're welcome. I'm glad you're here." Melinda held on, standing well within Olivia's personal space. The warm feeling of blush swelled into Olivia's face. Her resolve not to think of, or react to Melinda any differently than she had before she knew she was bi, faded. *Dammit, just because she held my hand doesn't mean she's making a pass at me. Some women are just touchy-feely, for crapsakes. Whatever.* That little self-chat seemed to help, and "whatever" felt like a comfortable perspective.

Melinda let go of her hand and stepped back with no amorous gesture. Nothing had changed. She was just being Melinda. They ate their lunch, avoiding the obvious draw to discuss the formidable virus raging across America.

"Charles is staying at my apartment for a couple days," said Melinda.

"And that's a good thing, right?" replied Oliva.

"Yeah. I like the company, and yes, it looks like we're a thing—again."

Olivia thought for a moment. She wanted to ask about Gwen but smartly kept it to herself. "That's great." Her words didn't quite match the tone.

"I know we don't have time right now, but I want to tell you about our trip to Tiptonville. There was a little more to it than visiting my parents."

"We should be done around six, then I'll be waiting for Alex, so we can talk then, if you want."

"Okay. Sounds good."

Chapter 16

Charles managed to focus on setting up his online teaching platform and notified his students by email. Only a handful responded. Completing classwork was rapidly becoming a fading concern. The semester ended May 20th, just over a month away. It was unlikely he'd get in any class time before then. Melinda called, interrupting his thoughts, to tell him she hoped to be home around 7:30. Planning dinner was a welcome distraction. Before long, chicken parmesan and mixed vegetables were ready for the oven and Caesar salad was in the fridge.

The jar of river sand sat next to the garlic flakes in the spice cupboard. His eyes were drawn by curiosity. He took out the jar and set it down on the counter. Then, on his way back to Melinda's well-used sofa, he picked up Doc Stevenson's first journal.

Charles was too curious and prone to impulsive behavior. These personality traits got him into trouble more than a few times since his teenage years. One such escapade took place in New Mexico when he was researching Navajo spiritual rituals. He drank more than his share of peyote tea, which left him teetering on the edge of reality for over a week. That didn't dissuade him from jumping headfirst into other hallucinogen-fueled tribal ceremonies around the globe. All in the name of science, of course.

The river sand was an irresistible temptation. Charles thought about trying it on himself the first time he perused the journals. As he re-read the first one, he was really just making sure there wasn't a danger he'd overlooked. For Charles, it took a lot to scare him away from experimenting on himself. However, cutting himself to see if the sand caused rapid healing didn't appeal to him. He was too squeamish. Concern for his father slipped into the background. It was the other effects he was interested in— enhanced virility, strength and intellectual prowess. He made the reasonable but simplistic assumption that the sand was responsible for Doc's transformation, ignoring the possibility of a "true, true, but unrelated" scenario. Once again, he was allowing beliefs to trump scientific thinking.

He read, "I took a pinch of the sand…" A pinch sounded specific enough. Charles decided that swallowing it would be as good as rubbing it into a wound. Doc never mentioned swallowing it. For five minutes, he sat looking at the jar, intermittently shaking it to even out the mixture. As he shook it, the grains broke down into a dusty powder. Slowly, he unscrewed the top, put his nose into the jar, and sniffed. It had a very faint earthy smell, which was what he expected, but there was also an odd aroma he couldn't identify. Then he took a pinch, dropped it on his tongue, and washed it down with water. No sooner had he done it, he began to panic, damning himself for being so cavalier. He anxiously paced the room for several minutes until a thought came to mind.

Many Chinese were big believers of traditional and alternative medicine. If the sand had any of the purported effects, he could sell it. If it only took a few grains to do the trick—he could get rich. Virility never went out of fashion—even during a pandemic.

During one of his academic forays into African tribal culture, Charles spent time with the San, who were believed to be the oldest tribe in existence. They were hunter-gatherers with a vast array of botanical medicines, including many hallucinogens.

Archeologists believed they had been in South Africa for over 20,000 years. Killing large game for food, hides, and jewelry was common before it was considered poaching. Their favorite hunting ground in Limpopo became Kruger National Park in 1929. Anti-poaching programs frustrated the San because, throughout history, they never killed enough animals to threaten them with extinction.

At first, the San tried to chase away outside poachers, hoping they could convince authorities to grant them their age-old right to hunt as they wished. It seemed like a logical bargain, but they were ignored. So, when they were offered gifts, money, and food by Chinese black-marketeers in exchange for elephant tusks and rhino horns, it was an easy decision. Charles posed as a middleman for several American buyers in order to meet the Chinese and document the illegal trade first-hand. He told them he could transport the contraband to the coast of Mozambique, eluding authorities because of his connections. Live animals, pangolin scales, elephant tusks, and rhino horns were then taken to China or Malaysia by boat. They offered him twenty thousand dollars for a trial run. He was about to back out, but when tribesmen brought him twenty-eight tusks, the allure of easy cash was too much. He justified it on the basis that the animals had already been killed, and of course he'd do his part and anonymously turn the Chinese into authorities—eventually. That never happened. Their contact information was on a USB he kept hidden at his house.

✧✧

Maggie looked out the living room window, watching the stillness. No kids playing outside. No soccer moms driving in and out of driveways. Their house was positioned in the middle of a cul-de-sac, giving her a view straight up the street. She could see four homes on either side. She was terrified. Her husband, Ron, was having severe bone pain. His pain medicine wasn't touching it. They wouldn't dare go to the emergency room for fear of catching the virus. Ron and Maggie were elderly and Ron was immunocompromised due to chemotherapy. She was afraid to even go out for food. If she brought the virus back with her, she might die, but Ron didn't stand a chance. They were desperate. For the first time, she was willing to convince Ron to take whatever natural remedy Charles suggested. She decided to call him after the five o'clock news.

At that moment, Charles was more caught up in his get-rich-quick fantasy. Besides, he didn't want to give the river sand to his dad unless he had at least a hint that it may work. Then it dawned on him: if he didn't cut himself and test the dust for healing properties, he'd have no idea if it could work for his dad's multiple myeloma. Assuming wound healing had anything to do with treating multiple myeloma was yet another huge leap. Cutting himself remained a formidable obstacle until he came up with a plan. He'd ask Melinda to test it on a lab rat. Problem solved.

❖❖

Olivia's staff had gone home. Melinda rocked back and forth on a black vinyl-covered office chair in front of Olivia's desk. The office was quiet for the first time since 6:00 a.m. The hum from a dying fluorescent bulb could be heard during lulls in conversation. Olivia listened intently as Melinda told the Doc Stevenson story. It was just too fantastic for Olivia to take very seriously. What got her attention the most was that Melinda had been to the area Miss Jenny referred to as the "green spot," which was right where the Madrid fault had ripped across the Mississippi. The journals sounded fascinating, but they weren't proof. Having the jar of river sand, however, was as good as it gets. A simple experiment would settle the mystery.

"Charles is obsessed with this whole thing. I don't know. Maybe he's just passionate about his work," said Melinda.

"Well, it is a pretty compelling story, and it's right up his alley."

"Oh hey, Alex," said Melinda as Alex came into the office. He smiled, pulled his N-95 mask to the side, and gave Olivia a kiss on the forehead.

"Did you guys get any results from my samples?" he asked.

"Not yet," answered Olivia. "The gel has to run overnight. It's a bit tougher to prep a tissue sample compared to blood,"

"I bet. Did you see today's numbers?" asked Alex. "Close to 50,000 deaths."

"We didn't look. Trying to avoid being terrified for a few hours."

"How'd that work out for ya?"

"Well, at least we could concentrate a little better. Melinda just told me an interesting story."

"Oh yeah. I love a good story."

"I'll let Melinda tell you."

After hearing the Doc Stevenson story, Alex came to the same conclusion. "Try it on a rat. Hell, maybe it kills viruses too." He snickered while biting into an apple left on the desk.

"Alex," snapped Oliva. "That's Melinda's apple."

"Oh shit. Sorry."

Melinda waved her hand. "I don't care. Eat it. Please."

Olivia got a good chuckle at Alex's expense.

"We sent a batch of BN27 off to the inhaler company. Private jet. We might even get the prototype back by tomorrow," announced Alex.

"My God. That's so tremendous," said Olivia.

Melinda punched the air with a fist, then said, "Great work, Alex. It's after eight. I better get going."

"Goodnight, Melinda. Be careful," said Alex. Olivia smiled a ditto.

◇◇

Melinda could smell the chicken parmesan on the other side of the door as she dug through her purse for her key. Charles was busy setting the table when she walked in. City lights speckled the view from the living room window as if all was well. The TV spewed horrific news, making it clear that it wasn't. After two years of COVID-19, social unrest, and political ridiculousness, they'd almost been desensitized. Almost. After a few bites, Charles got up and turned off the TV.

"I was thinking," said Melinda. "I can take a little bit of the river sand to the lab and try it on a rat. Make a small incision, rub in a little magic sand, and see what happens. It seems silly, but it's the only way to settle this old mystery."

"Great idea. I was going to ask you if you could do that. Can you bring it home so we can watch it here? It'd be nice to have a pet around. Can we, can we, please, pretty please? I'll take special good care of it."

Melinda rolled her eyes. "Cute. I'll bet management would be thrilled to know we have a pet rat in here."

"Ah, yeah. Hadn't thought about that. But I doubt they'll be coming around much."

"That's true, but what if Mr. Rat turns into Mr. Super Rat and eats you while I'm away?"

"Then you'll know my hunch about the sand was spot on. Pass the pepper, please?"

Melinda stopped eating, put an elbow on either side of her plate, and rested her chin in her hands. "Charles, what do you think about us...our relationship? I mean, if we live through this viral holocaust, where are we headed?"

"Okay. I'm taking a risk here, but I'll spill the beans. Ready?"

"Don't I look ready?"

"Ah, I like that. Anyway, I love you. I've never stopped...except for the times I hated you, I've always loved you. I got a little weirded out about you being bi, but that hasn't changed anything for me. I admit that I feel uncomfortable with the fact that I could lose you to a man or a woman. If you are loyal, that's all that matters. I also want to jump your bones so bad, I can hardly stand it...and you?"

"First things first. I was pissed at you when I first left for Yale, but I got over it. I know you wanted what was best for me once you had time to let it sink in past your sophomoric hormone-powered egocentricity."

"Wow, if I wasn't so impressed, I'd think I'd be pissed off. Good one."

"Charles, my being bi didn't happen overnight. Like anyone who's not straight, I hid it from myself...from everyone. I didn't act on it until I got to Vermont and met Gwen. I've often wondered if it was just an experiment. In reality, I'm drawn to the person, not the gender. I'm drawn to you. I do better if I don't dwell on it. I love you. I'm a little old-fashioned in the respect that if I say I love you, that means I'm loyal. You have nothing to fear. So... after we do the dishes—my bones are yours."

His pupils dilated. "I'll get the dishes. Where's the dishwasher soap?"

"Aren't you going to finish your dinner?"

✧✧

Immediately after the last tingle of sex, they fell asleep, both exhausted by the barrage of unexpected and unimaginable events. Almost overnight, everything had changed. Maybe sleep would make it all go away. Charles stayed in bed after Melinda's phone alarm convinced her to get up and get ready for work. She was dressed and in the kitchen by the time he decided to get up. He sat on the edge of the bed trying to sort out a confusing flood of thoughts and bits of dreams. None were related to the Zoom classes he needed to teach that morning. The night had been filled with overdue passion, yet all he felt was the coldness of a lingering resentment. *Will she ditch me like she did before?*

"Don't forget the sand sample in the baggie," Charles yelled down the hall.

"I won't." Melinda slurped down the last of her coffee. "See you tonight."

"Bye. I'll think of something for dinner. Call me later."

The scene outside was the same. National guard and ambulances. EMTs reserved their sirens for intersections. There was no traffic for them to warn. Charles turned on his computer and prepared for his first morning Zoom class. He would teach even if only one student showed up. While waiting, he glanced at the news. People were scared. Fear turns to rage and it was starting to boil over. The first riots had started. Protesters accused the government of numerous iniquitous acts. A mob in DC claimed the government purposely released the virus to destabilize society so a new world order could be forced upon them. Another mob surrounded the National Institutes of Health in Bethesda, claiming a secret treatment was being given to only the political elite. The local news showed a crowd forming in front of Vanhusse's research building. Word was out that scientists were working on a treatment. The crowd wanted it now. Charles grabbed his phone.

"Melinda. You okay? I just saw demonstrators outside your building on the news."

"Yes. I'm alright. Soldiers escorted me in."

"I can pick you up. Walking home at night may not be safe."

"You're probably right. I'll call you."

"And I was thinking, maybe we should move out to my house. The kids around here are still being careless. We're sharing air with the whole building. Not only that, we'll be safe from rioters."

"Okay. We'll talk about it tonight. I gotta go."

Not one student checked in for his class. He decided to give them a little time. But after ten minutes of staring at his unattended Zoom app, he gave up. His mind easily gravitated back to the river sand. The only possible effect from his dose the day before was a bizarrely intense dream. As he tried to recall the details, vivid images jumped from his memory into real time. For a few minutes, he couldn't shut it down. It wasn't a dream anything like he'd expected.

Yet in the dream, it was clear that he'd done something that led to him being chased by sleazy Chinese businessmen and US government officials. Just a bad dream, a nightmare, he thought. But it was nothing like Doc Stevenson's brilliant premonitions. He made a mental list of Doc Stevenson's behavioral changes. Virility was the one he could sell. *How am I going to know if it affects sexual prowess? I'm young. Everything is working just fine. More drive, I suppose? If that happens, I may wear out my welcome.*

He opened the jar and dropped a pinch on his tongue, and then a second for good measure. Instead of washing it down, he went to the bathroom and looked at his tongue in the mirror. Within thirty seconds, it dissolved. *It's not sand. Sand doesn't dissolve like that. It dissolves on my tongue, but it didn't dissolve buried in a riverbank? Must need some electrolyte or a higher pH.* Bodily fluids contain sodium, chloride, potassium, and glucose, etcetera. Hydrogen ions and bicarbonate maintain our pH at roughly 7.40. Water has a pH of 7.00. First, Charles dropped a few grains into a glass with a small amount of water in it. The sand didn't dissolve. He added a little salt—no luck. Then after a pinch of baking soda to bring the pH closer to the pH of blood—it dissolved.

By the time he picked up Melinda, the crowd had dispersed, but soldiers and EMTs were putting stretchers into the back of ambulances and Humvees.

"What the hell? Did they shoot them?" asked Charles.

"Don't think so. We heard that a bunch of the protestors were too sick to leave. At least one died."

"That fast?"

"They were probably sorta ill when they got here, but yeah, they went downhill over several hours. Horrible. I don't want it. We may have treatment soon."

"Really?"

"Yes, but you can't tell anybody, not even your parents. We'd be over-run by a mob for sure."

"Let's pick up some food and clothes and go to my house. Okay?"

"Alright."

◇◇

The roads were empty. Gas stations and markets were dark. They turned left onto Charles' lightless two-hundred-yard-long driveway.

"You do live in the middle of nowhere," said Melinda

"It's pretty private but growing up quickly. You'll see more in the daylight."

"Yeah. Olivia said that everywhere around Nashville has taken off."

"Here we are. It's mostly renovated but be careful on the porch. It's got some rotten spots."

"Wow. I love old farmhouses. When was it built?"

"Sometime around the turn of the century; before World War I. I'll get the lights."

Mango was underfoot the entire time they were putting groceries away. They made a quick dinner of grilled cheese and soup. Melinda explored the old three-bedroom, two-story house and made comments as she went. She particularly liked the random width pine floors and the large stone cooking hearth. The house was simple and built for function. So far, Charles had redone the kitchen and bathrooms, doubling the size of the once tiny rooms.

But as they settled in on the couch, more grim news on the TV faced them. China claimed the virus didn't originate there. The Russians accused the United States of letting it loose. Iran agreed with Russia but denied having any cases. CNN reported 128,000 US deaths in the last twenty-four hours. Videos of protests, looting, and burning buildings made journalists believe they were doing something important. The White House pleaded for calm.

Charles retrieved the USB drive from under a board on the porch. He then sat in a chair facing Melinda so she couldn't see what he was pulling up on his laptop. While waiting for it to boot up, he asked her if she had a chance to start the rat experiment.

"I did. I took four of them. I made a small incision on the abdomens of two of them and rubbed in a little sand. The other two will act as controls. Small sample size, but I can't just help myself to a bunch of them."

"Great. Can't wait to see what happens."

Melinda tilted her head and raised her eyebrows. "Don't get your hopes up."

The USB drive opened up and the contact information for the two Chinese smugglers was where he remembered it to be. He looked back over at Melinda, who was deeply immersed in the day's lab data, and was struck by the urge to take her violently. Not just the rough playful sex enjoyed by many but... He shook his head, trying to extinguish that fantasy, and looked back at his computer screen. Then he wondered why he cared about the smugglers' contact information. Was he really entertaining the idea of contacting them? *What the hell is up with me? I have no reason to believe the river powder-dirt-dust-whatever does anything at all, yet part of me is a hundred percent convinced.*

It was a good feeling for both of them. They were safe and together. Mango was the most content, lying blissfully on Charles' lap. Melinda closed her laptop and gazed at the hearth.

"How's your book coming?" she asked.

"I haven't done a thing on it since last week. I'm going to work on it now. Looks like I'll have plenty of time. None of my students have shown up for our Zoom class."

"That's scary. I guess when you're worried about survival, a college class doesn't seem really important."

"Maybe kids are taking this more seriously than we thought," said Charles while rubbing Mango's chin.

"That's exactly what I was thinking. Either that, or they're enjoying playing a little hooky."

"I'll try again every day. I'm obligated to at least try to do my job. I really want to get the book done in the next couple of months, but it's slow going. I have so much information. I should have had some contributing authors do some chapters. Too late now. If it gets good peer reviews, it may be the thing that gets me full professor status."

"Wouldn't that be awesome? I'm afraid I'm a long way off from that."

Charles nodded and avoided empty platitudes.

He returned to his laptop as Melinda went back to her papers. Getting back up to speed with his writing was effortless. He expected the usual hour of opening files and rereading what he'd written, followed by a painful mind-raking before even typing a single sentence. Instead, he found himself trying to type as fast as he could to keep up with the flow of words, sentences, and paragraphs.

Before he knew it, Melinda had been in bed for three hours. He wasn't tired, but it was 2:00 a.m. and he had a class to teach at 8:00. Reluctantly, he headed for bed. As he finally started to drift off to sleep, dreams crowded his mind.

Chapter 17

Alex tore into the box of inhalers containing BN27, venting his frustration that it'd been a week when two-day delivery was promised. Levi set up the lab with the equipment needed for another trial. This time, Alex had three groups of Wistar rats. One group had been exposed to Nipah late the previous evening. They would be treated with inhaled BN27 to see if it could treat active infection. The second group would be exposed after they received the drug. The third would be given a placebo via the new inhaler.

Dr. Bullock and two drug manufacturing experts worked out a method for mass producing the anti-viral. A team of engineers and nanorobotics experts put together a series of machines that were specially designed to create BN27's tetrahedral DNA nanobot.

Olivia and Melinda were thrilled the assay had detected BN27 in tissue samples. Separate immunofluorescence tests revealed that the drug was present not only in the cell's cytoplasm, but also within the nucleus. That was a surprise. Dr. Bullock's data never mentioned that possibility.

"It's probably a harmless finding. It may even be a postmortem effect or..."

Melinda piped in, "Artifact from freezing and thawing maybe?"

"Yes, but if it gets into the nucleus, there's a tiny risk it could alter the host's DNA. If this wasn't such an emergency, I'd push hard for further study. I'll call Shane."

On the fourth ring, Bullock answered. Olivia put it on speaker so Melinda could listen. "Hey, Olivia. You won't believe this. In four days, this bunch of geniuses have a viable mass production method figured out. Amazing. Anyway, what's up? I'm with the team, so give me the short version, okay?" Machines clattered and hummed. "Speak up. It's noisy here."

"Shane, the assays work, but we see evidence for BN27 in the nucleus of lung cells. To be specific: alveolar type II cells. Have you suspected it could cross the nuclear membrane and do you think it could be a problem?"

There was a pause. "No. Based on the delivery system, we never suspected that would happen. BN27 deteriorates along with the RNA it binds. I wouldn't worry about it. It may be artifact, right?"

"Well...yes, we thought of that," replied Olivia.

"Tell Alex to treat a group of healthy rats so we can study them over time, but right now, we need to move along."

"Will do."

She turned to her computer, carefully documented their findings, and saved the samples. She typed in her conversation with Dr. Bullock and added a time stamp, noting Melinda as a witness. Olivia plopped down on her chair, fiddled with her long blonde ponytail, and rested her hand on her upper lip. "I hope to hell this doesn't come back and bite us on the ass." Melinda nodded.

◇◇

The President, fearing complete pandemonium, contacted Cunningham and ordered him to orchestrate a press release concerning BN27. Director Cunningham called Bullock and told him to compose a press release for his review, leaving out most of the details. Within hours of Bullock's approved press release, the news shot around the world. Every country now knew that the

US had an effective treatment—maybe. Doctors treated patients with corticosteroids, convalescent plasma, Remdesivir, and monoclonal antibodies, among numerous other experimental therapies. Nothing worked, and if it did, it wasn't fast enough. By evening, China and Russia were demanding to know why they'd been kept out of the loop. And why wasn't the process shared with them so they could work on setting up labs and manufacturing? This was exactly what Alex and Shane had feared. Director Cunningham came to the lab that night to meet with them.

◇◇

Jan Whitorsh, the lead lab technician, led Cunningham into the cramped conference room, closing the door as she left. Alex and Bullock were sitting across from each other. Two empty pizza boxes and a half empty liter of diet Coke had been left behind by exhausted lab techs catching some quick nourishment. It was strewn about at the head of the table where they expected Cunningham to sit.

"Gentlemen," started Cunningham. He sat down, sweeping the pizza boxes aside with an almost imperceptible grin. The shine was off his shoes. His signature blue blazer, khakis, and white shirt were wrinkled and in need of a wash. An angrily knotted tie hung a few inches below his neck. "I'm here to remind you that the United States cannot risk sharing the BN27 process with our adversaries. That's from the President. We've already stirred up enough with that little press release. Our plan is to provide them with BN27 only after we've made enough for us. Hopefully, we'll have an effective vaccine before then. We'd prefer to give them that instead. If we have to give them BN27...there's the risk they'll reverse engineer it, and ten years of research goes down the drain."

Alex smashed his fist on the large cherry conference table and stood. "You damn well know we can't make enough of it fast enough for us, let alone the entire world! It's unethical, sadistic, not to mention majorly fucked up. Don't you brilliant politicians know this will have horrible consequences? What the hell are you thinking?"

Cunningham paused with a nod. "Alex...Dr. Winthrop, I completely understand your concerns. We don't want it to be this way. The problem isn't the BN27, it's the technology Dr. Bullock and his team have developed to create nucleotide nanorobots. The process is essential not only for BN27, but a number of other biologic agents critical to our defense interests. Dr. Bullock—your thoughts?"

Bullock pushed himself into the back of his chair. He had hoped for a cordial, if uncomfortable discussion. He did not expect to see Alex explode on the man who held their purse-strings. Even more confusing was that Cunningham took Alex's tirade in stride. He realized these two men must have some kind of history together. "The medical application for this technology is immense. Alex, you know, we've talked, my dream is only to advance medicine. I've done work for the government in the past. Of course, their agenda is different. It became apparent that this technology could also be used in biowarfare. China and Russia are investing heavily in nanotechnology and, of course, biological weapons. The last sev—"

"Shane. I know all this. What are you trying to say?"

"We both know why Director Cunningham is here. I don't like it any more than you do—but he's right. It would be a huge and potentially dangerous setback if the Chinese or Russians got their hands on our nanorobotics technology."

"So we let millions die?" asked Alex, now pacing back and forth, rubbing his neck.

Cunningham broke in, "Hopefully not. Like I said, a vaccine could be ready in a few months, they say."

Alex stopped pacing and stared at Cunningham. "Sixty days?

At the rate deaths are increasing, there could be ten million deaths in sixty days. And that's just in the States."

Bullock nodded. "Alex, we don't know how long it will take to produce enough BN27 for everyone in the United States. You've even said that right now it's a monumental task to get a million BN27 inhalers out in a day. That will improve quickly, but even then it could be at least a month…or more, and that's just for the US, right?"

Alex pleaded, "But if we give the process to all capable countries, there could be enough produced to treat most of the world in the same time frame."

Bullock tilted his head and drew his lips into a straight line. "It's not that simple, Alex. It's a complicated process. There are nuances that have to be taught one-on-one. We have three scientists that know how to make it. I've sent two to the U.K. to set up manufacturing at AstraZeneca. We can't afford to send the only other one to China…or Russia. Even if we give them the formula today, there's a good chance we'll have a vaccine before they can ramp up manufacturing. Then, we will have given them our technology for nothing."

Cunningham quickly agreed. "That's correct. We have to take care of our country…and our allies first. I hope you agree with that, Alex."

"Dammit. This is a pandemic, not a world war," said Alex. "I doubt our 'non-allies' will accept that they needn't worry about BN27 because it's too complicated for them to produce. Good luck selling that load of crap. They'll just tell us to give them the process and they'll take their chances. Shane, are you sure they can't pull it off without hands-on guidance?"

"No. Not absolutely sure."

Alex paused while the others waited. "So, the risk is too great to let them screw around with the formula and methods, no matter how you slice it?" Bullock avoided Alex's eyes. Alex sat back down across from Cunningham. "We already have riots and looting. People are dying in the street, the government's likely to run out of money, and crazy-ass Russia and China will probably nuke us...or eventually they'll offer someone enough money to hand over our little secret."

Cunningham grinned. "Nuke us? Not likely, but could there be an asset or a mole among us? Everyone involved with BN27 is being watched so closely, we'd know if you wiped your ass backwards."

"That's comforting," Alex smirked. "Since China owns our economy and everything we touch comes from them, hell yeah, you're probably right, why bother wasting nukes."

"We have an added disincentive." Cunningham leaned in as if to whisper a secret. "We know both countries are working on their own treatments and vaccines, and they haven't offered to share one shred of evidence with us, so why the hell should we share anything with them?"

Alex shook his head. "So, winning political games is far more important than human lives. I get it. Makes perfect sense. I'm stupid to even think these jack-asses would have morals. For chrissake, such fools."

"Okay, Dr. Winthrop, Dr. Bullock, I've told you how it's going to work. Like you, I hope we can find some way around it soon, but for now, that's the directive. I trust you understand...and will act accordingly. I will update you if anything changes. Good day, gentlemen."

They remained seated as Cunningham got up and left. Alex couldn't help feeling betrayed by Bullock, who seemed to be trying too hard to appease Cunningham. Neither of them spoke until the silence became too uncomfortable.

Bullock redirected his gaze from the pizza box to Alex. "Let's get to work."

"Yeah. Good idea."

◇◇

Four students tuned in for his Introduction to Medicinal Anthropology class, but they were too distracted to pay attention. One was crying. They all knew someone who had died from Nipah. Charles let them console each other and ended the class after ten minutes, wishing them well. He returned to his book, typing furiously for two hours without pause. *Man, I've really got my mojo going. But why? I've never been able to write like this. The river dust?* He decided dust was a more fitting term since the grains turned to a fine powder and dissolved so easily.

He closed his eyes and listened to the digital recordings he'd made during his trips to South America and Africa. Sights, sounds, smells, words, and feelings were all vividly recalled. It was like having a TV remote for his memories. He was able to stop and focus on details he had overlooked. Python in the brush. A hoatzin perched on a limb overhead. A deadly Brazilian wandering spider walking over his foot. Every step the shamans took to prepare their hallucinogenic concoctions was clear. Bewildered and excited, he felt pressed with a sense of urgency to capture the moment, hoping it wouldn't vanish.

◇◇

Olivia was very deliberate when she set up her lab. Equipment, supplies, and open space were strategically placed to keep workflow fluid and natural. Great laboratories ran like well-oiled machines. Smart people and good ideas aren't enough. The pandemic was the ultimate test. Without Oliva's structure, the lab would have degenerated into total chaos.

She looked up from her microscope. Melinda was sitting next to her scrolling through data.

"Melinda, take a look at this."

She adjusted the magnification. "Yup. I assume you're wondering if I see anything lighting up in the nucleus. Faint, but yes, it's there, but I don't see any in the cytoplasm."

"I was sorta hoping you didn't see it, that maybe I had eye strain or something. So much for that. Alright then, it looks like BN27 has degraded with bound RNA in the cytoplasm but remains stuck to nuclear DNA. I wonder what it attached to? I guess it doesn't matter right now. Manufacturing is off to the races."

Melinda just listened and let Olivia talk. An acceptable risk was one that was known. Neither of them knew if their observations posed any risk at all without extensive studies. Studies that could take several months.

"I'll get Dr. Bullock to look at this before we move on, just in case he wants us to dig a little deeper. Meanwhile, we can go over to Alex's lab and look at your rats," said Olivia.

"Great. I've been itching to check them out."

◇◇

Olivia and Melinda were greeted by pungent rodent odors, smells the men no longer noticed. "Hi, Levi," greeted Olivia. She looked at Alex and asked, "Do you mind if we take a look at our little rat experiment?"

"Excuse me, Levi," said Alex as he got up to join Olivia and Melinda.

"Holy shit," whispered Melinda, staring into the cage. Both control rats were dead. One of the river sand treated rats was biting into the neck of one while trying to have sex with it.

"Looks like we've got a crime scene here," said Alex, in his typically sardonic manner.

Olivia put on a pair of gloves and picked up the one that had been doing the hump and munch. "Rats do kill each other, and males will sodomize other males."

"So what do you make of it?" asked Melinda.

"It's likely that this one killed both of the others." Olivia turned the rat over to examine the incision where the river sand had been applied. Alex did the same with one of the dead ones.

"Oh my God. Look at this," said Olivia, as she revealed the rat's belly.

Chapter 18

Two ambulances were parked outside their apartment building. Instinctively, Alex slowed down and gawked at the scene.

"I don't even want to go in the building," said Olivia.

"We're going in the back entrance from the parking lot and up the stairs. We should be able to avoid anybody," Alex said.

The parking lot entrance opened onto the second floor. Alex opened the door for Olivia.

"What's that sound?" asked Olivia. They stood still and listened. *Thud, thud, thud.* Then they heard a snorting sound.

"Somebody's having a seizure down there," said Alex.

"What? How do you know?"

Alex took a step down the stairway and saw a woman's legs jerking spastically on the floor. His impulse was to run down to her. He stopped before the third step.

"There's nothing I can do for her, and I'll get exposed. Crap!" It went against every instinct he had as a doctor.

"No. Don't go." Olivia grabbed his arm.

He tried to convince himself while explaining, "When brain swelling from Nipah progresses enough to cause seizures, only five percent survive, and they're usually comatose. It's already too late for her. I'll run around front and tell the EMTs. They're in full PPE. Go ahead upstairs. I'll see you in a minute."

Alex stopped about ten feet from the scene. Two people were

being carried on stretchers to the ambulances. One appeared to be in a coma. The other moaned in pain. "Hey. Hey! Excuse me, there's a woman seizing on the first-floor stairwell landing. Go left, inside the doors, you'll see the Exit sign." The EMT only nodded.

He rushed back to Olivia's apartment. "Looks like a..." gasped Alex. "Like a whole family got sick."

"Did you run up the stairs?"

"No. I'm hyperventilating so I can get dizzy... Yes, I ran. All twelve flights."

"Smart ass." Olivia hugged him. He could feel her trembling.

Olivia piled several Tupperware of leftovers on the counter. One after another, Alex put them in the microwave. They stood in the kitchen, eating out of containers.

Alex finally paused between bites. "Did you notice the city getting darker and darker each night?"

"Yeah. Nobody's going to work, so they're saving power, I guess."

"Spooky."

"Everything is spooky," echoed Olivia.

"Come sit with me. Let's take a break from Nipah and talk about Melinda's rats." He sat on Olivia's black leather couch and patted the cushion next to him.

"Okay." She plopped down on the couch, just missing his hand. "The treated rats healed overnight. That is astounding, even if it's a four-rat study. The rapes and murders may have nothing to do with the sand, but I can't say."

"We need to try some more rats for sure. Meanwhile, the question is how the hell did it happen? What did the sand do to improve healing, and what if the sand did turn our friendly rats into sodomizing cannibals?"

"What's your theory, Dr. Alex?" She reached her hand around the back of his neck and rubbed his ear with her thumb.

Alex clasped her wrist and pushed her hand into his cheek. "Dr. Alex?" he asked. "Lordy. Do you remember when I first called you? Your Swedish accent was so intimidating, I almost hung up. You insisted on calling me 'doctor,' trying to keep your distance. God, I'm glad we didn't hang up."

"So am I. If you hadn't called, I wouldn't have found the love of my life. Not to mention getting out from under Altiva and getting back to Vanhusse doing what I love. It's hard to believe. Thank you."

"No, no, you're the one who deserves thanks. You may have saved my life. Anyway...Dr. Olivia, healing depends on white blood cell infiltration, epithelial cell growth, angiogenesis, collagen formation, extracellular matrix, oxygen delivery, etcetera. So each of these has to be ramped up. All of this requires cellular messaging with cytokines, TGF, PDGF, among others. Does the sand accelerate it? Maybe? As for the snuff porn—I have no idea."

"That stuff can be figured out. It would just take time. It could increase RNA transcription, or translation, or... We know circulating stem cells can differentiate into specific cell types as needed. If the sand somehow drew in more stem cells to the wound, couldn't that fire up the entire process?"

"Sure...I guess. You know more molecular biology than I do."

Olivia tapped her index finger on her front teeth. "Then the question is, what's in the sand, if it's even sand in the first place? It certainly isn't just grains of silica or quartz, that's for sure."

"Here's a stretch for ya: If it does what you suggest, could it stimulate antibody production and cellular immunity to a virus?" asked Alex.

"Who knows? Since we have no idea how the stuff works or even what it is, I'd say anything is possible, but yes, that's likely a stretch."

◇◇

Melinda had been driving on Highway 100 for twenty-five

minutes before turning onto Bush Creek Road. Google maps gave her instructions, but she looked for the landmark anyway. The further she drove, the thicker the fog. She strained her eyes searching for a church that marked Ivey Road. Fairview seemed a lot further away than it did the night before. Long stretches of empty road made her uneasy. *What if I break down?* She laughed at herself for imagining zombies coming out of the woods. The sound of her motor drew her complete attention. Ms. Google broke the silence with, "You've arrived at your destination," which would have been fine if her destination was a big old oak tree by the side of the road. A hundred yards later, she spotted Charles' mailbox.

"Hello. I'm home," she called from the doorway.

"Hey. Any trouble finding your way?"

"Oh no, except for fog dense as butter, zombies coming out of the woods, and Ms. Google telling me I'd arrived when there was nothing around but a big tree."

"Good. Glad to hear you had a pleasant drive."

"Hi, Mango." Melinda reached down and rubbed the underside of his neck. "You take good care of Charles today?" Mango lost interest and went to his litter box.

"Did you hear that China and Russia are talking trash about us for not giving them the cure for Nipah?" asked Charles.

"Ridiculous. I can't imagine that's true. We're not even sure we have one."

"Did you get a chance to check the rats?"

"Yes. I did, but don't get too excited."

"What do you mean?" Charles chafed at her parental tone.

"Okay. It looks like...yes, the wounds on the sand-treated rats healed."

"No shit! I knew it. That's amazing. It is real. Just like I told you."

"It's only two rats. That's hardly a study. Besides, what hap—

"

"I know it's just two rats, but it's one hundred percent of two rats, right?"

"Hear me out, Charles. One of the treated males killed the two untreated rats. When we went in to see them, the perp was sodomizing and eating one at the same time."

"That's gross. But you can't say it was due to the sand, right?"

"No, not for sure, but it's quite concerning."

"Oh, and it's not sand. It turned to dusty powder when I shook the jar."

She stood in front of the TV—transfixed. "I know. Same thing happened when I rubbed it into the incisions. Then it just dissolved."

Charles stepped in front of her, blocking the TV. "Also, it dissolves in water only if the pH is raised. I added a little baking soda and it completely dissolved. Weird, right?"

"Yes. Weird. What made you think to do that...to buffer up the pH?"

He walked away, jingling change in his pocket. "I don't know, really, except that I thought it might need to dissolve in order to be absorbed into a wound. And I wondered why it didn't dissolve in the river water. The pH of our blood is 7.4 and the water is 7.0."

"There's a lot of other characteristics that determine solubility besides pH."

"So? And? My simple mind wasn't bogged down with all those bothersome facts. I chose the one I knew. Sometimes not knowing too much is a good thing."

Melinda walked over to him, tilted her head, and looked into his eyes. "Is there anything else you want to tell me?"

"What do you mean? Well, yeah, I've had an interesting day. I don't know how to explain it. Maybe it's because I've been concentrating so hard on my book, but my memory has been working overtime. I started remembering things I didn't know I'd forgotten."

She nodded. "That's pretty cool. I've noticed that my mind works better when I'm going at something real intensely. It's a good feeling."

"Yeah. I've certainly had the intensity part. So," he said, half laughing. "It's either that or the ayahuasca I took with the Shipibo."

"Huh?"

"It's a psychedelic some of the Amazon tribes use, and yes, I took some...I took a lot. Just for research purposes, of course."

"Of course, she replied, tapping her temple with her index finger. "You're nuts. Hey, I'm really tired. I'm going to get ready for bed."

◇◇

Charles grabbed her arm and pulled her tightly against his body and kissed her hard with one hand behind her head. He unsnapped her jeans and yanked them below her knees. He turned her around and bent her over the couch.

"What, no dinner and a movie...or even a little foreplay?" she mused.

"Maybe next time." He banged his palm between her shoulder blades, pushing her further down.

"Hey. Lighten up a little."

When he'd finished, he went around and sat on the couch. "Sorry, I was a little rough. I just had an overwhelming urge. Like an animal."

"I don't mind it, but geez, not so damn rough next time. And make it more mutual... You started to scare me. I'm going to bed."

"Sorry. I'll be there in a bit."

She turned off the lights, leaving him with only the glow from his laptop. He opened his book file to chapter eleven: Ceremonial Use of Plant-Based Hallucinogens. His fingers sat idle on the keyboard. He expected a flood of ideas with a load of memories to form on the page but found only the usual trickle of thoughts. His mind had slowed, more like normal. After what he'd experienced, normal was inadequate.

He re-read some of Doc Stevenson's journal entries. Nowhere did Doc mention applying the dust any way other than through a wound. Charles' pharmacology knowledge led him to wonder if the dust's effects were wearing down quickly because he'd taken it orally. Substances taken orally may be altered as they pass through the gut. Gut circulation takes the substance directly to the liver where it is metabolized, detoxified, inactivated, or partially inactivated. In some cases, an inactive substance may become bioactive by liver processing. This is known as the first pass effect and is why some drugs need to be given intravenously, transdermally, or absorbed via mucous membranes of the mouth or rectum. If not, then it may require a higher dose or frequent dosing.

No longer worried about cutting himself, he searched for something sharp enough to do the job. In his tool kit, he found a box knife and new blades. By the light of his laptop, he chose a spot on his thigh to cut. Like Doc Stevenson, he hoped he didn't get caught with his pants down. Melinda would certainly think he was looking at porn. It might not matter, except they'd just had sex. She might wonder if he had a problem.

Blood dribbled down his inner thigh. He rubbed the wound with a pinch of river dust, as he now referred to it, just as Doc had described. Precision was not his concern. He sat back and waited a few minutes, half expecting to feel differently as if he'd taken a drug. That was his only point of reference and a drastic over-simplification. His thoughts turned to his Asian contact and the heinous traditional Chinese medicine market. *At least my product doesn't kill endangered species.*

◇◇

Li Jun traveled between Addis Ababa and Malaysia supervising the export of wildlife contraband. While in Malaysia, he connected with buyers from mainland China. His customers wanted both botanicals and animal parts that were used to treat any number of real or perceived ailments. The biggest sellers were anything Chinese men believed would enhance their virility. None of it had any true medical effects. All that mattered was belief. Rule number one was rarity equals potency. From snake blood to rhino horn, to various roots and herbs, many Chinese men would try anything to compensate for their perceived diminutive anatomy. They could care less if they wiped out an entire species. Nothing was more important than a hard-on.

A small portion of the contraband made its way to the United States, and into the hands of Asian-Americans. Most of it was smuggled in on container ships going to the west coast.

Charles saw an opportunity to make some easy money. He'd have to convince Li Jun that he had something very special that would turbocharge virility, sharpen the wit, and heal wounds. It would take more than just a claim. To sell, the dust had to be derived from some rare and preferably ferocious animal. He decided he would say the river dust was ground bones from Tyrannosaurus Rex and Velociraptors found during an archeological dig along the Mississippi. Li Jun would be inclined to believe it since he knew Charles was some kind of scientist. It all depended on whether or not Li Jun would be willing to get his traditional medicine buyers to try something new that had no known market value. *Once they try it, they'll be back for more.*

To deliver what he guessed was an appropriate dose, he needed to cut the dust with a filler similar to what drug dealers used. He decided that he'd fill small capsules with a few pinches

139

of dust, cornstarch, and a little "ground bone." *There must be hundreds of thousands of doses in that jar, and I can go back for more.*

It was 1:00 p.m. in Malaysia. Charles read the twelve-digit number and made the call. Li Jun spoke almost perfect English in addition to a few African dialects.

"Hello," answered Li Jun.

"Hi. Li Jun?"

"Who is this?"

"Charles. Charles Davenport, the American anthropologist who worked with you a couple years ago."

"Yes. Hello, Charles, what can I do for you?"

"I have something you may be interested in."

"Is that so? Tell me about it."

Charles took a deep breath before presenting his yarn. "There's a Native American legend passed down over the centuries that claims the ground bones of ancient animals gave their healers special powers. Not just any bones, but bones found by Choctaw Indians buried in the banks of the Mississippi River. I discovered some during an archeological dig and stowed them away. I ground them up to elude detection. They were the bones of Tyrannosaurus Rex and Velociraptor. I recently tried it myself. It works. It fucking works, Li Jun."

"What do you mean it works?" he asked.

"It jacked up my sex drive, sharpened my wit, and it heals wounds."

"I'm supposed to believe that? If so, why didn't you report it in one of your scientific journals?"

"For starters, I stole the bones, and I need some money. Of course, I know you may think this is a tall tale, but why would I take a chance on ripping you off? I'm pretty certain you wouldn't put up with that."

Li Jun laughed. "That's right, Charles, it'd be your bones ground up next. If you're willing to take that risk, I'll need some samples for my buyers. If they like it, I'll go fifty-fifty with you. How much do you have?"

"I might have a million doses. I'll go sixty-forty."

"Fifty-fifty or forget it."

"Okay," replied Charles. "Fifty-fifty."

"If it's worth a shit, can you get more?"

"Yes. I'm pretty sure."

"Where are you?"

"Nashville. It's in Tennessee."

"I know where Nashville is, Charles. I'll call you back when I've got someone who'll meet you. Don't waste my time, I'm a busy man."

"Of course."

"Good bye."

"Good bye." He went out to the porch, trying to slow his breathing. Sweat beaded up. He ran his sleeve over forehead and lips. *What am I doing?*

Chapter 19

There were no tourists to admire D.C.'s cherry blossoms. Their fragrance wafted into the breeze, unappreciated. Government buildings were surrounded by soldiers and military vehicles, giving the appearance of a military coup. Secretary of State Sean Finnegan waited impatiently for the President. He wanted to have a word with him before the meeting. Vice President Shaneaka Jackson, CIA Director Sam Espionto, and the Joint Chiefs of Staff were filing into the Situation Room. Tracy Jones, Secretary of Defense, had been waiting for thirty minutes. Everyone stood when President Phillip Triagin entered the room.

Tracy Jones started off. "Mr. President, as of yesterday, we have had twenty-two million Nipah deaths. Three out of four manufacturers have started distributing BN27. It's going surprisingly well. Almost ten million inhalers have been released in the first week. They predict they can make up to five million per day now, and thirty million when the other manufacturers come online."

"Good work," replied the President.

"Yes, sir. Mr. Espionto, your report please?"

Sam Espionto picked up his stack of paper. "First, as you know, we verified that China incorporated two vaccines during the COVID-19 pandemic. One for COVID-19 and one for a new coronavirus we haven't identified yet. We have pretty sound evidence this new one is genetically engineered. In addition, it looks like they've gotten hold of some of our nanotechnology."

"What the hell are you talking about, Sam? I thought we were talking about the Nipah virus," asked the President.

"Yes sir. Sorry for changing the subject, but I believe this is important. Espionto took a deep breath, nervously shuffled his papers and read from the first page. "We suspect the nanoparticles discovered incorporated within the Chinese COVID vaccine are similar to the type Dr. Shenberg developed at NIH. His lab has developed a nanoparticle that allows viruses to evade parts of our immune system. Blocks the antibodies, I think he said. The goal of his research was to better understand different components of our immune response. He didn't intend to make a more deadly virus, but with a few tweaks, he said it was possible. He believes the Chinese have figured it out. Some of the original technology was developed by Dr. Lieberman a couple of years earlier. Dr. Shenberg is prepared to explain this in detail at your earliest convenience, sir."

"You know my next question, right?" asked the President.

"Yes sir." Espionto turned to Secretary Jones.

"We fear they——."

"Wait a minute. Who's the mole? Was it Lieberman? Glad we've caught him at least. I'm sure you guys are on that, right?"

"Possibly, sir. Lieberman may be responsible for some, but not all of it. I'm short a few men, but we're working on it."

"I want that mole, Sam. All of them. Tracy, are we certain that they have a vaccine?"

Tracy Jones cleared her throat. "Yes, sir. However, according to Shenberg and Bullock, the vaccine identifies the nanoparticle and our scientists don't have a clue how they've done that, and if they have, it's likely very unpredictable. President Chen has threatened to release their virus in retaliation for our not providing them with BN27 technology."

The President looked back at Espionto. "Now I see why you

changed the subject."

Finnegan interjected, "If I may suggest, sir, it might help if we divert a couple million doses of BN27 to them."

"Nonsense, Sean. Where are we with the Nipah vaccine?"

"At least a month away, sir, by the end of May if we're lucky," replied Finnegan.

"So meanwhile, if Chen gets a wild hair up his ass, they can drop this new virus on us and we are absolutely defenseless? Am I understanding this correctly?"

"Yes, sir. That is correct."

"What about the rest of the world?"

"Our intel suggests they've shared their vaccine with Russia, Iran, maybe others. We suspect they have warned their other friends to completely lock down, even more stringently than now...as in shoot anybody trying to get in."

"What about our allies?"

Finnegan glanced at Secretary Jones. "You have a conference call with them at 8:00 a.m. to discuss the new development. Concerning Nipah, we have shared BN27 technology with several high security labs. Manufacturing will be done in England at AstraZeneca, GlaxoSmithKline, and Novartis," answered Jones.

"When China and Russia get a whiff of that, the shit will really hit the fan." The President paused and exhaled through pursed lips. "I know this doesn't fit the DOD's definition of an act of war, but we can't look at it any other way. We've never faced anything like this. If we cannot negotiate our way out of it, I will have no alternative. I trust that the NSA, CIA, and DOD will support me on this. I guess this brings us to you, General."

"Yes, sir. We are on high alert. Prepared for the worse. All branches are in line, sir."

"Maybe we should take this straight to the United Nations," suggested the President.

"I'm afraid that may be premature. We don't have enough

hard evidence. China would just deny the entire accusation...as usual," replied Espionto. "We all know that China is rattling their sabers, but they are not aware of how much we know."

The President pounded the table. "So how long do we pussyfoot around with this? What's the goddamned time-line, folks? This makes the entire Cold War, including the Cuban missile crisis, look like child's play!"

"Mr. President, your call with President Chen is scheduled for 5:00 p.m. We have a cadre of authorities for you to consult with between now and then. Here's the schedule." Finnegan turned his laptop around to show the President. "If you want any additions or subtractions, let me know."

Tracy Jones closed her laptop and addressed the group. "We need to be prepared for the worst, but I believe we can negotiate this thing out."

The President nodded. "If there's nothing else urgent, let's adjourn. If anyone leaks this to the press, I'll see to it you are air-dropped into North Korea for a special mission."

◇◇

Melinda closed the office door and sat behind her desk. There were now three desks crammed into Olivia's office. She attempted to bite into an apple before realizing she still had her N-95 mask on.

"Don't feel silly, I've done that a few times too," said Olivia.

"Thanks. It's good to know I'm not the only one losing their mind. Olivia, do you think...?"

"Think what?"

"Do you think, I mean, I was wondering if we used a smaller amount of the river dust on the rat wounds, they wouldn't be so aggressive?"

"It could be a dose effect...if, in fact, it had anything to do with their behavior. You just called it dust. I thought it was sand."

"Charles and I both noticed that it easily turns into a fine powder as soon as you disturb it, unlike sand. He called it dust...and I thought that was a more appropriate description too."

"Okay. Dust it is." Olivia grinned. "Here's some good news. Alex is swimming in rats. He said we could do some larger experiments, but I don't know. Don't get me wrong, I'm just concerned about getting caught doing this unsanctioned stuff. Shane would have a shit-fit. Be that as it may, I can't leave it alone after what we've seen. It's just too damn compelling, so we'll figure it out. I'll take the heat if he asks. After all, I'm the boss."

"I'll understand if you want to put it on hold," said Melinda with a mouth full of apple.

"Of course, BN27 comes first, but no, I don't want to wait any more than you do. Alex said he has some down time and it would only take him a couple of hours to set up our experiment. We don't have to do anything but run over to his lab and check the animals...at least at first."

"Good, 'cause I don't think we've scratched the surface. I've been trying to figure out how it might work. Can it get into cells and upregulate the production of repair proteins, or does it activate certain cytokines to call in other cells? I don't know. Any thoughts?"

Olivia took a deep breath. "Alex and I wondered if it could call up and boost production of stem cells. All the above may be true, but somehow, it can't just be the volume of repair elements; it also has to have an effect on reaction rate, right?"

"Yeah. It's easier to hypothesize about amassing all the needed cells and mediators for healing...like a hyperimmune response, but I don't know of any research that has revealed something that accelerates cellular metabolism to this extent."

"No, neither do I," responded Olivia. "Alex and I thought twelve rats would be enough, using half the dose of dust. I'll call him in a few minutes." Melinda perked up, excited that Olivia had bought in. "We should get a break soon while their preparing other BN27 samples for us. In the meantime, maybe we can check out some tissue from our rats under the electron microscope. We can stay late if we need to."

"Olivia, it's so amazing to have all this technology at our fingertips. Remember when we had to send stuff out then wait a week for results that we weren't sure were accurate?"

"I sure do. What a pain that was. Thanks for reminding me not to take all this for granted."

Olivia appeared to be studying her monitor. She wasn't. She was lost in thought. For almost a decade, she'd lived with chaos and fear. There'd been eight months of near normalcy, even though she was alone, waiting for Alex to join her, and COVID-19 was just starting to wither. Suddenly, she felt tired. There was always another hurdle. Now she had to set her sights on the end of Nipah, a very tenuous goal. Coming back to Vanhusse and having her own lab was great, but different. She was older and things had changed. Daydreaming came easy. A nostalgic escape back to her life before she worked for Altiva Pharmaceuticals. It was a lonely memory lane without Alex. Yet the memories that included Alex were the ones she fought to suppress. It was impossible to separate her love for him from the trials they'd endured together. Alex showed up and so did Nipah. A ridiculous notion. She resented her inability to separate Alex from these events. Her mind, like everyone's, insisted on tying things together. It was as if leaving any bit of information isolated or disconnected was a mortal threat.

◇◇

It wasn't dramatic, but the frenetic pace in the lab had eased off. They'd all been able to catch their breath since large-scale manufacturing started whirring along on the other side of the wall.

Alex had finished up his last group of BN27 rats when he brought out a dozen fresh ones for the river dust experiment. Levi didn't ask any questions. They got right down to work. Levi and Alex had their system down pat. Levi would place a rat in the anesthesia box, monitor it until it was sleepy enough, then hand it to Alex to make the one-centimeter incision and rub in half a dose of dust. Alex didn't have to ask Levi to stay mum. He'd learned that Levi never repeated anything he saw or heard in the animal lab. That was one of the reasons he'd kept his job for so long. He'd observed that those who gossiped didn't stay around very long.

When done with the twelfth rat, Alex carried the two cages into the animal storage area.

"Levi," hollered Alex.

Levi poked his head inside the door. "Yes, sir."

"We're missing the two rats we tested the other day. Be careful. They are more likely to bite than normal rats. Remember? I told you about one of them killing two others."

"I remember. I'll wear gloves to snatch them up…if I find them."

"They must have flipped the latch and escaped. Have you ever seen one do that before?"

"No, sir, that's a new one on me."

"Damn."

"Hey, Alex," said Bullock, causing both Alex and Levi to jump like two teenagers caught in the liquor cabinet. Bullock rarely came to the animal lab. He said he couldn't stand the smell.

"Yeah, Shane, what's up?" asked Alex. Motion drew Alex's eyes to the left of Bullock's right foot. One of the rats was meandering his way toward him. Levi nonchalantly shooed the rat away before Bullock saw him. Close call.

"Can you come to my office for a minute?"

"Sure." Alex nodded at Levi and followed Bullock out the door.

They walked single file between Bullock's piles of journals and personal jetsam. Bullock closed the door behind them before taking a seat. Alex had that "called to the principal's office" feeling for a moment. If Bullock caught on to his clandestine research project, it could get ugly.

"Cunningham called," said Bullock, while fidgeting with the string tethered to his reading glasses.

"And?"

"He said the Chinese have engineered a coronavirus using our nanotechnology to render it invisible to our immune system."

"Well, that's great. If that's the case, it could kill off the human race. That doesn't sound like a very smart move."

"That was my first thought as well. Cunningham said they gave out a vaccine for it along with the COVID-19 vaccine. How the hell do they have a vaccine for a virus that evades immune detection?"

"That's above my pay-grade, Shane, but...I'll give you an uneducated guess."

"Please do."

"Okay. Maybe their vaccine is an attenuated version that triggers some minimal degree of cellular immunity and not antibodies. That would require us to first figure out exactly how to copy their attenuated virus, which could be super complicated if they've designed it using nanotechnology and not our usual way of making vaccines. They might be hedging on all of us being dead before we could pull that off...I mean...if they were ever stupid enough to release their virus on us."

"That's brilliant, Alex. I know that just popped into your head, but it is totally worth considering. If it's feasible or not, I don't know."

"Thanks, Shane. I appreciate the complement. Ha. Get it...like immune system complement?"

"Yes. I get it. You're becoming an immuno-nerd. I've talked to Shenberg—"

Alex interrupted, "Who's Shenberg?"

"He's at NIH. Brilliant guy. He does a lot of work with nanoparticles and vaccine development. He said he has no idea how they've done it."

"Here we go again," said Alex, shaking his head in disgust.

"What do you mean, again?"

"Never mind. Let me guess, they're threatening to release it on us because we haven't given them BN27?"

"Yeah. The President might need to change his tune."

Bullock's face drew taut. The color drained. "There's something else," he murmured. Alex looked at him curiously and waited. "We're getting reports of miscarriages in women who've used BN27. The numbers are far out of the ordinary. More than suspicious. The FDA will feel obligated to put out a warning if it continues without some other explanation. Millions of young women will have to choose between having children or saving themselves."

"Oh God. That's terrible. Couldn't it be due to the virus? I'm sure you and others have already wrestled with that. I don't know what to say. It's just terrible."

"We've looked at that. Untreated pregnant women who've survived infection have not had miscarriages any more frequently than predicted. It's pretty clear, Alex...and I don't...I don't have any idea what to do about it. The pathologists are studying tissue samples. So far, there's some suggestion that the placenta is separating from the endometrium or not developing at all. If that's the case, I have an idea why it's happening."

"That's a start, right?"

"Alex. Do you know anything about the evolution of the placenta in mammals?"

"No, I don't. Ob-Gyn was my least favorite rotation in medical school."

"Okay, so there's a protein, syncytin, found in the outer layer of the placenta that has the RNA signature of an ancient retrovirus. You know that retroviruses incorporate their genome into our DNA as part of their reproductive cycle, right?"

"Yes. I know that much."

"Well, sometime around 150 to 200 million years ago, this viral interloper produced syncytin, which allowed the placenta to develop, and presto, hatching eggs became a thing of the past for prehistoric mammalian prototypes."

"Fascinating. So the same family of viruses that gave us HIV gave us the placenta?"

"Precisely. This isn't so hard to believe when you consider that at least eight percent of the human genome is of viral origin." Bullock's expression softened, and his eyes sparkled as his student lit up with an epiphany. "It's possible that BN27 is turning off the viral gene. Without syncytin, the placenta can't develop, and if one has developed, it may cause it to fail...and separate from the endometrium."

"Geez, Shane, that makes perfect sense," said Alex.

"And I believe it's right..." The animated professor look vanished as the gravity of it all hit again. "I just don't understand how it's happening. BN27 has to get inside the nucleus to bind to the retroviral fragment. I checked for that early on and never found that to be the case, but Olivia has found evidence that it does. How the hell did I miss that? Crap! My miracle cure has turned into a killer. Do you realize that this will scare the shit out of everybody, and they won't take the drug?"

"Shane. Calm down. You've created a life-saving drug. You've done good. It's bad news for some in this one way, but it's already saved millions of lives."

"You know as well as I do, we aren't remembered for the good we've done, we're remembered for our mistakes."

Alex paused. He'd been there, and wanted to escape from Bullock's pain. "Um...yeah, sometimes it seems that way."

Bullock crumpled into his chair.

They sat in silence, their minds racing. Alex thought about the dust. *It speeds up healing. It somehow gets cells to go into overdrive. That requires firing up protein production and that requires gene activation. Could it turn on the retroviral gene?* He had to fight the urge to share his crazy thoughts with Bullock. *How can I not tell him?*

"Shane. I'm sorry. I wish there was something I could do."

"I guess we better start working on it. We'll need a bunch of pregnant rats and that may take a while if we breed them. Levi can get you the phone number for our rat source. Obtaining supplies is getting tough. We've had to scramble to find suppliers that haven't shut down."

"Okay," replied Alex. "I'll figure it out." He had no idea how to breed rats, monitor their pregnancy, or interpret dissections. Those inconveniences were nothing compared to Bullock's issues. But the greatest thing about working in a big university research setting was that he could always find somebody who had the answers he needed.

◇◇

"Olivia. Can I come over for a minute?" asked Alex.

"Sure. What's up? You sound sorta agitated."

"I'm walking over as we speak. Bye."

He wiggled his way through the maze of lab workers standing at their benches. Olivia had just walked into her office. She was standing too close to the door when he pushed it open, banging her on the shoulder.

"Good grief, Alex."

"Sorry. Bullock just got news that the miscarriage rate in women taking BN27 is through the roof."

"Good lord. No. Are you kidding me?"

"Yeah. I thought I'd try to ruin your day just for the hell of it. Of course, I'm serious. He said he believes it may be due to deactivation of that retrovirus gene that codes for syncytin. Do you know about that?"

"Yes. Without that protein, the placenta can't develop. So he thinks BN27 shuts it off?" asked Olivia.

"Yes. The river—"

"This is horrible. What a disaster."

"Listen to me. The river dust speeds up healing, so it must upregulate, meaning activate genes, right?"

"I know where you're going with this. It may be a matter of dissociating it from BN27, or somehow repairing a damaged sequence. I don't know, Alex. That's really a leap."

"I thought you'd say that, and, yes, it may be a crazy idea, but I'm going to be setting up some pregnant rat studies to see the effects of BN27, so why not test some of them with the river dust as well?"

"Let's play this through, shall we?"

"Okay. Shoot."

"Suppose Shane is right, and we find that the river dust reactivates the syncytin gene. Then what? We don't know what this stuff is or how it works. We don't know what it could do to people. It could cause more problems than BN27. Honestly, it scares me. As a scientist, it's hard to believe I'm saying that. I know I can't keep myself from trying to figure it out...but we're getting ahead of ourselves. And if it works, we tell Shane, right? What do we tell him? That we found some magic dirt that he should mix up with BN27 and give it to the public? What about the FDA?"

"Wait a minute, Levi's calling me. Hey, Levi, what's up?"

"Doc, I caught the rats," announced Levi.

"Good."

"But they're acting mighty mean. I had to put on gloves to keep them from biting me. And I swear they look bigger. That's not all of it either."

"Maybe they're just scared. Put them—"

"I did, sorry for interrupting, but I put them in their cage and they walked right over and flipped the latch. It's not a tricky latch, but I've never, in forty years, ever seen a rat do that."

"That is strange. Levi, for now, would you just secure the latch? Wrap a twisty-tie around it or something. I'll be back in a few minutes."

"Okay, Doc."

Olivia watched Alex with her head cocked sideways. "What's that all about?"

"Oh nothing."

"Nothing?"

"I need to get back. Love you." Alex turned to leave with Olivia staring at his back.

◇◇

Sean Finnegan notified the President that the FDA was issuing an official warning for BN27 minutes before his call with President Chen. The warning specified the risk to pregnant women and women who may get pregnant. Some on the committee pushed to stop the use of BN27 altogether until more safety data was available.

"Ed, this is bad news, but it gives me some cover with Chen," said the President.

"What do you mean?"

"I can tell him about the warning and suggest that we may stop production. That BN27 may be too dangerous."

"Yes, sir. He's got more ammo now that he has the support of the World Health Organization, arguing that we should share with the Chinese and Russians. Those WHO bastards don't care if we give up our classified technology. But they may back off when they hear about the risks. Not to be a smart-aleck, sir, but when Chen hears it kills fetuses, he'll probably want it more."

"Hadn't thought of that. I wouldn't be a damn bit surprised if you're right. If so, I think we should offer to pledge a supply. I don't see any way around that."

"Yes, sir," replied Finnegan.

"I want you, Espionto, Dr. Shenberg, and Holdsworth in the Oval Office with me during the call."

"They're all here. I'll bring them right over."

Forty-five minutes later, the President hung up the phone. It didn't go well. Espionto was pacing and Finnegan was looking out the window. Shenberg and Holdsworth remained seated. The President leaned back and pushed his fist into the tip of his nose. President Chen had said they'd release the virus in seven days if the US didn't hand over clarified BN27 production methods, or send someone over so they could get the process going without trial and error. He didn't trust the US would send them enough final product fast enough. The President and his team realized that the truth was President Chen knew there was new technology involved, and he wanted it. Period. Its ability to cause miscarriages didn't concern him in the slightest.

"Any thoughts, gentlemen?" asked the President.

"We may have a vaccine in a month. It'll take them longer than that to replicate BN27, and he's right, we can't manufacture enough quickly enough to supply them, Russia, or anybody else with much more than a trickle," said Shenberg.

"That may be true," said Finnegan. "But remember, Doc, his primary concern is not the Chinese people. He wants it for himself and his government officials. After that, he wants the technology."

Holdsworth cleared his throat. "From a public health standpoint, I think letting them have it is the right thing to do."

Espionto's face reddened. "You don't realize what's at stake here, Doctor. Sometimes your do-gooder garbage is just plain ignorant."

"I think billions of lives trumps secret technology by a long shot."

Espionto fired back, "They're Chinese. Who gives a shit?"

"That's enough," interjected the President. "Of course, that's your stance, Holdsworth, that's your job. Sean, tell what's-his-name to send the process."

"It's Dr. Shane Bullock at Vanhusse, sir," said Finnegan.

"I'll get Director Cunningham to handle the transfer," said Espionto.

"Fine. Oh, Sean, have one of the European manufacturers divert a million doses to Chen. I'd like to choke that mother-fucker. Don't quote me on that, okay, fellas?"

"Yes, sir, answered Finnegan. The others nodded in unison.

Chapter 20

Dr. Bullock sat at his desk eating a bologna sandwich while his mind jogged down memory lane. He perused the many framed pictures that filled the wall across from him. Pictures of him receiving his Ph.D., accepting his first grant from N.I.H., a department Christmas party, on and on. Of course, his favorite was the one of him and Dr. Shenberg when they were awarded the Nobel Prize seven years earlier. His eyes welled up with tears. He'd just turned sixty-eight, and had made some bad personal choices in the last few years. Not even his wife mentioned his birthday. He was exhausted. Years had flown by in a blur. For forty-five years, he practically lived in the lab unaware of the outside world, his wife, or his children. The ringing landline jolted him back to reality. Before answering, he stared at the aging phone. Its ring had become quieter over the past twenty years. He reached to his left ear and slid his finger across the volume dial on his hearing aid.

Sandy's bulletproof cheery voice made it hard for him to be annoyed by phone calls he preferred to avoid. She'd been his secretary for eighteen years. Discreet, caring, and professional, she was his most loyal fan.

"Dr. B, it's Director Cunningham." A good example of a call he'd like to avoid.

"Thank you, Sandy."

"Bullock here."

"Dr. Bullock, I'm passing on a message from the President."

"THE President?" Bullock asked.

"That's what I said. I need a complete set of methods for the production of BN27 within a week. I'll be there in person to pick them up."

"I can do it, but that's years of my work."

"I know that. I also know it kills babies." Cunningham pushed that button hard to shut down any discussion from Bullock.

"For the Chinese, I suspect?"

"You're a genius, Dr. Bullock. Call me when it's ready."

The line went dead. He paced back and forth in front of his desk, rubbing the back of head, scared and confused. *Thousands, millions—sterilized, now it'll be a billion, and it's my fault.* He clasped his hands, squeezing the color out of them. *They already have most of the technology. They just don't know how to apply it. BN27 will give them the missing link. If they can't make it work, they'll come after me.*

✧✧

"Sandy," he barked as he shot past her, not turning his head. "Tell Dr. Nilsson and Winthrop to meet me in the conference room in five minutes."

"Yes, sir."

He passed several techs on his way to the conference room, most of whom had been with him twenty years, give or take. They'd seen him angry and frustrated but never looking like he did now when he pushed his way by.

Nipah was killing their friends and relatives. Bullock had given them hope. His pained expression triggered fear in them. They went mute trying to process the mix of concern for him and the shame they felt for being more worried about themselves.

Melinda sat at the far end of the table by the white-board in the conference room. She was looking at a cryptic drawing of a dendritic cell in the midst of immune havoc. Her back was facing the door when he came in. Alex and Olivia walked in a few seconds later.

Bullock wasn't looking at either of them when he began to talk. "I know we don't have definitive proof that BN27 shuts off the syncytin gene...but I'm sure of it. I can't understand why I didn't think of this immediately...but if it shuts down the gene, why and how would it ever get turned back on?" Olivia and Alex shared a stunned glance. "The FDA warning is for pregnant or potentially pregnant women. That's not enough. For shit-sake, it will most likely shut down the gene in all women. It could render every woman who takes it sterile. Sterile for friggin' ever, for all I know. I've sterilized millions of women..." He buried his head in his hands, unable to conceal his anguish. Olivia came around from the end of the table and sat in the chair next to him. They waited for him to compose himself.

"Shane, could I have a moment with Olivia?" asked Alex.

"Sure."

"We'll be right back," said Alex. Olivia didn't budge. "Olivia, please?" They walked down the hall to Olivia's office. They could feel the eyes of everyone they passed.

"What gives?" demanded Olivia.

"Settle down and hear me out. Shane's about to lose it. I think he needs, hell, we all need something to hope for. Let's tell him what we are working on."

"I don't know, Alex."

"I've got eighteen impregnated rats. Six controls, six have received BN27, and the other six got BN27 plus river dust. We'll know something in a week. Actually, sooner. Rats drop their hCG really quickly."

"If we tell him...he'll either go nuts on us, or if he's as beat down as he looks, he just might go for it."

Alex smiled and patted her thigh. "That's the spirit. Let's go."

Bullock had pulled himself together. When the door opened,

he greeted them with an embarrassed grin. They sat down across from him and leaned in.

"Shane. We have something to discuss with you," started Alex.

Over the next twenty minutes Alex and Olivia revealed their experiments and explained the story behind the river dust. Amazingly, Bullock just sat and listened, not saying a word until they were done. He nodded silently for several seconds before asking questions.

"You two and Melinda believe this dust stuff has definite effects. So, I'd be stupid to ignore you. Your premise, well, all I can say about that is it's as unlikely as anything I've heard, but it's not like I have anything else to go on. I agree, if it accelerates healing like you say, then yes, it must activate...upregulate the needed mRNA. Of course, connecting that to turning on the syncytin gene is...well...not a hypothesis I'd ever accept without more data at any time—except right now. Olivia, I need to take you away from your other work. Focus on determining if BN27 is shutting down the gene. I'll help you extract some mRNA from the rats treated with BN27. We'll see if they can make any syncytin. Alex, continue working on your BN27/dust treated rats and give nitrogen frozen samples to Olivia. Go ahead and enlist Melinda if needed. Before you go, I need to tell you Cunningham called."

"And what did Captain Sunshine have to say?" asked Alex.

"President Triagin has decided to send the entire process for manufacturing BN27 to the Chinese. I have a week to prepare it for Cunningham to hand over."

Olivia tapped her pen on her cheek. "Of course, it's only ethical that we let them have it even with the warning. Maybe we'll nail down a way to make it safe so we can get back on track saving as many humans as possible, no matter who the hell they are. That's our calling. We must keep politics out of it, right?"

"Yes, of course," answered Bullock. "Also, I've got to tell the FDA...I've got to tell them that BN27 could possibly make all women infertile—permanently. They'll realize what that means for the millions who've already taken it. That'll be ugly. It puts them in a terrible spot, and they'll rip me a new asshole in the process. I can hardly bear it, but the public has to know."

"Shane." Olivia paused until he looked up at her and held eye contact. "Don't lose sight of the fact that you've saved millions of lives and it'll be billions before this is over. They know that. They'll settle down after a while. They're not stupid."

◇◇

Full-time air-conditioning was a luxury for many in Malaysia. Li Jun kept his thermostat at a cool sixty-six degrees. Kuala Lumpur has numerous enclaves where the rich can distance themselves from the hot and dirty poor. His condo in Binjai on the Park provided every luxury and offered a direct view of Petronas Twin Towers. These matching monoliths are two of the tallest buildings in the world, serving as headquarters for the state-owned Petronas Oil, the largest and richest company in Southeast Asia.

New products were not something Li Jun usually took on, but he had a hunch that Charles was onto something. Unfortunately, Charles didn't ask about Li Jun's business model. If the dust got negative feedback from buyers, or if he balked at Li Jun's profit demands, Charles would simply go missing. But first things first. He had Chiamaka Abebe already north of Atlanta on his way to make a delivery to a consortium of Chinese buyers in Chicago. Li Jun requested a slight detour first. Like many, Chiamaka started as a poacher to provide money for his family. Over the years, he moved up the chain to a top-ranking international smuggler. His loyalty got him most of Li Jun's US deliveries. Those assignments were highly coveted because the risk of being robbed or murdered was minimal.

✧✧

Charles looked at the unfamiliar number ringing on his phone. He answered one ring before it went to voicemail. "Mr. Davenport, Li Jun has asked me to pick up a package from you. Where shall we meet tonight?"

"Tonight?" asked Charles as he turned away from Melinda and walked into the living room. He had the capsules ready but was caught off guard. *Drive back to Nashville to meet some shady character, alone, at night?* "I'll text you the address. It's an apartment in Nashville. How's 9:00 p.m.?"

"Good. Be there at 9:00."

Charles guessed the man was Nigerian based on his dialect.

"Melinda, hey hon, I need to run to my office and get my other laptop. It's got stuff on it I need."

"Tonight?"

"Yes."

"Okay. Watch out for zombies." That became their term for anyone who might not be taking extreme Nipah precautions. Having a BN27 inhaler staved off Charles' fears considerably. Melinda desperately did not want to use hers. When she first met Gwen, children were not on her radar. Over the past year, she thought about it more and more. She was hurt by Charles' lack of concern. Assuming he wanted their relationship to go in that direction was evidently premature.

Except for two ambulances, he didn't see any other cars on the road until he turned onto Broadway less than a mile from Vanhusse. Even then, he only passed a few military vehicles and no police. Nipah had spread quickly among them before BN27 was available. In some areas, forty percent of the national guard troops had died. Those remaining rarely stopped anyone to check essential worker status. Not catching Nipah was their first priority.

The lobby at Music Square East was empty. There was no guard at the desk watching the security cameras. The faint smell of garbage in Melinda's apartment rudely reminded him that he'd forgotten to take it out before they'd relocated to his house. He stood at the kitchen counter and slid a clip into his 9mm. Tightening handgun laws was an issue he promoted—for everybody else. The gun promptly slid down his butt when he tucked it into the back of his pants. He tightened his belt and tried again. The river dust capsules were in an overnight bag he'd left in the apartment tightly packed in plastic bags wrapped in cellophane.

The door buzzer startled him. He looked at the small security screen. A tall thin man with espresso bean-colored skin looked into the camera. *There's no security guard to ask questions. Good thing.* He pushed the "open" button, picked up the overnight bag, and stood in front of the door.

They exchanged greetings, Charles handed Mr. Abebe the bag and closed the door. It was over in five seconds. Charles sat on the couch, his heart pounding in his neck. A small plastic bag of river dust was left over from his capsule-filling marathon. Without a second thought, he placed at least two pinches of dust between his gum and cheek like a dose of snuff. Once dissolved in saliva with its pH of 7.4, it would be absorbed into his mucus membrane in much the same way it was through an open wound. *Why the hell didn't I think of that sooner?*

When he got home, the lights were off and Melinda had gone to bed. His body ached for sex. The bedroom window was open just enough to let in a faint stream of cool, damp night air. He started to reach for her shoulder. His hand froze in place. Doc Stevenson's journal entry popped into his mind. The image of Doc punching his wife during the exact same circumstances sent him back to the living room. He sat at his computer and just stared at the screen, trying to calm himself down.

✧✧

Mango plopped down on his chest. He had become his alarm

clock since MTSU had shut down. School administrators sent an email to teachers reporting a student death rate of fifteen percent. Unlike COVID-19, people under fifty were at increased risk of dying from Nipah. Charles stared at the ceiling, chilled by his damp t-shirt. Bits of vivid dreams still lingered, but he couldn't make sense of them. The disconnected fragments left him with an uneasy feeling, somewhere between fear and curiosity.

He picked up Mango and went out on his porch to get some fresh air. To his left, a set of hanging chimes rang in the breeze. The weathered blue Adirondack chair wobbled under his weight. It had been in the weather for too many years. He sipped his coffee and squinted from the morning sun. Spring brought renewed life, rich in its display of color and smell. Azaleas had begun to bloom around the edge of his porch. A Savannah sparrow chirped, marking his territory. The dawn chorus was in full swing. Mango eyed a squirrel going about her daily business at warp speed. *Do they know that the earth's top predator is in decline? Is that why they're so happy?*

Two hours later, his book had seventeen more pages with references and several images. He sat back, curious why his perception of time had slowed. Usually, being immersed in something made time appear to fly by. The difference, he thought, was that time seemed short when information came from within, but crept along if the source of information was external, like listening to a lecture. It was as if his rapid-fire thoughts were coming from outside of himself, leading him along ahead of his awareness. *It's gotta be the dust. This is what Doc Stevenson meant when he wrote about being led by his dreams. But what's it doing to me? This is crazy...but I love it!*

Chapter 21

Olivia grabbed her phone out of her lab jacket, shaking it loose from folded up paper and a piece of string that was supposed to remind of something she'd long forgotten. She was still holding the western blot results up to the light when Bullock answered.

"Shane, there's no syncytin. You were right. BN27 shut it down."

"Great, great, now to figure out how to turn it back on. I've been working on it, but so far, the only hope...crazy hope, is your magic dust. I just wish we had a handle on how it works."

"Crazy. Maybe, but we do have some good evidence on wound healing, stem cell recruitment, upregulation of growth factors, and cytokines. It doesn't seem as far-fetched as it did when Alex first suggested it."

"True. I'll be over in a couple of minutes."

"Okay, I'll see you in a bit."

Melinda checked Olivia's office, then walked halfway around her lab before she caught a glimpse of her white blonde hair in one of the genetics labs. Melinda headed toward her, bumping into a lab technician along the way. The short respite they had after BN27 had gone off to mass production was gone—now they had to fix the problem after the fact. She came up behind Olivia and waited for her to finish staring at the western blot before speaking.

"Are you going to eat lunch in your office?" asked Melinda.

"Yes. Why?" Olivia's forehead wrinkled as she looked over her reading glasses.

"I wanted to talk to you for a minute."

"We can talk now. I'm waiting for Shane to come look at this blot. Geez, I didn't tell you. The BN27-treated rats aren't making any syncytin. That's gotta be why there's no placenta, or if there was one, it failed."

"That goes with what I'm seeing under the microscope."

"Yes. We can talk about it a little later. What's on your mind?"

"So, you know Charles and I are a thing. If we live through this pandemic, I'm hoping we'll get married, have kids, and live happily ever after."

Olivia nodded her head slowly. She wanted to ask Melinda some personal questions, but knew better. "Are things going along okay?"

"Not sure. I think, well, I'm pretty certain that he's taken some of the river dust. He's acting differently, which makes me think he's dosed himself with it."

"Oh God, no. That's not good. Is he out of his—? Sorry, that's rude. We have no idea how to dose it beyond what we've seen with the rats. One milligram appears to make them predatory rapists and 0.01 mg per kg doesn't, so… We will need human trials, but it wouldn't be right to—"

"Dammit, Olivia, would you stop being a scientist for a minute? I'm not telling you this because I've found a study subject, for chrissakes."

"I'm sorry. That's so callous of me. Forgive me, please?"

"Yeah. I need to confront him. After I took out some to bring to the lab, the jar had a smidge over six inches in it. Now there's less than four. I know he'll get mad. He's been weird about this since the start. Remember when I told you his dad's dying from multiple myeloma. Well, Charles said something about giving him some river dust...after we had proof the stuff did something. I hope he hasn't already."

"Do you want Alex and me to be with you? Sorta like an intervention?"

"Intervention? Olivia, you're having an awful hard time saying the right thing."

"What do you want me—"

"Don't! Don't ask me that!"

Bullock was several feet behind Melinda. He stopped short and asked, "Is this a bad time?"

Melinda spun around to face him. "Oh no, Dr. Bullock, I was just leaving." She walked past him. Without turning back, she said, "Olivia. I'll be in cryo."

"Okay. We can talk more at lunch," said Olivia in her "everything's fine" tone.

Bullock looked even more uncomfortable. After a pause, he asked Olivia to show him the blots.

◇◇

Li Jun got up from a bench in front of the fountains at KLCC Park. His phone battery was at twelve percent and he had several more calls to make. On his to-do list was a call to Charles Davenport, lining up a prostitute for a Chinese buyer, and a call to a smuggler bringing in ivory on a container ship due to arrive at 8:15. Li Jun had things worked out with three customs officials who in turn gave the green light for all shipments to Li Jun's company, National Medical. The success of this arrangement depended on timing. Shipments had to coincide with the work schedules of those on his payroll.

It was a twelve-minute walk from his condo. He'd timed it. Two Japanese children ran by, oblivious to the sweltering heat and humidity. He paced himself, walking slowly through the thick air to slow the flow of perspiration. Quiet time was not his friend. When he had a lull in activity, he drank. He was a rock star with a very small fan-club. No true friends, no children, and his idea of a serious relationship was having the same prostitute twice. Money gave him what looked like a happy life. It was all he knew, and he was too old and frightened to change.

The parking lot in front of Binjai on the Park was packed with expensive and exotic cars. The new pearl white Porsche Carrera 2 that was delivered to him a month ago sparkled in the sunlight. He pulled out his key and got in, started it up, and turned on the air conditioner. Soon he felt a chill as the cold dry air met his sweaty hot skin.

◇◇

Charles heard his phone. He bolted to the kitchen and grabbed it off the counter. Mango ran for cover under the couch. A long list of numbers meant it was a call from Li Jun. He took a deep breath.

"Hello. This is Charles."

"I didn't expect to be calling so soon, but I've already received a report on your dinosaur bones."

"That was fast."

"The man who picked up your samples gave a hundred capsules to our buyer in Chicago. He took it three days in a row. Fool, he'd try anything. I guess he trusts me. He doesn't really have a choice. He liked the results. Really liked the results."

"Glad to hear it. I was sure they would," said Charles.

"I need a hundred thousand doses. I trust you can do that."

Charles turned his phone away as he caught his breath. "Yes. I can handle that, but it'll need to be in bulk, not capsules. I don't have a mechanized way to do that many."

"I can take care of that. I'll give you twenty-five thousand dollars."

"Is that forty percent?"

"It's twenty-five thousand dollars."

"Okay. How do I get the money?"

"You can meet Mr. Abebe and get cash, or I can wire it to an account. I suggest you get a shell company in the Caymans. I'll call it your consultation fee. You have the credentials. Your choice, but I need a decision by tomorrow. And, Charles, if I'm getting into this, I expect a regular supply. Probably a quarter million doses a month."

"Yes, yes, I should be able to do that." Charles went out to the yard for some air. "I'll call you tomorrow."

"Goodbye, Charles."

I may have to take a trip out to Jenny's farm. There could be an almost endless supply out there. My only money worry will be how to spend it. He walked back into the house, picked up his laptop, and typed in: "Banks in the Cayman Islands," followed by "Setting up a business in the Cayman Islands." *Dammit. Everybody does this. Our government is fully aware of this ploy. Wait a minute, it'll be a legitimate consulting business. I'm not money laundering. I'll pay taxes on it...at some point, and that's all the US cares about.* National Medical did do some legitimate business in the traditional Chinese medicine sector, which gave him some good cover.

◇◇

Simone Johnson, his literary agent, had died from Nipah. Nobody from the agency had notified him. He found out when he'd called to let her know he was three months ahead of schedule with his book. The man who answered the phone promised him that her replacement would be in touch. Charles asked for the replacement's name and number. When the man said he had neither, but he'd pass on the message, Charles realized his book was in trouble. Like most businesses, Thames Literary Agency was falling apart.

Oh good Lord, I hope Angie hasn't croaked too. Last he'd heard, she was locked down and doing all her editing from her rural home outside of Asheville, North Carolina. Charles was looking for her number when Melinda called to say she was leaving work early.

Entire families were dying in their homes. They rotted where they lay. The tent hospital at Centennial Park was gone. In its place were men in bulldozers digging mass graves. Several dug, while others pushed dirt over truckloads of bodies. Cars with dead family members were in line with trucks of every description. The stink of death hung in the air. Melinda closed her windows as soon as she got in the car, but, even then, the stench found its way in. It was a stark reminder. While at work, she could lapse into denial. It was hard to fathom that the human mind could deny such a horrific reality even for a minute—but it could. There were moments when she could forget that a third of the country was sick, dead, or dying.

Melinda stopped at the end of Charles' driveway to check the mailbox. Deliveries had dwindled to once a week at best. A letter from Gwen, dated two weeks earlier, was sharing space with a deserted bird nest in the doorless mailbox. She looked into the closest trees to see if she was being watched. A blue jay hopped from branch to branch in an old maple tree sporting new leaves. A crow pecked the ground. Neither seemed interested in the human invader. Melinda sighed and got back in her car.

The letter from Gwen struck her as intrusive. *Not now!* She felt busted. With all that had been going on it hadn't been hard to bury her past with Gwen. She threw the letter on the seat and drove up to the house.

Charles' car was gone. The back door wasn't locked. There really wasn't much reason to lock it. Mango was sleeping on the porch. She opened one eye to watch Melinda.

"Hi, Mango. Looks like you've kept the zombies out of the house." She managed a faint dark chuckle and walked into the kitchen. Charles left a note saying he'd gone to try to find some groceries. His laptop was sitting open on his small antique desk by the front window. She sat down and tapped the mouse-pad. Account information from Derbyshire Bank of the Caymans popped up. *What's this? A wire transfer from National Medical in Malaysia to a company called Indigenous Medicine Consulting for twenty-five thousand dollars? Charles, what are you up to?*

"Melinda. What are you doing?" Charles was standing at the back door watching her.

She winced. "Nothing. Just checking the news," she said, quickly bringing up a new search page and typing in "news."

"Why are you on my computer?"

"What's the big deal, Charles? Why would you care unless you're hiding something? Okay. Let's stop playing games. What's up with this bank in the Cayman Islands?"

"It's none of your business."

"What are you selling?" The moment those words came out of her mouth, she knew. The hair on the back of her neck went up. His frozen glare shot through her as his chest rose with a rage-filled breath. "Well, maybe I'm wrong...why don't you explain it to me?" He started to come toward her, his pupils constricted and his jaw clenched. "You look crazy. I'm going outside." The front door was within her reach. She pulled it open and ran out to the front yard, went around back, and locked herself in her car.

"Shit!" she shouted, pounding her steering wheel. Her phone was in her pocket, but her keys were on the kitchen counter. "C'mon, answer," she yelled into her phone while watching the sun drop below the tree-line, leaving an orange glow seeping between partially leafed trees.

"Hello. Hi, Melinda."

"Olivia, hey, I'm at Charles house and…"

"You okay?"

"Probably. I'm not sure. He'll cool down. He just scared me for a minute."

"What are you talking about?"

"I think Charles may be selling the river dust. I—"

"Selling it? Who to? Why?"

"On his laptop, he had a site open to a bank in the Cayman Islands showing a money transfer from a company in Malaysia called National Medical. It had real account data, at least it looked authentic. I'm pretty sure it's his account. He caught me looking at it and he got a bit scary. Wait a minute. He wants to talk to me." She put the phone on her lap and opened the car window a couple of inches.

"Honey, I'm sorry. Come in and we'll talk about it, okay?" She studied his face.

"Okay. No more scary stuff, right?"

"Right."

"If you start yelling, I'm going home."

"No yelling. I promise."

"Okay. Just a minute."

"Who are you talking to?"

"Nobody. Just checking a text."

He went back inside. Melinda left the phone on her lap and turned away as she spoke.

"I'm back. Okay, he's cooled down. I'll talk to him and let you know."

"Melinda, are you sure you don't want to come over for the night?" asked Olivia.

"I'm sure. I'll be alright. Besides, my keys are in the house. He wouldn't touch me. He might scream and yell, but he won't touch me."

"If you're so sure of that, why'd you call me?"

"Just to talk… I'm good. I'll call you later."

"I'll be waiting…and keep hold of your keys."

"Thanks. Yes. Bye."

✧✧

"Something wrong?" asked Alex, looking up from the cryo-electron microscopy pictures Olivia had taken.

"Melinda just called me. I forgot to tell you that yesterday she came to me concerned about Charles."

"Yeah?"

"She thought he'd taken some of the dust and dosed himself. She said he'd been acting differently like—"

"Like how?"

"Later in the day yesterday she came to me and said he was sexually aggressive. At first, she chalked it up to being 'playful.' But after watching and listening to him, she said he was hyperactive, cocky, like he was on speed or something. That's what tipped her into the concern category."

"Maybe he's just bored or frustrated with Nipah lockdown...or he's freaking out like most of mankind."

"Sorta don't think so...I mean, that's a good thought, but— not. Remember, it was his idea to go to west Tennessee in the first place?"

"No, but okay, so?"

"He was obsessed with Melinda's story about the old country doc's magic powder."

"Well, he was right about that. It's beyond amazing," said Alex.

"Yes. For sure. Hear me out. His dad's dying of multiple myeloma and treatment is failing. Charles had this hair-brain idea that maybe the river sand...dust, could heal him. Anyway, he seems to have, in her opinion, forgotten all about his dying dad. Tonight, she found some banking stuff, a wire transfer from a company in Malaysia. She's convinced he's selling it—the dust. He—"

"Selling it! Oh for shit-sakes, you're kidding. We can't let him do that. No telling what the hell will happen if someone takes just a little too much." Alex stood up, paced, and rubbed the back of his head.

"Hold on." Olivia put up both hands like an after-school crossing guard. "She's going to talk to him. There's probably some other explanation. He can't possibly be that stupid. Let me finish. He caught her looking at the banking stuff, and apparently got pretty crazy. Didn't hit her or anything, but scared her."

"Oh lord. I knew there was a reason I never liked that guy. Now I wanna shoot him."

Olivia stiffened. "I've had enough of that."

"No, no, honey. I'm just trash talking."

"What exactly did Cunningham have you doing at Camp Perry?"

"Just some training."

"Training?"

"Yeah, you know, like how to keep my mouth shut. I don't think it matters now. Nipah changed everything. So, Melinda's going to call you as soon as she's done talking to him?"

"That's what she said."

"Good. Let's go over our data. It's phenomenal. Oh, one more thing. Do you know where Charles lives?"

"Somewhere in Fairview, or Fairfield...that's all I know. Don't you even think about it."

"Think about what?"

"You know exactly what I'm talking about."

Chapter 22

President Triagin rubbed the edge of the old desk, marred by chair arms that sat a little too high. The Resolute desk was the only bit of decor that hadn't changed in the Oval Office since 1879. Ten American presidents worked from behind the 1,300-pound hand-carved oak symbol of grace and bravery. It was a gift from Queen Victoria to the United States when Rutherford B. Hayes was President; twenty-two years before viruses were identified as human pathogens. Triagin groaned. *I used to measure time relative to wars and great accomplishments, now it's viruses and pandemics.*

A lot had changed since the Resolute desk had been built. He wondered if the nation was really any better off now. Like a genie's lamp, he rubbed the old wood, wishing that he could go back in time. For a moment, he was lost in the story of the famed British Navy ship. In 1853, along with three companion vessels, the H.M.S. *Resolute* became trapped in an ice floe in the Canadian Arctic. They were on an ill-fated rescue mission in search of two ships that left England in 1846 in search of the fabled Northwest Passage. Two years later, the *Resolute* broke free and floated a thousand miles into the Davis Strait. The ghost ship was discovered by an American whaling vessel and taken to Connecticut, where she was repaired to her former glory. The restored H.M.S. *Resolute* set sail back to England, where she was presented to the Queen.

At the time, western Europe was in the throes of rampant

tuberculosis, typhoid, and cholera. Infectious disease had plagued mankind for millennia, but society persevered. Humans are resilient, and resolute, continuing on with their daily lives despite extreme adversity. President Triagin, like so many before him, would not be defeated. *I may die, but I will not be defeated.*

The *Resolute* was finally decommissioned and dismantled in 1879. Some of her timbers were used to construct a desk that was sent across the Atlantic and delivered to the White House. President Triagin wondered if anything like that could ever happen again. His fingers were still tracing the desk's carvings when Secretary of State Sean Finnegan walked into the Oval Office.

"Dammit to hell, Finnegan, what do you mean they say it doesn't work? It's only been a few days. I thought Bullock said it would take at least a month for them to make any?"

"Zhao called me. Their scientists claim the methods aren't feasible…that we purposely sent them misleading information on BN27 production, sir. He didn't give me any details. He said his office was transmitting complete information as we spoke and that his call was just an advance notice. Tyler Edmond in communications is cleaning up any translation errors. It should be ready any minute."

"Zhao, Minister of Security, right?"

"Yes, sir."

"That little prick. Is there any way it's true? Who on our end handled it?"

"Well sir, Dr. Bullock and his scientists prepared it. Director Cunningham hand delivered it to his tech team. I…I don't know their names offhand. They encrypted it for ultra-secure transmission to Chen's Chief Science Officer. From there, I imagine it went to the appropriate scientists."

"Okay, so we need to talk to Cunningham and his team, right?"

"Yes, sir. Also, you should be getting a call from Chen."

"I am getting, or you just think I should be?"

"Sir, Zhao said he'd pass on the message that you would want to discuss this misunderstanding...but…"

"But what?" Triagin shouted.

"He didn't think there was any room for negotiation. He said today was the day for a yes or a no." Finnegan sat down in one of the two Queen Anne-style upholstered chairs several feet from the President's desk. The weight of the disastrous news pressed him into the chair. Informing the President made it unbearably real.

"And what's that supposed to mean? What?"

"I'm afraid they may release their virus. The genetically engineered one. The coronavirus that they're already vaccinated for. They'll give us the vaccine when they have enough BN27."

"You can't be serious. They're just posturing, right?"

"I don't know. I don't know. Before hanging up, Zhao's interpreter said...and he sounded uncertain...that Chen would reconsider if he didn't get your pledge of full cooperation today. We've told them our Nipah vaccine could be ready in two to four weeks. It's pretty obvious it's the technology he's after."

"Then there is room for negotiation? I thought you said there wasn't."

"I interpret that to mean that we have to accept their terms with no discussion."

"Terms? What terms?" he said, thumping his desk. "How can I accept terms when I don't know what they are, for chrissakes?"

"I don't know what they are. Please check your e..."

"You don't know. Well, who does? Email!?"

"The corrected transcript should be there."

The President scanned his email. Finnegan looked on, clasping his hands. "I don't see anything. The call is in ten fucking minutes, Sean. Don't you think I should know what the hell is going on before I decide on going to war with China?"

"Of course. I'll call down." Finnegan got up, punched at his phone, and walked to the window. "This is Finnegan, get me Edmond. To the hospital? Nipah? He was working on a memo from China for the President. He needs it now! Quarantine? Uh huh. Yeah. No! It can't wait. Somebody suit the hell up, get in there, get his notes, forward any emails he has from China today to the President in the next sixty seconds or… Passwords…shit, get I.T. The President better have what he needs in under five minutes!" He hung up, tapped his phone on his forehead, and plopped back into his chair.

"Well, Sean, I guess I just pick up the phone, completely uninformed, and make a life and death decision for the entire free world. Piece of cake. All in a day's work, right?"

Ten minutes passed. No call and no transcript. They looked at each other with identical expressions.

The President broke the silence. "Sean, are you sure you got the time right?"

"Yes, sir."

"I'll give Chen until I've read the transcript," said the President. "Then I'll call him. While we're waiting, get Cunningham on the line. I don't know about him. On the other hand, if Espionto got in the middle of this, I might have reason to worry. He's a patriot…but he scares me sometimes. Tracy Jones, she's solid as a rock."

"Yes, sir. Good people." Finnegan thought it was an odd time for a staff review.

"Speaking of good people…go ahead and fire whoever dropped the ball in communications."

Finnegan chanced a grin. "That's above my pay-grade, sir."

"Well, Mr. Secretary of State, you just got a promotion." They both chuckled. "And stop calling me 'sir.' Right now, it's just you and me. That reminds me, have you briefed Tracy?"

"Yes, sir. She's got everybody on alert."

Five minutes later, the President's computer dinged. The transcript containing the conversation and the demands popped up. They both read it. Finnegan stepped back, preparing for Triagin to explode.

"Ed," he said in a metered calmness that comes before a total meltdown. "It says I was supposed to call him within thirty minutes or they would take action. It does not say he was going to call me. It also says that when I called, I should be prepared to accept their terms and there would be no compromise or negotiation. How long has it been, Mr. Secretary?"

"Forty-five minutes."

He picked up the landline. "Get me President Chen's office immediately." He stared at Finnegan. "Ed, the only reason I haven't pulled the pistol out of my top drawer and shot you between the eyes is because there's no sense in it, except maybe I'd feel better for a few minutes. The single most important thing that we are supposed to be prepared for around here is disasters like this, right? We screwed up on Pearl Harbor, and 9/11; why should this be any different? Why can't we learn from our mistakes, Sean?"

"I don't know."

"From now on, stick with 'yes, sir.'"

"Yes, sir."

"And we have failed." There was no meltdown. His phone buzzed. He remained calm. "Yes? He can't be disturbed? What? Okay." He gently placed the receiver back on its base. "Chen's office said he wasn't available. Not available even if it was the President of the United States. So, we are led to believe that China has done something, but we don't know what. Did they release the virus? If they're sending nukes, we haven't picked up on it...unless of course there's nobody minding the satellites. What the hell are we...? Answer the door."

"Yes, sir."

"Hello, Tracy. Maybe you have some ideas?" asked the President. "Let me get you up to speed first."

She sat in the chair across from Finnegan and nodded her head silently as the President filled her in. When he finished, nobody had anything to say.

◇◇

Jan Whitorsh and a few others were still working in the lab. Of course, Bullock hadn't quit for the day. Staff that couldn't guarantee a Nipah-free home were sleeping on cots and couches scattered around the building. At first, it was just three or four people. Now, twelve of sixteen weren't going home. They all had BN27 inhalers, but the younger women were panicked by the thought of taking it.

Olivia and Alex were huddled in front of two computer screens. The sheer volume of experimental data was overwhelming. They had to make sure it all remained coherently documented and analyzed. Not one of them understood all the information. The three of them had to review every finding together to make sense of it. Bullock joined them to lead the discussion. Since Olivia and Melinda had a similar knowledge base, Melinda got a bye for the night.

"Alex, let's hear your summary. Short version. We'll fine-tooth comb it in a bit," said Bullock. His crumpled white shirt, splattered with various reagents and an assortment of organic muck, made it clear he was working too fast, too hard, and for too long.

Alex pulled his laptop around so Bullock could follow along. "Okay, starting at the top, BN27 was effective in preventing and treating Nipah. Our secret experiment, sorry about that, with the river dust as a wound healing accelerant was profoundly positive. Although we can't prove it, our original dose appeared to cause hypersexual and predatory behavior among treated rats. And they apparently gained some cunning as well. Levi observed them pushing up their cage latch. One tenth that amount promoted healing equally as the higher dose, but without the behavior changes, at least so far."

"Go on," said Bullock, flinging his hand like swatting a fly.

"So," Alex continued. "None of the pregnant rats that received both BN27 and the river dust lost their pregnancies. You two have the mRNA data. I also did another mini-experiment."

"Okay. Let's hear it," Bullock sounded impatient.

"I gave four rats river dust only, no BN27, and exposed them to Nipah. None became ill."

"What?" Bullock asked. "Are you sure?"

Alex nodded. "I'm beginning to wonder what this stuff doesn't do."

"Olivia, what do you have?"

"Melinda and I have been studying the dust using several analytical approaches, and I don't know what to make of it." She brought up her data and spread out 3-D photos derived from her cryo electron microscopy images, and nuclear magnetic resonance (NMR) studies. "First off, we found that the dust recruits stem cells, and just the right combination of cytokines at a rate one hundred-fold normal. I also looked at cells from Alex's rats that were given dust and exposed to Nipah. It looks like once viral RNA enters the cell, it doesn't get transcribed. It just sits there, and no new virus is formed. Now get this, when I added the sequence for syncytin to cells with cleaved out syncytin gene components, the dust treated cells incorporated the functional sequence into the cell's DNA just like retrovirus probably did 150 million years ago. The next thing I want to tell you about is...almost incomprehensible. From what we've seen, it can literally initiate reactions that result in the formation of nitrogenous bases, both pyrimidine, and purines. It's..."

"Oh my God." Bullock was visibly shaken. "Have you found

nucleotides?"

"Yes."

"And you're positive there were no DNA or RNA fragments already present?"

"Yes. Only a few amino acids, trace metals, and simple carbohydrates were present. I don't know what the catalyst is. We've isolated a twelve base pair strand of RNA. There must be an RNA enzyme involved. We'll have to work backwards to figure this out...when there's time. This is early data. It'll take more work to know if we have what we think we have."

Bullock rubbed his hands together. "This could be the biggest discovery since DNA."

"It really does look like the dust may initiate the formation of RNA," added Olivia.

Alex listened intently. "If I'm hearing you correctly, it sounds like you are unraveling the mystery of how life began."

"That phrase is just too big to claim. We can say that we may have discovered a putative agent possibly involved in the production of RNA," said Olivia. "The biggest problem is that we don't know what the river dust is. Before it crumbles into dust, it is coated in a thin carbon veneer as if it were burnt or exposed to lava. Once dissolved, I can't find anything but some trace metals. Nothing organic at all."

"I know we'd prefer to drop everything and work on this, but we can't." Bullock paced in front of Olivia's desk while flipping his reading glasses between two fingers. "Right now, we have to decide if we are going to propose giving the dust to all premenopausal women. Do we have enough of it? Can we get more? How do we administer it? We have one huge problem—we can't even tell the FDA what this stuff is, let alone tell them we think it is safe. Do either of you have any answers?" He looked back and forth at Olivia and Alex.

"We know it's soluble. Why can't we incorporate it into the

BN27 inhalers?" asked Alex.

"Good idea," answered Bullock. "Now, do we have enough for a couple billion doses?"

"Melinda knows exactly where it came from. I'll ask her," said Olivia.

"Has she called back?" Alex asked.

"No."

"Maybe you should check on her?"

"Alex, I will. As soon as we're done here."

Bullock nodded. "Alright. We'll worry about the FDA later. Alex, get Darnell from manufacturing to make a couple inhalers with BN27 and dust. Test it on your rats to see if the dust works as an aerosol. Olivia, can you find out from Melinda if we can get more of it? Meanwhile, keep trying to figure that stuff out, even if you have to get creative... Right now, I need to go home and get some sleep. Maybe you should too. We'll get started early tomorrow."

"Sounds good. Goodnight, Shane," said Olivia.

Alex gave him a thumbs-up. Olivia picked up her phone to call Melinda.

"Are you okay?" asked Olivia.

"Oh yeah. I'm fine. I may have overreacted," answered Melinda.

"Overreacted?"

"Yes. He calmed down. We're good. Really."

"Did you ask him about the dust?"

"No. I'll work up to that. I can bring more in tomorrow," she said, quickly changing the subject. "It's at my apartment. We've been avoiding going there. Half of the tenants have been wiped out."

"Mostly young people?"

"Yes. They weren't safe enough fast enough. We saw that coming."

"Melinda, be careful. I'm not convinced."

"Don't worry. See you in the morning."

"K. Bye."

Chapter 23

A cloudless sharp blue sky blanketed Boston. A great day to be out, but nobody intent on leisure could be found. Boylston Street was empty. EMT Chuck Riley was going close to sixty. With no traffic, the road was his. They were carrying their fifteenth patient of the day to Mass General. She was a twenty-five-year-old nurse who'd gone home sick the night before. Every few blocks, a military vehicle or police car would be parked at the corner. They unenthusiastically attempted to discourage thieves from breaking into shops. Several homeless people sat on a bench in the Commons, surrounded by protesting pigeons frustrated by the lack of handouts.

Grocery stores were heavily guarded. Reports of ambushed and hijacked eighteen wheelers carrying food to supermarkets began to mount. Pop-up "thieves' markets" had become the new convenience stores. Police looked the other way. City mayors came to the realization that food, stolen or otherwise, was being distributed in a timely manner. That had to take priority over chasing thieves into hiding—with the food.

"Chuck, she's coughing up blood. A lot of it. Hurry it up."

"I'm pushing it. Just be a few minutes. Put in an airway."

"If we're that close, I think I can manage it with suction."

"Okay. We're at the Commons. Be there in a minute."

Jordan Simpson was a nurse at the Mass General. She was wearing the same scrubs as the night before. After getting to her apartment, she'd gone straight to bed with shaking chills, headache, cough, and shortness of breath. Sixteen hours later, she called 911. Blood ran down her cheeks and matted her dark brown hair. Her gray eyes stared at nothing. The EMT had seen her expression on several hundred faces. Pure paralyzing fear. Some fought like cornered cats, others lay perfectly still—in defeat.

Jordan tested negative for Nipah before leaving work. At 2:00 a.m., she pulled her inhaler of BN27 out of her purse and took two puffs. Logic and risk became irrelevant. Fighting for every breath while slowly drowning in her own blood made fertility a far-off concern.

"Hey, Chuck, this is the first time I've seen anybody coughing up so much blood. None of our Nipah patients have done this, have they?" Those words came out before he realized they were far from reassuring the already panic-stricken patient.

"No. John. Haven't seen it. Her Nipah test was negative. I don't have a clue. Okay, here we are."

They got in line behind five ambulances. Abandoned stretchers and their lifeless cargo had rolled into the nearest curb. People died waiting for care. A pile of dead bodies fumed at the edge of the hospital's parking lot. Jordan fought for every breath.

◇◇

From the Oval Office window, Tracy Jones didn't expect to see cherry blossoms bursting with color or fat and sassy white-winged doves flitting about. Dead flowers and a birdless sky would have been more fitting. Her mind was twisted by the incongruity. Nature isn't just. Nipah and China's new threat were human problems. In the grand scheme of things, people aren't that important. Humility for the sake of humility was a wasted lesson. She turned to face the President, even more pissed off and scared than she had been moments before.

Dr. Holdsworth from the CDC was notified to be on the lookout for a new virus, possibly an engineered coronavirus. They couldn't formally go to the WHO without evidence. Holdsworth set about contacting their allies' health leaders, asking them to look hard at all the viral-like deaths where Nipah wasn't found.

Two days after EMTs brought in Jordon Simmons, Holdsworth got a call from the Mass General. Doctors there reported the death of a young nurse due to a new strain of coronavirus. Their ICUs were filling up with Nipah-negative patients, presumed to have the new virus. BN27 was completely ineffective. Scores of young women who did have Nipah but refused BN27 were also being admitted at high rates. As the day wore on, patients recovering from Nipah or other illnesses were becoming ill and dying from pulmonary hemorrhage. Doctors and nurses were continuously being splattered with blood. Boston was the epicenter for the new coronavirus. COVID-H had arrived, far more deadly than Nipah or COVID-19.

The death curve for Nipah was beginning to flatten for all demographics due to use of the BN27 inhalers except for females of child-bearing age. BN27 manufacturing was getting up to speed and distribution around the world was underway despite the stern pregnancy warning. Conspiracy theories were rampant, claiming the fertility warnings were a hoax. Up to eighty percent of women who could get BN27 used it. Just like during COVID-19, people didn't listen to health experts. Population control was in full swing, one way or another.

Dr. Holdsworth called Dr. Shenberg at N.I.H. to discuss strategy before their conference call with the President. For the moment, they agreed that Jordon Simpson was the index case. Her boyfriend was sure the only place she had been for three days prior to becoming ill was work. That meant she caught it at the hospital, but from whom? Within twenty-four hours, nearly half of the patients and staff that worked on her shift were sick, and it wasn't Nipah.

Besides the President and Vice President, the situation room was crowded with members of the Joint Chiefs of Staff and National Security Council. Holdsworth and Shenberg were on speaker. Everyone knew who was responsible for the outbreak.

"We need the names of anyone who was on that floor," said Espionto. "We'll interview them. I'll send a couple people up there tonight to run the investigation." The President nodded in agreement.

"We've sent a blood sample to Dr. Bullock. Hopefully, it has some live virus in it," said Shenberg.

"COVID-H has been sequenced. Based on that alone, the COVID-19 vaccines are unlikely to be effective. We haven't yet been able to verify if it can evade immune detection. If that's true, developing a vaccine will be quite a challenge. We understand that you have information suggesting it carries a nanorobot that somehow provides that capability."

Tracy Jones leaned into the closest microphone. "That's correct, Dr. Holdsworth. Dr. Nilsson has developed some preliminary methods for identifying nanobots. Dr. Bullock will—"

"Yes, we know her work. So far, she's shared her progress with us, but she's made it clear that her methods aren't ready for prime time."

"Unless you have an alternative, it's all we've got. Follow every move this virus makes," said the President. "You will have full cooperation and support from the DOD, homeland security, the military, and the C.I.A. Now, tell me about containment."

Shenberg cleared his throat. "We need to lock down Boston—completely."

The President looked around the room, daring any dissenters. "So be it."

◇◇

Dr. Holdsworth called Bullock as soon as he got to his car. Holdsworth's southern drawl had gone into hyper-speed. Bullock had to listen extra carefully. When the call ended, Bullock had said two words—okay and goodbye.

Five minutes later, Director Cunningham called to brief him on security protocols involving COVID-H. Bullock felt a surge of anxiety as his to-do list pushed the needle into the unmanageable range. He held the sealed package containing blood samples from Jordan Simpson in his hand. Olivia would be the first to handle the lethal virus. If she died as a result, it would be his fault. Several deep breaths later, he headed over to Olivia's office.

The Boston outbreak hit the news that morning. They'd picked up on the fact that there was something different going on. Something inconsistent with Nipah infection. Bullock wondered if people had grown numb to bad news or if anybody was even listening.

Olivia was in her lab engrossed in the task of characterizing the river dust. She hadn't felt that connected with her work since before going to work for Altiva Pharmaceuticals. Bullock sat in her office, waiting. He didn't mind a moment to organize his thoughts. He was in the middle of some of his greatest work, although it was more misery than excitement. He had other worries. Having to answer to Cunningham and DOD was worse than the usual intrusions from university administrators. At least they listened and negotiated. They knew he could take a position anywhere he chose.

Like a life raft taking on too many passengers, the weight of responsibility had him teetering on the edge of uncontrollable failure. He wanted it all to vanish like a bad dream. He longed for the past, when life was simpler, his brain more agile and fresh. When he could drink a six-pack of beer with his buddies, sleep a few hours, and work the next day without missing a lick. Undaunted by challenges or missteps, he had always persevered. Co-workers were infected by his optimism. For the first time in his career, he was plagued by doubt. Maintaining the appearance of confidence and integrity felt like a full-time job.

Olivia walked into her office shaking several pieces of lined paper and talking to herself. She didn't notice Bullock until she almost ran into him. Startled, she clutched her chest as if protecting her bosom from an oncoming projectile.

"Ahh! You scared me." Her attention went from his eyes to the small box sitting on his lap.

"Sorry," he said flatly. He held up the box. "Olivia, this just came from the CDC. It contains blood samples from a patient who has died from a new virus. They're—"

"The one in Boston, I presume?"

"Yes, a new coronavirus is believed to have been engineered by the Chinese. COVID-H. H stands for hemorrhage. People die from pulmonary hemorrhage. They drown in their own blood."

"Well, shit, Shane, that's not news I want to hear. Why don't you start over...tell me something else? Something good."

"Me either. I've been sitting here trying to wrap my head around it...but I need more head."

"Can't help you there, Shane."

"Forget I said that. The reason I've brought this to you is that it may have a nanorobotic component. The spike protein that triggers our immune response is similar to COVID-19. Shenberg believes the nanobot is at the base of the spike and binds up antibodies in a way that alters them so there is almost no immune response."

"Okay. Scary, very scary. However, there's got to be more to it than that."

"I know what you're going to ask. There's much more. The viral genome may be engineered to replicate and incorporate the bot into the virus's protective shell, the capsid."

"Oh my God. That's brilliant. A genetically engineered bot...probably a novel glycoprotein that can be naturally replicated. It's functional, but not like a typical glycoprotein.

That's a new twist on nanorobotics...blending with genetic engineering. Wow."

"I agree. Shenberg reminded me of ribosomes. So…"

"Good point. We do think of our cell's ribosomes as naturally occurring nanobots. I get that. It's a pure biorobot, no metallic component. That will make it a lot harder to detect. Wait a minute, they've sequenced its genome. Can't they identify the strange additional sequence?"

"Yes, but there's a hundred or so strange additional sequences put in there to throw us off."

"Damn. That's even more brilliant," said Olivia. "I'll have to see if I can identify its structure with cryo, then model possible structures likely to fit the mess of genetic products."

"Your knowledge base has certainly grown beyond biochemistry," said Bullock.

"My research required it. No different than you. You've mastered several disciplines."

"Are you brown-nosing me?" Bullock grinned as he set the box on her desk and started to stand up.

"Don't think so. We're past that."

"Yes. Okay. I'm not done. Shenberg said that he believes that the Chinese vaccinated its populace against their COVID-H at the same time they vaccinated for COVID-19 and that they likely provided it to all their friends, like Russia and Iran, etcetera. Early data suggests the vaccine is not directed at the spike protein like the COVID-19 vaccine. Apparently, it triggers antibodies to an unknown engineered surface molecule. If some spy could get us a sample of the vaccine, we'd have decent chance of copying it. Without that, he said, they can probably figure it out, but it will take months. This virus is way too contagious and fatal to wait that long."

Olivia glared at him, trying to comprehend what she heard. Fear overwhelmed her scientific mind. "Is this all because our government assholes stalled on showing them how to make BN27?"

"That premature press-release caused this mess. I knew it was a stupid idea. I don't know any other details beyond the fact that the President believes that they'll give us the COVID-H vaccine when we help them make enough BN27 for their own people."

"This could wipe us out. We've lost nearly 50,000,000 people here, and we are finally flattening the Nipah death curve with BN27 and a hint of herd immunity—and now this? Geezus!" Olivia threw a handful of articles across her desk, and looked away, tears forming in her eyes. "Why didn't we...? It doesn't matter."

"Why what?" probed Bullock.

"Why didn't we know about this sooner?" asked Olivia, just louder than a whisper.

"The spy reported to the CIA. They went to Shenberg first, a few days ago. Olivia, we need you to work on identifying the COVID-H nanobot...or biobot. Melinda and Alex can stay on the river dust for now."

"Yes, Shane. Understood. But I want your opinion on something."

"Okay. Shoot."

"We've verified that the dust stops Nipah replication, at least in rats. I wonder if it could work for COVID-H?"

"I've been wondering the same thing. Seems so unlikely. What the hell? The only way to know is to try it. We can use the Boston sample. Right now, we don't have any other good options. We know BN27 doesn't work on COVID-H, and even if we have a best-case scenario, modifying BN27 could take a year. Figuring out a vaccine could take just as long. Meanwhile, we gotta do what they're asking. I'm waiting to hear from Cunningham about sending a team to China. He was supposed to notify me this morning...I wonder if something's come up."

"Go to China?"

"Yeah. They claim the methods we sent them don't make sense. I warned Cunningham that there are nuances that Chinese scientists might have trouble with. However you slice it, we have to comply. In the meantime, I still need you to find the biobot. Let's take these samples over to isolation and get to work. We can infect several rats and see if your river dirt has any effect, assuming these samples contain viable virus," said Bullock, regaining his usual exuberance.

"Melinda has spoken to the lady that owns the property where the dust was found in 1907. You're right, it looks like dirty sand, but when the sandy part is separated from the dirt, it is easily crushed into a fine powder that Charles called 'dust.' The name stuck. Also, it dissolves in water that's buffered up to a pH of 7.40 - 7.50."

"Who's Charles?"

"Melinda's boyfriend. He's a medicinal anthropologist over at MTSU."

"Okay. Whatever. Anyway, great, perfect. Let's get on it." Bullock clapped his hands. Olivia jumped. "On edge, huh?"

"Hell yeah. You do that again, I'll either fall on the floor or bite your fingers off...Dr. Bullock, sir." Bullock grinned and quickly stuffed his hands into his pockets.

Chapter 24

Traffic signals and streetlights were the last to go. There was no world beyond the glow of their headlights. Two dogs tore into a fresh corpse. Olivia and Alex kept talking without pause. The terrifying sight didn't even register a comment.

"Slow down, would ya?" barked Alex. "Are you trying to kill us, or just practicing?"

"You drive like this all the time, so…"

"Yeah, but I know how to drive."

"You think so." Olivia rolled her eyes and pushed on the gas. She zipped through the last two intersections on Hillsboro Avenue without turning her head. There was no attendant and the two zebra-striped gates were pointing straight up. The lot was empty when she pulled in at 5:07 a.m. Their mouths were dry with anticipation.

It had been seven hours since Alex exposed four rats to Jordan Simpson's blood. He'd aerosolized it into their lungs along with the river dust. If the rats weren't sick or dead, Melinda and four twenty-gallon canisters would be heading to west Tennessee. Miss Jenny gave her permission to retrieve as much river dust as she needed, if indeed the green spot still existed after so many years had passed.

Erosion and dredging had slowly eaten away at the hairpin turn that marked the course of the Madrid fault as it slithered under the great river. The green spot had always been directly over the fault on the eastern side. Melinda had GPS coordinates for the fault, but if the green spot was gone, they'd be out of luck.

The four rats exposed to COVID-H and river dust were romping about in their cages, not appearing to be the least bit sick. Olivia and Alex stared in quiet amazement as the active rats turned to them and came to the edges of their cages. The four that hadn't received river dust were dead, lying in dried pools of blood.

"I'll get Levi and we'll draw blood for analysis," said Alex. "Why don't you call Melinda? Tell her to hit the road. She'll be thrilled to hear about the results."

"Will do," replied Olivia, still transfixed on the rats, whose beady eyes watched them with an uncanny intensity. Melinda's phone rang and rang, finally going to voicemail. "Dammit. She didn't answer."

"Try again."

"I am." Olivia pushed her phone into her ear and groaned. "Come on, Melinda, pick up. Shit, shit, shit."

"Give her a few minutes. Go ahead and call Shane."

"Alex, I am. I don't need your moment-by-moment instructions."

"No, I don't suppose you do."

Two hours later, Melinda still hadn't answered her phone, nor had she shown up at the lab. Olivia left two voicemails while walking back to the cryo room to prepare a sample from one of the healthy dust-treated rats.

Reports came in from Boston. COVID-H cases soared. It was showing up in neighboring states. Nipah's case numbers hadn't increased. Ninety percent of new deaths were from COVID-H. Thousands of people were dying of pulmonary hemorrhage. Olivia pounded the lab table, too rattled to concentrate. She called Alex.

"Alex, I'm worried."

"Me too. What do you think?"

"Charles. I'm worried this has something to do with him."

"Where does he live?"

"You want to go check on her?"

"What else can we do? The police won't do anything. I'm sure thousands of people are MIA. We'd be lucky to even get somebody to answer the phone."

"You're probably right. I'll let Shane know what's going on. Take somebody with you."

"I can't take anybody away from their work...plus I don't want to involve anyone else. I've been carrying my gun. Nobody checks anymore."

"I figured as much. Does all this...I mean, could this trigger you? Could it trigger a flashback?" She'd seen them before. They started after his family was killed, and recurred when in the heat of the Altiva firefight in Mexico. He'd gone from physician healer to killer almost overnight. The intractable emotional whiplash infiltrated his psyche like an insidious infection. Their work battling Nipah and COVID-H had restored his faith in the good he could do. But now, he carried a gun.

Alex turned away as if concealing the painful memories. "You mean by walking into a threat, or finding another dead woman? How do I know? No, I don't think so. Haven't had a flashback in months."

"Another dead woman? Don't say that. I'm sure she's fine."

"Then why are we freaking out?" He gripped the bench with both hands.

"Because we're not sure," answered Olivia at twice the volume. "But going from not answering the phone to dead is a bit much, don't you think?"

"Maybe. Maybe not. Sensitive subject, right?"

"Right."

◇◇

Melinda slid her car to a stop in Charles' back yard and ran to the house. She usually walked around the two most precarious boards, but when Charles didn't answer her greeting, she walked straight over them and flung open the screen door. Mango's meow was different, higher pitched, as if he were in pain.

"Charles!" she screamed. "No. No! Charles! Wake up!" He lay motionless. Partially dried blood covered his face from the bullet hole in his forehead. She kneeled by his side, ignoring her ringing phone, and put her ear to his chest. Nothing. No heartbeat. No breathing. Mango stood between his legs, meowing his call of grief. Frantic to do something, she wiped blood off his face and out of his eyes.

The sound of tires on the gravel drive caught her attention. A Ford Explorer slid to a stop directly in front of the porch steps, followed by a cloud of dust. A moment later, someone stood in the doorway.

"Director, what are——"

"Come with me," demanded Cunningham.

"Charles, he's dead. Who shot him? Did ..." her eyes widened, "you shoot him?"

He walked up to her and grabbed her arm. "Come with me, Melinda. I'm not giving you a choice."

Melinda stood up slowly, staring past Cunningham in a frozen trance. A momentary fugue state. She shook her head hard as reality pushed its way back into her consciousness. Grief turned to rage. Adrenaline, epinephrine, and cortisol surged in her veins.

When Cunningham pulled her through the doorway, she swung around and grabbed the door frame. Cunningham wrapped his arms around her chest, yanked her down the porch steps and wrestled her into the Explorer.

He drove through Brentwood toward Nashville, searching for a car to steal. He needed to ditch the Explorer. A small used car lot with barely a shed for an office caught his eye. He turned in and spotted a 1990 Ford utility van that fit the bill. There was no one there. It was almost too easy.

Minutes later, the explorer was parked next to the van, and he reached under the van's dashboard, yanked the ignition wires free from the column, and touched them together. After a couple sparks and a crackle, the van sputtered to life.

When he was out of sight, Melinda listened to Olivia's voicemail. "Please make the trip ASAP. The dust stops COVID-H." Things just got a lot more complicated. Cunningham got out of the van and ordered her to get in just as she pulled the phone away from her ear.

"You drive, and give me your phone," he ordered. The discarded Explorer was soon out of sight. Who knew how long it would be before somebody at Johnny's Used Cars realized they'd been traded a 2007 Ford Explorer for their 1990 Ford van?

◇◇

Alex floored the accelerator when he got on Hillsboro Avenue. Travel time to Fairview was thirty-two minutes according to Google maps. The Route 40 exit was only a couple of minutes away. *Maybe I can attract a cop if I'm hauling ass.* The V8 in his BMW SUV was perfectly happy going a hundred miles per hour. Fifteen minutes into the drive and still no cops. He'd hoped to pick one up as back-up in case there was trouble at Charles' house. He turned left onto Brush Creek Road and wiggled down a back road until he heard, "Your destination is on the left." There was nothing there but the same old oak tree that had stumped Melinda. He crept forward until a mailbox came into view. A plastic oval hung below the box with the number 212 printed in white. *This is it.* The gravel lane crunched under his tires. He stopped when the house came into view. Melinda's car poked out from behind the house, flanked by two maples. To his right, he could see roof trusses above several shorter trees. Construction had halted over a month ago. The exposed wood had turned gray from repeated soakings by that year's frequent spring rains.

He called Olivia. "Hey. I'm here. I see Melinda's car, but I can't see behind the house from here. Maybe she's sick in bed."

"Yeah. Maybe," replied Olivia.

"Okay, I'm driving down to the house. I'll call you when I know something."

"Be careful."

His eyes were drawn to a patch of purple irises that had metastasized from the end of the lane to the front of the house. *No. No, not now. Dammit to hell!* He began to breathe deeper and faster. A flashback.

The mind makes connections without our permission. A joyous picnic with his wife Julie and their twin girls in a field of purple wildflowers became the memory link tied to their fiery deaths, branded into his subconscious, just waiting to be exposed. Once triggered, dark distorted memories of that picnic would flash before his eyes.

They were killed when their home exploded in a ball of fire, due to a gas leak. Alex was unloading the car when Julie and the girls went inside and flicked a light switch. A tiny spark was all it took. The gas had accumulated for a week while they were away on vacation. For months, he blamed himself for not calling a repairman to replace a dubious connection in the oven gas line. Months later, he learned that wasn't the case. The leak was intentional. Someone wanted him dead.

It was too late to look away. Images of his girls making a bouquet and presenting it to their mom came vaguely into focus. He saw himself giving Julie a kiss as she passed out sandwiches and chips. Then, she turned to ashes, and blew away in the breeze. He turned to the girls. They were gone. Vanished into the ether. He hyperventilated. Sweat bled into his shirt, and then it stopped as quickly as it started. He hated himself for not being able to control it——for being so weak. Suddenly, he felt something in his hand. He looked down. The cold steel felt good in his hand. Safety off, cocked and loaded.

✧✧

Olivia sat with her eyes glued to the lenses of the five-foot-tall cryo electron microscope. It was connected to a video monitor, but she felt she could see better when her peripheral vision was blocked. She used the same settings as she did with Nipah to visualize COVID-H. In the presence of river dust, free viral RNA could not replicate. The mRNA would not remain intact. She stared until her eyes hurt but couldn't find anything else specific. In the process, she identified the biobot structure that was somehow keeping the virus invisible to the cells of our immune system. *Oh my God, that's it...but what is it?*

✧✧

Dr. Bullock put his phone down on his desk and covered his face with his hands. Dr. Shenberg had just told him that China's vaccine was failing. He went to his window and peered down at the usually crowded courtyard. It was empty. The shrubs were untrimmed. Trash blew by in search of a resting place. His chest ached. For a moment, he wished he'd drop dead from a heart attack. After several anxious deep breaths, the pain faded, but his heart continued to race. He forced himself to plan his next move. The thud-thud of his heart pounding against his ribs gradually subsided. He pulled his ever-present handkerchief out of his shirt pocket and wiped the sweat from his forehead before reaching for his cell phone.

Paula scanned the kitchen for her ringing phone. It was on the counter by the sink. Her hands began to shake when she saw it was her husband, Shane. He didn't usually call from work.

"Honey, you okay?" she asked.

"Yes. I'm fine, just wanted to hear your voice."

"Then...I think something's wrong. What is it?"

"Stressed, I guess. I try not to think about what's going on in the world, but it seeps in. It's too awful. I know you must be feeling the same."

"Honey, I love you. Yes, I feel the same way. You're doing amazing things. I'm so proud of you. Everybody is."

"That's the problem, Paula. The responsibility is…"

"It must be overwhelming. I'm sorry…I didn't mean to put more pressure on you."

"It's okay. We'll get through it. The sound of your breathing is the most soothing thing I've heard in a while. Thank you. I love you. Gotta get to work."

"Alright. I'm so glad you called. Goodbye."

"Bye."

He walked through the maze of anxious workers and lab benches, ignoring questions, on his way to the cryo room. Olivia didn't notice he was there until he tapped on her shoulder.

"Did you hear from Alex?" he asked.

"He called when he first pulled into Charles' driveway. It's been a half hour and he hasn't called. I'll call him. Where's my damn phone?" she asked, rifling through her stuffed lab coat pockets.

"I hate to think of how much time I've wasted searching for mine." He stepped back as she dumped pocket fodder on the floor.

"Okay. Got it." They locked eyes as Alex's phone rang. "No answer. It went to voicemail. Shit! Something's wrong."

"He probably left his phone in his car or something."

"No. He said he'd keep it with him. Something is wrong, Shane. I have to go there. Come with me, please?"

"Of course. Do you want to call the police?"

"Doubt we can find one. Anyway, what would I say? They won't do anything based on a hunch." She stood up and grabbed the back of her stool and shook it violently while yelling, "I want to kill him!" Bullock took another step back.

"Kill who? Olivia, settle down. I'll drive."

"Charles. That mother fucker!"

"What are you talking about? What did he do?"

"Melinda was afraid of him. She thought he'd stolen some of the dust. Maybe even sold it."

"Good God. You're kidding? You're not kidding."

Olivia shut down the microscope and grabbed her purse. "Let's go. You can drive. Don't dawdle. Let me get my gun."

"Gun? How'd you get a gun in here?"

"Alex showed me a few tricks. Nobody is checking anyway. Don't tell him. I fussed at him for bringing his."

"I've wondered about you two."

"Well, don't."

◇◇

Bullock was going over eighty-five miles per hour in a forty-five mile per hour zone. Bush Creek lay one hundred yards ahead on the left. Suddenly, flashing blue lights appeared in the rearview mirror.

Oliva turned around to see a police car gaining on them. "I guess there are still a few police around. Don't slow down. Lead them to Charles' house."

"Are you sure?" asked Bullock.

"Yes. We can't screw around for ten minutes on the side of the road, for chrissake."

The tail end of Bullock's car slid around the turn. Olivia watched Google maps. They crested a small hill and almost hit a black Mercedes sedan head-on as it sped toward them.

"Geezus, those two Asian guys are sure in a hurry. I hope that cop stays with us."

"Wave him our way before he turns around," she shouted.

Bullock rolled down his window and waved his arm. It worked. The cop stayed on them with his siren blaring and blue lights flashing.

"Okay, go right, just after that church," said Olivia, pointing ahead. A few minutes later, she yelled, "Here, right here!"

Shane hit the brakes, skidding past the old oak tree, and stopping just short of Charles' mailbox. Cop in tow, they turned in. After a curve and a rise, they came up on Alex's SUV, sitting in the middle of Charles' gravel driveway, engine running. The cop slid to a stop behind them, turned off his siren, and sat in his car while a cloud of dust ran over them.

"What the hell? Why is Alex's car just sitting there? I'll go check. You can have a chat with the cop." She threw open the passenger door so hard, it bounced back and hit her hip as she jumped out, rushing to Alex's SUV. The cop got out of his patrol car, wary about the scene unfolding in front of him. He was at the back of Bullock's car when Olivia screamed. She stepped back from the SUV, almost falling. Bullock got out and ran toward her. The cop stayed behind the car and watched, with his gun raised.

"Oh God. No! I think he's dead!" she shouted, shaking, tears streaming down her face. Bullock opened the door and saw Alex's bloodied face. He checked his pulse. He saw Alex's chest rise and fall.

"He has a pulse. He's breathing."

The officer joined Bullock. Olivia stepped toward the SUV, reaching her hand in to touch Alex's hand. Through the blood, they could see a small hole above Alex's left brow and a second larger hole, an exit wound, behind his ear.

"Let's get him in my car," the cop said. "We'll never get an ambulance anytime soon." He pulled his car along the side of Alex's. As they wrestled to slide Alex out of his SUV, a gun bounced off the running board and onto the gravel. With less than a graceful flop, Alex's head landed on the back seat of the cruiser. The cop went back to the SUV and picked up the gun, placing it into a plastic bag. Oliva was silent, watching, with her hands pressed against her cheeks. As soon as Bullock and the cop were out of the way, she climbed in and put Alex's bloodied head on her lap.

"Officer, there may be something more down at the house," said Olivia.

He bent over to look at her. "What?"

"I'll tell you on the way. Shane, go look." He nodded in response.

"No," blurted the cop. "You stay here. I'll check it out." He called for backup. His pleas went unanswered. "Sir, get in the car. Now!" he yelled. "Sir!" Bullock continued to walk toward the house.

"Just get to the fucking hospital! Drive!" shouted Olivia.

The cop hesitated, bit his upper lip, and squinted, trying to force a decision. "Okay," he said, putting the car in reverse, bouncing it backwards into the field, his tires tossing clods of dirt as they sped away.

Bullock reached under his shirt and pulled out the gun tucked in his waistband that Olivia slipped to him when the officer wasn't watching. He surveyed the field, and the house with all his senses in overdrive. The irises yielded to his footsteps. Sliding along the side of the house, he took a deep breath and held it before peering around the corner into the back yard and porch. Charles' burgundy Toyota Rav 4 was parked in the driveway. Melinda's car was parked carelessly on the grass. Suddenly, Mango darted in front of him to hide under the rickety steps. Bullock lurched backward, stiffening as if shocked by a live wire. He tripped over a dying boxwood and landed on the newly bloomed irises. Disgusted, he got up and walked around to the porch. The door to the house was open. He stood to the side and called Melinda's name. No reply. No movement. No sound.

Another deep breath and he creeped across the threshold into the house. A sight he'd never seen shook every fiber in his body. He stepped back and froze. Charles lay crumpled on the floor. His face was covered in blood that flowed from a bullet hole in his forehead. Bullock saw red on the doorframe leading into the house; smeared blood in the shape of three fingers and a clear thumbprint.

He searched every room. Someone else had done the same. Charles's wallet was on the floor by his feet. His desk drawers had been rifled through. When he bumped the desk, Charles' laptop's screen lit up. It opened the website for National Medical in Malaysia. He clicked the other tab and Derbyshire Bank of the Cayman's came up. Neither of these meant anything to Bullock. He called Olivia.

Chapter 25

The White House had been converted into one big slumber party for the Joint Chiefs of Staff and the National Security Council. Members and their families had been moved in once COVID-H broke out of Massachusetts. There were no complaints. Everyone was scared. Knowing they and their families were safe, for the time being, helped them concentrate on the greatest disaster that mankind had ever known.

BN27 distribution was coming apart now that COVID-H was the bigger threat. People were shying away from health departments, fairgrounds, and hospitals that had been providing millions of the coveted inhaler canisters each day. Truck drivers refused to deliver food and medical supplies to Massachusetts. Police, firemen, hospital workers, and government service workers were abandoning their posts.

The National Guard and other branches of the military were diverted from other states. Commanders were given approval to use whatever means necessary to keep men and women from deserting. The fear of death from Nipah didn't compare to the panic resulting from the sight of bodies drenched in blood. In Boston, the only people on the street were dead or dying, ignored by police and EMTs. Being splattered by a COVID-H victim's blood, even if only on their skin, could be enough to cause infection.

Tracy Jones, dressed in jeans, white blouse, and a casual tan twill sport coat, knocked on the Oval Office door. President Triagin was considering a drink.

"Come in," snapped Triagin, without asking who it was. A tall, broad-shouldered secret service agent opened the door for the Secretary of Defense. "Hi, Tracy. Come in, have a seat."

"Mr. President, I have a little good news."

"And what might that be?"

"Dr. Shenberg called. They've got a vaccine for Nipah. They're testing it now, and it looks very effective. In the ninety-four to ninety-eight percent range, he said."

"That is good news." He shot her a thumbs-up. "Too bad it doesn't work for COVID-H."

"I know. I wish. We all wish. I heard that Dr. Nilsson at Vanhusse is making some progress with her analysis." She looked away, focusing on the eagle carved into the President's desk.

The President put down his notepad and clasped his pen with both hands. "Have you heard anything from China? Has anybody heard anything? I haven't. Not a peep. I've tried to reach Chen twice a day."

"No, sir. No official statements. Mr. President, I do have some concerning news to share."

"Go ahead."

She took a step closer to him as if she was about to whisper. "Intelligence reports suggest that China's COVID-H vaccine, best we can tell, has completely failed."

"That's about as concerning as you can get. Now what?" He smacked his Mont Blanc pen on the desk, breaking it into pieces. "Well, I guess I don't need to suck up to Chen anymore. He's got nothing to offer us now. Nobody does. We can't go to each other's funerals. Our allies haven't come up with any good news either. For most of them, the death rate is worse than ours. We'll come up with a plan, Tracy. We always do, right?"

Tracy nodded. She was patient with his rambling. "Our

scientists will come through with a vaccine or a treatment soon. They've really come a long way since COVID-19 hit us." The President didn't respond to her patronizing encouragement.

"What's going on in North Korea?" he asked.

"It's hard to know, sir. They might be the least affected by this."

President Triagin grinned. "One of the many benefits of isolation and absolute dictatorship."

"That's what I like about you, sir, you always find the bright side in everything," Tracy mused.

"Madam Secretary, you're blowing smoke up my ass, and I...I sort of like it."

"My pleasure, sir."

Like a pressure release valve, they vented steam with a chuckle. Levity quickly faded into glazed stares, followed by an uncomfortable silence as they waited for word from Espionto.

There was little doubt that Zhang Lee had released COVID-H, but proving he acted on behalf of the Chinese government was dicey. COVID-H had reached almost every country except New Zealand, Iceland, Japan, and most of the Caribbean. They'd locked their borders even tighter than they had for Nipah. The President had already notified the allies that he was planning to formally present evidence to NATO and WHO showing that China purposely released the deadly virus. The military had every nuclear weapon dialed in and every defense system double-checked. One phone call and the earth could be wiped clean of every living thing except for creatures many leagues beneath the sea. China and Russia were doing the same. Who would draw first?

"Nuclear war would at least put an end to the misery. I'd rather be instantly incinerated than die from COVID-H."

"Sir. I take back what I said about you and the bright side."

"Duly noted," replied the President.

◇◇

Sean Finnegan looked out the window of a makeshift office facing the White House front lawn. Normally, desks were not in front of windows. He watched bored soldiers protecting the perimeter, guarding against an invisible enemy. Pennsylvania Avenue was deserted. He tried to imagine the normal hustle-bustle. The nation's capital was not supposed to look like this. Shrubs went untrimmed. A Walmart bag lofted across the usually impeccable lawn.

His thoughts were redirected when his phone rang. It was Espionto reporting that technicians had found evidence on Zhang Lee's laptop showing that he had been in contact with Chinese authorities. Finnegan called the President and gave him the update. Triagin hung up the phone and looked over at Tracy Jones, shaking his head.

"What's wrong, sir?" asked Jones.

"Espionto said they've found a definitive trail implicating the Chinese. Now we can take it to the UN and WHO. Call Shenberg. He should be the one to address those mamby-pamby WHO doctors." The President stood and began to pace the floor. Jones made the call. A few minutes later, she hung up.

"He said he'd get right on it. He also said it would help if we could prove it was an engineered virus."

"Good point, but we can't wait for that. I'll contact our allies...see what the odds are of getting NATO and WHO behind us. I suppose Chen could respond by digging in his too proud heels even deeper...but—we've got nothing to lose."

"You know what else Shenberg said?"

"No, Tracy, I don't. Am I supposed to guess?"

"Sorry, sir. He said the technology they're using had to have come from Dr. Lieberman."

"That would be my first guess. I still can't believe the DOJ couldn't make those espionage charges stick. This time, we'll put that bastard away. If we can get enough to suggest it had to be his work that led to this, we could let him plea down his sentence by helping us. Then hang him."

"He'd never admit he knew anything about it, sir."

◇◇

Jan Whitorsh found herself the de facto boss while all four doctors were MIA. One of the lab workers had taken ill with fever, cough, and body aches. She immediately had him put in a negative pressure isolation room. Everyone else went into quarantine in offices throughout the building. The busy lab came to a grinding halt.

Finally, she got a call back from Bullock. "Jan, sorry I didn't answer. I'm tied up and can't come in right now. How are things?"

Jan closed the door to her office. "Dr. Bullock, Tate Bond is sick. I have him in isolation. Everyone else is quarantined...and the lab is shut down."

"Oh God. No. Jan. You did the right thing. Now, please call Holdsworth at the CDC and let him know. Just tell him I'm busy. I can't break away right now. Sorry." Bullock walked out to the porch to avoid staring at Charles' bloodied body.

"Okay," she answered.

"Jan, listen to me. There is a sealed test-tube in Dr. Nilsson's top drawer. It contains a sandy-looking powder. I want you to take several grains and swallow them—now. Give the same amount to everyone else, including Tate."

"What is it?"

"We haven't figured that out yet, but it works. It treats COVID-11."

"Really?"

"Well, it worked in rats."

"Okay. I'm walking into her office now." She rifled through the drawer. "Shane, the test-tube is empty except for a few grains."

"Take some and give it to as many people as you can, even if it's only a few grains. Be careful. Handle it gently. It turns to dust

210

really easily. If it does, it'll be harder to dose."

"Will do."

"Good. Talk soon. Bye. Oh, don't mention the powder to anyone other than those you give it to."

"Got it. Bye."

◇◇

There was a pause after Holdsworth listened to Jan explain her situation. She didn't mention the dust. He felt the need to offer some advice. All he could think of was a list of precautions she already knew. She thanked him and hung up. He dropped his head and sighed. He was holed up at the CDC headquarters in Atlanta. It was eighty degrees outside and at least that warm in the building. The air-conditioners were shut down to save power. It made more sense for him to be in Washington, but he wanted to be near his family. He went to his office every day even though he could do a lot of work from home. How would it look if the boss stayed home?

He took the steps down to the parking garage and jogged to his car. Redbuds and Bradford pears were done for the year, replaced by heavy seed-pods and foliage. The May sun was slowly warming their backyard swimming pool. It was clogged with catkins that had fluttered down from tall oaks several weeks earlier. His wife loved to leave the pool open all year so she could see the water from the house. Every fall and spring, he'd fuss at her about having to scoop leaves, sticks, and catkins. This year, he didn't scoop and she didn't complain. When he turned on to Arden Drive and passed mansion after mansion, once well-manicured yards and weeds reached toward the sun, free from human interference. Two blocks from his house, "Dawn" showed up on his phone. His body reacted instinctively like a traumatized combat veteran to a car backfire.

"Hi, honey. Y'all okay?"

"Ambulance showed up next door. Sorta far away, but it

looked like they carried out two bodies. Tom, I'm scared."

"I know. I'm almost home. Did the kids see it?"

"I don't think so."

"Good."

He was pretty certain his neighbors had taken BN27, which meant they likely died from COVID-H. There had been no reports of COVID-H in Atlanta. Of course, no one would expect it to start in the wealthy Buckhead enclave. A flash of demographic bias entered his mind, followed by a prompt self-scolding. His next question was where did they catch it? Bad timing or not, he had to talk to the family. Finding the index case was critical. Probably too late, but it was the only chance they had to contain it.

Before he could get out of his car, his phone rang again. It was Anne Crawford, one of his team of epidemiologists. *Dammit. I know why she's calling.*

"Tom. This is Anne. I just—"

"Hi. Let me guess."

"You're right. I just got a call from Grady. They've got three dead, two on ventilators, and three about to be intubated. They're all coughing up blood."

"I bet two of the dead are my neighbors. My wife just saw them being carried out on stretchers to a Grady ambulance ten minutes ago."

"Yes. They are from Buckhead."

"Any idea how it got here? Who's the index case?"

"A kid came down from Connecticut to visit his girlfriend who works at a grocery store up your way."

"There you have it. Contacts?" asked Holdsworth.

"Working on it. But, Tom, who knows how many people got exposed to her at the grocery, especially with those jackasses that pull their masks below their noses, or sneak in with no mask at all."

"Close the store. Quarantine workers. Notify Channel 5, the paper, etcetera. We've got to find as many contacts as possible."

"That won't be too hard. Most of them will be dead," replied Crawford.

"I'll work on getting some political pressure on the police and military to make a perimeter ten miles around Atlanta."

"Good luck with that, Tom."

"Well…?"

"You're right. I'm sorry."

"Anne, don't give up."

"I won't."

"Bye. Call me with updates."

"Will do. Bye."

Holdsworth called Rex Shenberg at NIH in Bethesda, Maryland, to keep him in the loop. Holdsworth knew that Rex had the President's ear.

"Rex."

"Yeah, Tom."

"COVID-H is in Atlanta. I'll send you the latest."

Shenberg looked at the ceiling, exasperated. "Tom, it's in twelve states…probably twelve more before we're off the phone. It'll be across the country in a few days at this rate. Did you hear that Bullock's lab has been shut down?"

"Yes. Their lab manager, Jan…Jan something, called me. She also told me that Bullock, Nilsson, and Winthrop had all left the lab this morning. Bullock had just called her and all he said was that he was tied up. I hope they're okay."

"Yeah, me too," replied Shenberg. "I haven't heard anything. We'll have to move their operation, and any unexposed lab workers. We have most of the equipment they need at Mount Weather. I'll notify the President. He'll get someone to handle the logistics. Damn, we're going to lose a lot of time getting them set up."

◇◇

Two EMTs wearing full protective garb knocked on the lab's main entrance door. Jan buzzed them in. She described the situation as sweat dripped into their widening eyes. When they arrived at the isolation area, Jan stepped into the ante room and wrestled her way into a suit similar to theirs. Government issue, made in China. The sealed steel door made a sucking sound as she pushed it open, leading them into an area that circled a series of glass-walled cubicles. On the other side of the glass lay Tate Bond covered in blood, taking his last few desperate breaths. The EMTs froze in place. Jan shrieked, spun around, fought with the door lock, and staggered into the ante room. Fifteen minutes earlier, she'd dabbed a few grains of dust on her tongue, then went to give some to Tate, but he was unconscious. She was too frightened to enter the room. Instead, she called 911. By then, it was too late. She pulled off her head gear, slid down the wall to the floor, and sobbed.

The EMTs shared an eye-phrase as they headed back to the truck to get a body bag and stretcher.

A moment later, she ran back to her office, opened her desk drawer, and took out the test-tube of dust. She poured out the remainder onto her desk blotter, pushed it onto a sticky-note with an index card and shook it into her mouth. *There's no way I'm ending up like Tate. No way.* She sipped some water and picked up her phone.

"Shane. This is Jan."

"Yes. Are you okay?"

"I am, but Tate is dead. Covered in blood. In blood, Shane! It's horrific! I just heard from Levi's wife—he died this morning. Shane, I'm so scared."

"Of course you are. It's terrible. Did the others get the dust?"

"No. Not yet." She paused to come up with a lie. "I mean, I can't...I bumped the test tube onto the floor by mistake after I took some. It spilled. I can't even find any." She winced with shame. "I'm sorry. I'm shaking…clumsy. I'm sorry."

Bullock put his phone against his thigh, hoping she wouldn't hear his rapid breathing as panic washed over him in a hot prickly wave. Mango sniffed at Charles' face, looking for signs of life. Bullock turned away.

"Listen, Jan, Dr. Winthrop is in the hospital with an injury. Dr. Nilsson is with him, and…and Melinda has gone to gather more river dust. It's a long story. I don't honestly know, Jan. Try to get some help getting food and water to our quarantined workers. Can't have them going out for it."

"Okay…I will."

"I'll get back to you. Bye."

It was the first time she'd heard him say "I don't know" without a specific plan. She chose to believe he just didn't feel like going into it. Nothing else was acceptable.

"Also, it might be better if we don't share anything about the dust until I have a better idea of…of where we stand."

Jan whispered, "Okay." She wanted to ask why.

✧✧

The President mustered up a quorum of NATO representatives. During the online meeting, he asked President Chen to explain China's role in the release of COVID-H. As expected, he denied having anything to do with it. Instead, he blamed the United States. Russia supported their accusations. To make matters worse, Chen ranted about the US not sharing BN27 and then he dropped a bombshell. He claimed the US had a cure for COVID-H as well, and threatened military action if it wasn't shared immediately. As expected, Russia said the same. Nothing the President said had any effect. All eyes were on him.

Reports of America's alleged COVID-H cure ricocheted around the globe. Allies became suspicious of each other. Within five minutes of the meeting's end, France's President, Jean

Deveroux, called President Triagin wanting answers. Conspiracy theorists came out of the woodwork. Professional-appearing presentations claiming direct evidence of America's guilt clogged social media. The US's adversaries had a field day.

Espionto sat in the backseat of a black Suburban SUV yelling into his phone at his FBI subordinates. "I want everyone in the Chinese embassy questioned. Don't let any of them try to leave. Shake down any academics…researchers, anyone on our watch list. I don't care if you have to resort to torture. Do I make myself clear? Get on it. Now!" He was convinced Chen had to have some basis for his accusation. Neither Director Cunningham nor his spy, Dr. Chau, answered their phones. For a fleeting moment, he wondered if Cunningham was up to something. *Nonsense. He's the most devoted man in the agency.* He called Dr. Shenberg, who reassured him that no American or allied laboratory had come up with anything even close to a cure.

In the meantime, every available reconnaissance aircraft was put into the air. Nuclear attack submarines were in position. Even with thinned-out troops, the mobilization was massive. Nothing since World War II has been comparable.

"Mr. President, Secretary Jones is here to see you."

"Show her in."

A too-young-looking Secret Service agent opened the door and led Tracy Jones in, then waited to be dismissed. It was a forgotten protocol designed to provide the President with protection in the event he or she wanted a witness when no one else was present.

The President looked at the young man and nodded. "That'll be all."

Standing a few feet from his desk with her back straight and her feet together, Secretary Jones announced, "Mr. President, all defensive and offensive strike capabilities are up. We are strike ready. In approximately three hours, we will have maximum recon and secondary forces amassed."

"Good," he said as he walked to the window for the umpteenth time that day. "Want a drink?"

"A drink? No, sir."

"So how do we turn this lose-lose situation around? Chen's a hot-head, but he's not a total idiot, for chrissakes. He says we have a cure. I would say he's blowing smoke, but it's too strong of a false claim to make, even for him. I worry there's some truth to it. If so, where is it? Anything from Espionto?"

"Nothing, sir. He's shaking every bush."

"What about that bunch at Vanhusse...Bullock, and the other one?"

"Sir. Dr. Shenberg said he's called but has no response yet."

The President flushed with frustration. "Well, get on it, Jones. Don't just stand there looking at me. Do something!"

"Yes, sir."

Chapter 26

Clouds covered the sun moments before the sky opened up with torrential rain. Melinda held the pedal to the floor as they drove onto Route 40 West, ignoring the downpour. The aging six-cylinder struggled its way to seventy miles per hour. She peered through two four-inch swaths of rain-cleared glass. It was all the worn wipers could accomplish. The van's bald tires slipped in every puddle. Melinda gripped the wheel.

"Why are you doing this?" asked Melinda, breaking the silence.

Cunningham rested his pistol on his lap and said, "Why am I doing this? I think you've got it backwards, doctor." For the first time, he noticed how attractive she was. Her high cheekbones, black glossy hair, perfect lips, and amber-washed skin. "What are you, Brazilian?"

"No."

"Indian?"

"Yeah. My father's a Maharaja and my mother is a Cherokee chief. I was raised in a teepee in New Delhi, where we hunted buffalo."

"Don't be a smart-ass. How did you get involved in this?"

Melinda suddenly turned her head. "What are you talking about?"

"Keep your eyes on the road."

"Involved in what, Director?"

"In Vermont, when you were working under Dr. Nilsson, what did the Russians offer you? A hundred grand? And what about the Chinese, did they offer more, or is this just something you and Charles cooked up?"

"To you, everybody's a spy. So, Director Cunningham, who do you spy for? The Russians? I'm confused. I've always thought you were just a prick. You had Charles killed, didn't you?"

"No," he replied, even though he wouldn't have minded doing it himself. "You didn't answer my question. Don't you think it's a bit coincidental that China's President Chen accuses us of having a cure for COVID-H right after you all discover that the dust can do exactly that?"

"Where'd you get that idea?" She let her foot ease up on the accelerator without thinking.

"Dr. Bullock told me this morning and Chen just made his accusation—for the whole world to hear."

"So why do you think I have anything to do with it?"

"You're the one who brought it to the lab and your boyfriend Charles is…was a bit sketchy, to say the least. I know he made calls to Asia."

"Why don't you just have me arrested?"

"Well, there is something we both have in com—"

"I doubt that," she murmured, while forcing the accelerator back down.

"I beg to differ—we both want the dust. I can't be bothered with anything else."

"Then you are crooked," she snarled.

"I guess that depends how you look at it, Melinda. I'll leave it at that."

For the next hour, they drove without speaking. The noise from the motor, windshield wipers, and the pounding rain gave their thoughts some privacy. Both were convinced they knew what the other was up to. The road was empty. She slowed to sixty-five miles an hour, biding time to come up with a plan. The one she came up with was iffy. *"If I see a cop parked along the side of the road, I'll pull up on him, get out, and walk over to him—Cunningham would have to back down...maybe, or maybe he'd shoot us both."*

He rolled up the sleeves of his white shirt, concealing his blood-splattered right sleeve.

"Don't try to take me on a wild goose chase. I expect to see your friend Jenny's white Victorian home in a few hours. I have a general idea what the area looks like, so if need be, you're expendable."

Melinda stiffened. *Expendable?* "I suspect you're planning on shooting me anyway, so why should I do anything you ask?"

"Because you believe there's a chance that I won't. How could an old CIA agent, an upstanding American citizen at that, shoot you in cold blood, right? It's just a job, Melinda. Another day at the office. As long as you have hope— you will do as I say." That answered her question. "Who, besides you and Charles, are involved?"

"Involved in what? Selling the dust to the highest bidder? Like you? Or do you expect me to believe you are acting on behalf of the United States?"

"It doesn't matter what you think. It won't change anything."

In Jackson, they got off on 412 W and headed toward Lake County. The highway took them through several small depressed towns. Most of the abandoned and boarded-up businesses had been that way before the pandemic. Rural America began to die in the late nineties. A handful of essential businesses like grocery stores, gas stations that sold beer, and pharmacies remained. The larger towns could boast a McDonalds or a Dairy Queen. A place where young people thought high school was higher education. Melinda recalled how anxious she was to escape Tiptonville and go to college. Now she was being sucked back into it like a bad habit.

Melinda stopped at the beginning of Miss Jenny's driveway. "I can't just drive up to her house unannounced."

"Well, beep the horn—that should do it—then introduce me to Miss Jenny. You will need to explain that I'm a scientist and we are studying the dust as a possible treatment for Nipah virus."

"She calls it river sand."

"Whatever. If you so much as wink at her, I'll kill you both." He lifted the pistol off his lap.

Melinda studied the house and glanced around at the fields. They hadn't been cut. The old Victorian didn't look at all like it was a hundred and forty years old. Nothing was amiss. No extra cars. No tractor in the field. It looked exactly like it did when she was there with Charles. The clouds parted and the setting sun shined in their eyes. She had the urge to jump out of the car and run, or find a way to get the canister of pepper spray from her purse. "Can I get my sunglasses out of my purse?"

"Sure. Don't bother searching for your pepper spray." He grinned.

"Wouldn't think of it."

She drove slowly up the drive and parked in front of the house. Melinda began to wonder if Miss Jenny was home when she didn't appear at the door as usual.

"Get out. Act like I'm your best friend." He groaned as he climbed down from the van. "Good lord. Stiff in all the wrong places."

"What?"

"Nothing."

A cerulean warbler watched them from the old willow tree. Above the house, a bald eagle soared in search of a meal before sunset. When Melinda was a young girl, she'd sit on the porch and birdwatch with Miss Jenny. The memory caused her to pause before walking up the porch steps.

"Well, are you going to knock?"

"Yes. The doorbell doesn't work. Never did. She said it startled her."

"Fascinating. Now knock."

Melinda rapped on the screen door three times. No response. She knocked again. Still no response. She turned the knob on the worn mahogany door that had been touched by six generations of family and friends.

"Miss Jenny," she called through the four-inch opening. "Miss Jenny, it's Melinda and a friend." She pushed the door open and put one foot in the foyer. This time, she yelled, "Miss Jenny!" No answer.

"Okay, let's check the house and get on to the river. We don't have much more sunlight," said Cunningham.

Melinda went first, taking a step into the parlor. "Miss Jenny! Oh shit! Miss Jenny! She's dead. Oh God!" Melinda covered her face with her hands and turned away. Miss Jenny lay face down. Her silver hair, blackened in a pool of drying blood. The left side of her face was smooshed into the red gel. Cunningham stared at her open right eye. Her sparkling gray eyes— extinguished by the glaze of death. A history book, thrown into the fire.

Cunningham bent down to have a closer look. "Shot in the head. She's cool but not stiff. The blood isn't completely dried. It hasn't been long. Dammit. Someone got here before us." He stood up and grabbed Melinda by the shoulders and shook her. "Who's been here? Who?"

"How the hell do I know? Do you think I'd have someone kill her? She was like a grandmother to me."

"Yeah. Okay. Well, we don't have to worry about her getting in the way. Let's go. Now!"

He grabbed her by the arm and forced Melinda back to the car while wiping sweat off his forehead.

"Get in. Drive."

Tears streamed down Melinda's face. It took effort for

Cunningham to ignore her. He wasn't sure she was sincere. The road to the back of the property had become part of the field. Only a faint impression remained.

Melinda wiped away her tears and cleared her throat. "What makes you think there is any left after years of wear and tear by the current?"

"I can ask you the same question. But I doubt you two would have planned to come if there wasn't. I suspect you or Charles have been back here. Am I right?"

"No. I was coming alone. Charles had nothing to do with it."

"Of course."

"I have a few questions, Director. Why did you steal this truck? What—"

"I don't need to explain anything to you," said Cunningham, raising his voice. "Your motives are the problem here."

Melinda stopped the van and surveyed the levee. "This is it. Somewhere near here—I think."

"Stop screwing around. Just take me there."

"I haven't been here since I was a kid. Is it safe to say you will contact your boss when...if we find it? Are you going to take me back to some dark little room and waterboard me for information?"

"No, but that could be fun."

A brisk warm breeze blew in from the river, blowing sand in their faces when they got to the levee's crest. They stood where the river made a hairpin turn. It had widened since she was a young teen. Melinda looked up, down, and across the river, searching for landmarks. She spotted Island No. 10. The forgotten site where Union General Mackall's army attacked the Confederate stronghold in 1862. The battle effectively gave the Union control of the Mississippi. Not something the people of Tiptonville wanted to remember.

An empty barge twisted in the current, temporarily hung up

on a sandbar. She knew they were close. To her right, the field had become so overgrown, it was too difficult to see the once unique area of growth. They trudged through tall grass. Blackberry thorns snagged their clothing. The soil turned to mud. She wished that a water moccasin or copperhead would sink its fangs into Cunningham's leg. About fifty feet ahead, she spotted a cluster of orchids.

"Listen," she turned to meet his frustrated gaze. "If we find it, why don't we share it?" She veered away from the orchids and waited to see if he took the bait. "You think I'm a spy and I think you're a spy...so..."

"Maybe we can work something out. Geezus, isn't there any way around these thorns?" Cunningham began to think Melinda might keep him wandering around until it was too dark to continue. If she believed they were partners, it might get a lot easier for him.

Even if he agrees, how can I trust him? They'd just maneuvered into a no value position.

"Okay," he said. "Let's split it. Fifty-fifty."

"Deal," she replied, stopping and pointing toward the river. "See that patch of orchids?"

"No."

"There. To your left."

"I see them. So what?"

"Orchids don't grow around here. That marks the 'green spot'."

As they neared the patch of pink orchids, Melinda muttered, "What? Crap."

"What?"

"It's a hole. Nothing but a hole where the green spot was."

They peered down into a ten-foot-wide hole that the river had filled in. The area around it had been trampled. Shoe prints outlined the perimeter. The opening went beyond the borders of the green spot. The small patch of orchids hung half suspended by undergrowth. The soil that hosted their roots was gone. Melinda looked out to the river. Cunningham stared at the water-filled hole.

"Well, Director, I guess you were right. Somebody beat us to it. The cure for COVID-H is gone."

Chapter 27

For two days, Olivia called the hospital where Alex had been admitted. She'd been turned away ever since she and the police officer brought him to Billington Medical Center's emergency room. It was the closest hospital to Charles' home. Visitors were not allowed in due to COVID-H. Her phone calls went unanswered. Getting him transferred to Vanhusse was an impossible wish. The news reported severe staff shortages. Only a handful of doctors were still standing. She didn't even know if Alex was still alive. Olivia called Billington Medical Center's main line for the third time in two hours, and hung up one syllable into the recorded message. *I can't fall apart now. I just can't. God help me.* She rocked back and forth, cradling her head like a beaten boxer trying to protect his face.

At 5:00 p.m., she turned off the light and locked her office door. All day, she'd struggled to focus on her work but finally gave up. Alcohol and pungent disinfectant fumes stung her eyes as she walked through the empty lab. The entire floor had been fumigated and scrubbed the night before. Bullock had been in with some men packing up equipment to take to a secure lab at Mt. Weather in Virginia. The DOD determined that their research was too vital to remain in the public domain.

The parking lot in front of Billington Medical Center was empty except for a handful of cars, three ambulances, and a police car. She waited until dark, getting up her courage to try out her disguise. The airtight PPE covered every bit of her body. She looked official. Within minutes, sweat ran down her chest, giving her a slight chill. The N-95 mask stifled her rapid, anxious breathing. She eased open her door and walked toward the entrance, hiding from view by keeping an ambulance between her and the large double sliding glass doors.

A man with a bandaged head and no shoes was leaning against the outside of the building, fifty feet or so from the entrance. *Oh my God. Alex?* She jumped back into her car, tore off her mask, and drove up to within five feet of him. He didn't see her get out and walk toward him.

"Alex?" She moved slowly toward him, half scared and half desperate to hold him.

"Oliv-vi-a?"

"Yes. Get in the car." She put her arm around him and helped him to the car. He staggered like a drunk. While holding him against the car with her shoulder, she opened the car door and clumsily got him into the seat. Once behind the wheel, she turned off the motor, hugged him and started to cry. He didn't respond.

"How the hell can you be up walking around two days after being shot in the head?"

"Don't take me back in there. What happened to me? I'm beginning to remember a bit, but I don't know what's real."

Olivia studied his bandage and gently put her hand on the back of his neck. Through tears, she whimpered, "You're alive. You're alive. Thank God, you're alive."

Slowly nodding his head, he whispered, "Good to hear. I wasn't so sure." He looked at his arm where blood from the IV he'd pulled out seeped through his shirt. "I'm hungry."

Olivia hit the gas and rushed toward their apartment.

"Slow down. You're giving me a headache."

"Sorry. I'm a little excited. I thought you were dead. I'll ask you again—how can you be walking around two days after being shot in the head?"

"Maybe I'm a zombie."

"Not funny, Alex. You must be coming around. Your inner smartass is up and running."

"Remember, I told you that'd be the last thing to go. I am coming around. Memories are flooding in like a tsunami. Olivia, I've been in a dreamworld, or hallucinating. Like those near-death experiences you hear about, only much more involved...detailed."

"What about your wound?"

"The bullet ran between my brain and skull. It caused swelling but didn't puncture my brain. I don't know how I know that...but you are right, I should still be in a coma."

The usual downtown smell of traffic exhaust was gone. When the wind blew in from the east, a foul odor of decaying flesh wafted down from Nashville General Hospital, where bodies rotted in dumpsters. Nashville General was a dilapidated hospital that served the inner city. For years, it provided Whitney University trainees with an opportunity to work alongside top-notch Vanhusse house staff. Politicians eventually destroyed the collaboration.

Olivia held her mask in place as they walked to the apartment elevator. They didn't have to wait. The elevator was just sitting there with its door open. A couple of cockroaches scurried out as Olivia and Alex approached.

They made it to their apartment without encountering a soul. She helped Alex onto the black leather couch, even though he was quickly regaining strength. From twelve stories up, Nashville looked no different than a sparsely populated countryside. She brought Alex some water and downed nearly half a bottle of wine herself.

"I'm sorry. I shouldn't guzzle wine in front of you."

"You probably shouldn't drink it at all, but I have no interest. Just don't get too drunk to do anything."

"As revved up as I am, I doubt I'd even feel a whole bottle."

"Whatever. Olivia, listen to me. In my dream...I learned about the dust. You probably think it's crazy, but I believe what I experienced. Yes, it is crazy because there's no logical explanation. It's spiritual, or supernatural, or something."

"Spiritual? Okay, I'm listening, but don't expect me to make any big decisions based on your wacked out spiritual experience."

"I do expect you to believe it, and I expect you to act on it with me. You have...we have no plan B."

Olivia shook her head. "Oh shit. This sounds familiar..."

Alex was no longer sluggish. His mind was crystal clear. Olivia half thought she might be the one who was dreaming. After all, she was sitting with a man who had been shot in the head two days earlier. A man who had gone from almost mute, confused, and weak, to speed talking, alert, and fit, in under an hour. *Maybe I should believe him?*

"Let me take a quick shower." Alex quickly got up and walked by the dinner table, stopping in front of the sparsely populated aquarium and said, "Melinda's gone, right?"

"Right."

"And she's with Cunningham."

Olivia turned around, grasping the back of the couch. "What are you talking about? Why'd you say that? How do you know she's with Cunningham?"

"I just know, that's all. I just know. I'll be right back."

"You can't just walk away after saying something like that." She stood up and walked after him still wearing her protective gown.

"Just give me a few minutes. Take off that gown. You can help me with my bandages when I get out of the shower."

"Yes, sir." An unsure grin appeared. Alex grinned back.

Olivia went to the kitchen to see what she could scrounge up. They'd been getting most of their food through work. Almost all the grocery stores were closed or foodless. Smeared fingerprints covered the handle of the stainless-steel refrigerator. Dirty dishes were piled up in the sink. She flipped up the top of the coffee maker to pour in the precious remains of their Seattle's Best. She lost interest when she was greeted by used coffee grounds growing mold. One of the few things in the freezer was a box of Stouffer's Lasagna. *Score!*

Alex came down the hall with a terry cloth towel around his waist. He'd removed the bandage. Olivia turned to face him when she heard his footsteps. Her eyes opened wide at the sight of his near-naked body. They hadn't had sex in weeks. That was the first thought that came to mind. Bad timing, but not unusual. Sex would have been a great temporary escape. In a moment, her desire was quelled. Alex was too focused. After all, he had a bullet hole in his head.

"Olivia. I know why I've healed so fast. I—"

"Let me guess. You took some of the dust, didn't you?"

He looked at the floor, then out the window. "Yes. I took two puffs from one of the inhalers we made. That's still a small dose. I brought some home for you, but things went to shit in a handbasket so fast and—"

"So how do I know you won't kill, rape, and eat me like those rats?"

"Olivia, I only took a little more than we're trying to give to the public. I was fascinated by the old doc's journals...when he became passionate about his work, and his mind went into overdrive. Also, it was almost like craving a drug. I wanted to feel different...better. I didn't want to die from COVID-H either."

"Oh lord. I wish I understood all that addiction stuff. You sure picked a good time to go down that road."

"That's how it works, Olivia. That's exactly how it works. But never mind, I'll get the inhaler for you. You have to be protected from COVID-H too."

"So, you're pretty convinced it works...in humans?"

"Absolutely. My nurse and neurosurgeon died. I was exposed to them these last two days and haven't gotten sick, and it worked on our rats, right?"

"Seemed to."

He handed her the inhaler after explaining how to use it. She shook her head as if to say no. After a very long five seconds, she looked him in the eyes and studied his face. She kept her eyes on his as she dosed herself with the most bizarre bioactive substance ever discovered.

"Okay. Back to my crazy dreams. I was transported back in time. Didn't know where I was, except that I was walking on a levee by a large river. There were no houses, nothing in sight. The earth began to shake. An earthquake so violent, it knocked me to the ground. All of a sudden, the earth split, and the side I was on jerked into the air. A fault ran across the river, rising up so high, it stopped the river. Chunks of smoldering rock and debris shot up into the air. It looked like it all landed back in the water except for a stripe of superheated dirt that wafted over me. Suddenly, the water overflowed the levee and rushed into the low fields to my right."

"The earthquake of 1811. You witnessed it...well, you dreamed it anyway. The Madrid fault split apart under the Mississippi, pushing water over the levee, flooding the fields, creating Reelfoot Lake. I mean, what else could it be?"

"Of course, that's what it was, but there's a lot more to it. For one, parts of my flashback with Julie and the girls were intermingled. They were in the field coming toward me when the flood washed them away. Then, I went further back in time— millions of years per second, at least that's what it seemed like."

"That must have been wild."

"...and so real. The dust. I think there's more to it than we imagined."

"It's strange enough already."

"Yeah. So far, we've recognized its ability to direct stem cells, modulate cytokines, repair RNA errors, and accelerate the hell out of reactions. It almost seems like it does whatever you want it to...except the aggression stuff. I have a strong feeling that it affects people differently. Almost as if it works off of who you are to start with."

"Concerning RNA, there are a couple start-up genetics labs that have some pretty interesting preliminary data, but nothing like the dust. Finding and correcting random RNA errors is still way off. We probably don't know half the potential the dust has."

"No. I don't think we do. At one point, I could see on a molecular scale, like I'd been shrunk down to the size of a carbon atom. Like that movie *Honey, I Shrunk the Kids* on steroids. Crazy. Not unlike Doc Stevenson's dreams. I saw short strands of nucleic acid spontaneously forming into what I think must have been RNA and DNA. It didn't look like you'd expect, but somehow I knew what I was looking at. Then, it...the RNA replicated. It was so powerful. I don't know why, but I'm convinced the dust was driving the reactions. I—"

"Alex. It was a dream, right? You've had head trauma and you inhaled some of the dust yourself. Sounds like a good set-up for some wild dreams to me."

"What did I tell you? Hear me out. Anyway, of course, molecules and atoms aren't labeled in real life. I could identify them by their form, or some kind of essence. It was as if I was an atom with a brain. I could identify structures based on their effect on me. I could tell what things were, relative to me...relative to what I wasn't."

Olivia sat down and rested her chin on her hand. "You were feeling charge, radiation, magnetic field, etcetera. God, I wish I'd dreamed that with you."

"Precisely. And, yes, you would have loved it...that part

anyway. The river dust is a physical structure, right? A physical structure we can't figure out."

"Right."

"The reason we can't figure it out is because it doesn't have a charge, or any other characteristic we use to identify atoms or molecules. It has its own forces, its own properties, that allow it to exert its effects. Now here's the hardest part for you to swallow."

"Try me," said Olivia, tapping on her teeth.

"When the dream took me back to now, I was overwhelmed by a calm feeling. A feeling of understanding, of safety. Then it hit me. I knew what the force was. I witnessed the creation of genetic material. Olivia, the dust is divine—I saw it for a reason."

"Alex. I need some more wine."

"No, you don't."

Chapter 28

The sun turned fiery red as it neared the horizon. A fine dense line of red separated earth from sky. Clouds changed color, reflecting the light differently as they crept northward. Melinda and Cunningham turned their stares from the water-filled hole and fixated on the sunset. But who had dug up the green spot? They each remained convinced the other knew the answer.

Melinda sat on the edge of the hole, leaned back on her hands, and said, "Does it really matter?"

Cunningham squatted a few feet away. He looked at her with tired eyes and a blank expression. Enough to convey that he'd heard her, but wasn't ready to consider defeat.

"The list of suspects, as I see it, isn't very long," said Cunningham. "Charles' Malaysian buddy, Li Jun, that so-called traditional medicine dealer, is at the top of my list. Tell me if I'm wrong, but here's a possible scenario: You and Charles had a deal with him, but you screwed up and gave him too much information. Either you told him or he magically figured out it works for COVID-H. You two thought you could mess with the pros and come out on top. Really?"

"Screw you!" She threw a clod of dirt at him, hitting him in the chest. He showed no reaction. "Unless you stole some dust from the lab, I suggest you start eating handfuls of dirt and pray there's a little river dust in it. I'd just hate to watch you die a miserable death from COVID-H. Yuk. It's a disgusting sight, isn't it?"

"I didn't have to steal it."

"Why am I not surprised?" Melinda continued to sift the loose dirt through her hands. "I'm sure you extracted every bit of data from Charles's computer, right?"

"Of course. Our tech team did it remotely." said Cunningham, shaking dirt off his shirt.

"I suspect you found a way to contact Li Jun yourself."

"We've known about him for a long time. Guys like him usually have their fingers in a lot of jars. He's connected to the Chinese government and I know he's connected with the 14K Triad. I don't suppose you heard that we got the Triad's kingpin, Broken Tooth, busted a few years ago. Didn't have enough to nail Li Jun. I've been to Malaysia. Li Jun knows who I am. If I have the dust, he'll play along. He'd be a fool not to. And if he has it, and knows I know, he'll make a stupid mistake."

"Well, Director, you don't have the dust and I doubt your cat and mouse secret agent shit works the same during an apocalypse. And unless you can convert this Ford Econoline into a jetliner, I'd say you're…we're screwed. As it stands, you are nothing more than a powerless annoyance. As I see it, the 14K Triad or the Chinese government could have sent men to steal it. I doubt you are the only one who can put pressure on Li Jun. Then, of course, you may have your own band of mutinous rogues."

"Right or wrong, our 50/50 split rides on the assumption that we are both bad guys, remember?"

"You kidnapped me. You had Charles killed. Yes, I assume you're a bad guy," shouted Melinda.

"Any way you slice it, Melinda, here we are and the dust is gone. All because of you two."

"That's your version."

"This conversation isn't getting us anywhere. There's one thing we agree on—we're both liars. Let's find the damn dust.

We'll stay at the house tonight." He got up and started to walk back to the van. "Come on. Let's go. I don't want to get lost in the dark."

◇◇

Miss Jenny's house faced south-east, letting the morning sun shine partly into the front bedroom where Cunningham slept. Melinda was in one of the two back bedrooms. The upstairs floors were slanted like a "fun house." A common problem in old houses where the vertical studs, sometimes twenty feet long, ran from the ground to the attic, allowing the weight of the house to slowly bend them over time. The well-worn, narrow-cut chestnut floors tilted toward the outer wall facing the river. Realtors call it old country charm. During the 1800s, chestnut was common in Tennessee. Disease wiped them out by the late 1900s.

The sun woke Cunningham at 5:00 a.m. while Melinda snoozed in near darkness. He'd let her sleep unguarded. They were in the middle of nowhere with no cell service. If she managed to find someone out on the road, they either wouldn't believe her, not care, or wouldn't want to get anywhere close to her. Three times during the night, she started to creep down the stairs, trying to formulate an escape plan with each step. Each time she returned to the bedroom, frustrated. Escaping wouldn't help find the dust, nor would it absolve her guilt.

Cunningham rummaged around for some coffee and made a pot. The milk was spoiled, the orange juice tasted okay. He poured some bran flakes in a bowl and drowned them in OJ. Melinda walked into the kitchen, went directly to the pantry, and pulled open the two narrow doors. Inside were rows of Ball jars filled with vegetables and fruit. Store-bought canned goods took up the bottom shelf.

"Damn. This place is better stocked than a bomb shelter," said Cunningham. He'd shed his dirty, blood-stained white dress shirt. She curiously watched him slurp OJ and bran flakes in a t-shirt, khakis, black socks, and a bad case of bed-head.

"It's standard old school country. See that freezer?" She pointed toward the outside wall.

"Yeah."

"I'll bet it's full of meat. Neighbors kept Miss Jenny well stocked since she hadn't had any animals in a while. Guess you're pure urban."

He got up and poured them both a cup of coffee. "There's no dogs here, are there?"

"Not since I left for college."

"Good. I'd hate for them to dig up Miss Jenny."

"You should have dug a deeper grave," snapped Melinda.

"I what? Last night, in the dark? Be grateful I didn't just throw her in the field."

"She needs a proper burial," said Melinda as she sat down and wiped the gray and white Formica table off with her hand. He set a coffee cup in front of her.

"Oh, for shit-sake. You can't be serious? Go ahead, dig her a nice six-foot grave if it'll make you feel better."

"I mean in the family cemetery. It's just up the hill, near the tree-line."

"I'll make a note." He sighed and shook his head.

"What's the plan, Director? How do you plan to catch our thieves?"

"They came and went by water according to the tracks in the mud. I suspect they went downstream. The river flows at around two miles per hour, but I'm sure they're motorized. Has to be a fairly big boat. Maybe ten, twenty miles per hour, I'd guess. So they could be around 250 miles away by now...give or take a couple hundred. We should have left last night. Seems I'm getting older and need my sleep. Stupid. They should have about 700 miles to go to get to the Gulf."

"Excellent, Director. Piece of cake. We just have to drive a hundred miles per hour, pull up to the river, say, what, 500 miles from here? Then, if and when we see a boat, we yell, 'Hey you, come over here and give us the two tons of dirt you stole.' Is that how it's gonna work, Mr. Super-Spy CIA Director of the Universe?"

"Yup. You've got the general idea...unless you've got a better one?"

Melinda walked to the sink and put her hand on the old windowpane. The image outside was partially distorted. Her eyes locked on Doc's wise old willow tree. *A true survivor.* Without changing her gaze, she spoke. "How about an airplane or a helicopter with machine guns?"

"Very funny," he murmured through clenched teeth.

"I'm serious, except for the machine gun part. There's an airfield nearby. Used to have a bunch of private planes and a couple helicopters."

"Let's go. Why didn't you tell me?"

"I just did."

Cunningham stood up, downed the rest of his coffee, and put his gun behind his waste-band. "Nice t-shirt."

"It's Miss Jenny's. She was a big Elvis fan. I didn't have much choice. Every t-shirt in her drawer has Elvis on it."

Chapter 29

Olivia poured a glass of wine and walked to the couch. Alex sat next to her, giving her time to process what he'd just said. He tapped his foot like a speed-metal drummer. In the distance, they saw an explosion. Bright white light and sparks flew from a transformer. Their lights flickered. A section of town, to the southeast, went black. Neither commented.

Alex was too impatient to wait. "You don't have to respond. It doesn't matter if you accept my spiritual experience as reality right now, but we have to do something—tonight."

"Like what?" Her voice sounded tired. "Alex, you better move away, my mind is about to blow...like that transformer."

"We have to find the dust ourselves. We can't expect Melinda to bring any back. I'm sorry."

"So you don't think Charles hurt her?"

"No. Like I said, I think she's with Cunningham. I don't know. They're both gone, right? Maybe it's just because of Charles, but something about Melinda bugs me. Cunningham's a little hard to read. Be that as it may, I just have a feeling. Can't explain it. Get ready, we need to hurry. Let's grab what we can find to eat, some bottled water, and get your pistol. I've got a bunch of ammo. We have to get what we can from Charles' and Melinda's laptops first."

"You mean go to his house?"

"Yes."

"Wait a minute, I think Bullock brought them to the lab. I'll call him."

"Hello...Olivia?"

"Yes. Shane, did—?"

"Are you okay? Any word on Alex?" asked Bullock.

"He's with me. He's okay."

"What? With you? How can that be?"

"Tell you later. Listen, do you have Melinda's and Charles' laptops?"

"Yes. They're with me. We're just finishing up. Heading to Mt. Weather tonight. You two need to be there."

"Can't right now. Alex is convinced Melinda isn't coming back. Looks like it's up to us to find the dust. Please leave the laptops in my office, okay?"

"What are you talking about?"

"Shane, we can't do a damn thing without the dust, right?"

"Right."

"Just leave the laptops. We'll explain later."

"Okay...okay, I will. What do I tell Cunningham, Shenberg, etcetera?"

"Have you heard from Cunningham?"

"No. No one has."

"Crap. Alex might be right."

"What?"

"Never mind. Tell them about the dust and that we're trying to retrieve a supply. That should make them happy."

"Well yes, but I don't think they'll like two of our main scientists running off."

"Probably not. Talk later. The laptops. Don't forget to leave them."

"Got it. Good..." Olivia had hung up.

Alex was pacing in front of the window. Olivia stuffed granola bars and water bottles into a backpack. She was shaking, fighting off a wave of paralyzing anxiety.

"I just thought of something." Olivia waited for him to stop pacing. "There may be some dust at Melinda's. We can search Charles' house as well. It'll give Shane something to work with while we're gone."

"If we could find some, that'd be great. Really great. You better call Shane and tell him to wait for us."

"Where's my phone?"

"Right in front of you."

"Good grief. I'm losing it."

Alex went to the hall closet and grabbed a large gym bag containing a disassembled AR-15, clips, and an extra pistol. "Take a deep breath. Look at me! It's gonna be okay."

"I'm sure it is...General Custer."

"There ya go. That's my Kung-fu fighter," he said, patting her on the shoulder. "I'll take that as a vote of confidence."

"You must have slept through history class. And I haven't practiced my Taekwondo for months."

"Like riding a bike, it'll come back to you."

"I thought you'd gotten rid of your weapons."

"I did, but after my CIA 101 training, I sorta got back into it. Once a shooter, always a shooter."

"Not sure I'd brag about that."

"Our dirty little secret. It's almost like Cunningham knew I'd end up in some crazy shit again."

"It's your nature." She paused with her wine glass between her lips. "To do the right thing...at any cost. He could smell that."

"Yeah. I guess."

"Deep down, maybe, you still want revenge...for Julie and the girls?"

"Thanks, Dr. Phil. I think you nailed it."

◇◇

"We'll take my car...wait, is it still at Charles' house?" asked

Alex as he hit G on the elevator floor selector.

"Yes."

"We'll pick it up there, then. I'll drive."

"Really? You sure you want to drive? After being shot in the head?"

"It's okay. I'm good. Can hardly feel it." He screeched the tires pulling out to the road.

Olivia watched Alex continuously for the first ten minutes of their trip out to Fairview. First worried, then with adoration, and then with memories. This was the Alex she knew best. Balls to the wall crisis mode. Aggressive, decisive, and in control. Sexy. She never knew him as a practicing doctor, husband, or father.

Olivia's father had abandoned her family when she was nine, leaving her mother to raise Olivia and her younger sister, Rikki. They lived near Igelboda Station in East Stockholm Sweden, where her mother taught school. By age thirteen, Olivia had amassed quite a collection of figure skating trophies from Sweden's many amateur competitions. Much to her mother's relief, Olivia's first love was science. Skating was a hobby, nothing more.

Despite her stunning appearance, she rarely dated, frustrating a long list of suitors. During her final year at the Karolinska Institute, she believed she'd found her mate. Unfortunately, she also found him in bed with another woman. As soon as she completed her Ph.D. thesis, she took a job at Vanhusse University Medical School in Nashville. She hocked the diamond engagement ring that covered her airfare, deposit, and first month's rent in Nashville. For a year, she dated a string of men, spending their money and seed. Two proposed. Both times she said no and walked out the door. Revenge didn't resolve her trust issue. For the next ten years, she never got involved. Then, out of the blue, she received a call from Dr. Alex Winthrop, who had a question about a drug she had worked on while working for Altiva

Pharmaceuticals. A call that changed her life.

"What's Charles' address?" he asked. "I have no memory of driving out there.".

"Two-twelve Ivey Road. I remember. I'll direct you."

Highway 100 looked like a set-up for an ambush. Uncut grass, weeds, and tree-limbs reached tauntingly into the road.

"Look." Olivia pointed. "The church. Burnt to the ground since we were here. Please don't tell me that's an omen."

"Okay, I won't."

Alex stopped at the end of Charles' lane. They could barely make out his house in the pure darkness. There was no light from their surroundings. The moon was hiding behind stagnant clouds. Olivia pulled her pistol from her purse and loaded a bullet into the chamber. Alex reached into the console for his.

They inched up the driveway with the lights off, stopping fifty feet from the house. Nature was beginning her process of reclaiming the land. The moon came out from behind the clouds, casting shadows, spreading a gray light over the house.

"Let's go," said Alex.

They were greeted by howling coyotes. It was almost impossible to guess how far away they were. Olivia wondered if they'd snatched up Mango. The air was damp. They could feel the dew on the tall grass wetting their shoes. As they neared the back porch, Mango ran out, causing both of them to jump. Olivia let out a muted squeak. The back door was open. The stench of death sent them both reeling.

"Oh, for chrissake. I guess the police have never been back," said Oliva, trying to shake off the pungent odor hanging in her nostrils.

"Guess not. I wonder why the coyotes didn't come for a feast."

"Maybe Mango scared them off."

"Ah, yeah. Sure. Grab a foot. Let's drag him out into the field.

The coyotes will find him and leave nothing but shredded clothing."

"Alex, this is disgusting."

"Way."

"What's this?" asked Olivia, as she picked up a piece of paper sitting by Charles' laptop.

"Check it out."

Dear Melinda,

I'm so sorry. I didn't see any way out. The dust changed me. It got so I didn't know what I might do. I didn't want to hurt you. There's so much going on in my mind. I can't handle it. I swear I've gone crazy. Yes, I've been taking the dust every day, I can't stop. I should never have contacted Li Jun, and I never should have convinced you to let me make us some easy money the day we fought. I was afraid of what he would do if I didn't deliver the quantity he demanded. Eventually, he'd send someone after me. Asking you to get more of it from Miss Jenny was wrong.

My mother called this morning and told me my dad overdosed on pain medicine—on purpose. I gave him a capsule of dust last week. It's my fault. I can't live with this.

Melinda, stay away from Li Jun. Stay away from the dust. Ignore his calls and messages. Don't end up like me, my dad, or the others.

I love you. I'm sorry.

Forever yours,

Charles

"Oh my God, Alex, I wonder if Melinda saw this? Where the hell could she be? Why doesn't she call us?"

"Only two possible answers—she can't, or she doesn't want to, right?"

"Yeah. Rhetorical question. Here's what I think about this: someone came to see Charles. I assume to kill him, but maybe not. Maybe there was another reason. Like Charles said, someone would eventually come for him. Then you show up uninvited and get in the way."

"Olivia, they wouldn't kill Charles unless they knew where the dust was."

"Or they planned to torture it out of him. I'm going to try Melinda again."

"Olivia. Focus. We need to get going. Go ahead and start searching the place."

"Okay. I know. I know."

"Looks like somebody's beat us to it," Alex yelled back from the master bedroom.

Drawers were pulled open. Closets were searched. Under the bed, Olivia found a Ziplock bag containing four unlabeled capsules.

"Alex, what do you make of this?"

"No labels. All real medicine capsules have some form of identifying imprint. Supplements don't."

He opened one and poured some of its contents onto a piece of paper. "Dust. It's dust. Probably a hundred doses in each capsule. Crap. If people are taking this much...hell, they'll be eating babies."

Olivia leaned on Charles' desk, sighed deeply, and dropped her head. "Thanks for the visual...like people hemorrhaging every drop of blood out of their lungs isn't bad enough."

Alex slammed the top desk drawer shut, rocking the lamp behind Olivia. "'Bad enough' is the end of mankind, don't you think?"

"Yes, Alex. I get your point. It can always get worse. I know that. Don't bark at me. We're on the same team, remember?"

"Yeah. Sorry. There's nothing here, let's get over to Melinda's. You can drive."

"What about Mango?"

"What about Mango? Okay, put some food out for him. And

no, we can't take him with us. This is his home. He'll be better off here."

◇◇

Melinda's apartment building was dark except for lights showing through the shades from two apartments. Before Olivia could swipe her pass key, they looked at each other. The familiar smell of death and feces. The elevator door opened and a blood-soaked torso fell at their feet. Olivia jumped back, pushing herself up against the wall. Alex took her hand.

"Why don't we take the stairs? It's healthier."

"Good idea," she replied.

Melinda's apartment door was open. The door frame was shattered. Furniture was torn apart. Drawers and shelves had been emptied onto the floor. Olivia went straight to Melinda's closet while Alex surveyed the mess.

"Here it is." Olivia held up a Ball jar containing an inch of dust.

"Where'd you find that?"

"Whoever searched the place doesn't know much about women."

"What do you mean?"

"It was in an Aldie's bag, in her closet. Women always stash stuff in bags in their closets."

Alex tilted his head and nodded. "Good to know."

Chapter 30

Reelfoot Lake Airport was thirteen miles from Miss Jenny's, at the north end of the lake, where Kentucky, Missouri, and Tennessee rub together. The publicly owned airport had been built to lure well-off fishermen and hunters to the lake. It was a massive failure, left to rot. Over time, local flying enthusiasts brought it back to life, building a new hangar with facilities for lessons, repair, and restoration. Before COVID-19 hit, there had been plans for a second runway.

"Since we are going to an airport, I assume you know how to fly?" asked Melinda.

Cunningham gave her a "that's a stupid question" look. "I flew choppers in Nam and...shared a Cessna with my best friend until he was killed flying over the Smokies in dense fog two years ago."

"Sorry."

Phillipy Road was a straight shot to the airport. Cunningham was entertained by the sight of Cypress trees mysteriously rising out of the lake to their right. A rusted F-150 was parked near a single-wide that served as the airport's terminal. Cunningham's eyes lit up when he saw a Mosquito helicopter sitting alongside several Cessna single engine planes. Two fuel tanks sat in front of the hangar.

"Park here and give me the keys."

A man wearing jeans, t-shirt, and a University of Tennessee

ball cap stepped out of the terminal. "Hey there. Let's keep a distance," the man said, holding up one hand.

"Certainly. Does that Mosquito fly?" he asked. "It looks bigger, like a newer model. I see it's a two-seater. Nice."

"Yeah. Why ya askin'?"

"I need to borrow it."

"We don't lend nuttin'. It belonged to Buddy Perkins. He died of that virus. Don't know about his wife."

"I'm CIA," Cunningham said, waving his ID.

"Can't see that from herra."

Cunningham pulled out his gun and aimed it at the man's head. "Do you see this?" The man's eyes widened and he nodded. "Good. Now get the keys."

"Hold on, I'll git 'em. Don't 'spose his wife care a bit anyways."

"See that woman in the car?"

"Yup."

"I'm going to test fly around the field for a few minutes, then you're going to fuel it. If anything goes wrong, or you make one wrong move, she'll blow your head off."

"Yessir."

Cunningham got in the chopper and familiarized himself with the controls and gauges. The flight clock only had twenty hours on it. "Nice," he said as he turned the key. The helicopter jerked awkwardly off the ground and wobbled a few feet in the air before rising about ten feet.

Within a couple of minutes, he was handling it like a pro. He set it down by the fuel tank and waved the frightened man over to pump it.

"Come on," he yelled to Melinda. "Let's go, and get that cornhole's cell phone."

The tiny airport faded into the distance. Cunningham followed the Mississippi, flying just above the treetops. Melinda had never seen her hometown from the air. She spotted Miss Jenny's farm just past New Madrid.

"What are you crying about?" asked Cunningham.

"Miss Jenny. She meant so much to me, and Charles, the man I loved, you didn't have to kill him, you bastard."

"Melinda, I didn't kill Charles. Think about it. I didn't show up until right after you found him."

"Bullshit. That's just how you set it up. You're CIA. You do shit like that. That, or you had someone else do it."

"I had nothing to do with it. Maybe someone else knew what you two were up to."

"What *we* were up to? To you, everybody's a bad guy. Jerk. There is no proof Charles sold dust to that traditional medicine dealer. He was a consultant. He was an expert. He'd done more research into indigenous medicine than almost anyone."

"No proof? We found deleted files that were pretty explicit."

"Prove it."

"Get off it, Melinda. Your ridiculous lies don't change anything, even if they were true."

"Why haven't you called in for help, if you're trying to save the world?"

"We've been through this. I couldn't wait. We don't have enough men...and it would take too long. They'd call me in for questioning. With that delay, we'd never get the dust back. I thought we decided not to have this fight anymore. I'm about to push you outta this thing. Just shut up."

"Maybe not," said Melinda, barely loud enough for him to hear.

"Maybe not? Maybe not, what?"

"Maybe you're not lying. I think I believe you."

"Sure. Just like that? You are still my hostage until we find it...unless I decide to throw you out of this damn helicopter first!"

"For God's sake. You—"

"Blah blah blah. Stop looking at me. Watch the river."

The twisting ribbon of water below them looked lost and desperate, sniffing its way south, in search of an ocean. Cunningham flew straight, making up for lost time, until they were over Greenville, Mississippi. He dropped altitude and followed the river's slalom course. Water traffic was scant. A few fishing boats and abandoned barges were all they saw. They had no idea what kind of boat the thieves would have, or even if they were in a boat. Cunningham envisioned a forty to sixty-foot-plus boat heading south with several crewmembers. Melinda studied the vessels and their movements. After a while, she could see a pattern. Most of the boats were still, others traveled at odd angles, searching for better fishing spots. Almost none were on a steady course south. While Cunningham focused on finding a boat that fit his mental image, Melinda watched for aberrations.

A couple of hours later, Cunningham said, "We need fuel. This thing doesn't hold much. Look on that guy's phone for an airfield nearby."

Melinda scanned the phone app. "Okay, there's one nearby. Thompson-Robbins Airfield. Just a little ways into Arkansas."

A few minutes later, they spotted the airfield. Several small planes were parked near the terminal, but they couldn't see any activity. They assumed it was abandoned. Cunningham landed next to the fuel tanks. He got out and started to refuel. Before he could finish, a rotund balding man drove up in a golf cart and yelled, "Hey, what the hell are you doing?"

Cunningham pointed his gun at the man and said, "Getting fuel. I'm CIA. Appreciate your help."

"CIA? Bullshit," the man yelled.

Cunningham shot a hole through the front of the golf cart. The man put his hands up and begged not to be shot. When they were about fifty feet in the air, tanks full, Melinda looked down. The man still had his hands up. They flew back to the Mississippi and resumed their hunt.

"It's too wide here for me to see boats near the shore. How about you?" asked Cunningham, shouting above the motor noise.

"Ditto. I'm sure it'll narrow soon. Either way, Director, this is like trying to find a needle in a haystack."

"Do you have a better idea?"

"Below New Orleans, it's mostly bayou, not many people. Generally, it's only barge traffic. Port Sulfur is a tiny town. Maybe land there, use your charm to commandeer a boat, and search by water."

"I like the first part of that. We could go straight to Port Sulfur, then fly back upriver. We'd be less likely to miss them, in case they're a lot further ahead of us."

"If all the stars line up and we find them, then what? And who do you think they are?"

"When we find them, I'll call for help. I suspect they're Chinese. They're most likely going to move the load to a larger boat and make their way back home. Either that, or they will off-load near an airfield and fly it out."

"Good. I'll know if you can be trusted when the good guys show up. If they don't, then I have to trust your fifty-fifty offer, which, of course, I don't. Why can't you believe I'm just trying to get it back to the lab where it belongs?"

"Look, I know Charles was selling it. You were his lover. Lovers are always involved."

"Just like that. Black and white. Not this time. Your concrete view of human behavior is stupid, but you know that, right?"

"Profiling is spot-on eighty-five-percent of the time. That's good enough for me."

Melinda craned her head around to keep sight of a boat that didn't fit the pattern. "Hey, turn around. We just passed by a big speedy-looking yacht. I haven't seen anything like that so far, and it's going almost as fast as we are. See it?"

Cunningham swung the helicopter around. "Yes, I see it. Looks like an Azzurra, sixty-footer, great for running drugs, especially if you gut it for cargo." He made one pass over the boat, then flew toward shore, trying not to look too obvious. "We've got to get a better look. If it's them, I'm sure they're already suspicious. I'll keep some distance and hope they dock soon. When they do, I'll land. We can try to get a better look on foot."

◇◇

The Azzurra turned left, traveled up the Yazoo River in Greenville, Mississippi for a half mile, and docked at the Delta Marina. Cunningham found a clearing in a wooded area less than two-hundred yards north of the marina and landed. Melinda unbuckled her seat belt and quickly climbed out before Cunningham got his door open.

"Where are you going?" he shouted.

Melinda was walking toward the woods. She turned her head and yelled back, "You don't have to shout. I have to pee. Don't you?"

"Well, yeah. Don't try anything."

"Tell me, Director, just what could I do that matters?"

He scratched his head and mumbled to himself, "Good point."

Once relieved, they stared into the woods. Nothing but dense undergrowth. When Melinda saw cypress trees further in, she knew they'd be trudging through marshes infested with water moccasins and maybe a few alligators. The air was hot and thick with humidity and mosquitoes. They found themselves breathing harder despite their oxygen-rich habitat. Spanish moss shrouded the oaks along the pre-marsh perimeter. Before their first step in they were dripping in sweat and swatting madly. The smell of wet life and rotting vegetation gave Melinda a wave of nostalgia.

"Smells like Reelfoot Lake," said Melinda, breaking the silence.

"Smells like misery to me," replied Cunningham. "Let's go. Hopefully, they're spending the night, and not just fueling up or changing boats."

It took an hour to climb through the two hundred yards of tangled ankle-deep muck. From the air, he'd guessed it would be a fifteen-minute stroll. The gnarly ecosystem spit them out fifty feet from the river. Delta Marina was packed with boats but not a soul was in sight. Cunningham spotted the stunning sixty-foot Azzurra yacht with its bright metal-flake blue hull and white deck.

"It'll be getting dark soon," he whispered. "See that houseboat about ten boats down from the yacht?"

"Yeah."

"When it's dark, we'll get in it. Maybe there's some food and water on board. Then, we'll check out the yacht. In and out as quickly as possible. If the dust is there, we go back to the houseboat and make a plan."

"I don't see anyone guarding the yacht."

"There's no one around, and they must have decided we weren't a threat when we flew past them."

"Let's get out of the sun and wait." Cunningham pointed to a fallen tree near the edge of the woods. "How much battery is left on that guy's cellphone? Yours and mine are dead."

"Twenty-eight percent, and good news, it doesn't need a passcode."

"Set it down where I can see it."

The sun cast a golden beam along the glass Yazoo River, widening until it vanished into the shoreline. Melinda rested her head on a sandy log. Exhausted, she rubbed the salty sweat from her eyes and ignored the stinging scratches on her arms. She recalled a poem she'd written in high school. Her muscles relaxed with a resigning sigh.

I sat by the river's edge

And cast a wish, but not too far

To lose it in wandering water's deep

Might a minnow or catfish

Take it home to keep

◇◇

Melinda stood on the pier scanning the marina for movement while Cunningham climbed into the weathered Gibson houseboat.

"No one here. Come on in. I found some stale hotdog buns, petrified granola bars, two warm beers, and some water."

She clumsily stepped down into the boat. "Sounds like a party to me."

Cunningham cracked open a beer. "Shouldn't you drink some water first?" she asked.

"Now you're my mother? What? No. Beer on an empty stomach helps me think clearly."

"I don't think your mother taught you that one." She got up, walked a few steps, and peered into a bedroom. "Hey," she whispered. "Can I take a nap? This looks pretty comfortable."

"No. Finish eating and let's go."

It was dead quiet. Every step and breath seemed too loud. There wasn't a single light on in the marina or on the piers. The moon provided just enough light to see where they were going.

"Stay on deck. I'll go below," he ordered. "Dammit, it's locked. Run back to the houseboat. I saw a toolbox in the cabin."

After five minutes of hacksaw work, the lock gave in.

"Melinda. This is it. Come here."

"Oh my God," whispered Melinda as they surveyed ten fifty-five-gallon drums.

"I'd guess that's about four or five thousand pounds?"

Melinda nodded. "Yes. More than enough."

"What would be the most we'd need for treating COVID-H?"

"Probably a barrel...two at the most."

"Give me the phone. Shh, I hear something."

She pulled the phone from her jeans pocket and reached toward him. Before she could hand it to him, two Asian men walked in behind them, guns aimed. Cunningham threw up his hands and said, "Hey there. We were just admiring the boat...thought it was abandoned. No need for guns."

"Who are you?" asked the man to their left. He was stocky, balding, about five-ten, wearing a white shirt, black slacks, and muddied black dress shoes. The other man was smaller, wiry, wearing a striped button-down shirt, pressed jeans, and black dress shoes, even muddier.

"I'm...."

"Search them. Get their IDs," ordered the larger man. The other man quickly frisked Cunningham. "A gun? Checking out the boat? Bullshit!" He pulled open Cunningham's wallet "Director Robert Cunningham, CIA. Well, Director Cunningham, it looks like you have a problem. Where's your ID, lady?"

"Don't have one."

"Is she CIA also? Doesn't matter. You two are going on a little trip with us. Tie them up." The wiry man bound their hands behind their backs with zip ties and wrapped their mouths with cloth he tore from a pillowcase. Melinda resisted until he punched her in the face. Blood quickly soaked her gag.

Chapter 31

Shane Bullock was in his office busily downloading files onto jump drives when Olivia and Alex entered the lab. Olivia went to her office to collect her data. Two men in full protective garb were anxiously carrying out boxes of equipment along with cages packed with rats.

"Shane," said Alex, walking quickly toward him.

Bullock looked over his reading glasses. "Hi. Are you two doing alright?"

"Okay. We do have some good news."

"What is it?" asked Bullock.

"We found some dust at Melinda's. Enough for probably thousands, maybe a million or more doses. Let me get you my records and methods. You'll need some equipment from the animal lab. Are you taking Levi with you? He knows the entire procedure."

"Alex."

"Yeah."

"Levi is dead. I'm sorry."

"Oh no, Shane. He was such a great guy. That's terrible." Alex looked down at the floor. "Dammit!" While looking down, his eyes were drawn to a picture Bullock had tossed in his trash can. It was of Bullock and another man shoulder to shoulder grinning in some laboratory. The man looked very familiar to Alex, but he couldn't place him.

"Yes, Levi was a rock. I never heard an unkind word come out of his mouth. Over the years, he contributed so much. Alex, I've studied your methods, but give me everything just in case."

"Will do."

"Hi, Shane," said Olivia as she came into his office, surprised to see him without his signature wrinkled and stained lab coat. You and Alex caught up?"

"Yes. I think so," answered Bullock.

Alex put his hand on Olivia's arm. "We need to go. Shane, take care. We'll stay in touch."

"Be careful. I know Melinda's your friend. Do you think she's up to something?" Bullock took off his tortoiseshell readers.

"Of course not," Olivia replied. "We'll keep you updated."

✧✧

"Have you ever been to west Tennessee?" asked Olivia, leaning forward to view the dash monitor as she scrolled through the never-ending list of options.

"Hell no. Why would I go there?"

"People say the same thing about Providence…right?"

"I suppose so. Can't help where you're born."

"And you're a Yankee snob. You never wanted to go to Memphis to see Graceland?" she persisted.

"Especially not to Memphis to see Graceland. Snob? You went to Yale."

"I've been to Memphis for a couple conferences," replied Olivia.

"Am I missing anything?"

"Nope. It might have been kind of cool fifty years ago."

Olivia got on Route 40 West and had the BMW up to ninety miles per hour in no time. Speed traps had been nonexistent for two months. An ambulance in the rearview mirror caught Olivia's eye.

"How's your head?"

"Dull ache. It's strange, I keep having odd thoughts—partial thoughts. When I close my eyes, I see images from my dreams, only from a different perspective. I—"

"What do you mean? Like what?"

"Olivia, we are both diehard scientists. All-out acceptance of God is extremely difficult for us. It's not science. Listen to me. Bluntly put, I believe the dust is the connection between God and science."

"Go on."

"No one knows how RNA or DNA were first formed, right?"

"Right, but there's speculation."

"A fairly accepted theory is that the first organisms were prokaryotes, bacteria that developed near underwater hydrothermal vents. They dust may have triggered the formation of DNA within one of those. Then, over three or four billion years, continents smashed together, possibly burying the dust. When that fault split in 1811, the dust may have escaped. It might have happened all over the world. I believe it guided life until evolution had a good foot hold. I call it God because that's what I felt and witnessed. At the time, in the dream it seemed so obvious, like I was being told it was right to accept the unexplainable 'unearthly' force as God. The dust was...is God's tool. Don't argue yet."

"Okay."

"If it was God's tool, should we be messing with it? I don't think so. Don't ask me why, but I think it served its purpose long ago and we aren't supposed to have it. We—"

"Alex. I'm trying to keep an open mind, but you're killing me. Okay. Phew," she fidgeted and tapped her fingers on the steering wheel. "I think I need some fresh air. So, if it is the tool God used to create life and we weren't supposed to find it, why didn't he just make it disappear?"

"Free will. Sin. Hell, I don't know, but it fits."

"It fits like all the other explanations religious people use to make friggin' sense out of everything they don't understand like: why'd the kid get run over by a car? It was God's will, or because there's sin in the world. I mean, shit, Alex, it's circular."

"Yes. Humans muck everything up. Maybe that's why it's still in the earth."

"Huh?" questioned Olivia.

"He's saving it for when it's needed? After we've destroyed life as we know it?"

Olivia pulled the SUV onto the shoulder, put it in park, and turned to face him. "Are you suggesting we don't use it to treat COVID-H?"

"No. I'm not suggesting that. Absolutely not."

"Alex, the God thing. It...it's just so weird, and you are so convinced? You've been shot in the head. It had to rattle your brain. I don't know. I'll work on it, okay?"

"Sure. Just trust my instincts like you did before."

"What can we do tonight, in the dark?" she asked.

"Go to your friend's property. See what's going on. At first light, we search for the dust. You have the address, right?"

"Yes."

"Okay." Olivia checked the address on her phone just as it rang. She put it on speaker.

"Dr. Nilsson? This is Bob Espionto, CIA."

"Yes. This is she." Olivia put the call on speaker.

"We have not been able to contact Director Cunningham. Have you seen or heard from him?"

"No. Dr. Bullock told us he was missing."

"We are concerned. Concerned to the point I have to ask you to be careful. If he tries to contact you, please call me before you meet him. Don't give him any information."

"What are you talking about?"

"For starters, he may have gotten someone to subtly alter the

BN27 protocol. That's why the Chinese can't manufacture it. That's partly why all hell has broken loose between us."

"Oh no. So that's your theory? From our dealings with him, he seemed like an obedient public servant. Bit of a bastard, but that's neither here nor there."

"Please call me if he contacts you or you have any idea where he might be. Also, Dr. Bullock informed us about some naturally occurring substance that treats and prevents COVID-H that he discovered. He said that you and Dr. Winthrop have been integral in getting it into treatment form. The President is, we all are, indebted to you all. There's one big problem."

"What's that?"

"The Chinese knew about it before we did."

"Oh my God."

"We understand you have gone to obtain more. That's good. Just hurry. Keep me informed."

"Yes, sir. Thanks for the heads up." She and Alex looked at each other. "So Bullock's taking credit for our discovery."

"He didn't get to his position without being a cutthroat on occasion."

Olivia drove back onto the highway. "Dickhead. What a dickhead."

"Doesn't really matter, does it?" asked Alex. "He's probably trying to improve his image after the BN27 fertility issue."

"That doesn't justify it. It's the principle, and that matters," Olivia fumed.

◇◇

No lights were on at Miss Jenny's. The moon provided just enough light to silhouette the house. Olivia parked in front. Alex walked to the side of the house and looked west to the river. A slight breeze made it difficult for the mosquitos. Fireflies blinked over the fields.

"I am getting some very strong feelings here. Something's not right," said Alex as he walked up the front steps to the porch.

"Alex, nothing is right," added Olivia.

"You know what I mean."

"Yes. You're communicating with the spirits."

"Who's the smartass now?"

The house still had power. They searched every room. Two beds had been used and there were two coffee cups in the sink.

"What do you make of it?" asked Olivia.

Alex sat down at the kitchen table. "There have been two people here. Jenny and Melinda? Jenny and a friend? But where's Jenny? Where would she go? She's like ninety-two years old, right?"

Alex got up and went to the kitchen window. He turned and leaned against the sink, peering into the parlor. "Wait, what's that?" he said, walking into the room. He knelt down and pushed his finger into a dark red stain. "Blood. It's blood." Olivia came up behind him.

"Sure looks like it," she said, bending to get a closer look.

"Someone may have attacked Jenny. That's why she's not here."

"Melinda wouldn't harm her. That woman meant a lot to her."

"Espionto thinks Cunningham is up to no good. Bullock thinks Melinda is up to no good. Crap. Somebody's up to no good." He went out to the porch. "Olivia, there's more blood out here. A smear, like somebody was dragged."

"So somebody killed Miss Jenny and dragged her off—somewhere."

"That's what it looks like. It's too dark to worry about it now. Let's get some sleep."

"Alex, this means someone's been here after the dust and I don't..."

"Exactly. Dammit!" Alex's fists were tightly clenched. He punched his thigh and slammed the porch screen door. "I knew it."

✧✧

The house didn't look much different than it did in 1879 when Doc and Edith Stevenson were alive. Much of the furniture was the same. Alex sat on a Louis XV chair across from the bed while Oliva undressed and slid between the sheets. From where he sat, the room looked like it hadn't changed in a century. He could imagine Edith walking in and wondering who they were. A pine corner cupboard caught his attention. He studied it, rubbing his finger along its sides. *If you could only talk.* Antiques, or anything old, fascinated him for just that reason.

The top shelf was packed with old notebooks, scrapbooks, and the family Bible. Bits of yellowed newspaper clippings poked out at various intervals across the shelf. One by one, he leafed through them. When he came to the Bible, he opened it where it was marked with a crumbling full-page article. Behind it, Acts 2:17–20 was underlined. *In the end times, God would pour out His spirit on all people and show signs in the heavens and on the earth before the coming great and dreadful Day of the Lord.*

The tattered article was from 1938. It reported the tragic death of Captain Simon O'Brien, Jenny's father—Doc Stevenson's grandson. He died in an apparent accident at the Army Intelligence Research Lab in Watertown, Massachusetts. There was a quote from Colonel Robert Cunningham expressing his condolences and sadness over the loss of a brilliant scientist, Captain Simon O'Brien. Alex's eyes widened. *Cunningham?* Alex sat back down, holding both the article and the four-inch-thick Bible. He unbuttoned his shirt and pushed his shoes off with his toes, letting them drop on the threadbare oriental rug. A warm breeze rattled the window screen as he started to stand. The sudden weight of the Bible caused him to pause.

Alex knew the basic history of the Army organization Simon had worked for: MI-8 was the first Army Intelligence agency, developed in 1917. This later became known as the Dark Chamber. Shortly before World War II, the FBI was given reign over intelligence operations by J. Edgar Hoover. During WWII, the Office of Strategic Services (OSS) was created. Hoover saw that he was in danger of losing control, and redoubled his fight to keep the FBI as the sole intelligence agency. He lost his grip when it became obvious that the FBI's tactics were archaic and ineffective. In 1947, President Truman signed the National Securities Act and the CIA was born.

"Holy shit. Could this be Director Cunningham's father?" he whispered. *What was Simon working on? What does Cunningham know?*

Chapter 32

Daybreak and mewing gulls pulled them back into their harsh reality. Awake to what should have been a bad dream. Their heads were leaning together, separated by a film of sweat. The heat in the closed cabin was unbearable. Zip ties cut into their wrists. Men's voices circled the boat along with the sound of a power saw followed by the high-pitched whine of a drill. The creaking of rubbing wood and metal was followed by sunlight bursting in along the edges of the cabin's ceiling. The men lifted the deck off the two-million-dollar Azzurra racing yacht and set it on the pier. Melinda and Cunningham looked up to see a large iron hook swinging from a crane, several feet above their heads.

"Now that's a novel way to get to your cargo," said Cunningham, wiggling a few inches away from Melinda, embarrassed that he'd been snuggling with his hostage.

"Melinda."

"What."

"Since we're their hostages and you are my hostage, that makes you a double hostage. Never saw that in the CIA training manual."

"You're pathetic. I've known you for three months and you never cracked a smile or a joke, and now you try to be funny? We're about to be killed, and your first ever attempt at humor bombs...sucks. You could at least be funny, for crap sake." She let her head fall back against the rusted fifty-five-gallon drum and slowly exhaled. "Director, are they going to kill us?"

"Not for a while. We're their security blanket, and I wasn't trying to be funny, just making an observation."

"Good grief. Why don't you observe us a way out of this mess?" Two men with deeply tanned and weathered skin, wearing t-shirts, and jeans, stepped into the boat.

"Get out," ordered the older man, probably in his forties.

Melinda and Cunningham struggled to push themselves up the side of a barrel. Melinda couldn't do it. The younger man laughed.

"Come on, lady, get up."

After a few more tries, he stepped down into the Azzurra and yanked her up by one arm. They then prodded them down the pier to a large fishing ship, a good ninety feet long with an upper captain's bridge, quarters for ten, galley, and mess hall. The crane was off to one side. Fifty-caliber machine guns were mounted on either side, covered with tarps. Melinda and Cunningham were directed to a bench along the port side opposite the crane. They squinted from the sun as the crew used the crane to offload the barrels into the cargo bay.

Cunningham whispered, "I don't know who they work for. It's possible they're MSS."

"Am I supposed to know what the hell MSS is?" snapped Melinda.

"Chinese CIA equivalent."

The ship's powerful Wärtsilä 31 diesel engine came to life. Black smoke bellowed out of the vertical exhaust pipes, turning to a lighter gray as the engine warmed up. With the Azzurra in tow, they headed down the Yazoo River to the Mississippi, escorted by seagulls.

Of the nine men on board, five, including the captain, were crew, and four managed the theft mission. It wasn't difficult to spot the leader. He looked to be in his fifties, crewcut, and average build. He wore a sports coat despite the heat, and carried himself like an officer. His men referred to him as Commander Feng. Cunningham was soon convinced they were soldiers. They all spoke fairly good English.

Commander Feng signaled to the ship's captain to leave the helm. He nodded and put the boat on autopilot. Feng directed Melinda and Cunningham to step down into the cockpit fitted with an array of high-tech equipment and down another step into the cabin. Walking into the air-conditioned cabin gave them some relief. The room was otherwise sparse and purely functional. The once splendid interior was gutted. He cut their zip ties and sat down across from them. In front of him were two folders. They contained information on both of them, including pictures. Melinda's eyes opened wide when she saw her picture lying on top of a folder with her name on it.

"Director Robert Cunningham and Dr. Melinda Taylor," he said, followed by a quick head bow. "I'm sorry for the inconvenience, but we have no choice but to take you hostage until our people have received treatment for COVID-H. If the US had shared it with us, we wouldn't have needed to steal it. As for BN27 for Nipah, we received the corrected methods and further assistance from Dr. Bullock. Our scientists are working to set up production. I don't understand why you would try to get away with sending methods that have been altered."

Cunningham pushed himself back and sat straight up. "Altered? What do you mean altered? I carried them myself to my superiors. You're lying." He turned to Melinda and asked, "Do you think Bullock or someone at the lab did it?"

"No. Bullock wouldn't do that."

"She's right, Director, we don't suspect him, so unfortunately, it seems more likely that you or your CIA superiors did it."

"That's impossible," snarled Cunningham.

Feng shook his head. "Please forgive me, but I believe you are incorrect, Director."

"Commander, what makes you think we have a cure for COVID-H?"

"My, my, please don't waste my time with your silly denials. We know everything that has transpired in your laboratory, except there was surprisingly little about the COVID-H cure. Your clever scientists hadn't gotten around to entering much data. Too excited, or just sloppy? That didn't matter; we figured it out ourselves." He stared at Melinda. "Honestly, I'm a bit surprised how easily our hackers got into your system. A DOD top security operation? You really do need to improve your security efforts. You should hire some Russians," he said with a sarcastic grin.

Melinda was seething with defeat. Cunningham glared at her. Neither had a comeback. Feng went back to looking at their files.

"Maybe my men left a little of your river dust behind, but I doubt it. They're very thorough."

"You bastard," yelled Melinda. Cunningham nudged her a "shut up" with his leg.

"Dr. Taylor, from your point of view, I'd think those words would have been better suited for your boyfriend, Charles."

"What are you talking about?" asked Melinda. Cunningham looked away in disgust, almost wishing he had been the one that shot Charles.

"Yes, yes, we are indebted to him, poor boy, and you as well," said Feng.

There was no denying that Charles had sold river dust to Li Jun. But that was the most she wanted anybody to know. How it got into the hands of Chinese government officials, and how they knew it treated COVID-H was a mystery. Only Alex's preliminary data was documented in the lab's computer system. *How did they know that Charles' 'ground T-Rex bones' were the same thing as what they were working on in the lab, unless somebody told them?* Feng leaned back and put his hands behind his head, enjoying Melinda's anxiety.

Cunningham looked around the cabin, his eyes stopping at a large map behind their captor.

Before responding, Melinda pushed her hair behind her ears, prepared her lie, and cleared her throat. "Charles? Yes, I suspected he'd sold what he said was ground T-Rex bones. He found the bones during one of his research trips. Apparently, he knew of some folklore passed on by the Choctaw Indians claiming that dinosaur bones had special powers."

"Why are you still trying to bullshit me?" Feng asked. "Dinosaur bones, dirt, dust, I have no idea what it is and you don't either, do you?"

Melinda gave him a piercing stare. "No. No, I don't, but you didn't have to kill him!"

"Kill him? Why would you say that? He was dead when we got there. Saved our man the trouble."

"You lying bastard," she yelled.

"Believe what you want, but I have no reason to lie, Dr. Taylor. We don't need him anymore. We are more interested in you. Our scientists want to know how to prepare your magic bone dust for safe human use. I trust you will show them."

"I don't know anything about that, Commander."

"I'm sure it will come to you...with a little incentive. I suggest you don't let it get to that." Feng collected the files and locked them away. "Ah yes, Director, I see you are studying the map. It's a long way to Malaysia, isn't it? Fortunately, most of our trip will be by air. By sea, it would take three to four weeks. We don't have that much time. Millions more of our people would be dead by then." He held up two sets of handcuffs. "Let's cuff your hands in front. I don't want you to be uncomfortable."

◇◇

The waters of the Gulf of Mexico were calm for the first two days. At sunset on the third day, waves suddenly began to slap the bottom of the boat. Rain and gale force winds came out of the south. The boat began to rise and fall on ten-foot swells. Melinda's stomach didn't cooperate. There was no horizon for her to focus on. The smell of diesel fumes made it impossible. She vomited what little was in her stomach then dry heaved relentlessly as Cunningham looked on helplessly. The crew smirked. Seasickness was a sign of weakness. For them, it was a vague memory they'd never admit. The man who dragged her out of the Azzurra handed her a bucket of sea water and a mop, telling her to clean it up. He chuckled as he watched her try to clean up her vomit while handcuffed.

At midnight, the storm vanished as quickly as it came. Commander Feng offered them a bunk to share. Melinda and Cunningham looked at each other with no expression. They were so exhausted, they'd sleep with a corpse. They maneuvered until they were back-to-back, cuffed in front.

Melinda turned her head and whispered, "I wonder where we're going."

"If we keep going west, we'll run into Mexico. I bet we'll fly out from there."

"Let's hope the crew haven't been eating handfuls of dust or none of us will make it."

"That is my primary concern, Melinda. It may be a cure, but it's deadly."

Like seals on a beach, they floundered their way over to face each other. Their cuffed hands were tucked under their chins. They shared mutually sour breath as they lay like two nuns praying for salvation.

Melinda furrowed her brow and squinted around several strands of black hair dangling over her eyes. "What do you mean, deadly?"

"You know exactly what I mean," he barked in reply.

"Not really. A couple of our experimental rats did seem unusually aggressive, but that doesn't mean it's deadly, especially if the dose is adjusted."

"It's deadly. Don't fool yourself. You mean to tell me Charles wasn't acting strangely?"

"Yes, sort of. I wasn't really sure what was going on with him. How do you know it's deadly, Director?"

He turned and stared hard into her eyes as if trying to read her mind. Melinda looked away. "I just do," he said. "Okay? I know what it can do to a person if they take too much."

She looked back at him, nodding her head. "And is that all you're going to tell me?"

"Yup."

Chapter 33

They were up at dawn. Olivia was already downstairs rummaging around for coffee and something to eat. The kitchen was a window into Miss Jenny's life. How she organized dishes, knick-knacks, and her favorite foods told Olivia what mattered to her. Pictures of at least twenty-five different children held by magnets on the refrigerator revealed her love for kids. Several unused Hallmark cards were in a neat pile just waiting to be sent. Each one was full of optimism and encouraging Bible verses. Shelves of Ball jars, packed with vegetables from her garden, were lined up and neatly labeled with the date and contents. "Good grief, where does a ninety-year-old lady get so much energy?"

"Are you talking to yourself?" Alex asked as he walked into the kitchen carrying the old family Bible.

"Yes. Doesn't everybody? What's that?" asked Olivia.

"Miss Jenny's family Bible. You've got to see this." He handed her the newspaper article. Her eyes widened as she sat down holding the astonishing find. Alex stood in front of her, watching her eyes run across the page, waiting for her response.

"What? I can't believe it. Cunningham's dad knew Jenny's father, Simon?"

"I also found notebooks and journals describing his work. Simon's work. He was doing research with the dust for the Army."

"So Simon did experiments with the dust while working under Cunningham's father?"

"That's what it sounds like. I think it was somehow tied to the *accident*," said Alex.

"Makes sense. Terrible sense," said Olivia, still staring at the brittle, yellowed clipping.

"Yes, it makes total sense. And it's fair to assume that our Cunningham has figured out that we are, in fact, working with the same material. Doc Stevenson's wonder dust. Damn. The question is, what does he know, what does he think about it? Not to mention, where the hell is he, and what is he doing as we speak?"

Olivia sipped her coffee to calm her racing mind. "Why didn't Cunningham tell us he knew what it was?"

"It was a top-secret project. His father wasn't supposed to tell even his son about it. If Cunningham had acknowledged that he knew, he would be betraying his father."

"Crap. You think so?" asked Olivia.

"That's my best guess. Also, he may know something we don't."

"Do you think he—?"

"Yes, and I don't know why. Ever since we got here, I've been thinking about him. For some reason, my mind keeps telling me that he is doing what he believes is right. I just don't know what that is."

Olivia reached across the table and took his hand. "Okay, Alex. Okay."

"Olivia. You must think I've lost it, but I haven't. My thoughts are clear, but they have a more convincing vibe than just random mind chatter. It is as if I've grown a piece of brain that knows more than I do."

"Sorta like schizophrenia, right?"

"No. Not at all, smart…"

"Sorry, but you've dropped a lot on me. I'm just trying to make sense of it, that's all."

"So am I. Hey, we better get going."

They spotted fresh tire tracks on the path leading to the river. Weeds and five-foot pines poked up from the once fertile field that yielded delicious corn and quality cotton for over a century. They parked where the tire marks ended and got out. Alex ran up the levee to peer across the great Mississippi for the first time. Olivia set out to see if she could find clues to where the previous visitors had gone.

"Hey. Wait up." Alex joined her and led the way.

"Do you know where you're going?" she asked.

"Not sure."

"Let me guess. You just have a feeling about it?"

"Yeah. You're catching on."

Soon, they were oblivious to the warm breeze and the morning sun shimmering off the river. Other senses were on high alert. Blackberry thorns tore at their flesh. The earthy smell of damp soil had them sniffing the air like hunting dogs. Their eyes stopped when they saw the clearing on the levee.

Alex pointed. "Let's have a look."

They were silent when they came to the gaping water-filled hole by the river's edge. Olivia suppressed a wave of panic. She swallowed hard around the imaginary lump in her throat.

"Dammit to hell," he shouted across the field. His yell died in the wind.

"Who did this?" Olivia asked, suggesting she expected him to know.

Alex rubbed the back of his neck and began to pace. "Melinda, Miss Jenny, and Charles knew about it, but it would take a team to dig this hole so fast. Did Cunningham know it was here?"

Olivia closed her eyes and shrugged. "Don't have a clue, Alex."

"They came and left by water; otherwise there'd be signs of something being hauled back through the field. I doubt they'd go upstream. Maybe we can catch up to them."

"Sounds like a long shot," murmured Olivia. "I'd do anything to stop that animal-murdering Li Jun."

"Okay, I have another idea. Let's go back to the house, get drunk, and screw. Who cares about that pesky COVID-H?"

"I doubt Miss Jenny kept any booze around, but I have to admit...that sounds like a whole lot more fun than what we're doing."

"Anyway, I saw an airport sign on the way in. Let's check it out. Maybe there's a plane we can steal."

"We can what? Steal an airplane? Are you out of your mind? You've watched too many James Bond movies. You never told me you could fly."

"Been a while. It has to be a pretty basic model."

"Oh great."

◇◇

Alex spotted several small planes, mostly Cessnas, ones he could manage. As they neared the terminal, a man walked out holding a shotgun. He was determined not to have a replay.

"Oh shit," said Alex. "Let's go talk to him. You can wait in the car."

"No. A woman's charm may help."

"Where are we gonna find that?" Alex grinned, still staring at the armed man.

Olivia punched him in the shoulder. "You're a jerk sometimes."

"Sir, excuse me," said Alex while walking toward him with his Glock tucked into the back of his pants.

"Yeah. Whadaya want, mister?" he said, raising the barrel a bit higher.

Alex cleared his throat. "Can I rent a plane?"

"No plane rentals. Already had a chopper stolen. I ain't fucking around."

"Chopper stolen? Right. That's why we're here." Alex hoped he could wing it convincingly.

"What?" asked the man. Baffled, he relaxed his grip on the shotgun.

"We're US marshals. Winthrop and Nilsson. What did they look like, sir?"

"Marshals? Shit. They said they were CIA. A man and a woman. He was thin, tall, wore a white shirt, and had short brown hair. The woman...she had black hair, pretty, darkish skin, looked like a Mexican or something."

"That's them. We believe we know where they are. Let me take a plane and we might be able to get your chopper back."

The man stood silent, processing Alex's story. "I think you're full a shit, mister."

"Of course, you do." Alex moved closer to him, within three feet. Olivia took a step to his side. The man glanced at her. When he looked back at Alex, Olivia pulled out her gun. The man froze. Alex pushed the rifle toward the ground and jammed his pistol under the man's chin.

Olivia poked her pistol into his kidney. "Drop it."

"Not again. Geezus. Not again."

"Sorry, buddy. We won't hurt you. Let's get some keys and fill up a plane, shall we?"

"This damn virus got everybody flippin' crazy. Okay. Crap. Take 'em all. Fly 'em into the river for all I care."

"Good man. That's the spirit."

The exasperated airfield employee retrieved the key and fueled the plane. Olivia kept the shotgun pointed at him every second. They boarded the plane. Before Alex shut the door, he called to the man as he walked away. "Hey, we're not marshals, we're scientists trying to get back the cure for the virus those two stole."

"Yeah, sure, and I'm Peter Pan," he shouted back.

After several bouncing attempts, Alex got the Cessna 172 into the air. Olivia was quiet as she watched Alex try to figure out the plane's instruments.

"Yes. It was Cunningham and Melinda," said Alex.

"It makes no sense. I know Melinda. She wouldn't steal the dust. Cunningham's such a company guy…"

"Couple of problems."

"What?"

"The man said nothing about cargo, but we didn't ask him either. I also didn't think to ask what model the chopper was. I doubt they'd have a big enough chopper here to carry all that weight, plus that's way too much work for two people. I'm sure the dust was taken away by boat."

"So, what the hell are Melinda and Cun—?"

"Olivia. I haven't figured that out yet. We'll fly down the river."

"And look for what?" asked Olivia in an angry tone.

"We've got a radio. We can ask people at all the airfields if they've heard or seen a chopper, probably a small one. They'd have to stop for fuel somewhere."

"Alex, why can't I just google those airport numbers and call them?"

"Duh. I forgot about that. Are you getting a signal?"

"Yup."

For the next couple of hours, they scanned the sky and watched the river below. Olivia began calling airports within fifty miles of the Mississippi. The third airport she called was Thompson-Robbins. A man answered the phone. Olivia handed it to Alex. After a few minutes, he hung up. Olivia could tell it was good news.

"Bingo. They landed there and stole some fuel. He said the man had a gun and shot his golf cart as he drove toward them. He also said they have a Mosquito."

"Mosquitoes and murdered golf carts? Are you sure you're

okay to drive?"

"I'm flying, not driving. The man was on the golf cart and the make of helicopter is Mosquito. Comprende?"

"Of course."

"We know we're headed the right direction. They're following the river."

Alex kept the plane low at three hundred feet. Olivia watched the river. They slowed down as they neared Greenville, Mississippi, searching for a boat being unloaded onto a dock or a larger ship.

"Alex. Look."

"At what?"

"You just passed a small helicopter in a clearing off to the left near that marina."

"Let's have a closer look."

Alex veered left and circled, flying as low and slow as possible. "I see it. That's it. I need to find a field to land on."

"Oh no, you don't," ordered Olivia.

"Got to. Don't worry. There, that one should do."

"Is this when I stick my head between my legs?"

"Whatever floats your boat."

"I'm ignoring you," she said while staring wide-eyed at the rapidly approaching field.

"That's weird. The top half of a racing yacht is sitting on a pier at the marina. We'll have to check it out. Okay, here we go. Hang on."

Olivia clutched her head and bent forward. The landing gear hit, bouncing the plane off the ground, listing to the left. Alex hit the throttle and rose back into the air. On the second attempt, the plane again hopped but remained level. The field smoothed out and they coasted to a stop.

Alex patted her on the head. "Piece of cake."

"I think I'm going to puke," said Olivia as she sat back up.

"Forget the chopper. I want to go to the marina and ask about that severed boat deck."

"Why do you care about a chopped-up boat? Never mind."

"The boat's important...I'll bet ya."

They walked quickly across the field to a shallow rim of pines separating them from the Marina. Once through it, they stopped and scanned the scene ahead. The only living thing in view was a turkey buzzard riding a thermal, overhead. The midday Mississippi sun burned into their scalps as they approached the sea of assorted boats moored to the docks like dogs chained to a tree. They walked down the weathered gray pier to the remains of a once fabulous craft.

"Why would somebody chop the deck off a million-dollar boat?" asked Alex. "I don't see the rest of it anywhere. Maybe we can find somebody inside the office or that restaurant."

A rotund, sun-dried grey-haired woman in her late sixties sat alone at a table in the restaurant, smoking a cigarette. She slowly turned her head, watching Alex and Olivia approach.

"Excuse me, ma'am," said Olivia.

"Yes, honey. Don't y'all get any closer. I'm one of the few around here still breathing.

"No, ma'am, we won't. We were wondering if you knew anything about that boat deck sitting on the pier?"

"Beautiful boat it was. Azzurra, worth over a million. A bunch of Chinamen or something just chopped it off. I stayed hidden. They looked scary, and I'm alone. They brought in a big fancy fishing boat with a crane and loaded up a bunch of fifty-gallon drums. They had two white-folk with 'em. A man and a woman. Didn't see them at first. I'd gone to the restroom a spell. They were on the fishing boat. Didn't look none too happy, tell ya that. Then they left, dragging the hull behind them. Oddest thang I ever did see...and I been around a while, honey."

"No idea where they were going, I guess?" asked Alex.

"Headed toward the Gulf, I s'pose."

"Ma'am?" asked Olivia. "Do you have any food or water?"

"Fish is all I have. Virus ain't kilt them yet. I'm just waitin' fer Jesus. He'll be here soon. Mark my words, child. What church y'all go to?"

Olivia knew the correct answer. "Baptist, ma'am." The old lady nodded her approval and disappeared into the kitchen.

◇◇

An hour and a half later, they were in the air, heading south over the river. The pandemic's ugly work was starkly obvious from three hundred feet. Empty roads, abandoned barges, and a burning house suffered alone. Forests, green and worry-free, offered scenic relief. Olivia imagined for a long five seconds that everything was okay.

"Two possibilities, right?" asked Alex.

"Yeah. They're either hostages or accomplices."

"The Chinese...seems they keep popping up wreaking havoc in our lives."

"Don't generalize," said Olivia.

"You know what I mean. Geez. Okay, I'll rephrase it. The evil government operatives that we've run into in the past just happened to be Chinese...or Russian. The civilians stuck in those shitholes are fine people. It's not them I'm worried about."

"I can't imagine they were sent by the Chinese government. How would they know where to find it? Would they really steal it all and watch us die?" asked Olivia, just to say it out loud, hoping her words would travel through the ether and fall on unwilling ears.

"You know we're in a pissing match with them over BN27? Who knows what else is going on? We're all paranoid. Trust is a distant concept."

"Yes. Sad."

"Li Jun..."

"What about him?" asked Olivia.

"He's the last one on our list who knows about the dust. We have to find him."

"Alex, he's in Malaysia. That's like six thousand miles away. And don't forget, the President's inner circle, and any number of people involved in manufacturing inhalers with our dust samples will all soon learn about it.

"They're on our side. They don't know what it is any better than we do, and they don't know it came from the banks of the Mississippi. Li Jun may know. Same goes for the Chinese."

"How far can this thing go on a tank of gas?"

"Eight hundred miles. Have to find a bigger plane even if we went to Hawaii first. A boat would take weeks."

"Wanna call Espionto?"

"And tell him what?"

"Do you know anybody else who can get a plane to fly us over the Pacific to somewhere in Malaysia?"

"No. Okay, okay, and tell him the whole story? About Cunningham? He'll flip. Then calmly ask him for an airplane that can make it to Malaysia?"

"True. He might get a little dramatic," replied Olivia.

"If he goes for it, he'll likely want to send special forces. We'd end up with a friggin' mess if China caught American soldiers. Well...yeah. Okay, call him but keep it simple."

"Yes, Dr. Winthrop," she said, pinching his cheek. "Here goes."

Alex listened to Olivia tactfully work Espionto. She pleaded with him to keep it secret for now.

"Dr. Nilsson, I can't. We can't put you two at risk. You need help."

"Please? If we're caught, we'll tell them we were stealing it for ourselves...that we'd planned on selling it to the highest bidder."

"You think they'll believe that?" asked Espionto.

"It's better than special forces being discovered. They'll know for sure it's our government then."

Espionto was silent for a moment, then began talking as if trying to convince himself, "I hear you. If you succeed, we can deal with China then. I may be able to get one of our contractors to help you, if any are still standing. We have several that ferry arms for us. Their relationship with us is well hidden. Dr. Nilsson, I know saving millions of lives and avoiding a final showdown with China are top priority—hands down. For now, it sounds like you and Dr. Winthrop give us the best chance of reaching those goals. Dr. Winthrop has training, so it's not like I'm handing this over to ill-equipped civilians. I can't believe I'm doing this, but okay. I'll ask for forgiveness later. I'll call you when, if, I find a plane. There's a reasonable chance you will need help at some point. That'll be tough on short notice, so I'll need updates. Got it?"

"Yes, sir," replied Olivia. "Thank you. Goodbye." Stunned by what had just transpired, she threw her head back against the seat and turned to see Alex's identical expression. "Can you believe that? See, you should listen to me." Olivia raised her chin to present her smuggest look.

"I never expected that kind of response. Good work. Wow. I do listen to you, like when you tell me dinner is ready or you're horny."

"If I wasn't a liberated woman, above pea-brained misogyny, I'd punish you with chastity."

"You wouldn't last a week," quipped Alex.

"Blah, blah, blah. Do you think he'll keep his word?"

"A little late to worry about that. He's up to his eyebrows with Washington, so he's giving us free rein, especially since his number one man, Cunningham, has disappeared. You didn't mention that we're pretty sure he's with Melinda."

"No. I didn't. You told me to spare the details."

"That's okay. I'm changing course for California. Can't see any reason to keep hunting for that fishing boat. Doubt we'd find it in the Gulf."

"If we somehow end up in Malaysia, then what?"

"We go to Kuala Lumpur and find Li Jun."

Olivia sighed. "Just like that?"

"Yup, just like that."

"What if they don't take the dust there?" she asked.

"You need to be more optimistic."

Chapter 34

At 6:30 each morning, Wade Espionto walked down Pennsylvania Avenue to the White House. He was staying at the Blair House along with FBI director Bob Banes and General Tousick. The home was once the closest neighbor to the President's residence. It was purchased in 1942 from the Blair family by the government after Eleanor Roosevelt wanted a little separation from foreign dignitaries. For her, the last straw was when Winston Churchill ambled from his quarters in the White House up to President Roosevelt's bedroom to chat at 3:00 a.m.

Espionto wore a shirt and tie every day even though most of the guests had gone casual. He described summers in Washington as hot enough to fry an egg on a bald man's head and humid enough to wilt a heavily starched shirt in under five minutes. The world of bricks, concrete, and asphalt didn't have time to cool overnight, making it hot even at 6:30 a.m. A blast of cold air greeted him at the White House. It sent a chill through his body when it hit the film of perspiration that coated his skin.

Not revealing all he knew about Winthrop and Nilsson shouldn't have bothered him, but it did. After all, it wasn't unusual for the CIA to lie by omission. They preferred to think of it as preventing the President from information overload. Sometimes it provided plausible deniability. It wasn't clear to him if it was withholding information or the nagging feeling that something was seriously wrong that bothered him now. He hoped nobody would ask him about Director Cunningham. He was trying to give his friend more time to surface, but he was having second thoughts.

The morning meeting in the Situation Room started like it had for weeks. First, the death toll: six to eight million a day. Dr. Shenberg neglected to mention that those numbers were likely only a fraction of the true sum. Then, he reported that progress on a COVID-H vaccine was slow. He chose to say "slow" rather than nonexistent. And finally, he gave the group some good news. There were only a thousand Nipah deaths reported the previous day. BN27 and the newly released vaccine were doing their job. A few people nodded and grinned. For the grand finale, he shared the news that Dr. Bullock's enigmatic substance was completely effective in neutralizing COVID-H, and hopefully, a supply was forthcoming. The room remained surprisingly sullen. Nobody believed it would arrive or be distributed soon enough to matter. When it was Espionto's turn to speak, he said he had nothing to add.

US allies were poised for war with China, Russia, Iran, and, of course, North Korea while waiting armies were being decimated by COVID-H. The faces in the room looked tired and discouraged. Sadly, the eyes of a few were vacant, like Holocaust victims being led to a gas chamber.

◇◇

Dr. Bullock's lab space at Mount Weather was three stories below ground. The seventh subterranean level was reserved for the President. Mount Weather Emergency Operations Center was completed in 1959 to serve as a secret installation to house the President in the event of a nuclear war. The 432-acre facility was capable of maintaining all essential government functions, including the command center for the Federal Emergency Operations Agency (FEMA). In 1991, the name was changed to High Point Special Facility. Nestled in Virginia, fifty-five miles from Washington DC in the Shenandoah Mountains, Mount Weather remained a secret until 1974 when TWA flight 514 crashed into the mountain, barely missing the compound. It made the front page of every paper in the country.

The sleepy secret mountain top retreat had morphed into a busy mini-city filled with essential workers and their families. A post-apocalyptic safe haven where the chosen few would take refuge. All communication was monitored. Family members were interrogated to assure loyalty. A flawed system at best. President Triagin remained in DC with his staff. He feared worsening panic if the nation found out he'd fled to his hideout. Dr. Bullock resented being cut off from the outside world. Spending all his time in the lab and not having outside contact was fine—when it was his choice.

In the meantime, Vice President Jackson argued that "dust" didn't sound scientific enough for the public. Bureaucrats agreed, and the initials, DX, were adopted. D for dust, and X for unknown. Now they could brag about their contributions to the fight against the pandemic. Close to a million doses of DX had been administered. It was required of all Mount Weather pilgrims. Nobody complained.

◇◇

Paula Bullock gazed through the east-facing window of their apartment from 1,800 feet. Western Loudoun County's beautiful rolling hills, valleys, and surrounding mountains had a calming effect. The well-to-do had been flocking there in droves to escape the crime-infested nastiness of DC, and its chaotic costly suburbs.

Her calmness turned dark. *Everything has changed. We are lost. My comfortable life and trivial worries are gone. Now it's survival. I can't imagine our world after COVID-H. We've gone too far. Technology has become our God. We are so damn stupid. Look at what we have done to each other—to the Earth.* She never broached the subject with her husband, whose very life-breath was exactly what she feared.

Something had happened to Shane. He had changed. Their checking account tripled. When she asked about it, he said it was consulting fees. An expensive red sports car appeared in the garage one day. He showered her with gifts of expensive jewelry she didn't want. Something had changed.

◇◇

Dr. Bullock had no idea that Jan Whitorsh had taken multiple doses of dust in the midst of her panic when Ned Tate died. She'd moved into her cramped utilitarian quarters at Mount Weather along with half the usual staff. The rest were dead.

She was forty-four, divorced, and one of Dr. Bullock's closest confidants. Over the years, the chemistry between them had grown. It took an effort to keep a professional distance. He loved Paula dearly, but Jan was fifteen years younger, smitten by his brilliance, sympathetic, and always understanding. Jan's not so latent attraction to him was a stimulating reminder of his younger self. A vestigial desire to go back in time.

Together, they busily set about organizing the new lab. The look in her eyes was different. Her progressive physical closeness was becoming a distraction. Within a couple days of her arrival, he thought he'd have to ask her to back off, but at the same time, he didn't want to entirely erase the fantasy. A couple days later, they'd worked late and were alone, three stories underground. Their stress and fatigue begged for relief. Jan made her move.

Chapter 35

Three eyes popped open. One of Melinda's was crusted shut. Men's loud voices punctuated by the arrhythmic thud of the boat bumping against a pier could mean only one thing.

"We're docking," whispered Cunningham, throwing his legs onto the floor.

Commander Feng poked his head into the cabin. "Come up on deck. We are leaving."

Resembling a seal trying to do a sit-up, Melinda threw herself into the sitting position to get on her feet. "Looks like our cruise director is taking us on an excursion."

"Yeah, maybe we're going to tour some Mayan ruins."

Three crew members struggled to offload the barrels with a winch built into the back of an old GMC flatbed truck. They ran a cable over a pulley attached to a makeshift support fashioned out of four-inch posts. Several smaller fishing boats were moored nearby. Small-time commercial fishermen worked their nets, hauling in the morning's catch. Nobody seemed to be paying any attention to the suspicious activity that transpired in their midst. They'd learned to ignore the unusual, fearing it was cartel business.

"They could decapitate us right here and I doubt those guys would react," whispered Cunningham.

A peeling blue sign read "La Pesca Hotel," about fifty yards from the dock. The hotel looked deserted. The hotel swimming pool, half empty and green with algae, was proof enough. Beach umbrellas lay crumpled on their sides, covered in sand. On the second floor, a lime-green shutter swung gently in the salty breeze. Gulls picked at the partially filled fishnets as the men pulled them from the water. Melinda stepped onto the dock, taking a moment to watch the busy fisherman, sandpipers, and gulls going about their daily routine. She was struck by the peaceful natural order of their harmonious foraging. There were no other signs of life as far as they could see.

La Pesca is a small fishing village, four hundred miles from Texas on the east coast of Mexico. Low-level tourism sustained several beachfront hotels and twenty-five percent of the local population of three thousand. In less than a month, the town had been decimated by COVID-H.

Without breaking her gaze, she spoke to the breeze. "Why are these three men alive?"

Cunningham gave her a questioning look and said nothing.

A short, broad-shouldered, emotionless man they called Chin pushed Melinda and Cunningham toward a sandy path that went along the side of the hotel. Out front, on the main road, there were two men in a Toyota Forerunner, waiting. Two other SUVs pulled in behind it as they were shoved into the back seat.

"Are we going to see the sea turtles?" asked Melinda. "I hear they nest down here."

Cunningham gave her a jab with his elbow and snapped "Shut up" in a spitting whisper.

"No, ma'am," replied the driver. "Not today," in perfect English.

"Well, just where the hell are we going?"

"You'll find out soon enough," answered the sweaty tan-skinned man in the passenger seat.

Melinda leaned into Cunningham. "I think he's Filipino...Indonesian, or something."

"So what."

"So why would these Chinese MSS, or whatever they are, have a…? Never mind, you're the secret agent here, I'm sure you're two steps ahead of me." Her whispering was louder than she thought. "Driver, excuse me, driver?"

"What?"

"Turn the AC up, would ya?"

In unison, all three men blared, "Shut the fuck up."

◇◇

Highway 52 ran along the Rio Soto La Marina. Homes of the wealthy dotted the river's edge to their left. They turned onto a dirt road that took them by forests of zapote and ceiba trees separated by desolate patches of desert. Thirty minutes passed before they turned into a densely wooded area and drove uphill on a road that required four-wheel drive during the rainy season. The forest ended abruptly, opening up to a runway and several men with automatic weapons. Two outbuildings and a fuel truck were partially hidden along the tree line. Melinda and Cunningham were surprised to see an aging Boeing 737 jetliner sitting on the tarmac. The unmistakable five-star red flag adorned its fuselage.

"This is no small-time operation," said Cunningham as the men got out and opened the back doors. "I wonder if your friend Li Jun is on board to welcome us."

"Very funny. I was about to ask you the same question."

They were directed up the ramp as men loaded the barrels into the cargo hold. They were seated in first class along with four well-dressed Chinese men who scowled at them. Two of them gave the obligatory partial body bow without thinking. Cunningham responded with an equally disingenuous head nod.

The idling jet engines grew louder, whining in the background. A man wearing a military uniform came out of economy class and fastened their seatbelts. The well-dressed men began to talk among themselves as the jet lifted into the air. Liquor began to flow once they'd reached twenty thousand feet. Cunningham strained his neck to catch a glance toward the back of the plane before the soldier closed the door. Five attractive young women sat together gabbing among themselves.

"How nice," quipped Cunningham. "They brought their own stable of mile-high hookers to help pass the time."

"Maybe you'll get lucky, Director."

"Maybe you will," he sneered.

"Yeah, I'm due for a little pussy," responded Melinda.

"Yuck," he said, looking out the window.

"I guess you slept through your LGBTQ sensitivity classes."

"I called in sick. Besides, I like the alphabet the way it's supposed to be."

Hours passed. The men took turns visiting the ladies in the back of the plane. Melinda and Cunningham grew weary of the alcohol-fueled adolescent behavior. Being amongst a group of care-free revelers didn't sit well, considering they were handcuffed hostages.

Besides sleeping, there was nothing to do. Neither felt like making conversation, especially with four jolly but unfriendly men in such close proximity. Melinda asked for something to read. The soldier brought her a few Chinese magazines.

Melinda scoffed, "Well, I guess I can look at the pictures."

The moon reflected off the wings as they flew over the pitch-black Pacific. The nine-thousand-mile, twenty-hour trip was long enough to let blood clot in their legs and cause bed sores if they didn't wiggle around every once in a while. That hadn't crossed Cunningham's mind until Melinda commented that dying from a pulmonary embolism would be better than their current situation.

The least drunk of the men sat down across the aisle from Cunningham. Melinda pretended to be engrossed in her Chinese travel magazine. His gray light-weight suit was worn to the point that the elbows shined. A black tie hung below his neck like an uncomfortable nuisance. His sculptured close cut black hair made him look like he was trying to appear much younger. He leaned toward Cunningham, reeking of gin.

"You Americans thought you'd outsmarted us. Fools."

Cunningham closed his eyes and shook his head.

"If you want to live, Agent Cunningham, you will cooperate."

Cunningham turned his head to face the man. "There's nothing I know that would change anything. You all only hear what you want to."

"Oh, I'm sure there is," he replied, rattling the ice cubes in his empty glass. "I'm curious, tell me why you wouldn't share your treatment for COVID-H?"

"I have a better question, sir," said Cunningham. "Why the hell did your country create such a vicious virus, and release it in the US?"

"We had no choice but to retaliate once it became clear you weren't going to share BN27 with us." Cunningham gave him the most contemptuous look he could muster. "No choice? Your little experiment could be the end of humanity. Good move. Real smart. And we didn't withhold BN27. Your scientists are just too stupid to understand the process. What happened to your vaccine that you thought would prevent COVID-H? And you call us fools? You're even dumber than you look."

Wang Wei huffed through a fading smile and said, "That doesn't matter now, does it, Director? We have the cure...and you don't."

"Doesn't matter? How many millions of your people have died?"

"You Americans pretend to care about every little person. Makes you feel superior. You think you are in a position to judge the world and dictate your way of life. Such arrogance. Can't you see that your country is failing? When this is over, you will be at our mercy, even more than you are already."

Cunningham wanted to gouge Wang Wei's eyes out, cut out his tongue, and crush his nuts, but all he could do was look away. For Cunningham, being helpless and not in control was tantamount to torture. He took three deep breaths and turned back to Wang Wei.

"How do you know the stuff in those barrels contains a cure?" asked Cunningham.

"Some politicians, even President Chen, were taking it as a supplement and they never got sick, even when coworkers and family died of COVID-H. The one thing they had in common was taking the supplement. Sounds like pretty good evidence to me. We had good intel on its location. A little old lady took our men right to the spot."

"Shit, Wei, I bet she led you to the wrong place, and your men dug up—"

"Don't think so; we have a test for it."

"A test?" asked Cunningham.

"Just drop it in water with a tiny bit of algae, and within minutes, it turns solid green, packed with algae. Simple."

"So how'd your people figure that out?"

"Apparently, something similar was written down by a doctor many years ago."

"Who told you that?"

"What's that expression you people use? A little bird told us? That's it, right, Director? We have many little birds."

Cunningham digested the information with no expression—cheating Wei out of any satisfaction. The journals; his father told him about Doc Stevenson's journals along with too many details to remember. Robert Sr. took great pains to send home the message that the strange substance was far more deadly than it was good. Director Cunningham never forgot the story about Doc's grandson, Simon, his research with the Army, and his progression into insanity. Wang Wei finished off another gin and tonic.

"How did your politicians get the stuff...the 'supplement' in the first place?"

"Director, you know all it takes is money. Many Chinese men are obsessed with traditional medicine remedies. I might try this or that. I've never been impressed. Not until now."

"Mr. Wei, you have no idea how dangerous it is. You must believe me."

Wei glanced at Melinda. "I'm sure Dr. Taylor can show us how to prepare and use it safely. Our scientists have just started to study it, but she can give us a jumpstart, right? Some say the effects are miraculous. Turns them into fucking machines. Yes, some have acted strangely, but people are strange anyway. It's just dinosaur bones. What harm could it possibly cause?"

"I suggest you and the boys take a couple cups full and see what happens. After all, being a fucking machine is the most important preoccupation you tiny-dicked fools care about."

Wang Wei stood up and backhanded him three times across the face. Cunningham spit on him, which got him a solid punch in the jaw. He tasted blood and felt it drip off his chin on its way down his chest and onto his lap. Wei went back to the front of the plane. Melinda pretended to ignore the entire exchange—until it got physical.

"You should take your own advice, Director, and keep your mouth shut."

Cunningham tilted his head back and squeezed his nostrils shut, hoping to stop the bleeding before throwing up a stomach full of swallowed blood.

Chapter 36

Olivia and Alex were flying over New Mexico after their second refueling stop when Espionto called. They felt like Bonnie and Clyde, landing at small airfields and stealing fuel. Alex would fuel the plane while Olivia held workers at gunpoint.

"I've got you a plane and a pilot," said Espionto. Olivia pushed the speaker icon. "He's a bit of a cowboy, but he knows C-47s like the back of his—"

"C-47? The WWII troop carrier?" asked Alex.

"Well, I couldn't exactly get you a Stealth bomber. It's been updated. You will have to stop in Samoa to refuel. It should make it that far. Don't worry. His name is Captain Randy Clarke. You need to meet him at our supposedly secret airfield twenty miles west of De Anza Springs Resort near Jacumba Hot Springs, not far from San Diego."

"Resort?" Alex's interest piqued.

"Yes, it's a nudist colony," replied Espionto.

"Good. Great. We are to meet a cowboy pilot with an eighty-year-old airplane at a nudist colony and fly across the Pacific to Samoa, if we don't run out of fuel or break down along the way. Perfect. We're on it."

"You don't sound grateful, doctor."

Olivia hollered out in the background, "Sorry, sir. Dr. Winthrop is a smartass. He can't help it. Getting shot in the head didn't help it a bit."

"Excuse me?"

Alex intervened, "Never mind. I think she's oxygen deprived at two thousand feet, sir."

"Okay. Whatever. I'll text coordinates. When will you be there?"

"Maybe three hours. I'll know better when you send directions."

"You have clearance to land at the Simpang Airport outside of Kuala Lumpur. For the last several years, Malaysia has once again been using it partially as an Air Force base. General Najib is in charge. He is no fan of China, but he's under pressure from their president to honor their wishes. He happily gave us permission, however, he said China has also used the base recently. He assured me that the runway you will be using should keep you away from any Chinese. He added that since COVID-H hit, it's practically a ghost town. Most surveillance and service workers have vanished. Your pilot is handling all the logistics."

Halfway between Albuquerque and Phoenix, Alex became restless and distant. Olivia studied him for several minutes.

"You okay?" she asked.

"Sorta. I mean, not so great. Why do you ask?"

"That expression on your face. It worries me. Not very comforting to say the least..."

"Sorry. You're right. There's a lot going on in my head right now. Images and thoughts come out of the blue, bouncing around but never fully resolving. I get a glimpse of something profound then it ends up confusing. Like some perverse twist of the Socratic method, I'm being given enough information to be intrigued or dismayed, but not enough to figure out what it means. I feel like I'm an observer. Like it's not really me. To make matters worse, images from my flashbacks keep inserting themselves into my chaotic revelations. Would you mind taking the wheel?"

"Are you kidding? I don't know how to fly."

"Nothing to it. Just keep heading west for about an hour, then I'll take over. You just hold the wheel and stay on course. Everything else is set."

"Well, okay, but if we die, you won't hear the end of it," threatened Olivia.

Alex did a double-take. "Huh? Just make sure you crash into a building, so I get my forty virgins."

"And what do I get?"

"I don't know...maybe you get to be a virgin."

"You better start practicing your Allahu Akbars."

◇◇

Monotonous desert creeped by below—empty, like the surface of the moon, peaceful and desolate. For the first time, Olivia found herself envious of those who lived off the grid, exposed to no one and self-sufficient. Alex leaned forward with his head in his hands, alone in his thoughts. Thoughts that he couldn't put into words.

"Does your head hurt?" asked Olivia.

"No. Not really. Olivia, I think we should pray. Pray for guidance and strength."

"What? Pray?"

"Yes. Pray. I know you think I'm delusional, but, Olivia, this is a battle between good and evil. God and the Devil. So far, we've listened to the serpent and eaten the apple. That's Satan, two; God, zero. Right now, the Devil has control over how man will use God's dust. I feel that I must make a choice. My mind is demanding it. I don't understand, but if I have to choose, it's a no-brainer. We need faith, science, and a few military tactics."

"Alex. You're freaking me out. You really do believe Satan is behind all of man's nasty shenanigans?"

"I didn't say that. My thoughts are strange, I admit, but I trust them. I trust them more than anything. Just do as I ask. It's not like I'm asking you to jump out of the plane. A while back, you said you'd trust my intuition, remember?"

"Okay. Okay. I guess it can't hurt anything. You said God's dust?"

"Yeah. That's right. God dust."

"Okay, God dust."

"And...my flashback. It was different this time. Everything was the same, but in the end, Julie took my hand and told me something—she told me to trust."

"Your deceased wife spoke to you from the spirit realm?"

"Yes. Something like that."

"What if it's really hallucinations from your head injury? You know as well as I do that's possible."

"Whatever. I think we've been over that already. It hasn't steered us wrong so far, right?"

"No, but it could. Alright, alright, I'll do it. But if you come up with anything too crazy, I'm calling you on it."

"I don't even know if I'll come up with anything, let alone anything drastic."

They sat in silence until they were nearing the airfield and Alex took the controls. Olivia was scared she'd lost the most important person in her life. Had he gone crazy from the God dust and his head injury? Distraught, she began to pray. She didn't know what else to do. A peaceful feeling came over her. A warm flush of well-being surged from her core to her fingertips, like hot cocoa and a warm blanket on a snow-day. *I'll trust him. If I die in the process, so be it. I don't want to live without him.*

"There it is," said Alex as he started to descend. "There's our plane." He circled the small runway once before making his approach.

"That's our plane? It looks like a museum piece."

"It is. It'll be fine."

Olivia put her hand over his and said, "Is this one of those times I'm supposed to trust you?"

"Yup."

Alex taxied alongside the proud C-47. The twin prop troop carrier had probably ferried the 101st Airborne into Normandy in 1945. A man wearing a brown Army t-shirt and camo pants stood under one of the plane's two engines. The cowling was half off and his head was deep inside the compartment. A puddle of oil spread between his feet.

"That's not a good sign," Olivia observed.

"Ah, he's just double-checking."

"You hope."

Randy grinned and shot them a thumbs-up. Light reflected off his bald head. He was muscular, five-ten, with dark brown eyes and sun-aged skin. He'd retired after a career as a pilot with the Army Rangers. That didn't last long. He craved the thrill and comradery. It was the only time he felt right. Like a character out of a Sylvester Stallone action film, he appeared fearless and jovial.

"I think I'm gonna like this guy," said Alex.

"Why am I not surprised?"

"You must be Randy Clarke," shouted Alex as he climbed out of the Cessna.

"That's right, Captain Clarke here. Call me Randy." He reached out his oil-soaked hand for Alex to shake. "And you must be Dr. Winthrop and Dr. Nilsson."

"Yes. You can call us Alex and Olivia," responded Alex, clutching Randy's hand with a firm shake.

"Will do. Hey, I hear we're gonna go kill some chinks. About time." He laughed. "Just pulling your leg...but if the opportunity arises, I'm your man."

"I'll remember that," said Alex.

Olivia whispered, "Good grief. A racist. Espionto wasn't kidding."

"Randy, I have something you need to take. It's a medicine that'll keep you from getting COVID-H," said Alex.

"I don't usually take shit like that, doc."

"We can't have you dying and leaving us stranded in Malaysia with no way to bring back enough of it to save our country. You're a patriot, right?"

"That's right. Sure. I'll take it. It ain't a shot, is it? I'd rather be shot with a bullet. Don't ask me why."

"No shot. You just swallow a few grains of it and you're good to go." Alex reached into his pocket and pulled out a little vial containing a tiny bit of God dust. He took out a pen, licked the end of it, and dabbed it into the vial, picking up just a few specks. "Here ya go. Down the hatch." Randy took the pen and licked off the barely visible dust.

"Is that it?" asked Randy.

"That's it," replied Alex.

"It won't get me high, will it?"

"Nah. If it did, I wouldn't be sharing it with you." Alex grinned.

Randy walked toward the open door on the side of the fuselage and pointed inside. "I didn't know what to bring, so I packed up the usual. Guns, ammo, explosives, food, tents, medicine for jungle rot, and some extra fatigues. I think I even got y'all some genuine US Army underwear. Got an added bonus too. A Minigun that throws out six thousand rounds a minute. Used them in Vietnam. Man, they were gook-splattering machines."

"Sounds good," said Alex.

Olivia walked curiously around the plane. Her wrinkled forehead and fake grin gave away her impression. She knew better than to say anything disparaging. It wouldn't help or change anything.

"Ya gonna kick the tires, doc?" joked Randy while she completed her inspection.

"Are you kidding? They might fall off."

"You're funny, ma'am. I like that," he added, handing them

coats and gloves. "The heater isn't great, and you'll need oxygen. She's not pressurized. Okay. Let's mount up and take to the clouds, shall we?"

"What about parachutes?" asked Olivia.

"There's a couple in here. We've got a raft, so as long as we don't get killed in the crash, we could at least float around until we starve or die of dehydration. I'd rather go down with the plane than parachute into the ocean and get eaten by sharks or flat out drown," answered Randy.

"Good point," replied Olivia, embarrassed she hadn't thought of that. On the other hand, she still liked the idea of parachutes.

◇◇

The roar of the two Pratt and Whitney engines was deafening. Plumes of white smoke blew back over the wings. Alex put one hand under Olivia's right butt cheek to help her into the plane. With little effort, he lifted her off the ground.

Olivia turned around and looked down at him. "What was that?"

"I don't know. It only felt like I gave you a little push, say, about enough to lift twenty pounds, not a hundred and thirty."

"A hundred and twenty, thank you." He turned away to avoid her glare.

The engine noise wasn't much better inside the plane even with the door shut. Randy began flicking switches and checking to make sure the ailerons and flaps were functional.

"What are you doing?" shouted Alex, as he watched Randy climb under the instrument panel.

"Tightening a cable. The left wing aileron's a bit sluggish."

Olivia tried to hide her dread. Alex felt it without looking at her as he climbed into the copilot seat. There were four seats behind the cockpit, two on each side, facing each other. Further down the fuselage were four cots with khaki blankets. Supplies, including food, water, camping equipment, extra H cylinders of oxygen, ammo, and weapons were piled up in the rear of the plane.

"That Minigun is a beaut," said Alex.

"Fuckin'-a-right, buddy. Sure glad the Taliban didn't have those suckers mounted on the back of their silly-ass Toyota pickup trucks."

"They still couldn't hit anything."

"Ha. You're probably right. A one-armed blind man facing backwards could out-shoot those losers. Okay, here we go," he said as he eased the throttle forward.

They flew into the setting sun. Bright white light shimmered and danced off the waves below, sparkling when lined up just right.

"We're going to settle in at twenty thousand feet. You'll need your oxygen. Hey, honey," he shouted behind him. "You can turn on the seat heater with that button near the right front leg."

"Call me Olivia, Captain."

He turned to Alex and asked, "Is she always so touchy?"

"It just takes her a few minutes to accept the idea of certain death."

Randy yelled back to Olivia, "Don't worry, honey, everything's gonna be fine."

Alex and Randy talked non-stop. Olivia couldn't hear a word they were saying and sleeping was impossible.

"Hey, Randy, do you have anything to read?" she shouted.

"There might be a *Hustler* or a *Penthouse* under the seat."

"Thanks, but I'm up to date on female anatomy."

Randy laughed.

"After we refuel in Samoa, we'll be landing at a remote private airstrip near Sungai Koyan, eighty miles from Kuala Lumpur. The owners catered to military flights, favoring the US or China, depending on the political climate. We'll have a vehicle waiting. Where to from there, doctor?"

"Let me first tell you the back story." Alex filled him in with selected details.

"That's some serious shit, doc. But one problem; it doesn't sound like you know where the barrels of medicine are."

"No. I don't know where they are taking them. I have an address for the traditional medicine dealer, Li Jun, in Kuala Lumpur. He's the one who sold the medicine that we call God dust as a supplement to improve virility. However, they realized that it prevented infection from COVID-H." Grinning, Alex said, "Anyway, I thought we could beat the shit out of him until he tells us something."

"That sounds like fun. I'll cut off his mini-dick and stuff it down his throat, then tell him it's good for his virility. That's pretty funny, right, doc? Besides that little distraction, I still don't hear much of a plan."

"That's all I got."

"Um...why do you call it God dust?"

"It's a long story, Randy. A very long and complicated story. I'll give you the condensed and somewhat redacted version."

"Well, we've got plenty of time to chat, doc."

Randy was accustomed to very precise operational planning. However, he also fancied himself as an expert tracker. "We have some people in Kuala Lumpur. If they haven't been snuffed by your virus, I could try to reach them and see if they could monitor some of the airports."

"That's awesome. Ah...Randy, it's not my virus."

Chapter 37

Monday mornings were no different than any other day at the White House. Bad news, problems without solutions, and nations biting off their fingers to point them at others were standard fare. The main air conditioner was down and body odor concentrated by stress, anxiety, and fear wafted into noses desensitized by the gift of habituation. The men weren't shaving and the women wore baseball caps. Nobody planned next year's vacation. An air of hopelessness crept in. That belief numbed frontal lobes and shot inhibitions over the bow of morality. Sex and alcohol competed with more appropriate coping methods, especially among younger staff members. It wasn't a big surprise to walk into an office and find a couple going at it on a desk.

Four things happened that Monday morning that got everybody's attention. The first three were: The President's condemnation of the sport-fuck, drunkenness, and bad hygiene— all while slinging a mug full of whiskey at nine a.m. Executive privilege. General Tousick delivered the fourth.

"Mr. President, General Tousick is here to see you," announced the President's secretary, Tim Smith, a twenty-four-year-old Harvard grad trying to make his way in government...when he wasn't working on Kate Kawalski. She was Sean Finnegan's aide, and too good-looking to be around powerful men. Tim was a safer dalliance, albeit a temporary distraction.

"Send him in, Tim," responded the President through the intercom.

"Good morning, Mr. President."

"Good morning, General Tousick."

"Our surveillance has picked up activity around nuclear weapon complexes in numerous countries. As you would suspect, China, Russia, North Korea, and Iran show the most activity."

"I thought Iran didn't have any nukes...just kidding, Tousick," quipped the President.

"They all know China has accused us of withholding a cure for COVID-H."

"So turning the world into ashes is a smart solution? Geezus! Where is this cure that Shenberg said we were working on? Don't those countries know our people are still dying by the millions?"

"I don't know, sir. But maybe we can play it to our advantage."

"How's that?"

"We don't want them to think our military has been weakened by COVID-H deaths. Why don't we leak information suggesting that all our military has been treated with the cure...that our military is strong, healthy, and ready? I know for a fact that theirs are being decimated."

"Tousick," said the President, tapping his chin. "It doesn't take a large military to launch nukes, now does it? I like the intimidation idea except that it could backfire."

"Yes, sir. Mr. President, concerning our ICBM defense systems...they're limited. China and Russia have perfected their maneuverable hypersonic glide vehicles. We don't have a reliable way to detect them in time. This is why—"

"Why we have to strike first, right, General? When do we know when that magic moment is?"

"I'm sorry, sir, but that is your decision."

"I know that. I know, but you are fully aware that I don't have any better idea than you do, General. I don't know if it matters who shoots first...does it? Does it matter if I die an hour before or after President Chen, or Putin? Does it?"

"I'm here to give you information, sir. Would you like to hear the details?"

"Shit. Sure. Let's see if it makes me reach for the Red Phone. I'm getting bored with all this anyway."

"Sir?"

"Just screwing with you, General. Don't be so damned concrete."

"Yes, sir."

◇◇

The burden of yet one more regret weighed on Shane Bullock like a sudden doubling of gravity. He avoided her eyes. Jan's aura of post-coital bliss repulsed him. He wanted to go back to the apartment and be with his wife, get drunk, and hope he forgot all about succumbing to a penis whisperer. *It's my fault. At least she's not married. Paula's been so good to me. So loyal and patient. Is this how I reward her?* He'd reached the golden pinnacle of his career. A time of wisdom and righteous pride. Then, over a mere two years, he'd systematically sabotaged everything that mattered to him. His only escape from a darkened legacy depended on COVID-H bleeding mankind to death. *Maybe my Wikipedia page will gloss over my total loss of integrity. Hell, there may not be any more Wikipedia!*

◇◇

Charles' body began to rot, melting into the cushioned chair like warm wax. Mango did not have to nibble on her master's corpse; she feasted on the rodents that did. The housing development on the other side of the tree line had been reclaimed by nature. Abandoned dreams of eager homeowners.

Back in Lake County, coyotes dug up Miss Jenny. Their celebratory yelps were muted by the river's wall of white noise. Becoming food for hungry animals was Charles' and Miss Jenny's final act of kindness. If critters could vote, they'd surely outlaw cremation.

Farmers had to turn their farms into high security outposts to prevent theft of field crops, cattle, chickens, and pigs. Sheep that had been used for wool became food. Goats and horses that had been pets were dinner. For the most part, farmers helped to feed their neighbors. People with a little land began to grow vegetables and raise a few chickens. Many hunted for meat. Families were drawn together to aid in the fight for survival. There was migration to the south to escape the upcoming winter cold. Power grids were failing. Fuel and potable water were scarce. Air pollution from cars and factories was replaced by smoke from burning wood. Diabetics and others dependent on medication died. The natural order of survival of the fittest had returned. Some religious leaders and philosophers called it "a cleansing."

People fled the cities, setting up camp wherever they could. Every RV and camper in the country was put to use. Those that had the means to purchase fuel and food at exorbitant prices often remained in areas of higher population density. As a result, they were dying at a much higher rate than those who were rural and isolated. America was quickly learning to live like it did during the pre-industrial age but without the lure of city jobs. A very steep learning curve. Many died in the process, unable to adjust to frontier life.

Gangs and militias began to form and conducted raids to obtain necessities. They were typically short-lived because COVID-H quickly spread rapidly among them. The virus made the rules and exacted swift punishment for those who didn't obey. COVID-H was a feared dictator.

As expected, the effects of America's dependence on China reared its ugly head. The death knell to the economy occurred when trade came to a screeching halt. Those that relied on government assistance became self-sufficient or perished. There was no further debate about entitlement. Nursing homes became morgues. Grand examples of how consequences that exceeded the pain point changed behavior. The arrogance of mankind—humbled.

COVID-H was no different than mankind. It did whatever it could to survive, and as its population grew, resources dwindled. For COVID-H, living humans were the necessary resource. Nothing lasts forever.

Chapter 38

The Feleolo Airport in Samoa runs along transparent turquoise waters of the Apolima Strait. One plane sat near a lone hangar fifty yards off the runway. The shore appeared to be only yards from the runway. Olivia began taking deep breaths, silently fearing they were going to end up surfing. Randy showed no signs of concern when a tailwind pushed the plane sideways, directing the C-47 oceanward.

"You never said anything about a water landing," said Olivia.

"Good thing I brought that raft, right? I'm sure the water's pretty warm. Sharks? Who knows?" teased Randy. "Just a little tailwind. I'll come around and try again. Ya get a pretty good breeze off the water."

"I'd tend to agree with that," added Olivia.

Alex admired how Randy handled the plane. Olivia didn't share his sentiment. When the plane landed and came to a halt, Randy sat still, looking carefully in every direction. Alex unbuckled his seatbelt and started to get up.

"Wait. Let's make sure nothing looks suspicious. Standard procedure," said Randy, putting his hand around Alex's arm.

"Gotcha. There's a fuel tank over there." Alex pointed out his window.

A Samoan man in shorts, t-shirt, and an orange nylon vest jogged up to the plane.

"Fuel, sir?" he yelled.

"Fill 'er up, bro," Randy yelled back.

Several tall palms had punched their way above the rainforest. To the south, Mount Tafua stood out above the flatlands, signaling to travelers that the shore was ten kilometers away. It was eerily quiet once the engines were shut down. Accustomed to shouting, it took a few minutes for the three of them to lower their voices. They began to sweat as the sun beat down on the plane's dark camo roof, and humid air entered the cabin. Fifteen minutes earlier, they were freezing at fifteen thousand feet.

The airport attendant banged on the side of the plane and yelled, "You're all set. Have a safe flight." Randy gave him a thumbs-up.

"We should be over Malaysia by morning," said Randy as the engines sputtered, puffed smoke, and came to life. Once in the air, he responded to a radio signal. It was one of the men he'd asked to monitor the airports. The man told him all but two airports had spotters in position.

"That's great, Randy. I've never been to Malaysia, but I can picture it vividly," said Alex. Olivia shot him a knowing glance. "Why don't you let me take over? Get a little rest. I can keep altitude and course for a few hours," offered Alex.

"I could use a little nap. I figure it'll take thirteen hours without a headwind to get to Malaysia." He went to the back and lay on one of the cots. He was snoring in thirty seconds. Olivia climbed into the copilot seat and curiously viewed the wall of vintage dials, switches, and knobs.

She wrestled with Alex's uncertain transformation. Overall, he was the same as always, but it was obvious there was something going on with him. It was frightening to not know. *How long will it last? Will it progress? Am I going to lose him?* Out of the blue, she asked, "Do you have premonitions?" Before he could answer, she added, "Is it getting stronger, or…?"

"No, it's not getting stronger. Premonitions? No. Not really.

It's hard to explain. Any little tidbit of thought or information conjures up memories I didn't know I had, and I get a sense about things, not a clear picture, like I'm getting a little nudge this way or that. It's made me realize just how much we forget over time. Maybe it has a survival benefit? I can see, in my mind's eye, hear, and smell every memory as it unfolds. It's a bit overwhelming. Seems I'm getting used to it, or it's slowly fading. I don't know."

"Do you feel aggressive, or vi—?"

"No, Olivia. No more than usual." He chuckled. "Thank God for that."

"Maybe it won't happen to you...you are sorta different. Special like. Ya know?"

"Ah, no, I don't. And I'm not sure I like the inference.

"On a serious note, you know my head wound healed almost overnight. I should still be in a coma. That's so amazing."

"Good thing. Otherwise, I'd be pushing you around in a wheelbarrow. Not sure I'd be up for changing your Depends. That's above my pay grade."

"Aw, baby, I know you'd do anything for me."

"Everybody has limits."

"Phssh. I'd change yours...well, maybe not #2."

They watched the sun set behind the curved horizon. Alex stared at the altimeter as darkness hid the ocean. The old C-47 didn't have autopilot or computer-generated audio warnings. It was up to him.

◇◇

Melinda put her handcuffed hands over her face when the pilot informed the passengers there was an engine problem and they needed to land. The pilot wanted to make it to Borneo, but a hundred miles off the north coast of New Guinea, the left engine dropped to half power, forcing them to land. Rendani Airport in Irian Jaya was the closest. They were grounded in New Guinea for most of the day to repair the Boeing 737's fuel control fault.

Fortunately for them, they found a mechanic who repaired the engine—at gunpoint. They took him hostage to assure he hadn't sabotaged the engine or blabbed about what he saw. Once they were in the air and the engine was running fine, they threw the mechanic out the door. Melinda screamed at the men as they laughed and sat back down in their first-class seats and swirled their martinis.

The 737 pilot pushed the throttle forward, settling in near the jet's top-end of 530 miles per hour. They'd passed the Manado peninsula and were over the Celebes Sea when Wei called to the copilot, asking how much longer they'd be in the air.

"Sixteen hundred miles to Malaysia. We'll be landing in about three and a half hours," shouted the co-pilot through the open cockpit door.

Cunningham looked at his watch. "It'll be around 8:00 a.m. when we get there."

Melinda nodded. "Tuesday, right?"

"Yeah. Tuesday, June 6th. D-Day. What a coincidence."

Their stop in New Guinea gave the C-47 time to get within nine-hundred miles of Malaysia. With a top speed of 240 miles per hour, Randy would be landing at about the same time as the Chinese.

◇◇

The sun rose behind them, illuminating the landmass that lay ahead. Alex stayed on course. A few minutes later, Randy shook off his nap and walked into the cockpit.

"Where are we?"

"Look ahead. I think that's Borneo," answered Alex.

"According to our coordinates...yup, that should be Borneo. We'll be over Malaysia soon. Why'd you let me sleep so long?"

"You'd been up for twenty hours. Figured you needed it," answered Alex.

"Aw, thanks...Mom."

A call came over the radio. It was one of Randy's spotters. "Captain Clarke, I'm here at the Sungai Koyan airport. Looks like your Chinese friends are coming in. A 737 just touched down."

"Perfect. Can we land a fair distance from them?"

"There's two runways. I'll tell the controller you need to land on the B strip. Captain, there's only a few people here. They say every last one of their security guards has died from COVID-H."

"Good. Don't need them snooping around anyway."

"Yes, sir."

"We should be there in twenty minutes. Keep me apprised of the 737 crew's activity, okay? Thanks. Over and out."

Alex reached for Olivia's hand and caught her index finger. That small touch calmed and excited him like a first kiss. Their eyes locked in a familiar way. A look that said, "It's real. There's no turning back."

Fifteen minutes later, Randy turned his head and shouted, "Buckle up. We're landing."

◇◇

Two SUVs and an old military troop carrier truck pulled alongside the 737. One man stayed on board the jet to keep tabs on Melinda and Cunningham. They watched several men struggle to remove the cargo and load it into the back of the truck. A limo pulled up and a rotund well-dressed Asian man got out. He was the perfect caricature of a rich gangster, sporting black sunglasses, fat gold chain around his neck, a floral shirt unbuttoned one button too many, and greasy black hair combed straight back.

"I wonder who the bigshot is," said Cunningham, peering out the window. "Maybe it's your buddy, Li Jun."

"Yeah, maybe it is. You won't let up, will you, Cunningham? Don't forget, I had a good reason to get the dust. A saving the world kinda reason."

"So did I, my dear girl. I suspect I'll know if you're telling the truth before they dispose of us. One thing we know for certain."

"What's that?"

"It doesn't matter what our motives are now."

"Come on, you two. It's time for another adventure," said their guard while poking Cunningham in the chest with the barrel of his rifle.

They were herded toward the first of two well-worn Land Rovers. As Melinda stepped in, she glanced at the man by the limo. Li Jun was already staring at her. Cunningham caught sight of the C-47 close to a hundred yards away. He knew it belonged to the US, but what really got his attention was that one of the three people facing him looked like a female with the same silver-blonde hair as Olivia's.

"That's Melinda," said Olivia, almost waving.

"I'll bet those barrels are full of God dust," added Alex.

"Hey, you two," said Randy. "I have an idea. But meanwhile, stop staring at them. They'll know we're up to something. I've got some GPS tabs. Wish I could get near them. Ha! I got it." He yelled to his spotter who'd just driven up in an airport vehicle that looked like a golf cart with an extra seat in back. "Chip, do you think you could stick a GPS tab on that truck? You look pretty official."

"I can go ask them if they need help, or if somebody needs a ride to the terminal, or if they're planning on refueling, etcetera. The worst thing they can do is shoot me. I'm packing, but I bet they all are too." He and Randy had served together in Iraq. They were cut from the same cloth.

"What the hell? A military Humvee?" said Alex as a Humvee with an enclosed rear bed approached them while they unloaded supplies.

"It's the only thing I could get," said Randy. "All the slick black Suburbans were taken. This is far cooler, and there's room for the Minigun. Speaking of which, I could turn them all into hamburger in about five seconds."

Alex nodded. "Man, that would be great, but there's one big problem."

"What's that?" asked Randy.

"They've got two hostages. A CIA man and the girl's a scientist."

"Crap. Alright, let's just load it up," said Randy.

Chip drove down the tarmac toward the 737. He nodded cordially at the men, pulled up behind their truck, leaned out, and stuck a GPS tab inside the bumper when he was out of view. Randy and Alex stopped and watched Chip walk up and talk with the men for about fifteen seconds. As he drove off, the men opened fire. Chip slumped over the wheel. The cart veered left and continued off the tarmac for around fifty yards before coming to a halt. Randy flew up the steps into the plane, yanked open the firing port, and started to push the Minigun into position.

"No! Randy, no!" shouted Alex. Randy ignored him. Alex ran toward him and kicked the gun's supports to the side, sending the gun toppling to the floor.

"Dammit, Alex, I sent him over there...now he's dead. Bastards. It's my fault. I can't let them get away with it."

"Randy, listen to me. You will get your chance, and when you do, you can kill them all twice." Randy dropped onto a cot and buried his face in his hands, hiding his tears.

Olivia poked her head into the fuselage, shouting, "Hurry up, they're getting ready to leave." Both men grabbed one end of the gun and lugged it into the back of the Humvee. The driver joined in and carried out the ammo cases. They were all in the Humvee when the convoy started to leave.

"Let's give them a minute or two to get some distance between us," said Randy to the driver. He put his hand on the Humvee driver's shoulder and asked, "Who are you, son?"

"Corporal Bill White from motor pool, sir."

"Good to meet you. I'm Captain Clarke. Can someone pick

you up at the terminal? You don't need to get in the middle of this."

"Yes, sir."

"Okay, Corporal, let's go."

Malaysia has two seasons, monsoons with sweltering heat, and stifling humidity with sweltering heat. They headed west on Route 102, traveling through miles of palm forest, harvested for palm oil. Thirty minutes into their drive, the GPS signal went off the main road, disappearing into the forest.

Randy was quiet, obviously shaken by Chip's murder. Alex and Olivia knew nothing they said would help. They turned onto an unmarked dirt road and slowly started to go uphill. Dust from the Chinese convoy was still in the air. Palm branches continuously swiped the Humvee. From a clearing, they could see Malaysia's main mountain range. The road was leading them toward Gunung Liam West, a mountain at the south end of the chain. They came upon a buffoonery of orangutans that scattered in front of them. A few moments later, trumpeting pygmy elephants could be heard in the distance, warning stragglers to catch up with the herd. By then, all the forest's critters within a mile were on alert.

Alex was checking over his AR-15 when he was struck by a surge of predatory rage. He could almost taste the blood of the men who stole the God dust, killed Chip, and abducted Melinda and Cunningham. Images from the explosion that killed his wife Julie and their twins darted before his eyes. He could smell their burnt flesh. Revenge would be exacted on these men.

Olivia saw his face and beads of sweat. She knew what was happening.

"Alex, Alex!" From the back seat, she reached her arms around his shoulders and squeezed without saying anything more.

He turned his head to look at her, and whispered, "I'm okay. I'll be okay."

Olivia fell back in her seat, wondering which of these two men would explode first.

Chapter 39

President Chen and Premier Zadong entered the main conference room at Zhongnanhai to join other top officials of the Chinese Communist Party. Beijing's Zhongnanhai Imperial Garden and Wanshou Palace were constructed in 1471 during the Ming dynasty. It was an opulent display of classic Chinese architecture, including strict adherence to feng shui. Chairman Mao Zedong moved to the site in 1949 after forming the People's Republic of China. It has remained the Chinese "White House" ever since.

They sat in ancient rosewood Quanyi circular backed chairs and made small talk while waiting for their president. Their expressions were flat, concealing any feelings of anxiety or fear. For men in leadership positions, composure ranked close to loyalty. Seven men and one woman stood and bowed toward Chen and Zadong as they entered the room.

"Gentlemen," said President Chen, ignoring the presence of a female. "We have obtained America's cure. After testing and packaging, we will begin mass distribution. This is for your ears only until I give further instructions. Nonetheless, I have not excluded the possibility of a full military assault on the United States and what's left of their allies."

Contagious grinning replaced emotionless posing. General Zao looked down to conceal his glee. The rules of composure still applied to him. The general had been admiring his country's growing cache of nukes for twenty-five years. He was itching to see them in action. The woman and three of the men believed that nuclear war should be off the table, yet they smiled in compliance along with everybody else. President Chen then announced that seven of the scientists who developed the failed COVID-H vaccine had been executed. That was much easier than admitting he was wrong to order the release of COVID-H in the first place. There's nothing like a few executions to keep your underlings loyal.

Zadong was an astute observer and concerned by Chen's increasing aggressiveness. Addressing it would be a delicate if not dangerous undertaking.

Through Li Jun's government connections, all of Chen's cabinet members had received a single capsule of dust. Chen, on the other hand, took as much as he wanted until he received word that higher doses could be dangerous. Of the first five government officials who took the dust-laden capsules for its alleged virility-enhancing capabilities, one had committed suicide, one was killed in an altercation, and the other three were locked up for psychiatric management. No one knew what would happen when the dust was widely distributed.

There had been no communication between Presidents Chen and Triagin. Chen wanted the American president to squirm with fear and uncertainty. President Triagin attempted to intimidate Chen with a continual presence of military jets along the edge of China's airspace. Chen had one major worry: He believed that the American military was intact and healthy since he assumed the COVID-H cure was in widespread use. The seas were thick with US submarines loaded with nuclear warheads. That much was certain.

Chen believed President Triagin wanted him dead for releasing COVID-H. In turn, he wanted to vaporize the United States in retaliation for the BN27 mishap and withholding the

COVID-H cure. Two mistaken beliefs.

✧✧

It was Tuesday morning and mothers chatted while their young children entertained themselves on slides, swings, and seesaws. Mount Weather's playground was built during the Cold War when entire families first lived on site. It was decrepit, but the kids didn't notice. Their only complaint was splinters. The weathered wood freely implanted little shards of wood into unsuspecting derrieres. Parents groaned at the thought of trying to restrain their child long enough to extract the tiny spikes from their tender butt cheeks.

Paula sat at the kitchen table with her coffee and watched the children play. *What does the future hold for them? Will they ever leave here alive?*

Shane was deep underground at a lab bench studying recently acquired data. Jan tootled around, not doing anything in particular.

She walked around the table and sat directly opposite from him. "Are you going to leave her?" she asked.

"Leave? Leave Paula?" he replied.

"Yes. Who else would I be talking about?"

"I never said I was, Jan."

"We had sex. Of course, I figured you'd leave her. I'm not just some cheap fling."

"I'm sorry, Jan, I had no idea you—"

"No idea? Well, now you know. For a genius, you sure make some bad choices…like leaving your computer on." She swiveled off her bench-stool and walked over to him, rapping a pencil on the back of her hand so hard, it reminded him of having his hands smacked by Sister Mary's ruler while attending St. Anne's elementary school. The nun's corporal approach to discipline was very effective.

"What are you talking about?" Bullock pulled off his reading glasses and let them dangle from their chain. He turned to face her.

"You're mine now, Shane."

"What the hell's wrong with you? You're not acting right."

"Leave her, or I'll have to share what I mistakenly saw on your computer a few months ago. Remember when we were talking in your office and you jumped up to tend to that leaking liquid nitrogen tank? You left what looked like an encrypted communication between you and some Chinese open on your laptop. I saw that they'd paid you thirty thousand dollars. I might be wrong, but I don't think you're supposed to be taking payments from the Chinese while working for the D.O.D."

He was silent, imagining a humiliating end to a brilliant career. "You don't have to do that. I'll leave her. Just give me some time," he pleaded, hoping she'd buy his ruse.

Jan grabbed his wrist with such force, he winced in pain. "Please me now, Shane."

Chapter 40

The little red GPS dot they'd been following came to a stop a little over a hundred yards ahead of them. Randy hit the brakes. There was no plan for what to do next. Embarrassed, they gazed out the window, waiting for somebody to say something.

Alex pointed ahead. "Look, on the right, ahead. Might be an old logging trail. We can find a place to lay low for a bit."

The logging road was overgrown. Randy struggled to maneuver over or around young trees until he realized that the Humvee could do more than he thought. He'd driven them in the desert, but never a jungle. Palms became less prominent, giving way to more typical rain forest flora. They'd gone about a half-mile when Olivia said, "Stop." She listened to the hiss of white noise in the distance. "Do you hear that? Water. There's water ahead."

Alex nodded. Randy shook his head. "I don't hear any...wait, now I do. Let's check it out."

The trees gave way to rocky terrain a short distance from a ravine. They parked and walked to the edge. Fifty feet below was a swift-running narrow river churning violently over boulders and drop-offs. Cool moist air rose up bathing their sweat soaked faces. An oriental pied hornbill flew down the center of the crevice.

"What the hell? That bird has two beaks?" asked Randy, referring to what appeared to be an auxiliary beak protruding from the hornbill's forehead.

"It's called a casque. It's an air-filled tube...like a horn," lectured Olivia.

"I didn't know you were a bird expert," said Alex.

"I'm not. I just saw a picture of one once and looked it up."

"Let's grab our guns and walk up river a ways...see what we can find," suggested Alex, looking up at the darkening sky. "I'd say we're about to get soaked."

Randy put a clip in his ASM/DT amphibious rifle while Alex got out two AK-47s. They loaded up backpacks with water and ammo and headed up a trail made by animals searching for a place to cross the river.

"Snake. Wait." Alex put out his arm like a school crossing guard.

"That's a pit viper. Nasty things," said Randy as he prodded it with his rifle. The snake recoiled and struck his gun barrel several times before slithering off into the forest.

"I don't like snakes," added Olivia.

"Just watch where you're walking," said Alex.

"Duh," she said, shaking her head.

"Let me walk ahead," said Alex. "I can smell them."

Randy looked at Olivia. "What'd he say?"

"You heard him. He's got a very keen sense of smell. Like a dog." Olivia assumed his heightened senses were all part of his transformation. *What else has changed?*

"Okay, Fido, lead the way. No argument here," chided Randy.

They'd been walking for twenty minutes when they heard voices. A clap of thunder startled them, and it began to pour, a welcome break from the heat. The sound of large raindrops smacking oversized leaves drowned out any noise they made climbing through the underbrush. From the edge of the forest, they could see a building overlooking the ravine. The one-story wooden structure was made partly from wood harvested from the site, but mostly from materials that had been hauled in. The roof was corrugated aluminum and the walls were wooden. A porch jutted out the back, giving the inhabitants a gorgeous view of the ravine and the river below. Next to the main building was a ten by twenty shipping container that had been converted into living quarters.

Once again, they stood silently, sizing up their dilemma. Randy had taken part in hostage extraction before. Espionto had connected them to the right man. Li Jun was outside talking with two of the well-dressed men that had been on the flight. The others unloaded the barrels and lined them up behind the converted shipping container. Cunningham and Melinda were escorted to the container and locked inside. They counted four men with automatic weapons standing guard.

The sun was beginning to set. They needed a plan—ASAP. Randy suggested they go back and get the Minigun. He and Alex grimaced at the thought of toting nearly two hundred pounds of ammo and equipment up the trail. The gun itself weighed eighty-five pounds, but the lithium battery used to power the rotor motor weighed in at thirty-five. Then there were the cases of 7.62 mm ammunition. It would take several trips.

"I can try to get the Humvee a bit closer. The rain should cover the noise," said Randy.

"Good. Yeah, let's get on it," said Alex. "Randy, would you man the Mini while we move in and scope out where people are, activity, etcetera."

"My pleasure. I can't believe those idiots are keeping your people in a separate building. Makes it a lot easier for us."

Just then, two men went to the container building and brought Melinda out to speak with Li Jun.

"What the hell? What's that about?" asked Olivia.

Alex looked into Olivia's eyes. "You don't want to hear what I think."

"No, Alex, she's not a bad guy. No way."

A few minutes later, Li Jun pointed to the main building. Melinda nodded and walked in. Alex curiously watched Olivia's expression. If Melinda stayed there, Randy's hopes of ending the siege by ripping the building and its inhabitants to shreds with the Minigun would be dashed.

"Olivia, take cover here while we get the gun," said Alex.

They were immersed in a dark, starless night by the time the intimidating weapon was set up and ready. Their enthusiasm waned with the realization they might never get to use it. Melinda had not come out of the building. Randy and Alex both wanted the satisfaction of a loud, exhilarating massacre.

"Olivia, do you know how to handle that thing?" asked Randy, pointing at the AK-47 hanging off her shoulder.

Before she could answer, Alex said, "Like a champ."

"So why would a lady scientist know how to use an automatic weapon?"

"Randy, it's a long story, but trust me, I know how," replied Olivia.

"She's also a Kung Fu master," Alex said with an expectant grin.

"It's Taekwondo," Olivia hissed.

"Well, okay then, why don't you two Ninja Turtles go do a little recon."

For the next ten minutes, Olivia and Alex inched their way closer to the building. Two guards stood chatting out front. Mosquitoes and biting ants swarmed them as they crawled through pasty mud. Luckily, or by evolutionary design, adrenaline, fear, and focus subdued the discomfort. Soon they could smell fish, garlic, and slightly burnt palm oil. Laughter lubricated by liquor gave them a modicum of confidence.

They approached the back of the building, using the porch as cover. Intermittently, they glanced into the window. The men were playing cards and passing a bottle of whiskey around.

Melinda sat on a stool thumbing through a magazine, unrestrained. After a few minutes, Melinda walked into what must have been a bedroom and closed the door. Several minutes later, the light in her room went off. Alex and Olivia assumed she'd gone to bed. They waited another ten minutes. Melinda never came back out. Soon after, guards who had been posted outside went in to join the others. Alex pointed to the container. They inched their way to the far side of the container and whispered through a barred window.

"Director. Director," said Alex. Cunningham must have been sleeping on the floor.

"Well, I'll be. What the hell are you doing here?"

"We were out for a stroll, so we thought we'd drop by and say hi," snickered Alex.

"Always a smart ass, right, doctor?"

"Sad but true, Director. Okay, listen, there's three of us. Captain Randy Clarke, retired special forces, is aiming a Minigun our way as we speak."

"Minigun? You mean the machine-gun-Minigun?"

"Yes."

"Good God. This could be fun."

"We think Melinda just retired to her bedroom for the night."

"Poor thing. I hope she finds the accommodations suitable," whispered Cunningham.

"Now who's the smartass? I'll go back and let Randy know what's going on. When I return, we'll signal him when to open up. I'll shoot off your lock and we'll finish clearing out the building. Got it?"

"Sounds good," said Cunningham.

Alex started back toward Randy. Olivia followed him a few feet and whispered, "Do you trust him enough to let him out in the middle of all this?"

"Yup."

"You're crazy. Let's just leave him there until it's over…or just shoot him now."

"Trust me on this."

Alex ran through the plan with Randy, hoping he'd agree. He listened but didn't answer for several moments, then he nodded. "Sure, sounds as good as anything I'd come up with."

"Remember, shoot to the right of the window on the far left."

"I'll try not to shoot your friend, bro."

"I need to signal you when we're in position. Watch for my flashlight by the container. When you see it, light 'em up."

"My pleasure," said Randy, snapping a roll of ammo onto the Mini.

Alex gave him a thumbs-up as he started back to the encampment. He retraced his steps back to Olivia. They crouched behind the container and double-checked their guns. Alex turned to Olivia and cupped her face in his hands, bringing her lips to his.

"Ready?" he asked.

"I'm always ready."

"Oh really? Okay, here goes." He pointed his flashlight in Randy's direction and turned it on and off two times.

Within ten seconds, over five hundred rounds from the Minigun ripped through the ravine-side lodge, nearly splitting it in two. Randy paused for a moment and then resumed with another fifteen-second burst. Two men came around from the back of the house shooting at the easy-to-spot muzzle flash. Alex aimed and took the two men down. Then there was silence.

"Did they get Randy?" asked Olivia.

"I hope not. There he is, running toward us. Great, let's go." Alex ran around to the front of the container and shot off the lock. Without stopping, he bolted around to the back deck. Randy was already inside. Olivia went around the front. Just as they stepped inside, they heard a single gunshot followed by a short burst of automatic weapon fire. Alex and Olivia hit the floor. From across the room, their eyes connected, sharing a questioning glance. After a few seconds of quiet, Alex got up on his knees and crawled along the wall, working his way to reveal the obvious. Melinda lay dead, riddled with bullets, with a pistol at her side. Randy was face-down, motionless, still gripping his rifle. By the time Alex got to him, his grip had faded along with his last breath. Olivia rushed past them to Melinda. She knelt by her side and wept.

Li Jun lay crumpled under the card table in the main room, wounded but alert. Olivia spotted him and came out of the bedroom aiming her rifle at his head. Scattered around her were four bodies shredded by the Minigun.

"You're Li Jun, right?" barked Olivia.

"Yes."

Suddenly, Alex shouted, "Cunningham! Crap, where is he?" He ran back outside, looking frantically through the darkness toward the container but saw motion at the edge of the ravine. Olivia poked her head out of the main building's front door.

"What the fuck are you doing?" yelled Alex, pointing his gun, but it was too late to keep Cunningham from rolling the last barrel of dust off the edge into the ravine. Alex took aim. Cunningham put up his hands.

"Don't shoot me until I have a chance to explain. It's important. You need to listen to me, Alex."

"For God's sake! Are you a spy or a friggin' lunatic?"

"No, Alex. Neither. Listen to me."

"Get inside," ordered Alex.

Cunningham stepped into the building to be met by the barrel of Olivia's AR. "You son of a bitch," said Olivia, taking a step closer to him.

"No! Olivia. Don't!" screamed Alex. Slowly, she let the gun fall to her side and then to the floor.

Li Jun let out a painful moan, drawing their attention. Alex walked over to him and crouched down beside him.

"Olivia, keep your gun on the Director. He twitches—shoot him."

Li Jun was hit in the right side, likely through his liver and kidney, before the bullet exited his back.

"If you want to live, tell us the entire story, asshole, from start to finish," demanded Alex.

Li Jun hesitated. Alex jammed his index finger into the entrance wound. "Start talking, big guy."

"I met Charles years ago in Africa. He ran some product for us…"

"Product?" asked Olivia. "You mean animal parts…endangered species…rhino horns, right? You dimwits are so pathetic. You murder rare species and ingest their tissue because you believe it gives you eunuchs a little virility. Pathetic," spat Olivia.

"He called me and told me of his discovery. Tyrannosaurus Rex bones. Claimed he had evidence of their amazing medicinal—"

"Dinosaur bones? Is that what he said it was?" asked Olivia.

"Yes. Then we realized it could prevent and cure COVID-H. That changed everything. Charles enlisted his girlfriend Melinda's help. He said she was directly involved with the research. Our government wanted it. All of it. They cut a deal with Charles. A deal that would make Charles and Melinda rich. I was able to get enough info on where it was from Charles...the government took over from there. They weren't willing to wait."

"Are you saying Melinda voluntarily got involved?" asked Olivia

"That's right, sweetie. She saw dollar signs. Works every time."

"You're lying!" shouted Olivia, pushing the barrel of her gun into his chest.

"Why would I lie at this point, sweetie?"

"Don't call me sweetie!"

Alex put his hand up in front of Olivia "Back off, please. Let him talk."

"What about him?" asked Alex, pointing at Cunningham.

"What do you mean? We thought he was with you, or up to something on his own." Li Jun looked confused. The three of them glared at the Director.

"I'll explain later. It'll all make sense when I do," promised Cunningham. "After that, Dr. Nilsson, if you still wish to kill me...go ahead."

"No, Director, I won't do you that favor. Now that you've destroyed mankind's last hope of surviving COVID-H, you get to die the same miserable death as everybody else, except for the few of us who've had a dose of God dust. I'll get to watch you drown in your own blood." They had no idea that Dr. Bullock had given Cunningham one of the prototype BN27/DX inhalers—that he never used.

Alex was surprised by her comments. "Olivia, please."

They heard a beeping sound coming from the bedroom. Cunningham and Alex ran in. Alex dug the phone from Randy's pocket. It was a text from Espionto.

I've had to share the details of the plan with the President. He's dispatched a military transport jet to Malaysia to be on standby. Notify me of your progress. He's directed me to work through you. Provide updates. If I've been relieved of duty, you will get a response, possibly from General Tousick.

Cunningham rubbed the back of his neck. Alex took the phone and texted Espionto back.

"He'll have to make do with me. Not sure he's too happy with you right now. Alright, Director, let's hear your story."

A shot rang out. Alex bolted back to the main room. Olivia was sitting on a wooden box, expressionless. Li Jun was dead.

"Why?" he asked.

"He called me sweetie again," she answered in a tone more fitting for a conversation about the weather.

"Okay. Okay," said Alex. "Promise me you won't shoot anybody else today?"

"Promise. I mean, I'll do my best."

The three of them sat at the card table. Alex and Olivia stared at Cunningham.

Chapter 41

Alex was at ease. An incongruous peace ran through his veins. It made no sense. He tried to resurrect a matching memory. As close as he could get was a Saturday morning in bed, lying next to his wife Julie, snuggling with their two beautiful daughters. At face value, Olivia's response was more appropriate. She was beside herself with anger and frustration. Why wasn't he? All of a sudden, it made sense. He got it. He no longer felt like a victim. He had faith.

Before Cunningham could start, Olivia said, "Alex, you knew Melinda was involved. I didn't believe you. I'm sorry. I trusted her. She was a dear friend for fifteen years. You'd think by now I'd learned not to trust anyone. What a fool I am."

"No, Olivia," said Alex. "You're not a fool. To love and to trust is always the right choice, whether it blows up in your face or not."

"What's got you all Gandhied up? Sorry, I think I know the answer...sort of. Anyway, let's hear your tale, Cunningham."

"My father—"

"Excuse me, Director. We know your father was in the OSS, and that he oversaw research led by Simon O'Brien involving a strange material discovered along the banks of the Mississippi by his grandfather, Doc Stevenson. I suspect you figured out that we were working with the exact same thing, but you never said anything about it even though you knew things turned out very badly for Simon and his co-workers. Why?"

"Shortly before he died, my father told me about the most terrifying experience he'd ever had. And yes, it involved Lieutenant Simon O'Brien and the dust, then known as SandX. My father was in charge of the research section that O'Brien worked in. At first, the Army was interested in it because O'Brien showed that SandX could improve wound healing. Shortly after that, he reported that SandX improved decision making and memory. O'Brien was a whiz at code-breaking, which he claimed was due to SandX. When he demonstrated that SandX could transform very average recruits into expert code-breakers, the Army took notice. Before long, other effects began to appear. O'Brien's volunteers became aggressive, physically stronger, and eventually, violent. My father tried to intervene. His superiors didn't listen. The military was gearing up for World War II. They saw the SandX as a way to create super-soldiers. He wrote O'Brien up for not following protocol which stated: Researchers are not to be exposed to experimental methods or substances. In other words, don't be your own guinea pig. It had no effect. He was told to let O'Brien continue."

Alex and Olivia shared a glance. Cunningham paused.

"Go ahead," murmured Olivia.

"It was no secret that Simon O'Brien had affairs. Several women claimed he was overly aggressive, using his rank and cunning to manipulate them into having sex. They were ignored and transferred to other departments and warned they would be tried for treason if they exposed any information related to classified Army research. One of his test subjects was accused outright of raping one of their secretaries. She too was ignored then transferred. My dad knew the woman well and was certain she wasn't lying.

"Shortly after the rape incident, a recruit was found nearly beheaded behind the research building. Both O'Brien and my dad knew that one of the other recruits in the study had done it. The Army decided there wasn't enough evidence for a formal trial. O'Brien remained silent. Fights broke out in the lab. The men were too strong to be subdued. About the time my father asked for a transfer, O'Brien was stabbed to death in the lab by one of his subjects. It wasn't until then that the research on SandX came to a halt. You see, don't you, that I couldn't let the world be exposed to it. Even if at first only one-time tiny doses were given for COVID-H, you know as well as I do that whoever possessed it would eventually push the envelope. The truth is, you don't have any idea what even a small dose will do over time. I had to destroy it."

"So you think it's better for mankind to be exterminated by the virus, except for the few of us who've already taken the dust?" asked Olivia. "You don't know...we don't know if small doses are harmful. Research is much more transparent than it used to be, Director. I doubt anyone would, as you say, push the envelope too far."

"Don't be so naive, Olivia," said Cunningham. "Let me finish. I didn't destroy it all. I just didn't want such an excess to be around to cause trouble later. There is some hidden away in Area 51. I know it's ridiculous, but I even wondered if SandX fueled scientists had indeed built the flying saucers that those conspiracy nut-cases talk about."

"There's more of it? You sure?" asked Alex. "Area 51, really? Sounds like a TV show. A bad one."

"It was the most suitable place for it...and that was before TV. Anyway, my father said it was hidden away in an area that became a long-forgotten storage room. He was sure nobody thought there was anything important there. All the men who knew about it are dead, along with all the records.

"I kidnapped Melinda to take me to the source...where the dust came from, so I could destroy it. I didn't know for sure if she was involved with Li Jun. Unfortunately, these dirtbags beat me to it," he said, pointing to the bodies strewn about the room.

"Enough to treat everybody on earth?" asked Olivia.

"A fifty-five-gallon drum full of it. I'm pretty sure that's enough."

"I suggest we get going to the airport," said Alex.

Alex started to hand Randy's rifle to Cunningham, but stopped cold. "What's that?" he asked, spinning his head towards the open door.

"My God, it sounds like…animals?" replied Olivia as they all went to the door. The air was still. The noise was nothing like they'd ever heard. For the next few minutes they stood in silence, looking in all directions. Every bird was singing. Elephants trumpeted. A seladang ox was standing eight feet away. A civet cat ran across Olivia's foot. Incessant high-pitched chatter came from behind the house along the ravine. Alex followed two wild pigs that sauntered by them on their way to the ravine.

"Come here!" he shouted.

Twenty-two excited monkeys were lined up along the edge of the ravine peering down into the abyss. Some were hopping up and down. Babies climbed on top of their mothers' heads for a better view. Alex, Olivia, and Cunningham walked to the edge and joined the menagerie. Downstream from where the first barrel of dust landed, there was no river. The river bed had split into a crevice thirty feet wide, consuming every bit of the powerful flow. The dust had been washed into the chasm. There were so many birds flying erratically to and fro, it was hard for them to get a clear view. The river bed below the crevice was dry and dotted with every creature that made the rain forest their home. Predators and prey stood side by side.

Cunningham shook his head. "Did Noah's Ark just empty out somewhere?"

Alex and Olivia were still too stunned to speak. Olivia stared at Alex, trying to read his expression. A smile grew so big, it pushed his cheeks into his eyes. His expression exuded the grand "aha" of spiritual connection. In a moment, she knew. She didn't need to ask.

"What the hell is happening?" Cunningham asked, not expecting an answer.

Alex and Olivia sat down with their feet hanging off the ledge. In an instant, the crevice closed and once again the river flowed. The animals scattered. The breeze the river once brought had returned.

"Must have been an earthquake somewhere...maybe shifting tectonic plates..." said Cunningham.

Alex stood up and put his hand on his shoulder and said, "He took it back."

"Who took what back, Alex? What are you talking about?" asked Cunningham.

"God took the dust back. Imagine what could happen to every living thing that drank or absorbed water laden with it? Director, it's the spark that created life, but it can also take it away. You were right. You did the right thing. It's not for us."

Cunningham sat down, then lay back on the moist undergrowth. "I know. I believe you. I don't understand any of it. As crazy as it sounds—I believe you. I just wish we didn't need the rest of it."

Olivia replied, "We have no choice. Dammit!"

"She's right. Unless we...somebody comes up with something else. Vaccine development has gone nowhere. Antivirals, antibodies, steroids, and a thousand others have had no effect. God help us."

Several minutes later, after the animals meandered off, they walked into the woods. "We need to bury Melinda and Randy."

"Of course," said Cunningham. "Besides, I doubt anyone knows what's happened here. But if they find Melinda and Randy, they'll have proof Americans were here. They'll suspect military. We don't have much time. I suppose we could ..." He looked back toward the river.

"Or take them with us," Olivia said.

Alex and Cunningham looked at each other and nodded reluctantly. They placed the bodies on the cart, leaving the Minigun behind, and trudged back to the Humvee, resting every twenty feet. Once they were packed up, they dug into the water and K-rations Randy had brought. For a few minutes, they chatted about anything but what they were in the middle of.

"Olivia, that picture I saw in Shane's trash can," started Alex.

"What picture?" asked Olivia.

"Oh, maybe I didn't tell you. There was a framed picture in his trash of him and another man yucking it up. I remember who it was. He's that Harvard scientist that got busted for spying— Frederick Lieberman."

"Scumbag," interjected Cunningham. "He gave the Chinese our latest info on nanorobotics, and molecular biology. Tools that could have been used to create COVID-H. He even set up a lab in Wuhan. And Harvard looked the other way while happily accepting millions of dollars from China's Thousand Talents project."

"Wait a minute. Alex, what are you trying to say?" asked Olivia.

"He and Shane were...are friends."

"So? That doesn't mean Shane's been involved in anything nefarious."

"I think he is. I hate to say it, but I think he is."

"Just like you thought Melinda was dirty?"

"Precisely, but I may be wrong."

"I don't want to believe it, Alex. Shane has always seemed so above board...so devoted."

"Crap. Dammit. You scientists are a pain in the ass," muttered

Cunningham. "Hiding behind that 'science is for everyone—knowledge should be openly shared' mantra. Nonsense! It all comes down to money. Scientists are just as greedy as anyone else. Has China shared anything openly with us? Hell no!"

"Cool it, Director, there's crooked, greedy people in the CIA too, right?"

"Of course." Cunningham grinned. "Never said there wasn't."

"We need to call Espionto…tell him what's happened and suggest he do a little reconnaissance on Dr. Bullock," said Alex.

"Give me the phone." Alex handed it to Cunningham, and he made the call.

Cunningham got a painful tongue-lashing from his boss for going MIA. He gave Espionto a brief overview of what had occurred along with their airport ETA, then they talked about Shane Bullock. He avoided telling him that he'd gotten rid of the dust.

"What did he say?" asked Olivia.

"Bullock is dead. He killed his assistant, Jan Whitorsh, then turned the gun on himself."

"Oh my God," whispered Olivia.

"They found evidence that he had indeed been selling secrets. Glad he made the right choice," said Cunningham.

"Right choice? What's wrong with you, Director?"

"Nothing. Yes—the right choice. He saved the government a ton of money in legal expenses, and we know he'll never be able to spy again. I'd say it was a very good choice."

"Okay, enough, you two," demanded Alex.

◇◇

An Air Force C-37 jet was parked alongside the C-47. Fortunately, there were no Chinese military craft present, nor were there any signs of life in the terminal. Major Turnble, followed by two enlisted men, jogged down the airstairs as the Humvee pulled up.

"Where's your cargo?" yelled Major Turnble, ignoring the two dead bodies.

Cunningham clenched his jaw. "There is no cargo, Major. It had to be disposed of."

"Director, I've been ordered to pick up ten barrels of high value material."

"I can't pull it out of my ass, Major. It's gone. I'll explain when we're in the air."

"I'll need to get permission to leave without the cargo."

"Screw that, Major. All hell could break lose any minute. We've got to get the hell out of here. These two scientists are critical in our fight against the virus. If you stall, you could be responsible for a lot more lives than just ours, capiche?"

Major Turnble reluctantly conceded, angry he'd been dressed down in front of others, especially the enlisted men. Once in the air, the first order of business was locating the last remaining stash of God dust. The Major listened in but really had no idea what they were talking about. Cunningham broke down and informed Espionto about the lost cargo. He had to in order to enlist help searching Area 51. The barrel of dust was transferred from the Watertown Research Facility in 1955.

Espionto still wasn't sure he could trust his old friend Robert Cunningham after his disappearing act, so he insisted on hearing the story from Alex and Olivia. They needed to see the complete blueprint for Area 51. It had never been shared with anyone but the President's cabinet. In order for Espionto to get permission, he had to tell the President everything.

"Robert, I've already been covering for you. Now I get to tell the President about the COVID-H cure being stolen by the Chinese and then thrown into a river by you? I doubt that will go well. We may both lose our jobs."

"I'm sorry, but I don't see any way around it," said Cunningham.

"I know. I'll do it, but I may not be the one calling you back if I get the axe."

"Understood. Listen, just blame me. I'm about ready for the glue factory anyway."

"Ha. No can do, Robert. I'll just tell it like it is."

"Okay. Later."

"Hope so."

The sun rose in front of them changing the ocean from black to blue. They drank coffee and ate everything that was offered by the air crew. Cunningham became increasingly nervous after two hours had passed with no word from Espionto. Then a notification dinged on Major Turnble's laptop. It was an email from the Secretary of Defense, Tracy Jones. The file required Cunningham's password to open. The Major acknowledged the snub and handed him the laptop.

Alex, Olivia, and Cunningham hovered over the computer. The Area 51 blueprints revealed an immense maze of tunnels and over a hundred rooms. Narrowing it down to the most likely locations was a formidable task. When they distilled it down to a dozen possible choices, Cunningham called Espionto.

"I guess you're still alive. Do you still have your job?"

"Yeah. For the moment. He said we'd discuss it later."

"Hope he's drunk...maybe he'll forget."

"Don't think so. He sounded pretty sober."

"Damn. Okay, here's a list of rooms. Can you get some folks and start searching now?" asked Cunningham.

"Yes. You said it's in a fifty-five-gallon drum, right?"

"Pretty sure, it may have SandX written on it, but I'd have them tap any unlabeled large container."

"Phew, who knows what they could get exposed to?"

"Oh, come on. Don't get all California on me. Put 'em in damn hazmat suits, give them a hammer and spike, and tell them to get on it. Tell them if they lose their hair or get a headache ten years from now, they can sue the government and be on *60 Minutes*."

"I hear ya. I might leave out the part about hair and headaches."

"Alright. We should be over Area 51 in about six hours."

"I'll have a jeep at the airstrip. They'll take you to the admin building. Colonel Harding will take you under."

"Got it."

"Stay in touch, Robert."

"Will do."

"One more thing."

"What?"

"According to our latest estimates, there may only be a hundred million still alive in the US"

"My God. No. It's worse than I thought. Docs Nilsson and Winthrop left some of the antiviral dust with Bullock. Did you get it before he blew his brains out?"

"Yes. Everyone in the White House and top brass got it last week."

"Good."

Chapter 42

Exhaustion and the steady drone of jet engines lulled Olivia and Cunningham into twilight sleep for a couple of hours. Alex woke Olivia and the Director thirty minutes before the California coast came into view. Man's coastal footprint quickly faded into parched desert after they passed over the Sierra National Forest. From twenty thousand feet, the pockmarked desert resembled the surface of the moon. They descended to ten, then five thousand feet when over Death Valley. The pilot steered toward the crystalline gleam of Groom Lake, a well-known landmark near Paradise Ranch, a.k.a. Area 51 in Lincoln County. Groom lake is in fact, a dry salt flat. The main runway extended to the edge of the lake. Their pilot made his approach, sticking an easy landing.

Dry sandy air, even at 101 degrees, felt pleasant in comparison to Malaysia's soggy 93 as they left the plane. As promised, they were whisked off to the Administration Building, where they were met by Colonel Harding.

"Colonel, sir, there appears to be a lot of activity here." Major Turnble attempted to make a bland observation but an edge of concern belied his real intent. Cunningham rolled his eyes at Major Turnble's inability to be direct.

"China," replied the colonel, turning to Director Cunningham. "Captains Miller and Jeffrey will take you under."

A group of Airmen familiar with Area 51's multi-leveled labyrinth had started the search an hour earlier. The significance of being allowed to traipse around Area 51 was lost on Olivia and Alex.

They followed the reverberating clackity-clack of hard-soled shoes hitting the floors of concrete tunnels. Two airmen kept guard outside the doors of each room they approached. Inside each, they climbed over aircraft parts, weapons and bizarre machines. Many looked like prototypes of failed experiments. Sealed rusty vats labeled with old-style skull and crossbones greeted them in the second room. One by one, timid airmen opened them up for inspection. Cunningham began to rethink his lost hair and headache slurs. By the third room, the odd menagerie of indiscernible machines rattled their belief that captured aliens and U.F.O.s were only pipedreams of the lunatic fringe. The fourth room, however, consisted mostly of discarded office furniture, phone systems, and typewriters from the forties.

"Dammit," said Alex, knocking an aluminum cart on its side. "It's got to be here somewhere."

Cunningham was making his share of noise on the other side of the room. Then, in the back of the room, Olivia spotted a pile of oversized khaki wool army blankets draped over something. Underneath were two file cabinets and an ancient fifty-five-gallon drum with the faded letters "SX" stenciled on its side followed by the name, Watertown.

"Guys. Guys, come here!" shouted Olivia. Alex and Cunningham pushed aside whatever was in their way to get to her find. They'd just pried one edge of the lid loose when they heard Colonel Harding's voice.

"Director."

"Yes, sir," answered Cunningham. He glanced at the colonel, taking in the man's excited expression and urgent tone.

"I have a message you all may be interested in. President Triagin reports that there have been no new cases worldwide of COVID-H in the past twenty-four hours. None."

Cunningham leaned against the concrete wall, staring at Colonel Harding in disbelief. Olivia turned and slid down the rusted barrel to the floor. Alex crouched down and gently took her hand.

He whispered, "It's over. By grace, Olivia. Undeserved grace." She stared back at him, shaking her head. Her eyes questioned, but her expression softened with welcome defeat.

"Alex," said Olivia, between exaggerated breaths.

"What?"

"Is grace ever deserved?"

"Good point."

Colonel Harding cleared his throat. "There's more. Secretary Finnegan also said the President is beginning negotiations with President Chen." No one responded. "Did you hear me?"

"Yes, sir," replied Cunningham. "We heard you."

Alex helped Olivia to her feet and wrapped his arms around the rim of the barrel.

"Watch." He tugged the lid off the barrel, and they peered inside.

It was empty.

Epilogue

Olivia and Alex were escorted out to the runway where they boarded a military plane for their trip to Fort Campbell, not far from Nashville. Director Cunningham was being flown to DC to meet with Espionto. More than half the earth's population had been incinerated, buried, or left rotting in stacks like cord wood. People were hungry. The economy lay in ruins. There was a lot to talk about.

They held hands but didn't speak until almost twenty minutes into the flight. Alex gently grasped her shoulder and turned to her. They studied each other's expression. The worry lines on the edge of his eyes and forehead were gone. His lips formed a faint smile. His eyes were soft but confident.

Olivia, however, had the look of desperate prey, eyes wide open—searching for an invisible attacker—hypervigilant. Her neck muscles were taut. Her lips momentarily restrained her thoughts.

"How did you know the barrel was empty?"

"Lucky guess, but it made sense. When the barrels were swallowed up in the ravine—it may sound strange, but I had a feeling that God took it back. He took all of it. Now it fits. Why would He just take the dust in Malaysia? Just to send us running around the world to find more? I doubt it."

"God? Vanishing magic dust? Alex, it's just too much. But...there's got to be an explanation."

"What about a vanishing pandemic? That doesn't sound very scientific to me."

"No. It doesn't. Let's just let those little details air out for a while." A smile came and went. "Alex. What...what do you think the dust is, or was?" she asked, not taking her eyes off his face.

"I have no more idea than you do about its composition, or how it works, but I'll tell you what I do think. Doc Stevenson was right. It came from the earth when the Madrid fault split. I believe it brought about the formation of RNA, maybe DNA, consistent with our research. Then sometime over the next three billion years, it ended up deep within the earth. And not by mistake."

"Yes, I remember your explanation...but I thought that was your injured brain talking. So why all the weird unpredictable effects? I can wrap my head around its ability to promote healing...maybe even gene modification. But all the other bizarre stuff doesn't seem to fit."

Alex thought for a moment, his ideas forming as he spoke. "My guess is that it had one specific purpose at one precise time— to begin the journey of life. But evolved organisms were never expected to be exposed."

"And when they were?"

"Well, I can't say for sure, but gene alteration would lead to changes in cell differentiation and function, right?"

"Yes."

"Once this occurred in the brain, anything could happen. Like all those unpredictable effects."

"What about behavior? Wouldn't it change everybody's behavior the same way?"

Alex shrugged. "Maybe it depends on who you were in the first place. I mean, what if it exaggerated certain tendencies each person already had?"

Olivia hesitated, gently tugged her earlobe, then said, "Like disinhibition. It gave deeply rooted thoughts or behaviors free rein. That sorta makes sense, but what about physical abilities?"

"The brain controls everything. You know we may never fully understand its capabilities. Maybe the dust causes the body to change physically in response to the brain's signals.

"That's scary," replied Olivia, twirling a lock of her silver-blonde hair between her fingers. "We don't know how many people have been exposed..."

Alex put his index finger to his lips then glanced at the four soldiers sitting in front of them. They pretended to be oblivious to their strange conversation.

"Alex?"

He looked up, his mind was racing, darting from one unknown to another. "I'm sorry. What did you ask?"

She stared into his gray eyes, studying the rays of muted color that circled his pupils. Her lingering fears were easy for him to see.

"This is only the beginning, isn't it?" she asked in a whisper.

His gaze drifted from her face to the small porthole window where he sought comfort from the familiar azure sky. Two thoughts resonated in his mind: they were alive and they were together. After a long few seconds, a confident grin chased away his damning premonitions.

"Olivia."

"Yes."

"Don't worry about it. We'll figure it out, right?"

"Right."

Book One in the Broken Cure series.

Find out where it all started.

In Broken Cure we meet critical care specialist Alex Winthrop M.D. and biochemist Olivia Nilsson Ph.D. who risk their lives unraveling an international bioweapons plot. We go with them from the depths of personal hardship to unsung heroes and renewed lovers. Their reward: a choice between criminal charges, death or providing their skills as indentured scientists for the CIA.

Amazon: Broken Cure
Website: dougkaneauthor.com

Acknowledgements

Special thanks to: Nancy Cross for her tireless ear. Valerie Walker and Kenny Scott for their feedback and support. My editors, Sandra Haven, for showing me my blind-spots, and Beth Lynne, for her astute proofing and numerous "fix-its".